Celebrity Skin

Breakthrough

C.E. Maras

Celebrity Skin: Breakthrough

Copyright © 2024 C.E. Maras

Publishing: Nine Live Press, LLC

To believing in yourself when it is the hardest thing to do and leaning on those around you when you need them the most.

One

"The November air was crisp, the days were darker earlier, and there was a smell of winter in the air. Gabriella clutched her tweed peacoat closer together and wrapped a large scarf around her neck and face as she dashed out from the building where her meeting had just ended. She had met with Desmond's agent, who excitedly discussed some possible projects. Gabriella had texted Desmond some options, which included an audition for Raul in Phantom of the Opera.

She hustled through a crosswalk by the Rockefeller Center area, where the feeling of Christmas was buzzing. Tourists crowded around the world-famous tree, which was delivered the week previous, but still undecorated. Shouldering her way through the crowds whose eyes never lowered from the towering buildings, she headed towards Liam's apartment near Columbus Circle.

Once she made it past the crowds and onto a less trafficked sidewalk, she pulled out her phone. "Hey!" She said when he answered the phone.

"What's up goober? How was the meeting?" He asked as he shouted over the video game in the background.

"It went really well. I'm heading over. Is Chinese cool for tonight?" She asked as she made her way up west fifty-first street towards tenth avenue.

"Absolutely. Want me to call it in?" He asked.

"Yeah, you know what I like. Call the place up the block from you. Extra eggrolls." Gabriella confirmed.

"Got it goober, later," he said before he hung up.

Gabriella laughed as she continued to walk and noticed a voicemail that she hadn't seen before. It was a message from Don Starr's office, about the Edge of Time movie. Confused, Gabriella called the number back in the voicemail.

"Starr Studios, this is Linda speaking, how can I help you?" A chipper voice answered.

"Hi, my name is Gabriella DiStella, I received a message saying to call back regarding the Edge of Time."

"Oh yes, please hold," the woman said, before twenty seconds of hold music played. "This is Gina Levine."

"Gina? It's Gabriella DiStella, Laurel Dolce's manager. I received a message to call Don?"

"Gabriella, hey! I'm so glad you called us back so soon. I'm here with Don, he just stepped out of his office. The studio was not a fan of how the movie ended, so April Brown is rewriting the ending. The film was supposed to be released in December, but now with the rewrites and having to shoot new scenes, the movie is being postponed until the summer. They are looking to make it a summer blockbuster now." Gina explained.

"Got it. So, when do you need Laurel to come back? She's in Vancouver right now, but I think that movie is due to wrap in December." Gabriella asked.

"Oh, yeah, we will need her to come back, but we actually need you to come back. The rewrite heavily involves your character and Jake Wilson's." Gina explained.

"Seriously? I thought this was done. What about everyone else? Aren't Riona and Henry both filming out of the country?" Gabriella asked.

"Yes, but like I said, it's really you and Jake." Gina repeated.

"When are you looking to have us film?"

"End of December." Gina answered.

"I'm not missing Christmas with my family. That's a hard no for me." Gabriella responded.

"No, after Christmas. Last week of December, maybe first week of January if needed." Gina stated.

"Okay. Can I get back to you to verify everything? I'm walking the streets of Manhattan right now, and it's really hard to concentrate."

"Absolutely. I am going to email you everything, for both you and Laurel. We will get the schedule put together so you know exactly what days you will be filming." Gina said before she ended the call.

Twenty minutes later, Gabriella opened the door to Liam's apartment, which he left unlocked for her, with her hands full of Chinese food.

"Goober!" Liam chanted as Gabriella walked through the door, his focus on the television as he played his video game.

"Goob," she responded as she made her way into the kitchen and dropped the bags on the counter, then tossed her coat, pocketbook and scarf on the back of a chair.

"How did the date go last night?" Gabriella asked as she shoved an eggroll in her mouth while Liam saved and turned off his game.

He rolled his eyes dramatically and sighed as he turned on the couch to look at her. "If someone would just get over her whole no dating rule, I wouldn't have to go out on these mediocre dates through that stupid app."

Gabriella walked around the couch with the two bags of food and placed them on the coffee table with the eggroll in her mouth.

"Couldn't wait until you sat down for that," Liam asked as he eyed the eggroll.

Gabriella shook her head in response as she sat down on the other end of the couch, "you know how I love my eggrolls."

Liam laughed and shook his head as he reached for his hot and spicy noodles. "Such a goober."

Gabriella smacked his arm and inhaled her eggroll before she reached for her lo mein. "So, what made the date so mediocre?"

"She was just so blah. She was attractive, but there wasn't much going on up top. I couldn't really have a conversation with her. I went to the bathroom, and I caught her taking selfies at the table." He said with a cringe.

"Are you setting your preferences to eighteen-year old's?" Gabriella asked with a smirk.

"You think you're so funny." He said with an eye roll as he threw a wrapped fortune cookie at her.

Gabriella laughed and dodged the flying treat, the wrapped cookie landing somewhere between the couch and the wall. "Seriously though, maybe you need to be on another dating app. What is the one for seniors?"

"I'm not that old, Gabby," Liam laughed.

"I dunno, thirty is pretty up there. Did you take her to an early bird special?" Gabriella asked as she attempted to keep a straight face.

"You're going to be the cause of any premature gray hair and wrinkles I get," he said as he pointed his chopsticks at her.

"Speaking of gray hair and wrinkles, I've got a new source for them," Gabriella segued to the next topic.

Liam watched her as he chomped on an extremely long bunch of noodles. "The Edge of Time needed a rewrite. They are postponing the release until the summer. They need me to go to LA and film new scenes."

Liam continued to look at her as he chewed his food. "Are you okay with that? Are you ready to see he who shall not be named?"

"You can say his name, you goob." Gabriella said with an eye roll.

"Are you okay seeing Voldemort?" Liam asked with a shit-eating grin on his face. Gabriella narrowed her eyes at him until he conceded. "Okay, okay. Are you okay seeing Henry again?"

Gabriella shrugged. "I mean, sure, it's been a while. I'm over it, I've moved on. Plus, I'll only be filming with Jake, so I won't even have to see him."

"Huh. You're really over it?" Liam asked.

Gabriella nodded. "Yeah, it's kind of like out of sight, out of mind. Plus, now that I don't have the tabloids talking shit about me, it's like my life returned to normal, like it was just some weird out of body experience."

Liam studied Gabriella as she sat there. Gabriella noticed his intense gaze and raised one eyebrow. "Why are you looking at me like that? Spit it out."

"You're really over him? If that's the case, why haven't you dated anyone then?"

Gabriella shrugged. "I've been busy. First with the apartment, then with juggling Laurel's schedule, and now Desmond's schedule is starting to fill out. I have to accompany him to a commercial shoot next week. I'm content with my life. We have our routine; I have down time to relax. Why mess up a good thing?"

"What's holding you back from dating me?" Liam asked as he placed his carton of noodles on the table.

Gabriella looked at him and started to laugh. He scrunched his face up in disgust. "Why are you laughing?" He asked.

"Because you made a joke?" Gabriella replied.

"I wasn't kidding. We didn't date because you said you weren't ready. You just said that you're over why you weren't ready. So, we should date." Liam said as he got up to refill his soda.

Gabriella sat there as a noodle hung from her chop sticks and watched Liam move around his apartment. She couldn't tell if it was a joke. Her eyes followed him as he came back to the couch, his glass filled with cola, a bottle of water in his other hand for her. "What?" He asked as he handed her the water.

"How are you not kidding? Didn't you say that you couldn't date because you are married to your job and travel constantly? Did something change?" Gabriella asked.

"Are you being serious, Goober? We spend all of our free time together. The only thing we're missing is the title and the physical part to a relationship." Liam said as he relaxed back into the couch.

"Hm," Gabriella verbalized as she considered Liam's words, then grabbed the leftovers to put in the kitchen.

"Are we watching the next episode tonight?" Liam called out.

"Yeah," she responded, his words echoed in her ears. He wasn't wrong, they did spend a lot of their free time together. She really was over the Henry thing, for the most part. And her and Liam got a long so well, she really felt like she found a solid friend in him. He made living in New York a little less lonely, since Desmond was so busy with the show and the commercials he was shooting.

"How you have never seen *Six Feet Under* is beyond me." Liam said with shake of his head as he set up the show and grabbed the blanket from the back of the couch.

Gabriella approached the couch, and Liam nudged his head to his shoulder and arm, which was draped around the back of the couch, where she usually nestled in while they watched television. Gabriella made herself comfortable as Liam covered her with the blanket.

She found herself not paying attention to the episode and considered what Liam had said. Rather than watch the show, she studied Liam and took in his sparkling brown eyes, which were a few shades lighter than her own. His black hair fell just above his eyes, and his tight beard was neatly trimmed to where it was almost stubble.

"You're not watching the show," Liam said with a smirk as his eyes were glued to the television.

"No, I'm not," she said, slightly breathy.

Liam noted the tone of her voice, and looked down at her, his hand gently glided up and down her arm. Gabriella stared into his eyes, her hand reached up to his face, her nails lightly scratching his beard. Liam slowly lowered his face to hers, his breath warm on her lips. Gabriella inhaled deeply, then lifted her chin and pressed her lips against his. She felt Liam shudder next to her as he sat up, his other hand weaved into her hair at the base of her head. He deepened the kiss; his tongue made his way into her mouth. Gabriella sighed with contentment as Liam pulled her on top of him, intensifying their kiss.

The show was long forgotten as their hands began to roam over each other's body, layers of clothes being reached under for better access.

"Gabby," Liam breathed out.

"Yeah?" She asked as her body grinded against his.

"Do you want to go in my bedroom?" He asked.

Gabby nodded her head, then stood up and straightened out her clothes as Liam turns off the television. He took her hand and lead her to the bedroom as the silence increased the tension and anticipation between them.

Liam walked into the room, and went to a nightstand, where he pulled out two candles and lit them. He walked back over to Gabriella and placed both hands on her face. "Gabby, are you sure about this? I don't want to pressure you into something you're not ready for."

Gabriella smiled up at him and nodded her head. "Yeah, I'm ready for this. I'm ready for you, Liam."

***

Gabriella woke up surrounded by and unfamiliar room. She looked around at the white walls, the dark green curtains, which matched the dark green comforter on top of her, and the dark wood furniture which was a stark contrast to the cream-colored carpet on the floor. She looked down at herself, and saw she was a gray t-shirt. She walked out of the bedroom and finally noticed the living room and realized where she was.

"Liam?" She called out.

"Hey, goober," he said as he walked out of the bathroom behind her.

"Hey. Um, what time is it?" She asked as she tried to comb her hair with her fingers.

"9:15. Why?" He responded.

"Oh, I'm supposed to meet Des for breakfast at ten. I have to meet him near the theater district. I hate to ask this, but could I borrow a sweatshirt or something?" Gabriella asked with a shrug.

"Yeah. Do you have pants to wear?" Liam asked as he headed back to the bedroom.

"I have leggings in my bag. And I'll wear my boots. I really don't want to re-wear my office clothes. Can I take a quick shower?" Gabriella asked.

Liam nodded as he grabbed her a towel. Gabriella smiled and entered the bathroom, stripped off the t-shirt and took the quickest shower possible. Wrapped in the towel, she walked out to the kitchen and grabbed her bag. Liam wolf whistled at her as she shook her head and closed the bathroom door. She noticed her clothes from yesterday folded and placed on the counter. She slipped on her bra, then pulled out a pair of underwear and leggings from her bag. After she was dressed, she took out her travel toothbrush and brushed her teeth. She wiped the smeared mascara from under her eyes, then went back to the bedroom, where Liam held up a red sweater.

"I thought you would look good in this, and I thought it would go better with your boots." Liam said with a shrug as he handed her the sweater.

She smiled sweetly as she put it on. "Thanks, goob. I appreciate it. You're saving me a shit ton of time going back to my place. And I won't have to hear shit from Des for being late." She stood in front of the mirror and threw her hair up in a messy bun.

"Gabby?" Liam asked, "you don't regret last night, do you?"

"No, do you?" She asked as she turned to look at him while she put her clothes into her bag.

"Not at all. I just wanted to make sure." He said with a sheepish smile. "Do you want coffee?"

"No thanks, I have to leave to meet Desmond now." She said as she started to walk towards the door.

"So, are we doing this, Gabby? Are we going to be a thing?" Liam asked as he followed her to his door. Gabriella turned before opening the door and kissed him.

"Yeah, I think we are. I'll call you after breakfast, okay?" She asked. Liam kissed her back and nodded. "I'm looking forward to it."

***

Gabriella walked up the subway steps and made her way to forty-third street to the café they dined at on Saturdays when neither one of them wanted to cook. She entered the café to find Desmond at a table in the back corner, with his menu open. Gabriella smiled as she draped her peacoat over the back of the chair before she sat down.

Desmond looked up at her and stated, "you had sex last night."

Gabriella paused, then looked at Desmond as she sat down and settled herself in. "What are you talking about?"

"Whose sweater are you wearing?" He asked, as he turned his attention back to the menu.

"Oh, it's Liam's. I passed out watching tv at his house last night." She answered as she looked at the menu. The waitress approached and took their orders. Once she walked away Desmond looked up at Gabriella and rested his chin on his fist, elbow on the table.

"So, what show gave you those hickeys on your neck?" He asked with a smirk.

12

Gabriella blushed as she raised her hand to her neck. "It's on both sides," Desmond informed her.

"Okay, Liam asked me out last night." Gabriella explained.

"It's about time." Desmond said as he flashed a brilliant smile. "Arnie and I were waiting for the two of you to finally get together."

Gabriella gave Desmond a half smile, tugging the sleeves of Liam's sweater to cover most of her hands. "So, how was the sex?" Desmond asked.

"It was good." Gabriella said shyly. Desmond's eyes flickered up, a look of horror on his face at her answer. Gabriella notices his reaction and quickly elaborated, "it was nice."

Desmond bit his tongue, his eyes slightly bulged as he contained his response while the waitress brought over their coffees. As soon as she was out of ear shot, the words exploded from his lips. "Good? Nice? Gabby, that is not good."

Gabriella vehemently shook her head in response. "No, it was good and nice. He made me feel good... cherished." Gabriella said as she searched for the way to explain.

"Did you cum at least?" Desmond asked with his face twisted in disgust.

"Of course, I did, a couple of times. What kind of a question is that?" She asked defensively.

"If I came a few times, I wouldn't describe the sex as nice or good," he exclaimed with a shake of his head. "Are you not into him? Was it weird, like fucking your cousin or something? You two have gotten very close in a short amount of time."

"Eww, no. I'm into him. How could I not be? He's stupid good looking, and he's so nice. He makes me laugh, and I feel comfortable around him." Gabriella answered.

"I'm sensing a but," Desmond stated.

"There's no but." Gabriella stated as their food was delivered to the table. She picked up a slice of whole grain toast and dipped it into her sunny side up eggs. She chewed her food as a quiet settled over the table as Desmond wrapped his hands around his large breakfast sandwich and almost unhinged his jaw to bite into it.

When they were halfway through their meal, Gabriella quietly stated, "there was no spark."

"I knew something was up," Desmond said before he took a drink of his coffee. "Explain."

Gabriella pushed some of her eggs around with her fork. "It's just, everything with Henry was so… hot. He could look at me and I would need a new pair of panties. Everything was electric with him. And it's not like there is no attraction with Liam. I find him very attractive, and the sex was good, but it wasn't life altering like it was with Henry. I think Henry broke me and ruined all men for me."

14

Desmond digested her words, then slowly smiled and laughed. "Gabby, I have had some fucking hot one-night stands with guys who rocked my world off of its axis. But that's not enough to stay with someone. Sometimes things are hot as hell with Arnie, other times I should have not missed out on sleep. I feel like you could have something real with Liam, but you need to give it a chance. Sometimes you need to strike a match a few times before it catches fire."

"I mean, I guess so." Gabriella said unsurely.

"Henry was your forbidden fruit. He was your celebrity crush, the unattainable. And you know what, bitch, you attained that. But you said yourself that you never truly felt comfortable with him, that you were always feeling inadequate. I think you got too close to the sun, you got burned, and now anything less than the sun is leaving you feeling cold. Give Liam a chance. He's good for you." Desmond said with a wink as he finished his coffee.

***

Thanksgiving passed quickly, as did the weeks that lead up to Christmas. Gabriella opened the door to her apartment and struggled with the giftbags both she and Liam dragged into her home and deposited them in the center of the living room. "Gabby, that tree is so sad and tiny, you couldn't even fit one present under there," Liam said with a smile as he nodded towards the two-foot-tall Christmas tree sitting on the edge of her desk.

"You know space is at a minimum in New York City apartments," she smirked in return. "You're staying over tonight, right?"

Liam nodded in response as he took off his coat and hung it on her coat rack. He helped her with her coat and hung it as she made her way to the kitchen to start dinner.

"What's on the menu tonight?" Liam asked as he walked behind her and wrapped his arms around her waist and kissing the back of her neck.

"Steak, potatoes, and green beans. Is that okay?" She answered.

"Yes. Can I get a bottle of red ready?" He asked as he continued to place slow kisses on her neck.

"Absolutely."

Liam patted her on her bottom before he walked over tiny wine rack and retrieved two glasses and a bottle. "So, did this finish your Christmas shopping?"

"For the most part. I sent a bunch of gifts directly to Patti in South Dakota. She gave us the number of gifts to send her, and she's planning some big gift exchange, so everyone will have the same gifts to open." Gabriella answered from the stove as Liam set up the peninsula with plates and utensils.

"Did you send Laurel and Matt their gifts? I thought you just got them stuff today." Liam asked.

"No, they are coming home for Christmas. Actually, I wanted to ask you something, but I didn't want it to seem like it was too soon. My parents always host a ridiculously huge Christmas eve party. Arnie and Desmond will be there,

Laurel and Matt are flying in for it. I know it's next week, but I wanted to ask if you would want to join us."

Liam sat there quietly, then gave her a sad smile, "I would love to go, Gabby, but my parents and I are going to Pennsylvania to visit my sister, she's hosting the holidays at her house."

"Oh, no, I totally get it. I wasn't sure what your plans were. Of course, you should be in Pennsylvania with your sister." Gabriella said with a smile.

"When were you planning on celebrating with the film crew?" Liam asked, which changed the subject.

"Two in the afternoon the day after Christmas. Patti said she didn't want to make it too early for the west coasters, but not too late in the day for everyone else. She plans on having this party go on for hours." Gabriella said with a smile as she checked the potatoes and the steak roasting in the oven.

Gabriella had managed to keep in touch with everyone from the movie, they held virtual meetings together every other week to catchup. Jem, Max, and Darius were all on different projects. Patti and Joshua were still in South Dakota, but they decided to open a restaurant together. Bob was over in Ireland on the set of Henry's new mini-series to take care of Leigh. It was rare when Bob was able to join the calls, but when he did, talk of Henry was kept to a minimum.

"I think it's really nice that you guys are all still close," Liam said as he opened the bottle of red wine. "When should we celebrate Christmas together? It seems like you're booked the twenty-fourth through the twenty-sixth."

Gabriella watched him as he poured the wine. "Well, when are you leaving to go to Pennsylvania?"

"Probably around nine in the morning on Christmas Eve. I know we are going to hit a bunch of traffic, but my mother does not like to wake up early, and she does not like to be away from home for too long." Liam said with a shrug. "When are you heading to your parents' house?"

"I was going to go a day or two before Christmas to help cook and set up everything. But since I'm so close now, I wasn't planning on staying over there, except for Christmas Eve." Gabriella said as she removed the string beans from the bag and washed them.

"How about we celebrate the night before Christmas eve. We can have a nice sleepover, spend Christmas Eve morning together. I can make you pancakes for breakfast," he said as he wagged his eyebrows at her.

"Yeah, that sounds like a plan to me," Gabriella said with a smile as Liam handed her a glass of wine. They clinked their glass together in agreement.

Two

Gabriella spent the day before Christmas eve at her parents' house and helped them set up the rooms for the large amount guests expected to arrive the next evening. After they cooked entire morning away, Gabriella sat at the kitchen island to decorate cookies as her mother flitted around the room and rechecked all the dishes for the celebration.

"I don't know, I'm not sure if I'll have enough food. Laurel and Desmond are bringing their boyfriends, your cousin Nick is bringing his fiancé, I think Gianna has a boyfriend she might bring." Marie worried out loud as Giuseppe made his way into the kitchen. He placed his hands on his wife's upper arms and held her steady.

"*Amore*, breathe. We have enough food to host three Christmas eve parties. The house is set, and thanks to Gabby's help, we are ahead of schedule. No rushing around tomorrow, we only have to get ice. Look, Gabby even made dessert." Giuseppe stated to try and calm his wife down.

"Yeah, mom, don't worry. I'm just finishing up the cookies. I already baked a bunch of cakes, there are a few down in the basement fridge, and I have two more that I'm bringing with me tomorrow." Gabriella concurred.

Maria nervously looked between her daughter and her husband a sighed, "great, so now I have nothing to do? What am I supposed to do the rest of the night?"

Gabriella laughed as her father shook his head. "Mom, why don't you have some spiked cocoa with me, and help me with the rest of the sugar cookies? Then we can draw you a nice bath, and you can relax until bedtime?"

Maria sighed and slouched into the stool next to Gabriella. She picked up a cookie and began to frost it. Gabriella patted her mother's head, then set off to make her a hot chocolate. "Why are you bringing more cake tomorrow, *Bambolina*? Aren't you staying tonight?"

"No, mom, I have to be home tonight. I'm celebrating Christmas with Liam tonight. I'll be back tomorrow long before everyone starts heading over."

"Ah, the elusive Liam. Are we ever going to meet this one?" Maria asked as she placed sprinkles on the cookie.

"Sure, mom, eventually. It's still new." Gabriella answered.

"If he was really serious about you, he would come here for you," Maria said with a sigh.

"Mom, enough. We aren't serious, and he has his own family to spend the holidays with," Gabriella warned.

"I bet you Henry would be here, and lives in England," Giuseppe said under his breath.

Gabriella slammed the mug of hot chocolate in front of her mother as she stared down her father. "Too far, Giuseppe," Maria whispered.

"Really, dad? You're still hung up on him?" Gabriella yelled.

"I just don't understand what happened, you just dropped him." Giuseppe said in defense.

"It's really not something I want to talk about with my parents, okay? He just wasn't who he claimed to be." Gabriella said with a sigh.

"Gabby, I..." Giuseppe started as Gabriella cut him off.

"I'm going to take off. I'm going to take the Corolla home so I can bring all of the gifts and the rest of the cakes with me. I'll see you guys tomorrow."

Gabriella made her way out of the house and ignored the flurries twirling around her head. She started the car and let it warm up as she dialed Liam.

"Goober!" He answered happily.

"Hey," she replied.

"Are you here already? I wasn't expecting you for a few hours," he said, as the game paused in the background.

"No, no. I'm leaving my parent's now. I'm going to head to home and get ready. I'll be over around six." Gabriella assured him as she put the car in drive.

"Okay, I will see you then," Liam said before he hung up.

***

Gabriella arrived at Liam's apartment a quarter after six with a small overnight bag and his Christmas gift. He opened the door dressed in the red sweater she had borrowed of his on the night they started dating, as well as a Santa hat and a giant smile.

"Merry Christmas eve eve, Goober!" He said before he planted a kiss on her lips. He took her bag and brought it into his bedroom as she placed his gift under his Christmas tree. He met her in the living room and helped her out of her coat. He whistled at her when he saw the midi-length red bodycon dress that she was dressed in.

"Wow, Gabby, you look phenomenal. Are you my Christmas present? Because in that dress, you totally could be."

Gabriella leaned in and kissed him, then wrapped her arms around his neck as she pushed herself against him. Liam dropped her coat on the couch, his hands gripped her hips as he deepened the kiss. The conversation her father had started earlier in the day was on repeat in her head, and she was determined to drown it out by any means necessary.

"Gabby, wait, we can't get straight to dessert without eating. I have dinner in the kitchen for us." Liam said after tearing himself away.

Gabriella smiled, "sorry about that. What's for dinner?"

Liam led her into the kitchen, where a candle was lit in the center of the two-top table, champagne in flutes and chicken franchise with pasta was on the plates. "Wow! What's the occasion?"

"It's Christmas eve eve, and we're celebrating the almost birth of Jesus," he said as he pulled out her chair.

"This looks so good. Where did you get it from?" Gabriella asked with an arched eyebrow as she settled in her seat.

"What, you don't think I made this for you?" Liam asked as he pressed his hand against his heart.

Gabriella tilted her head to the side as she stared at him. He laughed as he took his seat. "Okay, it's that place on Mulberry Street that you like."

Liam held up his champagne flute as Gabriella followed his lead. "To our first pre-holiday together, Merry Christmas."

The clinked their glass together as Gabriella smiled. After a sip of champagne, they both dug into their food, Gabriella moaned and did a happy dance in her seat. Liam jumped up, pulled garlic bread out of the oven, and placed it in a bowl onto the table. "I almost forgot the best part," he said with a smile.

"Oh! More carbs! Merry Christmas to me!" Gabriella said with a smile before she took a huge bite out of the bread.

Liam laughed. "You really are something, Gabby. You might be the coolest girl I've ever known."

Gabriella smiled with her cheeks full of bread. After she chewed and swallowed, she sipped her champagne and said, "I don't know about coolest, but I'll tell you, teenage Gabby is throwing a rager at that comment."

"Where do you come up with this shit? Like, coolest of the cool," he said with a smirk.

"You want cool, I've got cool. How much of a notice do you need to give work to take vacation?"

Liam hummed for a moment. "It's supposed to be two weeks, but I really don't take time, why do you ask?"

"How would you like to come to L.A. with me for a few days in the second week of January?" Gabriella asked with a twinkle in her eyes.

"L.A.? Why L.A.?"

"The studio got back to me with the dates they need me to come in. It's only about three days of shooting. We can stay an extra day or two? Make a little vacation out of it?"

"You're serious?" He asked cautiously.

"As a heart attack," she responded with a smirk.

He pulled out his phone, typed a few things, then a moment later he looked up with a smile and said, "fuck it, let's go to L.A.!"

Gabriella clapped her hands together and cheered as Liam reached across the table and kissed her. She grabbed her phone an booked their plane tickets. After they ate and cleaned up together, Liam poured a glass of wine for

24

Gabriella and grabbed a bottle of beer for himself and joined her in the living room, where she was waiting on the couch.

"You have a choice, Elf or Fred Clause," he said as he lifted the remote.

"Elf is a classic." Gabriella responded as she sipped her wine.

"Elf it is," Liam said as he started the movie. He sat next to her and put his arm around her shoulders as she snuggled into him, his beer in the hand leaning on the armrest.

Twenty minutes into the movie, Liam paused it. "What are you doing?" Gabriella asked as she raised her head up.

"We didn't open gifts yet. Movie is after gifts." He said with a smile as he took her empty wine glass and put it in the kitchen with his beer bottle. He came back in and went to the tree where he pulled out two gifts wrapped in shiny red paper and picked up the one Gabriella brought over.

"Thanks," she said as he handed her the two gifts.

"How do you want to do this? Should we open at the same time?" Liam asked.

"You go first. I'm really excited for you to see your gift," Gabriella said with a smile.

Liam nodded his head, then tore into the snowflake covered wrapping paper and disposed it on the floor. "No fucking way! Are you for real, Gabby?" Liam shouted as he stood up as he studied the box in his hands.

"Do you like it?" Gabriella asked, unsure as she tried to decipher the look on his face.

He blinked, then looked from the gift down to Gabby on the couch. "Coolest girl ever," he said with a giant smile. "What in the world made you get me a VR gaming system?"

Gabriella smiled with relief, "I know how much you love gaming, and I know you don't have one of these, so I thought you would enjoy it."

He placed the gift on the table, then pounced onto Gabriella and kissed her thoroughly. "You really are amazing," he said after he released her lips. "Okay, your turn," he said with a smile as he reached for her gifts.

Gabriella looked up at him and smiled before she opened a box the size of two bricks. When she removed the wrapping paper, she tried to keep the smile on her face when she saw the gift.

"Isn't it great?" Liam asked. "Now we can both play when you are over, so you won't be bored watching me play!" He excitedly said as he looked at the controller box in her hands. He took it from her and opened it to show her that he had a pink silicone cover on it. "I got a cover, so you know which one is yours," he explained as he took the controller over to his media console and placed it on the charger next to his controller, "we'll keep it right here, so it's accessible."

Gabriella watched him as she forced the smile on her face. "Yeah, good thinking."

26

"You need to open your other gift," he said as he turned his attention to the thin rectangular box next to her.

She unwrapped the gift, unable to keep the look of shock from her face when she revealed two scraps of red lace. She held them up and thought he must have purchased the lingerie set at least three sizes too small.

He scooted next to her, his breath hot on her neck. He placed a wet kiss on her neck and trailed his tongue up to her ear where he whispered, "I was hoping you would wear that for me tonight," then nipped her earlobe with his teeth as his hands began to wander over her body.

"Um, I don't think tonight is a good idea, too many carbs at dinner, I'm totally bloated." Gabriella said as she placed the sorry excuse for fabric back into the box. Liam looked at her, disappointment on his face. "Maybe we can save it for L.A.?"

He nodded, then resumed his seduction tactics on the couch. Gabriella sat there and allowed him to do his thing as the disappointment from his gifts sat front row and center in her mind. She was appalled by the complete lack of effort behind his gifts. She had searched for weeks to get him that gaming system.

Liam took her hand and placed in on his tented pants. "Gabby, I'm so hard for you right now."

Gabriella hardly registered what he said when her mind betrayed her. *I bet Henry would never be this inconsiderate with a Christmas gift.*

Absolutely horrified by her inner monologue, she gave an emphatic yes when Liam asked, "Let's take this to the bedroom?"

***

Gabriella woke up the next morning as Liam shook her at seven. "Gabby, come on, you gotta get up. Rise and shine Goober."

"What? What time is it?" She asked, hey eyes still closed.

"It's seven."

"Why are you waking me up so early?" She whined, then turned away from him.

"Gabby, are you for real right now?" Liam hissed in an annoyed tone.

"What?" Gabby asked as she lifted her head with one eye open to look at him.

"You need to be out of here by eight, eight thirty the latest. I'm making the pancakes I promised."

"Why do I need to be out of here at a certain time?" She asked, as she started to shake the sleep away.

"Because my parents rented a truck, and they are coming to get me at nine. Now come on, up and at them." He said as he left the bedroom.

Gabriella sat up in bed as she replayed what happened in her head. She grabbed her overnight bag and went to the bathroom to brush her teeth and change. She went back to the bedroom to pack the rest of her belongings, then placed her bag on the couch.

"Breakfast is ready Gabs," Liam called out from the kitchen.

She made her way into the kitchen and sat down at the table where a cup of coffee waited for her, along with a stack of pancakes and a side of breakfast sausage. Liam joined her at the table and smiled at her encouragingly, "eat up."

Gabriella cut into the pancakes and shoved them into her mouth as she stewed about his actions. Before she barely swallowed the first bite, she stuffed another chunk into her mouth. Liam chewed him breakfast as he watched her shovel the pancakes into her mouth. He chuckled then said, "wow, someone is hungry. Slow down, what's the rush?"

Gabriella looked up at him, held up one finger and gulped a mouthful of coffee to help aid as she swallowed her pancakes. "Hungry? No, I'm actually surprised that I have an appetite at all. I'm just making sure I get out of here before your parents arrive. I don't want to embarrass you in front of mommy and daddy when they see who you've been slumming it with."

Gabriella slammed her coffee mug on the table, stood up and stormed out of the kitchen, as Liam sat there in shock.

"Gabby!" He yelled out as she grabbed her coat from rack in the living room and gathered her bags. "Gabby, what the hell are you talking about? Where do you come up with this shit?"

He exited the kitchen to see her march to the front door. "Shit? Shit! What else do you call it when someone wants you gone before their family gets here?"

"That's not what I meant. I just need to shower and pack and get everything together before they get here," Liam explained as he followed her to the door.

"Sure it is. Merry Christmas, fucking jerk," she murmured as she left his apartment and slammed the door behind her. *I hope his uppity neighbors make a noise complaint*, she thought as she exited the building.

After the almost half an hour commute back to her apartment, along with a long hot shower, Gabriella had almost calmed down from the most humiliating morning on record. She felt like she was tossed out like a one-night stand and wasn't able to get the feeling of pure rejection out of her system.

She took the time to do her hair and makeup and slipped on her jeans and ugly Christmas sweater, which was mandatory this year. Once pleased with her appearance, she emptied her overnight bag and repacked it for her two-night stay with her parents. She placed the bags of gifts and her stuff near the door, then went to the kitchen where she spent the next two hours decorating the cakes for the party.

Around noon she cleaned up the kitchen and packed the cakes into containers. After everything was balanced in her arms, she locked up and walked around the block to the parking garage to claim her vehicle. Once all of her items were secured in the car, she linked her phone to the radio and started the commute to her childhood home.

With traffic heavier due to holiday, she emersed herself in her playlist as she slowly crawled her way through the Long Island Expressway. The eclectic mix of music made her mind stray back to everything that happened over the past twenty-four hours. *I can't believe Liam had the balls to be such a douche bag, especially after those sorry excuses for presents. Those were definitely more for him than for me. And who the hell does he think he is, he's too good for me? He's embarrassed of his parents seeing me. Fuck him! And mom is right, if he was really into me, which he obviously isn't as those gifts proved, his ass would have made time to come tonight. And if he really couldn't make it, he could have attempted to come after the holidays, my parents always have leftovers for weeks.*

I bet if it was Henry, he would have gone out of his way to come for Christmas Eve, and he would have given me such thoughtful gifts. He's always been so generous and thoughtful, always going to the extra mile to make everyone happy. No, scratch that, he did it to make me happy. And I went and fucked that one up big time.

Gabriella's thoughts were all over the place as she sat in traffic. *What the fuck is wrong with me, no, I didn't fuck that up. He did. He lied. It didn't matter what his intentions were, he lied. Just like that fucker, Brad. The douche who started it all. Talk about a liar. Oh, let me lead you on for a year, then let me destroy you in front of everyone, oh then years later I can admit that I was a douche of epic proportions and lied to everyone because I couldn't be seen with the fat chick.*

Speaking of fat chicks, what the hell was Liam thinking giving me that dental floss? I'd look like a tied up stuffed roast. That's not attractive. Hmph, speaking of not attractive, how about that Bryan idiot that wasn't even attracted to me. He was a piece of work. I've got some shitty track record. Even Jordan, God rest his soul, was a total pig. I mean, typical horny teenager, but still, he was a bit uncouth. Henry was a bit uncouth himself, with his dirty mouth and his photos. The way he would pull my hair and suck on my neck and tell me how pretty my pussy was. That time on set was definitely the peak of my sexual encounters for life. Ugh, why did he have to be so sexy? Why couldn't I resist him? I never would have had carnal knowledge of him, which replays in my head constantly.

A loud blare of a horn knocked her from her train wreck of a thought processes when she realized that she had exited the Southern State Parkway, and the light she was stopped at had turned green. She scolded herself as she turned into the neighborhood and observed the houses decked out in lights and decorations.

"Mom, Dad, I'm home," she yelled out as she opened the door as she dragged her overnight bag and presents in with her. She dropped the gift bag next to the tree, then made her way upstairs to drop her bag in her room.

"Gabby? You need help bringing anything in?" Giuseppe yelled out from the bottom of the stairs.

"The two cakes are still in the car, on the floor of the back seat." She yelled back as she left her bags and coat in the room. She tucked her phone into her jeans and made it down the stairs as her father entered the house with the cakes.

"I think you missed your calling; you should be a baker or a chef," her dad said with a smile as he walked over and kissed her cheek. "I'm sorry about yesterday, Gabby."

"It's okay, Dad, forgiven and forgotten," she said with a smile as she followed him into the kitchen. Her mom closed the basement door as she said, "Oh, *Bambolina*, I didn't know you were here."

"Hi mom, I just got here. Dad has the two cakes I brought." Gabriella answered as she kissed her mother.

"That is such a pretty sweater, Gabby. It's so festive with the green and red and white. I know the whole pattern thing makes it an ugly sweater, but those colors are so vibrant."

Giuseppe placed the cakes on the counter and turned when he took a good look at the sweater and started a deep belly laugh. "What is so funny, *amore*?" Maria asked as she looked at her husband. Gabriella bit back a smile and gave her father a knowing glance.

"Nothing, I was thinking of something I heard on a podcast earlier today. You are right, *cara mia*, that sweater is something alright." Giuseppe said while he wiped his eyes.

A few hours later, the house was filled with twinkling lights, Christmas music, and food spread out as far as the eye could see. The kitchen island, countertops, and the dining room table was filled with food. A table was setup against the far wall of the kitchen with all the drinks and booze. Tables and chairs were strategically placed throughout the living room, den, and sunroom, and the office had coat racks for everyone's belongings.

As tradition has dictated over the past few years, the Dolces always show up first, since they brought three of the seven fish dishes, not to be outdone by the Balvins, who come armed to the hilt with coquito. The two families arrived within five minutes of each other and brought an extra guest each of Matt and Arnie. Caroline and Dino followed Maria into the dining room to deposit the fish while Sierra, Marco, Elise, Desmond, and Arnie followed Giuseppe to the bar setup, all of them carried multiple bottles of coquito.

"Merry Christmas guys!" Gabriella yelled as she ran over to Laurel and Matt and threw her arms around both of them. Laurel pushed Matt away as she squeezed Gabriella. Matt laughed as he stepped away to allow Laurel to get her fill of Gabriella.

"I've missed you so much!" Laurel wailed as she sobbed into Gabriella's shoulder. "I've missed you too, Lau. Please tell me you're wearing waterproof makeup." Gabriella joked.

Laurel bit Gabriella's shoulder in response, which caused her to yelp. "Yes, I did, you bitch," she said as she loosened her grip.

Matt approached Laurel slowly, "are you done mauling Gabby now? Am I able to give her a hug?"

Laurel smacked Matt in the arm and let go so Matt could greet Gabriella. "Hey Gabby, how have you been. We miss seeing you in the sunshine."

34

"Oh, I miss you guys too. I've been good, Manhattan has been good to me. Busy, busy." Gabriella said with a smile.

Matt released her as Desmond and Arnie approached them in the hallway, their parents not too far in the kitchen. Gabriella turned to hug Arnie as Desmond took a good look at her sweater.

"Gabby, are those humping reindeer on your sweater?" He asked loudly. Gabriella began to respond as Giuseppe began to cackle in the kitchen, and Maria ran into the hallway to get a good look at her daughter's shirt.

"Oh my god, Gabriella!" Maria exclaimed over the collective sound of everyone's laughter and walked closer to take a look at the small, repetitive detail of two reindeer fornicating on multiple rows of her sweater.

Three

The party was in full swing as the three friends headed outside to the front patio with the two boyfriends in tow. Gabriella sat in the center of the sofa as Laurel and Desmond flanked her on either side. Arnie sat in one of the single rocking chairs as Matt leaned his back against the banister of the porch. Desmond revealed a bottle of coquito from his jacket as Laurel giggled to reveal one of her own.

"Gabby, tell me you took one," Laurel said with a twinkle in her eye.

"Sorry, but I do have sangria up in my room ready to go for later."

"Can someone explain to me why we are out here? It's freezing," Arnie complained as he breathed into his gloved hands.

"Tradition," the three of them said at the same time.

Matt shook his head and looked over to Arnie. "I think we have a lot to learn with this group. My Californian ass can't handle this weather. You better crack open that liquor or I'm going back inside. Screw tradition." Arnie nodded his head in agreement while the others giggled.

One bottle of coquito was given to Matt as the other was passed around. Watching the two men shiver in the cold, Gabriella ran back into the house to get throw blankets. After they were distributed and everyone was tucked in, Desmond cleared his throat. "In honor of the tradition to top Nonna Rosa's comment for Christmas wish list, I now ask, what do you want Santa to bring you for Christmas this year?"

"Let's start with the newbies! Newbie number one, Matt," Laurel said as she handed the liquor bottle to him.

"Um, I guess to develop the two storefronts next to the gym to expand to more clients? Like to have classes and maybe a pool or something." He said, then took a swig of the drink.

Desmond gave Matt a thumbs down as he handed his bottle to Arnie, "go on, newbie number two."

Arnie took a long swig of the drink and revealed, "I want a new career. I hate being on my feet for hours in a busy, hotter than hell kitchen. I just can't see myself doing this forever. I'm thirty-three years old, and I already have the feet and knees of a fifty-year-old."

Everyone sat in stunned silence as Arnie let out a deep breath, then took another swig of the bottle. "Baby, you never told me that, why haven't you said anything?" Desmond asked as he grabbed Arnie's hand.

"No offense, but I thought only one of us should be chasing our dreams at a time. We need steady income, and I didn't want to add any more stress to you branching out in your career," Arnie admitted.

"Baby, you don't have to put your dreams on hold for me. I'm solid. This bitch over here got me into two national ad campaigns, plus if the auditions go well, you're looking at the new *Phantom of the Opera* Raoul. We've never been in a better position for you to do something else. I want Santa to bring you your new career."

"What is it that you want to do?" Gabriella asked after she sipped from the bottle.

"I've always wanted to make unique foods and desserts and sell them, like at a posh shop or an online store. I could create my own foods and do things on my schedule. I've seen so many people be successful with this, and I think my foods would really be a hit," Arnie explained with a passion.

"Um, Arnie," Laurel said, "You do know my father owns a few cafes. My mom always wanted to be a small business owner, so after my dad retired from the police department, they started a little coffee shop, and over the years they expanded. They have two in Suffolk County and one in Nassau County. The first one they opened is on main street, like five minutes away."

Arnie looked at Laurel, unsure of what to do. Laurel nodded her head and said, "Yes, Arnie, you should definitely go pitch your idea to my father."

Arnie smiled, then hesitated and looked at the rest of the group. "What are you waiting for?" Laurel asked.

"You guys didn't say what you wanted from Santa," he responded sheepishly.

"The role in that streaming service series about a trio of female serial killers. Gabby?" Laurel stated.

"A new brain," Gabriella responded as she stood up and headed towards the front door. Everyone exchanged confused looks as they followed her into the house.

"Matt! There you are," Marco yelled from the living room when they walked into the house. "I was telling Roberto about your training and the tips you've been telling us. He doesn't want his brother to get in better shape than him, so he wants to pick your brain."

"Yeah right, that fat ass wishes he was in better shape than me," Giuseppe yelled out.

"*Fanabla!* This *stronzo* over here talks so much shit, I don't know if I should give him a breath mint or some toilet paper," Roberto responded to his brother's taunt.

"Duty calls," Matt said with a wink, then kissed Laurel and headed into the living room.

Laurel threaded her arm through Arnie's and dragged him to the den, where her parents were located. "Hey Dad, I've got a business prop for you."

Gabriella and Desmond finished off what was left of the coquito and put the empties under the bar. "New brain?" Desmond asked as his one eyebrow lifted.

"Arnie's career?" Gabriella asked as she mimicked Desmond.

He rolled his eyes in response and pursed his lips and shook his head. The then held up his left hand and wiggled his ring finger. Gabriella nodded in understanding, "yeah, that sounds more like it."

"Yeah, guess that won't be happening anytime soon. Not with this sudden mid-life career crisis." Desmond said with a sigh. "I know, fucking diva, I sound like a total shit. But we've been together for almost two years. I just thought since we've been living together for so long, the next logical step is putting a ring on it."

"We need to hit pause on this convo. I've got sangria stored in my room, we just need to get Laurel," Gabriella interjected.

"Laurel!" Desmond yelled, getting her attention. "We need you, bitch. Pronto dente."

Laurel looked up from her conversation with Arnie and her parents, which looked to be going well from where Gabriella and Desmond stood. She held up a finger to give her a moment, then turned back to the conversation, her hand rubbing Arnie's arm. Arnie flashed a bright smile at Laurel and nodded his head, she winked in return and made her way to the kitchen.

"That seems to be going well," Gabriella commented.

"Yeah, yeah. Save it. Upstairs, now," Desmond demanded.

After they made their way up the stairs and settled into their typical spots in the room, Gabriella erred on the side of caution and broke out one bottle of sangria since they all had their fill of coquito outside. "So, what happened downstairs?"

"My parents are going to give him a chance. He's going to make a few items that he would be interested in selling, and they are going to try it out. Test it on some customers to see if there would be a demand. If so, they said that they would carry his food. He said he won't quit his day job, but he's really happy, Des."

"Well, I do want to see my man happy, so yay." Desmond responded

"You're such a salty bitch. Can you please fill Laurel in?" Gabriella said with an eye roll.

"I thought that maybe we'd get engaged soon, but I think it's out of the question with this mid-life crisis." Desmond sighed and grabbed the bottle of sangria from Gabriella.

"You actually want to get married?" Laurel asked skeptically. "Since when?"

"It's just the next logical step," he responded in a huff.

"So what? Who cares if it's logical? Fuck marriage. I'm all about living my life the way I want to; societal norms be damned." Laurel said as she swiped the bottle from Desmond.

Desmond pouted in response, then turned to Gabriella. "Meh, she might be right."

"Is this a recent revelation from moving in with Matt?"

Laurel shook her head, "no, I love being in the house with him. We even set up a room for Matty. I just don't see the need to be married. We're happy the way we are."

Desmond nodded, then turned his attention back to Gabriella, "You're stalling. Spill about the new brain for Christmas." Laurel's eyes widened and she pointed at Gabriella in agreement while she drank.

"Yeah, my brain, totally broken. Like my bad luck with men thing, it isn't over. It has reared its ugly head once again."

Her friends sat there as if it was story time and waited for the elaboration.

"Okay, here's my tale of woe. Liam and I decided to celebrate Christmas last night, since he was going to visit family in Pennsylvania. We had a really nice dinner, we watched Elf, we exchanged gifts, I bought him this really nice virtual reality gaming console. He bought me a game controller for his gaming console so we could play games together," she said as Liam gasped and clasped his hand over his mouth and Laurel shouted no, "and skimpy lace lingerie in fire engine red, which I would be lucky if they covered one nipple, never mind both of my tits."

"Oh no, Gabby," Laurel squeaked out as she passed the bottle over. Gabriella took it and looked at her friends.

"That's not even the worst part. He tells me that he was going to make me breakfast. He wakes me up at the ass crack of dawn and rushes me out of bed because, and I quote, my parents will be here at nine and I want you gone before then."

"Stop it. He did not," Laurel gasped.

"Oh, he did. And the worst part about it, like way worse than having it insinuated that he's embarrassed for his parents to meet me, is all I could think of was that Henry would never pull this shit on me. The guy who lied to me, the guy who destroyed me, not looking so horrible against mister you-aren't-good-enough-to-meet-my-parents."

Gabriella tossed back the wine as Laurel blinked at her, Desmond still didn't move his hand from his mouth. After a few moments, Desmond removed his hand from his mouth and extended it in front of him. "Girl, you need to kick his ass to the curb. What a fucking douchebag. I'm sorry I ever encouraged you to date him. I should have seen the red flag when you complained about the sex."

"The sex is bad? Gabby, what are you doing?" Laurel asked.

"It's not that it's bad. It's just that it's not Henry. That man ruined sex for me. Nothing will ever be as good as it was with him." Gabriella sighed, then drained the rest of the wine in her mouth.

"Get the other bottle," Desmond instructed Laurel, who grabbed the next bottle and cracked it open.

"Gabs, if you aren't happy, dump Liam. I know you guys were good friends, maybe you can just go back to that?" Laurel suggested.

"It's not that I wasn't happy, I feel like I was just settling. But after the shit the pulled last night, deuces." Gabriella said as she flipped her hair behind her head.

"But if Henry is who makes you happy, why not be with him?" Laurel asked. Desmond looked over at Laurel, his eyes wide, then looked over to see Gabriella's reaction.

"Where is that even an option, Lau? He's not here. He's in Ireland filming. Besides, that shipped sailed and ended as a Viking funeral. Besides, I'm still broken over what he did. And I won't have to see him until the summer for the premiere, saying I go."

"You're going." Laurel said as Desmond said, "I'm going." The girls looked at Desmond who shrugged as he took a sip of sangria. "What? She's going to need a date. I trump any douche she's dating at the time."

"Sure Des, you got it," Gabriella said with a smirk as her bedroom door creaked open. Matt popped his head into the room and smiled, then shouted out behind him, "found them!"

He entered the room, quickly followed by Arnie and Elise. Elise sighed as she shut the door behind her. "You guys can't leave me down there with all of them. The adults are out of control and, no offense Gabby, some of your cousins are real assholes."

Gabby shifted over on the bed and patted the spot next to her for Elise to squeeze in between her and Laurel. Desmond got up from the desk chair and perched himself on the desk and offered the chair to Arnie. Matt sat at the end of Gabriella's bed, with his broad back pressed against her wall. "So, what did we miss?"

"Nah-uh," Laurel replied, "I want to know what happened with Arnie and my parents."

"Oh, well, I can't thank you enough. I'm going to make a few samples and give them to your parents next week. If it passes their quality check, then we are going to introduce them at one of the shops. Depending on how things go, we might expand to the other shops. Dino was saying that if the food sells well, we could even sell them like to-go on the shelves. It's just so exciting to get the opportunity to do it. I'm hoping it takes off and I can quit my damn job."

Desmond rubbed Arnie's shoulders in support. "You're going to be amazing, babe. Your food is phenomenal, and you are so talented. I can even be your sexy little sous chef at home while you're cooking."

"Oh, gross," Elise said in response, which made everyone laugh. Laurel grabbed the other bottle of sangria and

passed the two around in a celebratory toast to Arnie's new passion project.

"You guys were left alone for a while, I know we missed something with you three," Matt said.

"Gabby got a game controller and underwear for Christmas," Desmond said at the same time Laurel said, "Gabby isn't over Henry."

"What the fuck, Laurel?" Gabriella yelled and reached behind Elise to hit Laurel on the arm.

46

"That needs to be unpacked," Arnie said with a smile while Matt stared at Gabriella.

"Yes, Liam bought me scraps of fabric and a game controller for Christmas. Laurel has it in her head that I'm not over Henry and I totally am."

"Not." Laurel said to finish Gabriella's statement. "She said Henry was the best sex of her life."

Desmond hit his palm onto his forehead as Gabriella screamed, "Oh my god Laurel!"

"How could he not be? That man is a walking pheromone," Elise said before she bit her knuckle, which quieted the room at her response.

"She has a point," Arnie said with a laugh as Gabriella buried her face in her hands.

"I could call him if you want," Matt said as he took out his phone.

"Matthew Trammel, I will kill you where you sit." Gabriella threatened as she looked up from her hands and gave him the stink eye.

Matt put his hands up in surrender, "okay, okay, I won't call him, tonight."

"You won't call him ever," she retorted.

"You can't say that, he's my friend. I can't never call him again," Matt said with smirk.

"Ugh!" Gabriella yelled as she dropped her head back against her headboard.

"Hey Gabby," Arnie asked, then waited for Gabriella to acknowledge him with eye contact, "are you even a gamer? Do you ever play video games?"

"No! I totally don't. He usually plays them before I go over, but there have been times that I've sat there while he played. I've never shown an interest in wanting to play. I'm usually on my phone."

"And don't forget the skimpy underwear," Desmond reminded.

"Wow, it's like he bought himself a Christmas gift and said it was for you. That's pretty damn selfish." Arnie concluded.

"Yeah, that's pretty bad. A dude buying lingerie for a chick is never a gift for her. That dude just wants to see her in it." Matt stated.

"So, what are you going to do?" Arnie asked.

"Oh, nothing. We're done. He made sure he kicked me out of his apartment before his parents came to pick him up. Apparently, I'm not good enough to meet mommy and daddy. You know what?" Gabriella asked as she took her phone from her pocket. "He's blocked. Fuck him."

***

It was three in the afternoon when Gabriella finally awoke on Christmas day. She made her way downstairs and nursed a horrible hangover to find her parents on the couch in similar states. They grunted in acknowledgement to one another, then Gabriella continued their traditional hair of the dog and made coffee with Irish cream and gathered a box full of leftover pastries. She trekked into the den with the tray of treats, she distributed the food and made herself comfortable on the recliner. No one spoke as they tried to fuel themselves, and it wasn't until the pastries were gone that Maria broke the silence. "I'm getting the triple fudge cake you made, *Bambolina*. Does anyone want refills?"

"Are you crazy? Bring out the gallon of milk. You can't have anything with all that chocolate without milk," Giuseppe said before releasing a belch.

"Nice one, dad," Gabriella said with a smile.

Once the three of them were circled around the cake armed with only forks, Giuseppe asked, "when do we open presents?"

"Meh, we can do it later. Or tomorrow. Are you staying tonight?" Maria asked.

"Yeah, but I need to leave in the morning. Patti setup a virtual gift exchange and party tomorrow afternoon, and all of the gifts are at my apartment." Gabriella said through a mouth full of cake.

"Who is going to be on the call?" Maria asked.

"Probably everyone that you met at my graduation party, I'm assuming. She scheduled it for three in the afternoon, so it will be noon for the west coasters. She plans on having this party go on for hours. She was texting me that she had ideas for virtual games and whatnot. All I know is the size of the box that was shipped to me barely made it through my door."

"So, everyone from the movie is going to be on the call?" Maria asked.

Gabriella rolled her eyes. "No, mom, I saw the invite. Just the Americans are on the call."

"What did Liam get you for Christmas?" Giuseppe asked.

Gabriella shoved a large bite of cake in her mouth and shook her head. After she chased it with milk, she looked at her parents. "Liam? Liam who?"

"Okay, I'm not touching that one with a six-foot pole," Giuseppe said with his hands up in defense.

"I think it's going to be a new year, new Gabby," Maria said with a wink.

"Oh! Did I tell you guys that I have to go back to L.A. in two weeks? The movie needs a bunch of shoots for a new ending, so I'll probably gone for a few days."

"You are coming back, right? You're not doing your six months in California early, are you?" Maria asked.

"Yes, mother. I will be back in less than a week. I'm not heading out until maybe April or May. Speaking of which, do you think it would be a good idea for me to get a place there?" Gabriella asked.

"Are you planning on renting it out when you aren't there? It would be a good investment," Giuseppe chimed in.

Gabriella shrugged, "I guess I could. It could be a vacation home for you guys too. I can get a place with an extra bedroom so you can stay with me. We can summer in L.A."

"I think that would be wonderful," Maria said with a smile.

"Let us look for a place with you, maybe we can go in on it and you can get a bigger place in a nicer area. We could snowbird for some time in the winter," Giuseppe suggested.

"That sounds like a great idea," Gabriella agreed.

"I want a place near the water. I want to hear and see the ocean," Maria suggested.

"Mom, I'm not Laurel. I don't have movie star money," Gabriella said with a laugh as she shook her head, then took a huge bite of cake.

"You haven't had any more run-ins with the paparazzi, have you?" Giuseppe asked.

Gabriella shook her head as she swallowed a mouthful of cake. "No, thank God. Not since after the movie when they ran stories about me and mystery man Liam. I've had enough speculations of me cheating to last a lifetime. They lost interest in me when they saw my very real, very boring day-to-day."

They spent a few hours lounged around the house and as they picked on leftovers, then the DiStella's exchanged gifts. Gabriella bought her father some gym equipment that Matt suggested, which would be delivered later on in the week. Maria received a pair of classic black Louboutin heels and a black Dolce and Gabbana clutch, which she freaked out about. "*Bambolina*, this is too much. What am I supposed to do with these?"

"They are classic black accessories; you can use them for formal events. Maybe some Hollywood events, like the movie premiere when that happens," Gabriella said with a shrug.

"Wait, we'll get to go to the premiere?" Maria asked.

"Yeah, of course. I mean, Des already claimed to be my date, but you guys are definitely going to come," Gabriella assured them.

"Looks like we might need to start looking at a place in California soon, so we have a place to stay," Giuseppe said with a smile.

Gabriella opened her gift after her parents were done with theirs, and revealed a new iPad Pro. "You guys shouldn't have! This is so great!"

"Well, you keep making comments about not having a portable second screen to work off of, and we know how much you rely on your laptop, so we thought this could help." Giuseppe explained.

"It's perfect! Thank you!" Gabriella said as she hugged her parents.

"Do you realize it is almost midnight?" Maria asked.

Gabriella shook her head while she unboxed her gift. "What train do you have to take home?"

She looked up at her mother, "Anytime between eleven and one. I just need to be home by three."

"So, you'll have time for breakfast?" Maria asked.

"You mean I'm going to get a real breakfast while I'm here? Not just pastries and cake?" Gabriella joked.

"Never mind breakfast," Giuseppe said, "afternoon train means a night cap." He said as he walked over to the makeshift bar that was still set up from yesterday.

"Oh, Dad, no. Shouldn't we clean? We can wake up early and I can help you guys break down the tables and put the house back in order."

"No need, Gabby. We got the garbage out last night. You were a huge help with the set up. We can handle the breakdown. Can I interest you in a glass of wine? Some boozy hot chocolate?" Giuseppe asked.

Gabriella and her mother shared a look and responded together, "boozy hot chocolate."

***

Gabriella awoke to the smell of bacon, eggs and pancakes the next morning, which encouraged her to hop out of bed and run downstairs in her pajamas. Her mother placed the plates down at the island while her father was worked at the espresso machine.

"You better keep liquor away from my caffeine this morning, Dad. I don't think my liver can handle anymore. It's been an extremely boozy Christmas this year."

"And knowing Patti, I'm sure there will be some drinking game involved with your festivities today," Maria said with a laugh.

"Don't worry Gabby, I think I'm steering clear of booze until New Year's," Giuseppe said as he brought the coffee mugs to the island.

"Did you decide what train you were going to take home?" Maria asked as they began to eat.

"I think I'm going to take the 12:03. It will give me enough time to get home and shower and prep for the party." Gabriella answered.

"Are Laurel and Matt still here, or did they fly home?" Maria inquired.

"I think they were planning to stay for a week. You know Laurel doesn't make it home too often."

"What about Matt's son? Doesn't he celebrate with him?" Maria asked.

"They are Jewish, so he celebrated with them last week. Laurel actually celebrated with him and his ex-wife and her fiancé. She said that it was a really nice time, and they all get a long really well."

"I think those two are going to get married," Maria said with a smile.

Gabriella raised her eyebrow at her mother as she chewed her food. "If you say so."

"Are we placing bets? Because my money is on Arnie and Desmond," Giuseppe chimed in.

"Eh, I'm not sure about that one. Not anytime soon at least," Gabriella explained. "Arnie wants a new career. He's going to be working with Dino to sell some of his food at their cafes. I'm not sure if marriage is on his mind at the moment."

Gabriella's parents exchanged a look that she noticed. "I don't want to hear it. I'm very happy with my life right now. I don't need a man."

Gabriella's mother hummed in annoyance at her statement, then shook her head. "Well, I know what you do need. You need to take home leftovers."

"I'm not going to say no, but remember, I have to get this stuff back to the apartment using public transportation. And I have my overnight bag and whatever reusable cake cases I brought."

Maria hushed her daughter as she instructed Giuseppe to grab the large overnight bag so she could fill it with leftovers. Gabriella shook her head and cleared the island, then made her way upstairs to get ready to go home.

Four

The apartment was prepped and ready for the virtual holiday party. Gabriella made it home and lugged cartons of food and desserts back with her. As she put away all of the perishable items, she noticed a thermos in her bag filled with her father's holiday martini, the scent of cinnamon overwhelmed her when she opened it. She then showered, she straightened her hair, donned her Christmas sweater from Christmas eve along with a reindeer antler headband, and added a pop of red on her lips.

She settled down on her couch with the large box from Patti on the floor in front of her, her computer propped on the coffee table with her thermos of booze, a martini glass, and plate full of leftovers and dessert next to the computer. She turned on the computer and entered the virtual room but checked her hair and makeup in the preview before she joined. She was greeted by a yell from Patti and Joshua as their faces came into view.

"I knew you'd be the first one on here, don'tcha know," Patti said with a big smile. Her red hair was covered with a Santa hat, and she had tinsel with small Christmas lights around her neck like a boa.

"Am I early?" Gabriella asked as Joshua entered into the screen view with a drink in his hand, he wore a sweater with the body of an elf on it, and an elf hat with point ears on his head.

"You're punctual," he replied with a smile.

"I miss you guys so much! Thank you for putting this together, Patti." Gabriella gushed.

"I miss ya'll too. Joshua and I have been so busy with the restaurant, so it's nice to be able to relax and spend some quality time wit'cha." Patti said with a smile as she poured herself some bourbon.

Laurel and Matt showed up next, the two of them in her childhood bedroom, both of them wearing Frosty the snowman hats, complete with holly. Next was Max, who wore a sweater with the leg lamp on it, followed by Darius in a Christmas sweater print blazer with a white ascot. Everyone spoke over one another in excitement. "Patti, you should have made a talking stick so we could pass it around so we can hear each other," Darius joked.

"I organized this, set up the gifts, and got ya'll on here at the same time. Didn't I do enough? Now you want a dang talking stick?" She joked back.

"Who else are we waiting on?" Matt asked.

"I'm here!" Jem announced as she appeared on the screen, her usual black hair dyed white. She wore a headband made of fake holly and an off the shoulder red shirt.

"Whoa! Check out the hair!" Laurel exclaimed.

"Yeah, I decided to change it up for the holidays. There's no snow here in L.A., so I channeled Jack Frost," Jem said with a laugh.

"You look like Max," Matt commented, which made Jem to give him the finger while everyone laughed and agreed.

"Where is Bob?" Gabriella asked as she poured her drink into her martini glass.

"Check out the fancy bitch with the fancy glass. She moves to Manhattan and gets all highbrow." Max said with a laugh.

"If she starts drinking with her pinky up, I'm hiding her feed from my screen," Darius winked.

"I'm kinda surprised you're drinking Gabs, I know you've been drinking since we left you on Christmas Eve," Laurel said as Matt nodded in the background.

"Hair of the dog, part two," Gabriella said as she raised her glass to the camera and ensured to raise her pinky out as she took a sip.

The group laughed at her antics as Bob joined the call. "What did I miss?"

"Bob!" Everyone cheered when he appeared on the screen. His hair was longer and ended at the middle of his ears, his not so scrawny frame was covered with a green and white ringer tee with a message that said "Merry Drunk, I'm Christmas".

"Holy shit, Bob got jacked!" Laurel said while Matt whistled. "Looks like Ireland did you good."

Bob blushed slightly, then flexed to show off his bicep. Everyone on the call catcalled Bob as Matt asked, "So I guess you were training with Hank?"

"Yeah, since he had to be this jacked mythological warrior, he was constantly in the gym. He offered to let me train with him. It was fucking intense, but I'm glad I did it. I've been keeping at it since I've been home too." Bob said with pride.

"Yeah dude, you're looking good. Keep it up. I might have to come back to South Dakota and test you," Matt joked.

"Test him on what?" A British voice chimed in. Gabriella's smile froze on her face as she saw Henry appear on the screen. His Christmas sweater had red solo cups on it with a message that said it's the most wonderful time for a beer. He wore a knitted reindeer hat with antlers and flaps that covered his ears. Panic set in as Gabriella's eyes fixated on the new square on the screen that he occupied.

Her attention was torn away from the computer as her phone vibrated. She saw a message from Laurel as the rest of the call cheered because Henry was on the call.

Laurel: Breathe. Are you okay? Your face went pale.

Gabby: Just shocked, wasn't expecting him.

"I'm so glad you made it! I was afraid it was going to be too late for you," Patti said with a large grin.

"It's eight at night, Patti, nowhere near my bedtime." Henry said with a laugh as Leigh pushed her nose up under his arm. "Looks like Leigh wants to say hi."

Everyone said hi to Leigh as she barked excitedly at the noise. Gabriella smiled at Leigh, then took a long sip of her martini. "What happened to the fancy pinky, Gabby?" Max asked with a raised eyebrow. Darius chimed in, "she better not, I'm not good with this technical shit, I would have to put a post-it on my screen to block her bougie ass."

"What did I miss?" Bob asked.

"Gabby is all fancy in her Manhattan apartment, drinking martinis and whatnot. So, we were busting on her that she better not start drinking with her pinky up." Darius explained.

"You do realize that there is two Hollywood heavy hitters on this call? We're saying the Gabby is the bougie one?" Joshua pointed out.

"Eh, Henry is drinking a beer out of a pint glass, and I'm pretty sure Laurel is drinking a beer too." Max said.

"I'm only drinking a beer because I don't have martini accoutrements around me. Gabby, tell me your dad sent you home with martinis." Laurel said.

Gabriella smiled and nodded as everyone else laughed. "Oh man, Giuseppe is the best," Henry said with a smile.

Gabriella swallowed harder than normal as she went to tuck her hair behind her ear and hit her antler headband instead. She felt hyper aware that Henry was on the call and got nervous that he spoke about her father. She bit her bottom lip slightly and could swear that Henry started at her. She looked up, but it just looked like everyone was looking into the cameras.

"Hey, did you two plan to match?" Bob asked. Laurel and Matt looked at each other. "Well, yeah, we bought the hats together," Laurel replied.

"No, not you two, Gabby and Hank. Did you guys plan the reindeer theme?" Bob asked. Gabriella shook her head no as Henry said, "no, not planned. But it doesn't surprise me. Great minds."

Gabriella nodded slightly, then finished the rest of her martini, and poured another.

"Alright people, I've got some games planned, I've got some snack breaks prepped, and we've got some presents to open," Patti said to reign in the crowd. Everyone settled down and gave their full attention to Patti's instructions.

"If you open your boxes, you will find a bunch of smaller packages with numbers on them. Please locate package number one."

Everyone dug through their main box and held up a large package. "Okay, everyone, show me your package," Patti requested.

The call erupted in laughter as Bob, Matt, and Henry all stood with their crotches in the camera. "Great minds again, mates" Henry said with a laugh.

"You can open your packages. And I'm also speaking to you fellas. Maybe not Bob, because that's cradle robbing, but by all means, Matt, Henry, open them. Momma likey." Patti said with a wag of her eyebrows.

"I agree, that would make my Christmas very merry indeed," Jem shouted as Laurel said, "no, no, no, Matt's package is for me to unwrap only."

Laughter ensued as everyone opened a bag filled with chips, candy, and cookies. "Okay, so snacks are dispersed. Joshua, would you like to start the gift giving?"

"Sure thing. If everyone can open package two, this is my gift to everyone." Joshua said with a smile. The package was filled with a bound recipe book and a few non-perishable food items and a few cooking utensils. "The book is filled with some recipes from our restaurant, but it also has some recipes that I created with you guys as the inspiration. There is Max's Mexican Crema, Darius's Diva Eggs, Laurel's thousand calorie dessert, Jem's dark chocolate pudding, Bob's gourmet hot dogs, the big Patti melt, Henry's hoppy fish fry, Matt's protein pancakes, Gabby's Mediterranean delight, and Joshua's famous flapjacks. I just wanted to give you guys something a little something in return for what our time together gave me."

"Oh, fuck you. You sentimental asshole," Darius said sarcastically, "this guy starts us off with this shit? My gift is gonna suck compared to this."

"Aww, this was really sweet, Joshua," Jem said as she held the book to her chest.

"Thousand calorie dessert? Why do I get that?" Laurel asked.

"Because you eat so much junk food and dessert and your still so thin, so it was inspired by your sugar consumption," Joshua explained.

Laurel smiled and then rolled her eyes as Patti murmured, "you skinny bitch."

"Max's Mexican crema, isn't that illegal to serve in a restaurant?" Henry asked with a smirk. Joshua shook his head and laughed. "This one is okay Henry; it's not straight from the tap."

"Oh, eww," Patti said when she realized their innuendo.

After opening Jem's gift, which consisted of bottles filled with sand and water from the Pacific Ocean, each with a heart inside it, and framed picture of everyone at the beer garden, the group moved onto Bob's gift of Irish tweed scarfs and lemon soap. Package number five from Max was a basket full of facial cleansers, masks and lotions and some makeup for the ladies, which he claimed he got deep discounts for all of the name-brand products he gifted everyone.

"Onto a game!" Patti announced. "And of course, they shall be drinking games! Because how can we get together and not drink? So, make sure your glasses are full. Now is the time to do it. Maybe a bathroom break before someone gets to the point of breaking the seal?"

Everyone left their computers to get themselves prepared for the next part of the party. Gabriella checked her thermos, which she has already emptied. She made her way to her kitchen with a sigh, where she grabbed a bottle of red wine, a glass and an opener, then she grabbed the two beers that were in her refrigerator. Once settled, she opened the beer and looked at the screen, where Laurel remained.

"You good?" Laurel asked as Gabriella nodded her head. "No more martinis?"

Gabriella shook her head. "Nope, dad didn't give me a big enough thermos for this party."

"Hey sis, are you drinking a winter beer?" Bob asked. Gabriella looked at the beer in her hand and nodded.

"Well, that doesn't seem Gabby-like" Joshua said.

"It's really not. They were left in my fridge. Figured I'd polish them off before I move to the wine," Gabriella said with a smile as she held up the wine bottle.

"But a holiday brew?" Bob asked, his face wrinkled in disgust. "What would you possess you to buy that?"

"Asks the nineteen-year-old connoisseur over here," Matt said with a laugh.

"I didn't buy it, they're Liam's," Gabriella answered as Henry and Patti sat back in front of the computer.

"Oooh, the boyfriend. How's he doing," Jem asked. Gabriella shook her head slightly in response. "Patti, you ready to start your game?" She deflected.

"Yes ma'am. But first, how's Love Bug Liam?" Patti asked. Matt and Laurel exchanged a look as Gabriella took a swig of the gingerbread seasoned beer. "He's fine. Let's play."

"Okay," Patti said as she made a confused face. "Name of the game is worst Christmas gift I've ever gotten. We need to guess if you are telling us the truth or not, if you guess wrong, you drink. I'll start. Worst Christmas gift I ever got was diet pills from my ex. Raise your hand if you think it's true."

Max and Darius raised their hands. "I call bullshit. No one is that much of a douche," Jem said with a snort.

"It is indeed true my friends. Drink bitches." Patti said as everyone else took a drink.

"When the hell was that?" Laurel asked. "I might need to kick some ass."

Patti laughed, "I think I was in my sophomore year of college. Mind you, I was probably half the woman you see before you, but my freshman fifteen bothered him, so he thought he'd help me out by buying me some nice dress and a bottle of diet pills so I would fit in it better. Dumped his ass after that shit."

"I'll go," Matt volunteered. "The worst Hannukah gift I ever got was a regift of sorts. I was thirteen and I was big into gaming. It was the last night, and all of the gifts I got so far were lame, like socks and whatnot. The last night was the big gift. There were five small gifts wrapped up. My mom was ready with her camera to film me as I tore into my presents. I noticed they were games that I already owned. I went over to where my games were to double check… yeah, they were my games. My mom wrapped them thinking my dad bought them for me. So, I had no gift. They felt so bad; they took me to the store the next day and bought me new games."

Everyone laughed at Matt's story as Patti spoke up, "okay people, raise your hand if you think it is true." Everyone but Jem, Max, Laurel and Gabriella raised their hands.

"Matt?" Patti asked.

"It is a true story," Matt answered.

"No way, Laurel got that wrong?" Darius squealed.

"Hey, we haven't been dating that long," Laurel defended herself as she drank.

"Um, it's been almost six months," Jem pointed out.

"Shut it, Jem," Laurel said with a wink. "My turn. The worst Christmas gift I ever received was an etiquette book to accompany etiquette classes."

"What? That's bullshit," Gabriella scoffed.

"Raise you had if you think it is true," Patti instructed. Everyone looked at one another, no one raised their hand after Gabriella's comment.

"No one, really?" Laurel asked. Gabriella smiled. "Well, drink up, bitches, because that is one-hundred-percent true!"

Everyone groaned at Gabriella and drank as Gabriella stared at Laurel completely dumbfounded. "How is that possible? You never told me that."

"The last Christmas I was dating Marc, his grandmother got it for me to make sure I was classy enough to marry into the family. I obviously never took them. It was just so embarrassing." Laurel explained. "Since you didn't guess right, my bestie, chug the rest of that beer."

"Are you serious, it's pretty full," Gabriella hesitated.

"Chug, chug, chug!" Everyone chanted as Gabriella studied her beer, then shrugged her shoulders and drank the rest of the beer. Everyone cheered when she finished.

"Alright you hyaenas, what's next?" Gabriella asked.

"Package six people!" Patti shouted. "This one is from me!"

"Patti, is this the whiskey we drank at the beer garden?" Laurel asked.

"You bet'cha! And you got a shot glass, so you know what that means," Patti said as she wagged her eyebrows.

"Oh my god, beer pong!" Ben shouted.

"Yes, and a beer pong kit. I wanted everyone to take home part of the beer garden with them. Now, prepare your shot!" Patti instructed.

Everyone took their shot, most of them chased it with their drinks. Gabriella looked at her newly opened beer, surprised to see that a quarter of it was gone already. "Guys, I'm definitely getting drunk," she announced.

"I'm right there with you," Darius responded. Max and Jem raised their glasses in agreement.

"Max, worst gift," Patti said.

"Okay, worst Christmas gift I've ever gotten. There was a starlet I was working with on the set of a movie. She had just released her own fragrance, Risqué, it was a scent for women. She gave it to everyone and got mad if you didn't wear it, like diva meltdowns. So, everyone walked around the set reeking of this dead skunk hooker scent for a week, until someone claimed they were allergic." Max explained.

"Show of hands for true?" Patti asked. Everyone but Darius and Joshua raised their hands.

"Wow, you guys are terrible at this game. It's not true," Max said with a laugh.

"Bobby, my boy, worst gift," Patti said.

Bob took a long drink of his beer before he spoke. "Okay, this is kinda embarrassing. When I was a kid, like eight years old, I was obsessed with Pokémon. My grandma went and bought me the coolest stuff for Christmas that year. And the year after that, and the year after that. It's been eleven years, and she still gets me Pokémon stuff."

Everyone raised their hand to vote for true. Bob shook his head and scoffed. "I almost want to say it's fake because I think he still likes Pokémon," Matt joked.

"I feel like I should be insulted. Looks like everyone is drinking, because it's false." Bob said with a laugh. A groan ensued as everyone took a drink.

"I'm definitely getting drunk," Laurel commented after she finished her drink. Patti laughed, "alright, one more worst gift and then we'll open package seven. Joshy, my work husband, will you please give your gift?"

"Yes, my work wife. I had a bunch of regulars when I worked at a diner near the airport. One Christmas, a few of them decided to chip in and give me a gift, which was completely unexpected. This one woman, Sueann, she made a huge stink about what they got me. It was a one-hundred-dollar gift card to Walmart, which was super generous. One day I went shopping and remembered I had the gift card. I go to use it on a forty-dollar purchase, the cashier tells me I owe thirty-five dollars. I got a used gift card. I don't know who got the other ninety-five dollars but is sure as hell wasn't me."

"No way, that has to be made up. Like someone would pocket the money or use the gift car before giving it to you," Jem said as she waved her hand dismissively at the screen.

"Show of hands please," Patti reminded. Matt, Henry, Darius, and Bob all raised their hands.

"Right hand to God, that is a true story," Joshua admitted as he raised his right hand in the air.

As Gabriella took another drink, her eyes focused on Henry, whose eyes were slightly squinted from the huge smile across his face. He and Matt talked about an experience they had in a Walmart together. She could not help herself as she studied his face, and appreciated how attractive he was, even though he wore a ridiculous knitted reindeer hat. A small smile made its way onto her face as Henry winked at the camera during his story. Shortly after, Gabriella's phone buzzed.

Laurel: Someone is looking smitten

Gabby: I'm drunk, and so are you

Laurel: No way, I've seen that look. You're staring at Henry

Gabby: I'm looking at the screen, at everyone

Laurel: I think he noticed and winked at you

Gabby: He's telling a story. It's not at me. Lay off the booze.

Laurel: You're in such denial.

Gabriella scowled at the screen and Laurel laughed. She tossed her phone back on the sofa next to her. Patti's voice focused her attention back at the computer. "Moving on to package number seven."

Gabriella reached into the box and opened the gift. "This one is from me," Henry announced. Gabriella pulled out a book and found a post-it attached to the front of it. On it was a poor drawing of an eye, followed by an even worse drawing of a woman with a hand up and a ring on the fourth finger with a circle with a line through it over the hand, and then the letter u. After it was signed H. She studied the post-it while everyone gasped at their gifts.

As she still tried to decipher what he drew on the post-it, she opened the book to find it was bound book with all behind the scenes pictures from the movie. There were group shots of their outings, candid of them on the set and during parties, and on the last page there was a picture of the two of them with Leigh from the night of the storm. On the inside back cover, there was a note: Dear Ella, I'm sorry. Love, Henry

Gabriella tried to control her emotions as she flipped through the book and noticed a picture of her parents with her at her graduation and another of the group shot from the family dinner she invited him to. "Henry, this is amazing! I love these pictures! But the shirt might be my favorite! Patti's Bitchin' Kitchen!" Patti said.

Gabriella looked up at the screen to see Patti hold up her shirt. "You do realize in really small letters it says 'in the' before kitchen?" Darius said with a large laugh.

Patti looked closer at the shirt and began to laugh so hard she couldn't breathe. Joshua spoke up, "mine says best chef in the Midwest, and on the back, it says don't tell Patti."

"Mine says second best actor in Edge of Time", Laurel said with a roll of her eyes. Matt laughed and chimed in, "muscles by Anderson. Get the fuck out of here, dude."

"I make people less ugly," Jem read from her shirt. "Fluff and blow," Max followed up with a laugh. Bob cheered when he saw his. "Beer pong champion."

Darius chuckled as he read his, "this shirt is designer." "Gabby, what does yours say?" Joshua asked.

Gabriella looked down in the box as Henry spoke up, "I had to get her a little something different than you guys."

She unfolded the garment, and she bit her lip from a mix of laughter and tears. Without saying a word, she lifted an apron up and showed the computer that it said #kissthecook on it. Everyone started to laugh as Gabriella's eyes glistened. She wasn't sure why she was so affected by the gift. It was a silly gag gift, but everything from him was so personalized, which was the complete opposite of what she received from Liam.

She mouthed the words "thank you" to Henry as she neatly packed away his present. Henry smiled and winked at her as Patti instructed them to open the envelope marked with an eight.

"Okay, you sentimental assholes, let me explain my gift. My life partner, Samuel, started a clothing line with his sister. I gave you all gift cards to their boutique, which is in Santa Monica. They have a website, and they will ship anywhere. I was kinda hoping you guys would try their clothes, maybe spread the word. It would mean the world to me." Darius explained.

"Darius, this is a gift card for a thousand dollars," Laurel said when she opened the envelope.

"Yeah, I know. Happy shopping," he said with a smile.

"This is amazing, Darius. This is so generous," Jem said.

"Darius, you know I will wear their clothing when I know I will be photographed," Henry said seriously.

"Absolutely, I'll do the same," Laurel chimed in.

"Well, I just like free clothes, no one cares what accessories a cook in the Midwest wears," Patti said with a smile.

"Patti, my love, they have a plus size line as well. They cater to everyone." Darius said with a smile.

"Who knew this salty bitch had a heart this whole time," Max said with a laugh.

Patti laughed and instructed everyone to open package nine, an L.A. Raiders hat and a gift bag full of water bottles, towels, and shirts from Matt's gym.

"Patti, can we get a potty break?" Jem begged.

"Okay, but when we get back, we will open number ten." Patti instructed.

Gabriella gathered the empty beer bottles and brought them to the kitchen and then ran to the bathroom. As she was washing her hands, she heard her phone notification. With a roll her eyes, she made her way back to the couch but grabbed cannoli from the plate of pastries and shoved one in her mouth before she sat down. She looked down at her phone to see a text from Desmond.

"Well, that looks delicious," Henry said as she settled onto the couch.

"Are you talking about Gabby or the pastry hanging from her mouth?" Matt asked with a raised eyebrow.

Henry laughed in response and took a drink of his beer. "Did you make cannoli for the holidays?" Bob asked.

74

Gabriella shook her head, "no, I baked a bunch of cakes, but these are from an Italian pasty shop on the Island."

"What kind of cake did you make?" Bob asked.

"Triple chocolate fudge, cheesecake, a gingerbread cake, vanilla cake with caramel, and a traditional swiss roll yule log cake." Gabriella answered.

"She also made my favorite German chocolate cake," Laurel chimed in. "Is that the one with the coconut?" Matt asked. Laurel nodded her head in response. "Oh my god, guys, you missed out. You thought the dessert she made for the party was good, this blew it out of the water."

"Great, rub it in guys," Bob said with an eye roll.

"Since Gabby seems to be the topic of discussion, please open number ten. Gabby, care to explain?" Patti asked.

Darius started to laugh as soon he opened his gift, and lifted up an I love NY shirt, where a heart was in place of the word love. "Since you all had some choice words and opinions of me moving here, I thought I'd spread the love," Gabriella said with a smirk as she raised her full glass of wine to the computer.

"Touché, you snarky bitch, I love you," Darius said with a smile as he wiped a tear from his eye.

"Also, I got us friendship lamps. They work over long distances, over the internet. Everyone gets their own color, so if you're thinking of someone, you can light their lamp up with your color." Gabriella explained.

"I set all ya'lls up and gave everyone a card with everyone's colors. Joshua is teal, Jem is dark purple, Bob is white, Max is red, I'm green, Henry is blue, Darius is yellow, Matt is orange, Gabby is lavender, and Laurel is pink." Patti explained.

"This is actually a really cute idea," Laurel said with a smile.

"Gabby, worst Christmas gift ever," Patti yelled, surprising everyone.

"Um, wow, okay," Gabriella said before taking a large swig of wine. "Easy. Scraps of bright red lace disguised as underwear."

Laurel and Matt raised their hands right away with a smirk. In response, everyone else raised their hands. Gabriella's eyebrows furrowed as she frowned at the screen. "Really? No one drinks with my story?"

"Sure. You do, because we all guess correctly," Joshua said with a laugh.

Gabriella rolled her eyes and sipped her wine. "It's really a good thing I'm drinking at home. I can crawl to my bed after all of this." She reached onto the plate on the table and shoved a sugar cookie into her mouth.

"This isn't fair, Gabby has all of these amazing treats she keeps eating. I'm voting that next year she bakes for us and ships it. The friendship lights are cool and all, but I really just want to shove a bunch of baked goods in my mouth," Bob complained.

"It isn't fair, I think Gabby shouldn't be able to eat in front of us anymore," Max chimed in with a smirk.

Gabriella nodded her head in agreement, "you guys are right, I shouldn't eat this in front of you. I apologize." She then turned off her camera and instructed Patti to continue with the festivities.

After the laughter of her antics calmed, Jem shared her worst Christmas gift. "My aunt is one of those new age hippies, everything is all granola and namaste. Pretty much my complete opposite. She had moved in with some hemp wearing guy, somewhere out in the desert in Arizona. They were talking about how they remodeled their basement into some love den or whatever. So, I got her a lava lamp, figured it went with her vibe.

"She made a big stink out of it, saying how great it was going to look in love den. I think I sent it to her over the summer for her birthday. Anyway, that Christmas we all get together to exchange gifts. I open the one from my aunt, and it was a lava lamp. The same exact custom lava lamp that I bought her. I confronted her about it, and her hippy dippy boyfriend told me it didn't groove with their esthetic."

"Gabby, is your hand raised?" Patti asked to her blank screen. Gabriella smirked, then responded with a muffled moan.

Henry's eyes shot up to the screen, his ears perked at the sound that came from his computer. "Mmm, oh." A breathy voice came through again. Bob looked at the screen with his eyebrow raised as everyone else seemed to look at one another.

"Gabby? Girl you there?" Patti asked with a hesitant smiled.

"Mmm. Oh, that's so good," Gabby said softly, not in a response to Patti.

77

Henry licked his lips, memories of their night together flashed in his brain when he had her moans directly in his ear. He adjusted on the couch; the blood rushed and made his pants uncomfortable. He could picture the way she moved beneath him as he coaxed those sexy sounds from her. His breath labored slightly as his arousal grew.

"Uh, Gabby?" Laurel asked, her discomfort becoming apparent and Matt turned his attention to Henry.

"Ohhhh, yeah. Mmm. Oh, I'm making a mess," Gabby moaned quietly.

The mouths on all the guys dropped simultaneously as Jem began to giggle. A blush grew on Patti's face as she looked through the controls in the meeting to mute her line. "Gabriella!" Laurel yelled as Henry blurted out, "turn on your bloody camera!"

Gabriella had to stifle a laugh as she turned her camera on, chocolate on the side of her mouth as she bit into a large piece of her triple chocolate cake without a fork, as she tried to hide the thrill that Henry demanded she turned on her camera. She feigned innocence as she looked up from her cake. "What? You told me you didn't want to see eating."

A mix of laughter and groans filled the room as they realized what she did. She watched as Henry blinked a few times, then rubbed his face roughly with two hands, then blew out a deep breath. He held his beer up to the screen in a cheers, then slammed the beer and walked away from the computer.

"That was hysterical," Jem said through tears. "That made me feel weird," Bob admitted. "I've got a bloody semi," Henry yelled from off camera, which caused another eruption of laughter.

"No handies during the party, Henry." Matt yelled out. A middle finger appeared in Henry's screen in return. He sat back down with a fresh beer and shook his head as he said, "saucy minx."

Gabriella's insides did summersaults at his reaction as her face split into a huge smile. "Before I was so rudely interrupted by sex by chocolate over here, did we get a vote on my story?" Jem asked.

"I'm just going to drink because I'm always getting it wrong anyway," Gabriella said with a smile as she sipped her wine.

"Well, anyone who voted true can join Gabby in the drunk tank." Jem said with a wink.

"We have one more story and one more gift, what is it gonna be ya'll?" Patti asked.

"I'll tell my worst Christmas gift, it's fitting at the moment," Henry said with a smirk before taking a drink. "A few years ago, my ex-fiancé didn't like that I was going to be away for filming, so she gave me a wanker mold kit."

"Wait, like you stick your dick in plaster and make a dildo out of it?" Max asked curiously. Henry nodded his head in response.

"Isn't that more a gift for her than for you?" Joshua chimed in.

"Well, yeah. Plaster is not a kink of mine, mate," Henry said with a laugh. Gabriella raised her hand violently.

"Question from the chocoholic in the top right box," Henry said to Gabriella.

"Who me? No, I'm saying this is true," Gabriella said with a smile. Henry's face broke out into a shit-eating grin at her conviction that it's a true story.

Her enthusiasm had everyone except Matt, Bob, and Joshua raise their hands. "Ah, tough break, mates, it is a false story." Henry said with a wink.

"Who the hell comes up with shit like that?" Matt asked with a laugh.

"Oh, it really happened, just not the way I told it. I was approached by a sex toy manufacturer. They wanted to make a pun on the superhero movies and approached my manager. Apparently, they were asking all the men from the movie to participate." Henry responded.

"No fair, he cheated, it was a real story," Laurel complained as Matt tickled her.

"I would try out the Henry Anderson dildo," Jem said with a laugh. "Same, girl," Darius joined in.

"It would make a really good dildo," Gabriella said as she stared off into space, her lips touched her glass as she paused before she took her drink.

"What?!" Laurel yelled after a pregnant pause as Patti and Jem burst into laughter. The guys laughed along as Henry smiled wickedly at her response.

"Gabby!" Laurel yelled again, which drew her attention to the screen. "What?"

"Um, do you know what you just said?" Laurel asked.

A look of embarrassment and horror poured over Gabriella's face. "Tell me I didn't say that out loud," she said quietly. The response of muffled laughter and Henry's smile was answer enough as she put her nearly empty wine glass down on the table and buried her face in her hands.

"Maybe the apron wasn't the personalized gift Gabby was looking for, Hank," Darius said with a laugh. Gabriella walked away from the computer to dump the rest of the wine down the drain. She heard hollers of her name from the screen, but she was too mortified to say anything. She made herself a cup of coffee and grabbed a bottle of water, then worked up the nerve to sit back in front of the camera.

"Um, I'm drunk, and I am no longer drinking for the remainder of this party." Gabriella said as she rejoined everyone. "I cannot be held responsible for anything I do or say while intoxicated."

"Only she would say responsible and intoxicated while drunk." Bob said with a laugh.

"Okay, since Gabby has graced us with her presence again, let's move onto the last gift. Ladies and gents, I ask you to find the envelope in your box marked eleven." Patti announced.

"Fucking shit, these are airline tickets," Bob yelled out. "What?" Patti said as she tore open the envelope.

"It's not tickets, it's a gift card. I was thinking that maybe you guys can use it to come to L.A. for the premiere of the movie. And for the rest of you, it's just for whatever." Laurel explained.

"Wait, we're invited to the premiere?" Joshua asked.

"There is nothing official yet, but Henry and I discussed it and we want the whole gang there. I just thought this would help get you there." Laurel explained.

Gabriella smiled at the generosity of her best friend. She looked at the screen and she felt it in her heart that her family had really grown to include every single person at this party, Henry included. They may never have stood a chance as lovers, but she knew deep down that they had a connection, and that he was a good person, so it would not be such a terrible thing to have a friendship with him.

"I'm going to plug in my lamp and see if it works, who's with me?" Max asked.

A few people plugged in their lamps and went online to register and set it up. Gabriella had hers connected already and waited on the rest of them to connect. Everyone chatted and listened to Bob talk all about his experience in Ireland, and how Henry brought him to England for a few days where he met some of his family. Gabriella drank her coffee as she listened when a blue glow came from her lamp. She looked over and smiled that someone had set theirs up.

As Bob went into some of his experiences in the pubs in Ireland, Gabriella's phone buzzed. She glanced over at it, then sat up a little and put her coffee down when she saw who it was from.

Henry: Hey

Gabriella looked down at the phone and bit her lower lip, a bit of anxiety and excitement coursed through her veins. She realized that he could see her reaction and typed back.

Gabby: Hey

Henry: Did it work?

Gabby: What work?

Henry: the lamp.

Gabriella looked at the lamp and smiled, then nodded her head at the computer.

Gabby: you're blue I'm assuming?

Henry: Yes, and in more ways than one.

Henry: I'm truly sorry for what happened between us. It was never my intention to hurt you. It was a stupid move. I became extremely jealous of every man on that app. I needed your attention and I'm so incredibly sorry.

Gabby: I still don't get the logic behind getting to know me under a fake name, but I understand. I was letting my bias of your career stop me from letting down my guard completely. I'm sorry too.

Henry: No need to apologize to me, Ella.

Gabriella's face cracked into a smile at seeing his nickname for her. She looked up at the camera and saw him smiling back at her.

Henry: did you figure out my message?

Gabby: the post-it?

Henry: yep.

Gabby: I got I and You. Not sure about the deformed lady hand.

Henry: Come on, girl with a wedding ring on her finger with it crossed out. She's not a missus, she's a miss.

Gabriella shook her head at his corniness. Henry's laugh rung out on the computer at her response.

Gabby: Wow, Henry, that's something else. I miss you. Cute.

Henry: I do, Ella. I miss you a lot. I hate the way things happened with us.

Gabby: I miss you too. You're a good person, Henry Anderson.

Five

The party lasted for about four hours, everyone thoroughly enjoyed the company, but eventually people signed off due to other commitments. They agreed to try to sync up once every other month, and Patti promised to be the organizer of the gatherings. Gabriella stretched as she stood up from the couch then gathered all the junk that had collected on the table through the call. She deposited her dishes in the sink and threw away all the wrapping paper, then looked out of her windows as she made her way back to the living room. The dark winter sky, which had already settled in three hours ago, was brightened by large snowflakes that fell at a rather fast pace. Surprised by the snow fall, she settled down at her desk chair and stared out into the night.

Her phone rang, and she answered it without looking at who it was. "Hello?"

"Hey, so what did you think of the party?" Laurel asked.

"It was really nice to see everyone. I'm still feeling pretty good from all the drinking, but the water I've been guzzling down for the past hour and a half seems to have helped. And I already took my Advil."

"I should have stopped at your parents and had Giuseppe make me some martinis."

Gabriella laughed, "you know he would have. Then again, he may have not let you leave, especially if you brought Matt along with you."

"Oh, I know. He's like bros with all the dads now. So, was it really nice to see everyone on the call?" Laurel prodded.

"Yes, it was nice to see and speak with Henry." Gabriella said to placate her friend.

"Were you two texting each other during the party?"

"Why would you ask that?"

"I just noticed that after the gift exchange was over, the two of you seemed to be preoccupied. Kept looking down, partially paying attention to what everyone was saying."

Gabriella laughed. "We may have texted a bit."

"Ha! I knew it. You owe me a back rub." Laurel yelled victoriously.

"You play you cards right, I'll make it a full body massage," Gabriella could hear Matt say in the background.

"Oh, gross, I'm not listening to this." Gabriella said with a laugh as she hung up.

It was only seven in the evening with had no plans the next day, so she decided to change into her pajamas and get comfortable on the couch and searched through her streaming devices to find something to watch. She typed into the search bar and a list of Henry's films appeared on the screen. She scrolled through the list and sneered at the show he starred in with Riona. She decided to watch the action movie that he was basically shirtless and wet the entire time.

The ring for a FaceTime call interrupted her start of the movie. She answered the call without a glance at the screen. "So help me God if you're calling me during your full body massage."

"I've never thought of doing that, but it may be fun the next time I go if you're willing to reciprocate." The deep sound of Henry's voice responded.

Gabriella sat up and looked at the screen to see Henry's face with a smile stretched across it. "Oh lord, I thought you were Laurel."

"That is some friendship you two have." Henry said with a chuckle.

"Funny. No, I was talking to her before, and Matt was getting handsy so I hung up. So, what do I owe the honor of this call?"

"I enjoyed chatting with you before, and I enjoyed seeing you even more, so I thought, best of both worlds."

"Isn't it late by you?"

"It's not even midnight yet."

"Oh. So, how have you been?" Gabriella asked.

"I've been busy. Had a good time filming in Ireland. Spent the holidays at my mum and dad's house. Everyone was there this year, which was really nice. Saw some extended family as well. How was Christmas eve? Did Giuseppe get everyone drunk?"

Gabriella laughed, "yeah, that he did. It was good. Typical holiday at the DiStella's. It was nice that Matt and Arnie were there. It's always good when the family gets bigger."

"Were they the only newcomers this year?"

"No, some of my cousins brought their significant others. The parties are getting so big, my parents are considering putting an extension on the house for an all-seasons room to expand."

"That sounds nice. I have to admit, I was thinking about you and your family on Christmas Eve. They must throw one hell of a party."

"You know my parents, it's an open invite with them. I'm sure they would love for you to come if you were ever in New York during Christmas." Gabriella said with a shrug.

"But would you want me there?" Henry asked, the question burned in his eyes.

"Of course, I would invite all of you if I could get you here for Christmas." Gabriella said with a smile.

A look of disappointment flashed on Henry's face but was gone as quick as it came. "How has life been since you made the move to the big apple?"

"Busy. Very busy. Laurel has always kept my schedule pretty full, but now with Desmond in the mix, I'm lucky I have any time to myself."

"Desmond in the mix?"

88

"Yeah, I'm his manager now. He convinced me to stay in New York and take him on as a client. He auditioned for a huge part in the *Phantom of the Opera*. He's been in the ensemble for *Hamilton*, but this is a great chance for him to really make a name for himself."

"Wow, that is incredible. Good on him."

"What about you, any good projects coming up?"

"There is a new project that I've signed on for, about the knights of the round table."

"Let me guess, Lancelot?" Gabriella said with a smirk.

"Nope, his son, Galahad."

"Wait, they are going to have you be the pure, untouched grail-getter?" Gabriella asked incredulously.

"Yes. I don't always have to play the heartthrob. Shame on you, thinking I'm a piece of meat." Henry said with his hand to his chest as if he was offended.

Gabriella laughed as he continued. "Hey, I get to film in New Zealand, ride horses, and dress in a suite of armor. I'm okay not having to kiss an actress for a movie."

"Have you spoken with anyone from the film?"

"Sure have. As a matter of fact, I just saw a bunch of them on the computer not too long ago." Henry said with a laugh.

Gabriella rolled her eyes. "I meant other than them."

"Yeah, sure."

Gabriella nodded her head in response. A lull of quiet fell over them. Henry studied her face through the screen, then wiped down his face with his hand.

"Look, we both have things we want to say and ask. Can we just cut the shite and be honest with each other?"

Gabriella gnawed at her lower lip as she contemplated his ask. He was right, they needed to have an honest conversation with one another. Clear the air and move past what happened those last few days on set. Gabriella nodded her head in response.

"Ask me your question." He demanded.

"Have you been in touch with Riona?"

"Yes. Have you been in touch with that dating app guy?"

"Yes."

Henry nodded his head. "Okay, good. Have you been dating him?"

"Yes. Have you been dating her?"

"Not dating. But we do see each other."

"Okay," Gabriella said quietly, not sure what to make of that.

"Do you forgive me for that wanker thing I did with the dating app?"

"I already told you before that I do."

"Do you think we would still be together if I didn't fuck things up?"

Gabriella looked at him, her breathe caught in her throat. "I'm not sure how to answer that."

"Do you still have feelings for me? Because, bloody hell, Ella, I still think about you all of the time."

Gabriella's eyes began to water, her emotions choked her. Her head nodded slightly in response. "Yes. I think about you too, as much as I try not to. I compare everything to you."

Henry smile sadly. "I'm so bloody sorry, Ella."

"Me too." Gabriella said as she reflected his smile. "I was hoping that maybe we could still find a way to be a part of each other's life. I really do miss you, all of you."

"Tell me what to do, and it's yours."

"Maybe we can start over? Press reset on everything?" Gabriella asked hopefully.

"On everything?" He questioned. Gabriella nodded in response, her heart beating erratically.

"Anything for you, Ella."

Gabriella smiled at him as he smiled back. He then cleared his throat and said, *"hola señorita, mi nombre es Henry. Debo decir que eres hermosa. ¿Te gustaría ser mi amigo?"*

Gabriella could not hold her laugh back at his Spanish. She shook her head and smiled as she responded. *"Ciao Henry, sono Gabriella. Non parlo spagnolo. Sei molto attraente e mi piacerebbe essere tuo amico, ma gli amici non lo dicono a vicenda."*

Henry laughed at her response. "I'm not fluent in Italian, but I'm pretty sure you agreed to be my friend."

"That I did."

"You also said that you think I'm attractive," he said as he wagged his eyebrows.

"I also said that friends don't say that to each other."

"They absolutely do."

Gabriella rolled her eyes in response. "If I think that my friend, my best friend, is one of the most attractive women I've ever met, with the softest skin and the sweetest mouth, I can absolutely say that."

92

Gabriella's insides clenched as he spoke. This is what she had missed, a man who actually wants to be with her, who thinks she's beautiful and tells her so. A rush of feelings rolled through her body, the desire to be in his arms engulfed her desperately.

"Henry, you're treading dangerous water."

"I know, I know. I'm sorry. I'll try to be more friend appropriate. So, a friend appropriate question for you."

"Shoot."

"When did you get the tiny red lace panties, do you have them, and can I see them?"

Gabriella barked out a laugh. "I got them three days ago, I do not have them, and I wouldn't show it to you if I did have them."

"Gift from the dating app guy? Wait, don't tell me, I don't want to know."

"What did you think of the party? Patti did an awesome job." Gabriella asked to change the current topic.

"It was brilliant. She really went over the top. I need to ask; did you know I was going to be on that call? Because you looked like a deer in headlights when I got on."

Gabriella pressed her lips together and shook her head. "No, I didn't know. Which was wrong,"

"So how did you get me a gift?"

"Patti told me how many to buy and what size shirts there were. I didn't even think about it honestly."

"Was it okay that I was on the call?"

"Of course, they are your friends too. If it wasn't okay with it, I wouldn't be talking to you now."

"Ah, that is true. I will say, I was surprised by Darius's gift. I had no idea he was married." Henry said.

"I don't think he is. He did say life partner and not husband."

"Mmm. Those were some great stories with the worst gift ever."

"Oh yeah, that was a great game. Patti really knows what she's doing."

"So, you really think my dick would make a great dildo?"

A deep blush crept across Gabriella's face as she adjusted on the couch. "Um, that wasn't supposed to be said out loud."

"But you said it, and you think it. That might be the best compliment that I've ever been given."

"I don't want you to get too full of yourself. Moving on."

"Ella, for real. That was probably one of the hottest things anyone has ever said to me. I knew it was good between us, but you really think it was on that level?"

"Total transparency and honesty in the name of friendship?" She asked him hesitantly as he nodded in earnest as if he was imitating a bobble head. "You ruined men for me. Relationships, expectations, sex… totally ruined."

Henry groaned at her response. "I don't ever want to be inside another woman, Ella. They could never compare to you."

Gabriella bit her lip and stared at him, and watched his lips move as his sexualized words caressed her soul. "Henry, we're dancing through a field of land mines."

"I'm pretty nimble," he responded.

"I'm not."

"That's a lie. I've seen you move in many ways."

Gabriella closed her eyes and took a deep breath and tried to regain her composure. Her body was warmed from the slick words that came from Henry's delectable mouth. "So, how was it seeing your family?"

"Do you really think you are going to distract me with another topic?"

"Your mom must have cooked so much for your huge family. Does anyone help her, or does she do it herself?"

Henry huffed in frustration. "Okay, Ella, I give. Yes, my mum has help, we all come over and help her with the meal. My family is great, my sister won't stop talking about her wedding. She's elbows deep in the planning and keeps going on about how September is not that far away, and how she can't decide on bridal colors or if she wants it in a church. It's all very dull and I pity my future brother-in-law."

"Was that so difficult to answer?" Gabriella asked with a smirk.

"No, I was able to answer it fine, but all that I can think of were those sexy noises you were making when the camera was off. I'm getting hard all over again thinking about it."

"I think my friendship lamp is broken. I had a few flashes of colors, but it's been blue most of the time."

"That's because I'm constantly thinking about you. I think about you when I'm in the shower, and when I'm in bed. I think about you when I need a release. I think about you when I'm on set, or when I see a blueberry muffin. I think about you when Leigh does something funny or adorable, and I want to reach out and tell you. I think about you when I see Italian food. I think about if I had another shot with you, how I would make up for everything that I did to hurt you."

"Do you ever think about the logistics, Henry? Because I have. My personal insecurities aside, we are from two different worlds. Not just based on our jobs, but we are physically on two different continents. We have a whole ocean between us, and that's when we are home, never mind when you are traveling for work or when I'm in California."

96

"We would figure it out."

"Henry, please. If you don't think that I feel like a piece of me is missing, you're wrong. But I'm a realist. I do care about you Henry, as much as may have wanted it for a while, it hasn't changed. I also need to protect myself and protect you in the process. I think friendship is the only thing I can give you."

Henry was silent and he absorbed her words. He covered her mouth with his hand, breathed in, then rubbed his face with a long exhale. "Okay, Ella. I still think we could figure it out, but I am not going to push the issue. You are right, I am heading to New Zealand in a few weeks. I'd rather we be in each other's life, than go on the way we have. But I'm warning you, I don't want you hear about your dating app boyfriend."

A small smile broke onto Gabriella's face. "Well, I don't want to hear about you being with Riona."

"I won't say anything, but I can't help what you read in the tabloids."

Gabriella's face contorted as she exclaimed, "blech. I stay far away from the tabloids, you know that."

Henry chuckled. "Right. Well, the reality is, if we aren't together, we are going to be with other people."

She nodded in response. "That is true. We can be happy for one another, right?"

"Ha! I'm going to want to pummel every single man you are with."

"I'm not going to like seeing you on the red carpet with a gorgeous model on your arm."

"Well, just know that whoever she is, I'll be wishing it was you instead."

***

The sound of the door buzzer jolted Gabriella from a deep sleep. She cracked one eye open and saw it was already two in the afternoon. She spent hours talking with Henry, and didn't hang up until it was four in the morning in England. She was so revved from their conversation; she had a hard time falling asleep. They shared so many stories, spoke about their childhoods and families to current affairs and philosophical debates. There was a deeper connection between them after they came to terms about their feelings and the future of their relationship, like a large, weighted blanket was lifted off of them.

The buzzer stopped, so her eyes start to drift close again. She was jolted from her sleepy state when a someone pounded on her apartment door. She jumped from her bed, grabbed her oversized plaid robe and covered her baby blue fleece pajamas with penguins and polar bears having a snowball fight on them. She smiled at her pajamas and remembered how Henry had poked fun of them last night.

The brightness from the window caught her eye as she walked into the living room. She looked out on the same view that she observed the night before and was stunned to see everything blanketed in just under two feet of snow. The banging on the door started again and dragged her attention away from the winter wonderland outside. She looked through the peep hole before she unchained and unlocked the door, and saw Liam in her hallway, bundled up in a hat and scarf, his nose and cheeks a bright red.

"Liam? What are you doing here?" She yelled out.

"Gabby, thank God you are home. Can you let me in? I need to speak with you." He responded.

"You could have called."

"I tried calling; it said the number wasn't in service. Gabby, please, I'm frozen. There is an insane amount of snow out there and I just got here from taking the subway."

"That's a fifteen-minute walk from the closest subway," Gabriella stated.

"Yeah, I know. Hence the freezing. Please Gabby, it is important," he pleaded.

Gabriella huffed as she slid the chain and unlocked the door, then stepped aside as she held it open. He walked in, immediately dropped his backpack and overnight bag in the entrance, then hightailed it over to the radiator in the living room to warm his hands.

Gabriella stared at him dumbfounded as he thawed himself out for a few minutes. The uncomfortable silence encouraged her to walk into the kitchen and boil water in a kettle to make hot chocolate. The whistling sound from the kitchen brought Liam in as Gabriella reached for her mug and the cocoa mix.

"Can I get one of those?" Liam asked as he entered the kitchen.

She wordlessly grabbed another mug and fixed him a cup, then slid it over to him on the counter when she was done. "Are you going to tell me why you are here? Or do I have to watch you defrost for another fifteen minutes?"

Gabriella walked past him, not waiting for a response as she settled onto the couch. He sheepishly followed her and settled on the single chair. "I came to apologize."

"For what?"

"For being a complete ass. Gabby, I'm so sorry the way things happened before Christmas. It's not you that I'm embarrassed about. I know my mother, and she would be all over you, asking questions and being overly obnoxious. It's nothing I want to subject anyone to. And she would be hounding me when I was going to settle down with you and making comments about grandchildren. It's just too much. I should have explained it better, and I'm sorry that I let you leave thinking that it was you I was keeping away from them."

"Liam, give me a break, it's just what parents do. They all make their comments and whatever. I get it, and I'm not one to push you into an uncomfortable situation. I just wish you would have let me handle it."

"I'm sorry. You are such an awesome person, and I don't need my mother ruining what we have going on with her talk of settling down and relationships. Like, no thank you, don't mess up a good thing."

Gabriella sipped her coffee as his words danced in her mind. She wondered what he meant by a good thing. Instead, she stayed quiet and let him continue.

100

She watched him as he jumped up and went to retrieve his backpack where he removed a gift bag and placed in on the coffee table in front of her.

"Here, this is for you. Merry Christmas."

Gabriella paused as she looked at the red giftbag with a black Santa belt around it. He gave her an encouraging look and gestured towards the bag with his head. She slowly put down her mug and lifted the bag. She pushed through the tissue paper to find a silky black knee-length nightgown with a matching robe. Beneath the robe was a new iPad in the box.

"What is this for?"

"Proper Christmas gifts. I'm sorry for what I gave you, they really weren't gifts for you when it was brought to my attention. I thought about it, and I thought you would feel more comfortable with a sleep set like that and I thought the iPad might be easier for you to use while you're on the go. Instead of lugging around your laptop and phone, maybe it would make working on the plane better. Or at least give you a bigger screen to watch shows on during your travels." Liam said with a smile.

"They are very nice, thank you. Um, brought to your attention?" Gabriella questioned.

"Yeah, I was really in a foul mood after our fight on the ride to my sister's. When I got there, she pulled me to the side and asked what was wrong. I told her what happened with the whole meet the parent's thing. I told her how we had such a great night before, with dinner and the awesome gift exchange, but then what I told her what I bought you for Christmas, she actually hit me. She yelled that I was an asshole and that you would never want a game controller because you've never shown interest in playing. And then she said I was a pig for buying you the lingerie. She said that men buy that for themselves, that women never actually want that for men. She asked me to tell her about you, and she suggest buying you these."

"So, I should really be thanking your sister for these?" Gabriella asked.

Liam sheepishly rubbed the back of his neck. "I mean, kinda, yeah. I'm sorry, okay? There is a reason I'm still single, Gabby. I don't do this shit. But you don't deserve my half-assed attempt at gift giving, okay? And before I forget, I did do one more thing, and this I did all on my own."

He pulled out his phone and pulled up and email, then turned it to show a confirmation for two upgrades to first class for a flight to California that left the following week. "Um, what is this?"

"I upgraded our flight! I thought it would be awesome to fly first class." Liam said with a grin.

"You're still coming to L.A.?" She questioned.

"Of course, why wouldn't I be?" He asked, his smile wavered slightly.

"Um, because we broke up?" Gabriella stated.

"Gabby, we didn't break up, we had a fight. Come on, I left my sister's early and took the train back to come and apologize to you in person."

102

"I appreciate the effort, Liam, but it was more than a fight."

"Come on Gabby, what can I do to get you to forgive me? I said I was sorry; I explained the misunderstanding. We have a good thing here, Gabby, I don't want to lose it because I was a complete idiot."

"And what exactly is the good thing we have? We hang out and I fuck you from time to time?" Gabriella said, her voice raised from the anger she felt. Her emotions completely mixed up from her time with Henry the night before.

"Whoa, where is this coming from? We are seeing each other, right? What is going on with you?"

"What is going on with me is that my feelings are still hurt from that shit you pulled. It's only been a few days; you can't expect to just barge in here unannounced and expect me to fall at your feet because your sister told you to buy me better presents. We've been friends for a while, never mind the dating aspect, and you don't know me at all."

Liam sat there in stunned silence as Gabriella tried to control the rage that built in her chest. She couldn't help that in her heart, she wished that it was Henry with her, the man who knew her better than the man who sat across from her, the one who she was in a supposed relationship with.

"Wow, okay. Let me call an uber or something so I don't have to walk back in the snow. It might take a little while to get someone over here, but I'll be out of your hair soon." Liam said defeated, as he pulled his phone out of his pocket and opened the app.

Gabriella sat in silence as he typed on his phone and spied the overnight bag near her door. "Did you not go home before you came here?"

Liam sighed as he looked up from his phone. "No, I took the train from Pennsylvania into Penn and then took the subway over to here. I had no idea how much it snowed until I got out at the closest stop. There were no cabs, so I walked over. Apparently, it's snowing heavily again and there aren't many uber drivers out. One responded that he was trying to dig out his car."

Gabriella turned on the news to hear the weatherman announce that they were due to get five to ten inches of snow an hour for the next few hours. "You can't travel in that, it's too dangerous. Just stay here and wait it out until the streets are cleared."

"I appreciate it, thank you." Liam said as he put down his phone and drank more of his cocoa. They sat there for a while in silence.

"Would you like a refill" Gabriella asked as she stood up with her mug. "Yes, please." Liam responded as Gabriella took his mug. She made her way into the kitchen and prepared the drinks. A few moments later she returned to find Liam eyeing the large open box from the party.

"How was your party yesterday?" He asked after he thanked her for the drink.

"It was really nice. It's always good to see everyone, and it was really well organized. Patti really knew what she was doing when she coordinated the whole thing."

"Did you get anything good?"

"Yeah, you can look in the box if you want. Actually, there is a bunch of snacks in there that Patti sent if you're hungry."

"I'm starving. You don't mind?" He questioned.

"Not at all. As a matter of fact, I have a bunch of leftovers in the fridge from my parents' party. It's more than enough to sustain us through the snowstorm."

Liam smiled as he grabbed a bag of chips and a sleeve of cookies. "Save that for later, I'm good with this stuff."

***

The next hour was filled with strained conversation over the sound of the news from the television. Liam demolished the food he took from the box and pulled out another sleeve of cookies.

"Can I be completely honest with you?" Gabriella asked, as she interrupted the sound of plastic opening.

"I wish you would," Liam responded.

"After what went down the other day, I decided that I was done with you. I blocked your number."

"Guess that's why my calls wouldn't go through," Liam said.

"Sorry, I'll unblock it. I was just really hurt. It sucks to not feel good enough, and to have you kick me out of your apartment before your parents showed up was the ultimate you aren't good enough. I understand your reasoning of why you did what you did, but deep down, I think you really don't think I'm good enough for you. And that's okay."

"Why would I keep asking you to date me if I thought that?"

"Wanting what you can't have?"

"That's so insulting, Gabby. Seriously."

"I can't help how I feel, Liam. I have so many issues I could be a magazine. I think I need time by myself, no relationship, just time to focus on me and my career, for real this time."

"So, what are you saying? We are done?"

"I'm saying maybe we could go back to being friends? Maybe just until I figure things out for myself? We had such a great relationship when we were hanging out. I don't want to lose that, but I don't think I'm okay with continuing to be romantically involved at the moment."

Liam sat there and thought about what she was asking of him. "So, you still want to hang out?" Gabriella nodded her head.

"No sex?" She shook her head in response.

"No kissing?" She shook her head again.

"Cuddling allowed?" He asked with a smirk.

"Maybe, but not right away."

"Can we still go to L.A. together? We can do that as a friend trip. I've never been, and we already have the tickets."

"Fine. But we get separate rooms, or at least separate beds."

Six

The California sunshine blanketed her skin as soon as she stepped out of the airport. Gabriella lifted her face to the sky and inhaled the sunshine, with a side of smog. "I've missed this sunshine. New York winters suck."

"Yeah, you aren't kidding. After how much snow we just got slammed with, I'm happy we were able to get out on our flight," Liam agreed as he brought their luggage to the curb and searched for the driver the studio sent. Gabriella held onto their carry-ons as she searched around for a car.

"Well, hey there Gabby." A deep voice said from behind her. She turned to find the bushy mustache that she hadn't seen in months. "Duke! Oh my god, I didn't know you'd be picking me up!" Gabriella embraced him in a large hug. "Duke, this is my friend Liam. Liam, this is Duke. He knew everything on set. And he drove our drunk asses around from time to time."

"Pleasure to meet you Liam. And believe me, I drove them for the sheer entertainment of it. The money I could have made if I had a camera in those golf carts. It was like spring break some nights." Duke said as he took a bag from each of them and directed them over to the town car waiting for them.

"How are you still assigned to this project?" Gabriella asked as he drove them away from the airport.

"This movie has become a top priority for the studio. There is a lot of buzz about it, especially with Henry and Riona dating, the studio is eager to get this going. I made the call to say that I wanted to stay on board, and they had no problem with that. The more original staff to stay with this, the easier it will be to get the film completed."

Gabriella was taken aback by Duke's statement about Henry's relationship. Although they had been texting since the virtual Christmas party, it was agreed to not discuss relationships. It was easy to escape into their bubble where the outside world did not exist, where they could continue their friendship without everything that concerned Gabriella: the paparazzi, the fans, the other women.

Liam nudged Gabriella's arm and shot her a questioning look. "Did you know?" He inquired quietly.

She shook her head briefly in response. "Are you okay?" He asked. Gabriella nodded her head.

"The studio has you staying at the Sunset Tower, which is pretty nice." Duke said as he drove towards the hotel, "It's about twenty minutes away from the studio, so you'll have a car service drive you to and from. For you, Liam, I would suggest renting a car and enjoying your time here. I have a feeling that the few days the studio has their hands on Gabby, there won't be much time for the two of you to spend together. You remember the crazy long hours on set, Gabby. It's going to be all of that, just intensified. Be prepared to run on caffeine," he said with a laugh.

"Thanks for the warning, Duke," Gabby said with a smile. "I already warned Liam that he has to entertain himself while I'm working, but we're staying through the weekend to hang out. I'll probably show him some of the spots Laurel and I used to rough it at before she really made it."

"After the winter we've been having, I plan on spending as much time as possible on the beach," Liam joined in. "Hey, Duke, do you think it would be possible to go with Gabby on set? I would love to see what it's like to make a movie. See some of the behind-the-scenes magic."

"I think you would be bored to death if you went for the full days, but I don't see it being an issue for you to come the last day she is on set."

"Awesome, I'll definitely do that! Could I ask you how far away is the hotel from the beach?" Liam asked.

"Maybe fifteen miles? Like I said, your best bet is to get a car or get a service. The bus is going to take a while."

After a few moments of quiet, Duke spoke up again. "So, how's the big apple treating you?"

"It's good, Duke. I'm busy, I get to see my parents more often. It was definitely the best move for me. But I'm planning to look at some real estate while I'm here. My parents and I decided it would be a good investment, that I'd have somewhere to live while I'm out here, I could rent it out while I'm in New York, and my parents want a vacation place."

"I didn't know you were doing that," Liam said in surprise.

"Yeah, my parents and I discussed it on Christmas. I told them I'd look at some places while I was here, I hope you don't mind. We found a few places online, but I wanted to see them in person before we made an offer."

"Sounds good to me," Liam said with a smile.

"Looking anywhere in particular?" Duke asked.

"Near the beach. I don't care what my commute will be while I'm here. I want to fall asleep to the sounds of the ocean." Gabriella said wistfully.

"My daughter-in-law is a real estate agent. Let me get you in touch with her. I'll tell her what you are looking for, and you can tell her what places you want to see. She will work with your schedule." Duke offered.

"As always, Duke, you are a god sent. What would I do without you during this whole life-altering film?" Gabriella asked with a warm smile.

"According to what Duke's said, you'd be stumbling around drunk in the middle of America," Liam said with a laugh.

Twenty minutes later, Duke pulled up to the towering white art deco hotel. "Alright, kids, here we are. Gabby, I'll be back at two to bring you over to studio."

***

Gabriella entered the soundstage, dressed in a pencil skirt, button down blouse, heels and a white lab coat. Her hair was pulled back into an aggressively tight low bun, her makeup was minimal, and she wore black-rimmed eyeglasses.

"Ah, Gabby, I'm so happy to see you!" Don said as he turned from his director's chair as April Brown pointed in her direction.

112

"Hi Don, April, good to see you both again," Gabriella said as she approached the two of them. Her eyes moved past them at a mostly green-screened set, with some desks and other lab equipment staged throughout.

"We're just waiting on Jake to join us on set, and we'll get going," Don explained as he turned back to the cameraman.

"Party's here! Let's get these reshoots started!" Jake bellowed as he walked onto the soundstage, followed by Gina and Lloyd.

"Gabriella, nice to see you again," Gina said as she walked over and hugged her.

"You too, Gina. We're a far cry from South Dakota, huh?" Gabriella joked.

"Hey Gabby," Jake said with a smile as he kissed her on the cheek.

"Jake, are you ready to conquer this next task together?"

"You know it, babe. It's up to us to carry this film, ya know," he said with a wink as Don called his assistant to get the extras ready on the set.

Gabriella watched as the extras sat at laboratory workstations, everyone was instructed how to act once the scene started. Jake was placed at the largest workstation and Gabriella was instructed to wait beyond the laboratory doors. Don yelled action, and the laboratory doors slid open to reveal Gabriella. Jake approached swiftly as Gabriella entered through the doorway.

"Doctor Young, I'm glad you made it so quickly. We have reason to believe, from the trends on the monitors, that he is waking. You wanted us to let you know when it was about to happen." Jake said as they walked through the rows of workstations, then stopped at a mark on the floor. When they stopped, Jake was handed a tablet from an extra, which he passed to Gabriella.

Gabriella looked down at the green screen on the tablet and mimicked looking through the data on the tablet. "His heart rate is accelerating, breathing is growing rapid, and his eye movement is increasing as quickly as his breath. We believe he is being killed in the current life. He has run through multiple iterations, but his reaction to his death has not been like this before. We think this might be it for this sequence."

Gabriella looked up to two marks on the wall as Jake continued. "The others are still in suspended animation. We are waiting on your orders to put them through the program."

Gabriella looked down at the original mark with disgust. "It is your decision, Doctor Young. We can pull him out of the chamber and awaken him, or we can run him through another round of the program, but I warn you, his chance of survival lessens with each death he suffers."

Gabriella looked at Jake, who stared back at her. "Doctor Young? I know what he did to us. Do you want to run the program again?"

Gabriella stared a few moments, then nodded her head once, then turned away and walked back through the lab to the doors, which slid open, and she walked through them.

114

"Cut! That was good. But Gabriella, I want hate in your eyes. You want the subject to suffer. They wronged you. This is your ultimate revenge. I need to feel the pain in your eyes, the hate, the conviction to serve your justice. Do you get me?"

"Yeah, I get you. Let's go again. I've got some rage to use." Gabby said with a smirk.

***

Gabriella was moved to a small office, surrounded by photos from a life alien to her, yet she was prominent in most of them. There was a framed photo of her and Henry from the wedding scene on the desk. She studied the frames on the wall, medical certificates with the name Charlotte Smith. There were framed articles that Young Enterprises purchased Life Sciences. Another was a wedding announcement that the CEO of Young Enterprises married head scientist of the frontier research department, Charlotte Smith. More articles were framed about philanthropic endeavors and charities that the company were involved with, many of them having to do with children. Another article introduced Young Enterprises' new fertility department, because head scientist and wife of the CEO, Charlotte Young, has made her fertility struggles public.

"I see you're seeing some of your character's story," April said with a smile as she approached Gabriella on the set.

"Yeah, what is all of this?" Gabriella asked.

"I can't ruin anything yet. It's going to be a surprise for everyone. I promise, it's going to be amazing. I blew the balls off of the studio when I submitted the rewrite. Your character arc is badass." April said with pride.

"Sweet. If only you could make me a badass in real life," Gabriella said with a laugh.

"Um, going from being an actress' assistant to being an actress in your own right, without even wanting it, is pretty badass. Being thrown into the spotlight because a certain actor fell for you, and you held yourself together. You are a badass." April said, her hand upon Gabriella's arm.

"Wow, April, thanks." April looked up to see Don approaching with Jake, reviewing the scene. "I guess that's my cue. You got this, badass," April said with a wink as she made her way behind the camera.

"Alright Gabby, I need to get a few shots of you answering your phone and reacting to you being told something important. I need to then film you watching some upsetting footage on your computer. I want your reaction to throw things on your desk. Destroy whatever you want. The one item I need you to destroy is the wedding photo, I want you to take it and throw it against the wall across from you. Then we are going to move onto the scene where you call Jake into your office, and you show him some footage on your screen. You are going to have no reaction, but Jake will have his own meltdown. When Jake asks you what you want to do about what you have shown him, I need a slow, sadistic smirk, complete with an arched eyebrow, if you can do that."

***

116

It was two in the morning when Don finally called the day. He instructed everyone to be in at noon, stating that set was going to change drastically. Gabriella and Jake made their way to wardrobe together, changed back into their street clothes, and then made their way back to the car service.

The driver approached them as they reached the car. "I hope you don't mind that I will be taking you both in the same car. I will be dropping Miss DiStella at the hotel first before dropping off Mister Wilson at his home. I apologize that there is only one car available currently. If you would prefer to get your own ride, I completely understand."

"I'm cool with it. Jake?" Gabriella asked.

"Yeah, sure, I just want to get some sleep. Let's go." Jake said and gestured to the back door being held open by the driver.

Once the car was in motion, Jake turned to Gabriella. "Today went pretty well."

"Agreed. I'm glad the rewrites weren't too extensive. I'm looking forward to seeing the final cut."

"Me too. There is some serious Oscar buzz about the movie."

"I heard that. Have you been working on anything since last I saw you?"

"You're going to laugh, but I judged a competition show. It's like a battle of the bands. I don't know how I got invited to judge, but it was an awesome experience. I sat on the panel with Dr. Dre and Bon Jovi, with Jessica Simpson as the host. If the ratings are high enough for the show, they may make another season."

"That's amazing, Jake!"

"Yeah, we even had a few special guest judges like Stevie Wonder and Mark Hoppus."

Gabriella sat there with her mouth open. "You got to meet them? You don't understand, I have Stevie Wonder's greatest hits and all of Blink-182's music on heavy rotation in my library."

"Yeah, they were all super cool. I probably walked around looking like you the entire time, just in complete awe."

A few moments of comfortable silence passed as Gabriella stared out of the window. "I didn't realize how much I missed it here."

"That's right, you're an east coaster. How is over there?"

"Cold. We got almost three feet of snow two days after Christmas. New Year's was pretty horrible, it felt like negative ten, and people were still crazy enough to stand out in Times Square."

"Did you do anything good for New Years?" Jake asked.

"I was planning on going to my friend Desmond's; him and his boyfriend were going to throw a little party, but it was so windy and cold, I stayed home and facetimed a few people."

"Oh, that's sad, Gabby. You should have been out here, major pool party at Adrianna James' house on the hills. It was epic. So many people were there."

"It really doesn't sound like my cup of tea, but I'm glad you had a good time."

"Miss DiStella, we have arrived at your hotel." The driver announced.

"Thank you. See you tomorrow, Jake," Gabriella said as she exited the car.

"Have a good night, Gabby."

Gabriella made her way to her room on the eighth floor and quietly opened the door to find Liam asleep in the king-sized bed, with the television still on. She stepped into the bathroom and quickly changed into her pajamas, then turned off the television and got into the other side of the bed.

"Are you back? What time is it?" Liam asked, still partially asleep.

"It's a quarter to three in the morning. Go back to sleep."

"What time do you have to go back in?"

"Noon. Go to sleep. I'll see you in the morning."

***

Gabriella awoke the next day at ten to find Liam at the edge of the bed with a food cart next to him. "Morning sleepyhead, coffee?" He asked with a gesture to the cart.

"Definitely. But I need to shower first. What did you do for your first day in L.A.?" She asked as she grabbed her clothes and toiletry bag.

"I bummed out at the beach, but I made it a point to go to the Santa Monica pier. After a few hours baking in the sun, I walked the pier, I had an amazing burger for lunch. I did some fishing and then ate some amazing Mexican food for dinner."

"You had yourself a very full day. And that Mexican place on the pier is one of my favorites. Let me take a quick shower and we can get some breakfast downstairs if you want."

"Sounds good, I'll get dressed."

After a quick shower, Gabriella put her hair up in a bun, brushed her teeth and moisturized her face. There was no need to wear makeup when she would be having it done professionally if a few hours. She changed into a pair of jeans and a long-sleeved t-shirt.

They made their way down to the terrace bar for breakfast. "So, what are you planning for day two?"

"Oh, I'm going full tourist. Walk of fame, Hollywood sign, I'm even going to take one of those celebrity tours."

"No, you aren't." Gabriella said horrified, as she dug into her omelet.

"Totally am, you can't stop me, miss Hollywood." Liam said with a laugh as he bit into his toast.

"Laurel will be so disappointed."

"Of me taking the tour, or if she isn't on it?"

"Maybe a little of both." Gabriella said with a laugh.

"I was thinking that maybe I could catch a ride with you to the studio. There are a bunch of studio tours over by there, and I was thinking of checking that out."

"Sure. I could probably get you a studio tour tomorrow, if you want." Gabriella suggested.

"I'll take a tour of your studio tomorrow, but there are so many other tours over there too."

"Sounds like a plan. Looks like Duke is almost here, lets finish up and meet him outside." Gabriella said as she took a final bite of her breakfast.

Gabriella entered the soundstage, dressed in a pair of white shorts and a navy-blue tank top, her hair in a tight ponytail and boat shoes on her feet, shocked to see a giant pool. "No, this is all wrong, we need her to look distressed, the nicer parts are going to be filmed tomorrow." Don yelled when he saw her.

The makeup artist and hairstylist sat her down and roughed up her look. The stylist came out with a distressed version of her outfit and instructed her to change. She came back out and Don seemed pleased.

"Gabby, we need you in the pool. You are going to be hanging onto floating debris. We need you to be passed out and exhausted, like you just survived a horrific accident. A small coastguard boat is going to approach you and rescue you from the water."

"You are going to put a boat in the pool?" Gabriella asked.

"It's already in there, we just have the green screen in front of it at the moment." Don said as an assistant lead her towards the pool.

"Don't worry, the water is only a few feet deep, you will be able to stand in it." The assistant said as he helped her get into the water. Once she was in, he handed her a foam board designed to look like a piece of debris from a boat. She picked the upper half of her body up out of the water and placed it on the float with her arms draped over it and her cheek pressed against it. Dom filmed her in various positions on the board before they brought out the boat.

Gabriella was surprised to see small twenty-four-foot inflatable rescue boat appear when they moved a screen away. When the camera rolled, the boat was slowly pulled in her direction, the actor on board yelled to see if she was okay and shined a bright light in her face. She turned her head towards him and opened one eye, which was enough of a signal for the man to pull her out of the water.

After a few shots of that, Gabriella got out of the pool and was immediately given a towel to dry off, followed by a robe. She was then directed to go back to wardrobe, where she was dressed in the original outfit, and then her hair was dried and restyled and her makeup redone.

122

"That scene in the water looked great," Gina said as she approached Gabriella in the makeup chair.

"Thanks. Why am I dressing in my original outfit? Why wouldn't we save that scene for later?"

Gina rolled her eyes in response. "Apparently there was a scheduling conflict with the marina, but everything is okay now. We are going to head over there; Jake is already there. We will film a few scenes there today; we need to get the daylight for these shots. Then tomorrow we will be filming at night, so you will have the day all to yourself."

"Sounds good to me. Then tomorrow I'm done with my parts, right?"

Gina nodded in response, then lead Gabriella and some of the other crew members to the bus, which took them to Marina Del Ray. They arrived half an hour later to find the crew on a gorgeous luxury yacht. "We get to film on this today?" Gabriella asked to no one in particular.

"Yup, let's live it up!" Jake exclaimed as he approached her and threw his arm around her shoulder.

"Alright people, we don't have much time in the way of daylight, but the scenes we're shooting are quick. Jake and Gabby, we're going to be filming you on the dock next to the boat, then in a few key areas in the ship." Don shouted.

"I think I should get one of these bad boys," Jake said with a wink as he approached the yacht.

"You better hope this movie hits big if you're going to get one of these," Gabriella joked as she followed.

***

Gabriella was back at the hotel by seven in the evening. Liam was off doing his tourist thing, so she decided to order room service and soak in the bathtub while she could take advantage of being alone in the room. Once the food was delivered, she ran the bath and filled it with a bath bomb and some bubbles. After she soaked in the tub, she thought of Henry, and how he had the uncanny ability to contact her while she was in the bath. She tried to facetime him, but the call failed. She sent him a text, but he never responded. Disappointed, she called Laurel, and her voicemail picked up. She checked the time and hoped that Desmond would be out of his show and tried to call him.

"Hey bitch! Good timing, I just got out of the theater." Desmond said as he answered the phone.

"I'm so glad you answered, I'm getting a complex," she responded with a laugh.

"Who did you call before me?"

"Just Henry and Laurel."

"I see where I rate." Desmond scoffed.

"You just got out of work. I know your schedule."

"Whatever, how is the trip going?"

"Okay, just relaxing in the tub while Liam is out doing his tourist thing."

"How is that going? Is he behaving himself?"

"Yes, we haven't seen much of each other, but everything is very friend oriented."

"Don't be surprised if he tries something with you." Desmond warned.

"Yes, dad." Gabriella said. "Changing the subject, how is Arnie doing with the food stuff?"

"OMG, Gabs, the kitchen is a warzone. I swear I can't touch anything without getting yelled at. I've been limited to the fridge door and a shelf in a cabinet. Everything else is for Dino. It's so annoying."

"I thought you get to taste all of the food?"

"I do, and it's delicious, and that's why it sucks, he won't let me eat it after I'm done tasting it. He's lucky I love him."

"How are you getting such good reception in the subway? I would have lost you as soon as I walked down the stairs." Gabriella asked.

"Bitch, please, I'm in a cab. I can't just abandon you while you're soaking in a tub in L.A."

"You really are a savior, Des."

"Pshh, I know. So, what is the plan for the next three days?"

"Tomorrow is my last day of filming, it's at night. Then Duke hooked me up with his daughter-in-law, she's a realtor and she's going to take me around for a place. I want to stop by the old apartment and see if Darren and Mitchell are working. The rest of it kinda depends on what Liam did today. I was thinking maybe going to Disney or Universal."

"That sounds like it could be fun, can you make sure whatever place you get has two bedrooms. I'd like to pretend I have a getaway in California too."

"I told you my parents are going in on this, it has to have two bedrooms. So how is it there?"

"I do not want to talk to you about the weather. It's colder than a witch's tit in a brass bra here, and you know it. Don't be mean."

"I'll be freezing my ass off with you before you know it."

"I just got home, and I'm pooped. Love you, bitch. I'll talk to you soon."

"By Des. Love you too."

Seven

Since Liam saw most of the touristy things on his own, they decided to spend the morning at the Huntington library and visited some of the exhibits but spent the majority of their time outside in the botanical gardens.

"I don't care how lame it might be to hang out with a bunch of flowers, but I want to soak up as much sunshine as possible while I'm here. I almost don't want to go home. Maybe I could transfer out here," Liam said as they walked around.

"One, it's not lame to be here, this place is gorgeous. Two, California does have its charms, but you would miss the city too much."

"I guess that's true. But if we could have this weather at home, I'd be in heaven."

"So, did you enjoy yourself yesterday? I'm sorry that I fell asleep before you got back."

"I did. I met a few people on that cheesy tour of the stars and hung out with them. We went to dinner and went to a club for a while. It was a lot of fun."

"I'm so glad to hear that, I feel terrible leaving you to your own devises while I'm working."

"Goober, I'm a big boy, I can handle being on my own."

"I know. I'm just glad that we can hang out today before I have to work again."

"Yeah, but I'm coming with you. Speaking of which, do you think I could get a tour of the studio before you start today?"

"I'll check with Duke, he'll set it up."

"Are you ready for your last day on set?"

"I am. It's not as intense as it was while we were filming the entire thing. It's just me and Jake Wilson and a bunch of extras. I don't feel like I worked with Jake much before, so it's a nice change of pace."

"Well, I'm excited to see you in action. I've never been interested in how films are made, but now that I'm friends with an actress, I'm dying to see it."

"You're in luck, my friend. Duke said to head over by four and you can get your personal tour."

"It's almost noon. Do you want to get lunch and then maybe stop at the zoo on the way to the studio?" Liam asked.

"I think that sounds like an awesome idea. There is a brewery right near the zoo that we can stop at for lunch."

They quickly got a rideshare and made their way to the brewery, where they sat at the bar and immediately ordered two pints of craft beer. "Cheers, to our first trip together," Liam said as he lifted his glass.

Gabriella tapped her glass to his and then took a sip. "Wow, I'm not usually a dark beer drinker, but this one is pretty good. Are we ordering food?"

"Let's have this beer first, and then when we are ready for our second, we'll get the food."

"Okay, but I'm done after two. I have to work tonight. I can't be all drunk and sloppy."

"You got it. So, I was wondering, what is your favorite thing about the west coast?"

Gabriella took a sip of her beer as she thought about the question. "Hm… I really do love the sunshine here. It's just such a different vibe from New York. I like the mellowness of it, but then my inner New Yorker acts up and I can't stand it."

"I can see that. I feel more mellow out here. Like the worries of work melt away."

"That's called a vacation, Goob." Gabriella replied with a snort as she continued to drink.

"You want me to order you a second?" Liam asked as he looked at the mostly empty pint glass.

"Sure. But I really want a giant pretzel."

Liam laughed, "you got it. How about we get a pretzel and a burger, and we split them?"

"Sounds like a plan to me," she said with a smile as she finished her beer.

"Wow, you came to play, huh?"

Gabriella shook her head. "On the contrary, if I get my two beers in early, I can sober up before work."

The time passed quickly at the bar as they had their second round and ate their food. Their conversation flowed freely, a sure sign that their friendship was back on track. "Alright, Gabs, I got us a ride to the zoo. It should be here in ten minutes."

"Okay, I'm gonna hit the bathroom," she said, but when she stood, she felt a little lightheaded and stumbled slightly.

"You okay, Goober?"

Gabriella winked at him as she gave him a thumbs up and made her way to the bathroom. She was surprised to feel as intoxicated as she did, especially since she only had two drinks and ate a bunch of carbs. She returned to the table to find an amused Liam watch her make her way back.

"I don't know why, but those drinks really hit me."

"Maybe because the beer I ordered almost has a fifteen percent ABV." Liam said with a sly smile.

Gabriella gasped as she smacked him on the arm, which made him laugh. "Liam Jonathan Stewart! You are in so much trouble, mister!"

Liam threw his arm around her shoulders and lead her to the door. "Come on lightweight, we're going to sober you up at the zoo."

The zoo was considerably crowded for a Thursday afternoon, but the lines moved quickly. After they purchased their tickets, Liam grabbed a map. "Okay Goober, your choice. Where to first?"

Gabriella studied the map and decided the best course of action to see the animals she preferred. "Definitely the koalas. They are so adorable."

"Alright, koalas it is."

After visiting the koalas and the neighboring kangaroos, they made their way to the gorilla exhibit. As they did with all of the exhibits, Liam stopped in front of the glass to take a photo, then swapped with Gabriella.

"That is such an adorable picture, Gabby."

"Really? Let me see."

"Yeah, you can really see the strong family resemblance. I didn't know we were visiting your family today."

Gabriella's mouth gaped as she stared at Liam, as he desperately tried to hold in a laugh. "Seriously?"

"Yeah, but don't worry, you're not as hairy as them."

Gabriella chased Liam through the zoo as she yelled, "oh yeah, maybe we can visit some of your relatives. Is there a pig exhibit?"

Liam stopped by the elephant exhibit, he turned and waited as Gabriella ran after him. He scooped her against his chest and spun her slightly. "You know I'm only kidding." He said with a laugh as he kissed her on the top of her head.

She pushed against his chest and rolled her eyes. "Yeah, whatever. Keep it moving, jackass."

"Now I don't think they have a donkey exhibit here."

"They don't need one when they let them wander around freely."

Liam laughed heartily. "Touché, Goober."

They made their way over to the Giraffes, with Gabriella gave Liam the evil eye as he giggled at the chimpanzees behind them. "Don't even say they are distant cousins or something."

He held in a laugh, he asked. "What's next? We don't have time to see the whole thing."

Gabriella's eyes light up when she spotted an ice cream vendor. "Ice cream!"

Liam led the way and purchased them soft serve cones. Gabriella happily accepted, making little noises of delight as she licked the twist cone with rainbow sprinkles. Liam laughed and shook his head at her child-like antics.

***

After exploring most of the zoo, they realized the time and ordered a ride to take them to the studio. They made their way to one of the last exhibits before they left. "Finally, we are with your people," Gabriella said with a smirk as they stood in front of the sloth exhibit.

"How do you figure?"

"They are lazy and slow. Put a game controller in their hand and sit them on a couch. The resemblance would be uncanny."

"Alright, smartass, you've made your point."

Gabriella smiled brilliantly at him as she made her way toward the exit. Liam followed her, then shook his head. "One more request before we leave," Gabriella said as she turned to face him. He raised his eyebrows in response.

"We hit the souvenir shop on the way out. We have to buy each other something stupid to remind us of this trip."

Liam nodded, then dashed into the closest shop. Gabriella sighed, then followed. She knew exactly what to get him, and made her way over to the stuffed animals, where a long-armed sloth with Velcro hands hung. After she was rung up, she waiting outside until Liam reappeared.

"Do we exchange now?" She asked.

"Nah, let's get to the front gate and meet the car. We'll do it there."

They exited the park; the app informed them that their driver would arrive in five minutes. "Let's do this. On three." Liam said, as he held out the bag from the gift shop. Gabriella nodded in agreement. They exchanged bags on three, Liam let out a howl of laughter at the stuffed sloth. Gabriella looked in the bag and pulled out a shirt that had a gorilla on it, with a saying "Gorillas like to hum while they eat."

Gabriella looked up at him with a questioning look in her eyes. "I get the gorilla, but the humming?"

"Are you serious? You do it all the time! Not only do you hum, but you also happy dance!"

"Nah-uh. That's a lie."

"You make happy noises. You grunt and moan as you eat."

"That's not humming."

"Whatever helps you sleep at night. You have to wear it."

"Fine, I'll wear it if you wear yours."

Liam separated the arms of the sloth and wrapped it around his neck like a scarf. Gabriella laughed, then put the t-shirt on over what she was wearing. "The car is here, give me one second, I'll meet you in it." Liam said as he ran back over to the gates.

Gabriella waited in the back of the car while Liam came back and handed her large bag of cotton candy. "We need sustenance for the fifteen-minute ride."

Gabriella laughed as she teared open the plastic and dug into the sweet confectionary.

***

They were dropped off at the front gates of the studio, where she gave her name and identification. They were escorted onto the lot and began to walk to the set. "Welcome to where the magic happens," Gabriella said with flourish as she extended her arms out.

Liam laughed and threw his arm over her shoulder, the sloth hung over both of their shoulders. Gabriella wrapped her arm around his waist, a giant wad of cotton candy still in her free hand. "Seriously Goober, thank you for giving me the chance to come here with you. I know I really fucked things up back home, but it really means a lot that you haven't cast me out." Liam placed a kiss on the top of her head as they walked further into the lot.

Gabriella fed Liam and herself the remainder of the cotton candy as she pointed out some areas of interest. "Oh, our sound stage is straight ahead. Duke is going to meet us there, he said he can take you around while I'm in wardrobe."

"That sounds good to me. Hey, are you trying to finish the rest of that yourself?" He asked, eyeing the cotton candy.

Gabriella smiled. "Maybe."

Liam kept his arm around her shoulder, then grabbed her hand with the other arm and forced her hand to his mouth, where he tried to eat the last of the cotton candy. He shoved her thumb and pointer finger into his mouth as she released a fit of giggles.

"Oh my god, babe, look who it is! Hey Gabriella!" An Irish-accented voice called out.

Gabriella's head snapped to see Riona approach, her hand intertwined with no other than Henry Anderson. She froze up for a moment, then tightened her grip around Liam's waist as they approached. Liam's unclenched his teeth from around Gabriella's fingers, and she immediately sucked the candy off her fingertips and brushed them on her jeans.

Henry's eyes traced the path her fingers took from Liam's mouth to her pants; the hardness of his stare was obvious to Liam. Liam stood a little straighter as he left his arm hooked around Gabriella's shoulder.

"Oh, hi Riona, Henry. What are you doing here?" Gabriella asked.

"Well, don't just stand there like a carp with its mouth open!" Riona laughed as she approached Gabriella, pulled her out of Liam's grasp and hugged her. The sheer shock that Gabriella felt at that moment made her freeze in place and made it difficult to return the hug. Riona pulled back, her hands firmly on Gabriella's upper arms. She looked past Gabriella and smirked, then turned her attention back to her captive.

"And who is this lovely chap? Is this the boyfriend I read about in the rags?" She asked.

136

"Um, this is Liam." Gabriella stammered out.

Riona let go of Gabriella and made her way to Liam, where she extended her hand. "Riona Murphy, pleasure to meet ya."

"Liam Stewart. It's nice to meet you too. I'm a big fan." Liam responded.

Gabriella gave Henry a puzzled look as Henry shook his head slightly in response with a slight shrug of his shoulders. He was equally as baffled by the interaction.

"So rude of me, Liam, dear, this is my boyfriend, Henry Anderson."

Liam reached his hand out to Henry, who shook it in return. "Hi, yes, we've met before. Back in New York on set."

Henry nodded his head in agreement, "ah, yes, of course we did. It's nice to see you again Liam. I hope you have been well."

"Yup, can't complain. I'm looking forward to next superhero movie." Liam responded.

"Yeah, thanks mate." Henry said as he looked towards Gabriella, his eyes drank in the sight of her. "Hey, Ella."

"Hey, Henry." Gabriella said in response as Henry approached her and enveloped her in a hug. Gabriella relished the being in his arms and inhaled his scent, but it was short lived, the sound of Riona's throat clear made them step away from each other.

"Cute shirt," Henry said with a smirk. Gabriella looked down at the shirt and laughed. "Liam just bought it for me. He says that I also hum while I eat."

Henry laughed, "he's right, you absolutely do!"

"See, I told you." Liam said with a vindicated smile.

"So, um, what are you guys doing here?" Gabriella asked as she watched Riona reclaim Henry's hand.

Liam sensed the unease of the moment, so he reached out to Gabriella's hand, interlaced their fingers, and pulled her a little closer to him. She looked up at him and smiled gratefully.

"Same as you, we are shooting the new scenes." Riona answered.

"Oh, I thought it was just me and Jake this week." Gabriella responded.

"The studio felt it was imperative, their words, that we be here to film today. So, our teams made it happen." Henry replied.

"Hey, hey, the gang's all here," Duke said as he approached them.

"Hey, Duke!" Henry exclaimed as he pulled away from Riona to give him a hug.

"Alright, Henry and Riona, you are heading into wardrobe, Don needs a few scenes with the two of you. Liam, you are with me, I'll be giving you your tour. Gabby, you have about an hour before they need you in wardrobe, so you decide what you want to do."

138

Henry and Liam both looked at Gabriella and waited to hear her response. She looked between the two of them, then looked to Duke for help. Before she could answer, Riona approached Henry and wrapped her arms around his waist from behind. "I think a tour would be a great idea." Gabriella said as she tore her eyes away from Henry's waist and smiled at Duke.

"Well, alright, you chariot awaits," Duke said as he gestured to the golf cart.

"Just like old times, Duke," Gabriella said with a chuckle as she climbed into the cart with Liam. Henry stood there and watched her drive off as Riona whined. "Come on, Henry, we need to get ready."

"So… that was something back there," Liam said as Duke maneuvered through the lot.

"Oh, yeah. I was not expecting to see them," Gabriella said with huff.

"Are you good?" He asked gently.

Gabriella looked down at his hands, then reached out and interlaced her fingers with his. "Yeah, I'm good. Thank you."

***

Two and a half hours later, the cast and crew, along with Liam, were descending from the bus and made their way down the dock to the luxury yacht they would be filming on.

139

"Whoa, this is way better than the sound stage," Liam said as they approached the boat.

"You have no idea; this boat is ridiculous. I was on it yesterday, and from what I saw, it's beyond decadent." Gabriella responded.

They made their way onto the back deck, which held a pool, an outdoor seating area, which lead into a lounge and dining area. The cameras were already set, and the crew were prepped to begin the night.

"Alright, my cast, feel free to roam around for a bit if you want, just don't touch anything. We should be ready to go in about twenty." Don announced as he conferred with Lloyd and Gina.

"Let's go," Gabriella said to Liam and headed through the seating area and into the lounge. Everything was chrome with white couches and black accent pillows. They walked behind a couch and looked out towards the water when Gabriella's hand was grabbed and someone shouted, "Boo!"

Gabriella screamed and yanked her hand away and jumped towards Liam. Stunned, Liam grabbed a hold of her and spotted a petite woman with caramel brown hair laugh her ass off on the couch. "Gabby, I think everything is okay." He said into the top of her head.

Gabriella turned to find Laurel as she tried to catch her breath and stop her laughter. "What the fuck, Laurel? You scared the shit out of me."

Laurel put her hand to her chest and began to stand up. "I'm sorry, that was just so freaking funny."

Gabriella stormed over and pushed Laurel back onto the couch, which cause Laurel to erupt into another fit of laughter. Gabriella hit her with one of the pillows, then joined in on the laughter.

"You're such a bitch. What are you even doing here? You're supposed to be in Vancouver." Gabriella asked.

"Apparently my manager was too busy filming to get involved," Laurel said with a wink, "Gina called and asked for me to delay returning to Vancouver for a few days. Everyone was okay with it."

"God, you suck so bad." Gabriella said as she finally calmed down.

"So, is this the illusive Liam that I've heard so much about?" Laurel asked as she stood up.

"It is. The best friend slash movie star Laurel Dolce, it's nice to meet you in person," Liam said with a smile as he shook Laurel's hand.

"Hm, a charmer. Maybe there is still hope for you yet. Word to the wise, steer clear of the red lace." Laurel said with a smile.

"Jesus, Laurel." Gabriella breathed out.

"Oh, I've learned. She's making me go through the ringer." Liam responded and sent a wink to Gabriella.

"Places people, let's get this going." Don yelled out.

Liam kissed Gabriella on the head, then made his way over to where the rest of the crew was positioned. He gave Gabriella an encouraging smile when she was settled on the couch next to Laurel. Riona sat on the couch opposite them, as Jake stood behind her and Henry stood between the two couches. Once Don was satisfied with the scene, he started to roll.

"I wanted to thank you all for coming out to celebrate. This is a huge step forward for Young Enterprises. We would not be celebrating if it wasn't for my best friend and CFO, Chester, and of course the support of his beautiful wife, Mina. Without you, Chester, we would have never secured the funding for this project. And of course, we would not have a project to support if it wasn't for my brilliant wife, Charlotte. Your mind is one of the wonders of the world. And, thanks to her best friend, Abigail, who is always there to help us out when we need her."

Henry grabbed a bottle of champagne from the table and opened it, then poured some in everyone's flute. Laurel shook her head, "no, none for me, thanks. I have my water." She lifted the water bottle in response. Gabriella and Jake make eye contact in response.

"Cheers! To friends," Henry said as he looks to Riona and Jake, "to family" he says as he looks to Gabriella, "and to the future," he says as he looks to Laurel.

Everyone lifted their glasses and sipped the contents of their glasses, except Gabriella, who downed it in one shot.

"Whoa, easy Charlotte, don't drink too fast," Laurel said as she looked at Gabriella.

"It's okay Abigail, it's a celebration. I think my wife has the right mindset," Henry said as Gabriella grabbed the bottle of champagne and walked back to the dining area.

"Cut!" Don yelled out. "We need to focus in on Gabby and Jake. Let's set it up."

After they marked and did makeup touchups, Don called action again. Gabriella stood beside the table, and she filled her glass with more champagne as Jake approached. "Liquid courage?" He asked as he filled his own glass as Gabriella eyed him over the rim of her glass while she drank.

"Are we ready to start?" He asked. Gabriella gave a solitary nod, as Jake clinked his glass to hers in a celebration. "I'll grab the other bottles of champagne, there are only a few on board?" Gabriella nodded again. "I'll handle the drinks. Is it going to be a problem that Abigail isn't drinking?"

Gabriella shook her head, then pulled a pill out of her pocket. "Muscle relaxer? Is it safe to give her?" Gabriella shrugged, then crushed the pill with the champagne bottle and put it in a bottle of water. She walked away from Jake and made her way back to the couch, then handed the water to Laurel as she sat down on the opposite side of the couch.

"Thanks, Char." Laurel said as she opened the water and drank from it. "I don't know what is with me lately, I feel like I'm constantly thirsty and peeing."

Gabriella nodded at Laurel, then her eyes locked onto Riona and Henry. Although they were supposed were acting, it looked like they were in their own happy world as they chatted away and touched each other's arms. It didn't take much to stare them down when she while already battled her own jealous feelings.

"What do you think is going on with those two? Mina seems very handsy with Carson." Gabriella looked to Laurel, shrugged her shoulders, looked back over to Henry and Riona and continued to drink.

"Cut! Moving on!" The next hour was different shots of them partying on the boat. Henry walked over to state-of-the-art audio system to act as though he turned music on. Jake brought up bottles of champagne, which were really sparkling apple cider, and handed one to each person, except for Laurel. Henry, Jake, and Riona all drank directly from the bottle, Gabriella poured hers into the glass. The others partied and drank as Gabriella stayed on the couch and tried to keep a neutral look on her face.

At one point, Riona approached Henry, and began to dance with him and grinded herself against him. Henry danced with her as he continued to drink from his bottle. Jake saw this and jumped in and sandwiched Riona between the two men. Gabriella stared daggers at Riona and attempted to pretend that she was doing it for the movie. Laurel leaned into Gabriella and whispered, "you're lucky your character is salty about them. You may win an Academy Award for your portrayal of a wronged woman."

"Shut up," Gabriella said with a smirk as she gave Laurel the side eye. Don instructed Gabriella to make her way over to the side of the boat and have her path cross with the dancers.

"Do you think I could get away with starting a cat fight with her as I walk past?" Gabriella asked Laurel as she stood up from the couch. Laurel tried not to laugh as Don called action.

As Gabriella walked by the ménage trois, Henry threw his arm out at Gabriella's arm, which startled her. "Hey wife," he said with a drunken slur, "come dance with us."

Gabriella rolled her eyes and tried to continue to walk by, but Henry stepped away from Riona and pulled her back to him. Her entire backside pressed against the front of him as held her tight against him, his arm wrapped around her waist. "Where are you going, Charlotte? Your husband wants to dance with you."

He began to grind into her and slightly swayed to the inaudible music. He freed his pointer finger from the grip on the champagne bottle and brushed along her cheek, jaw, and neck, then hovered right next to her breast. His warm breath coated her neck as he nuzzled into her. Gabriella's eyes fluttered closed and her lips parted as his nose pressed behind her ear. She gently bit her lower lip as she pushed herself against his groin.

"Cut! Gabby, you can't look like you are enjoying this. You hate him, you want away from him. The thought of him touching you makes you sick. Turn off the chemistry for once." Don yelled.

Gabriella exhaled, completely taken out of the moment and Henry chuckled. "Shut it, Anderson," she snarked as Don started the scene.

Gabriella tried to pull away from Henry, but his grip tightened. "Stop being such a frigid bitch. You're my wife, act like it."

Gabriella looked to Jake, who had poured out the contents of his bottle overboard. She pulled away from Henry, then gave Jake a quick nod as she walked over to the side of the boat. "Hey, Charlotte, can we show him our surprise?" Gabriella nodded in response.

"What surprise?" Henry asked. Jake approached the sound system and turned it down.

"Charlotte and I made a video for you to celebrate this momentous occasion. It has some old and some never-before-seen footage of the company. You're gonna love it."

Laurel walked out from inside the boat, "what happened to the music?"

"We are going to watch some video," Riona said as she sat down on the couch.

"We need more refreshments before we start this thing," Jake said as he made his way back to the bar where the bottles were. "Hey, Carson, we're out of champagne."

"The bar is fully stocked, just drink something else." Henry responded.

"No way, this is a celebration, and we need champagne. There is a liquor store back on the island, I can get a crew member to pick it up." Jake suggested.

"No can do, I gave all of them the night off." Henry responded.

146

"Isn't the captain still on board?" Jake asked. Henry nodded. "I can get him to take me back to land, I'll get a few cases, and he'll bring me right back. It will take an hour, tops."

"Alright man, if you really want. Mina, are you going to go with him?" Henry asked.

"No, I don't want to ruin her good time. I'll slip out and be back before you know it." Jake said as he started to head towards the interior cabin stairs.

"Oh, Charlotte, you can start the video without me. I've seen it so many times I have it memorized." Jake said with a smile as he descended into the ship.

"Cut! Okay, Jake, you can come back out. We need shots of everyone watching the screen. I need the range of emotions from shocked, embarrassed, horrified, and enraged. We can't tell you what you are reacting to, but I'm sure you will figure it out eventually." Don explained. After he got the shots he wanted, Don prepared them for the next scene.

"Gabby, I know you don't have any scripted lines, but I want you to react the way someone would to an argument. We need to show you reacting, but don't worry, the audio won't be used."

Don set the scene and called action. "What is this?" Henry demanded as he looked at Gabriella. Gabriella stared blankly at him. "What the fuck is this, Charlotte?" He yelled as spittle burst from his mouth.

"It's pretty self-explanatory, Carson," Riona muttered from the couch, her anger boiled at the surface.

"Shut up, Wilhelmina." Henry snapped. "What do you think you're doing, Charlotte? What do you think showing this is going to accomplish?"

"I think she accomplished showing what a fucking douchebag you are," Riona snapped.

"Hi pot, I'm kettle, nice to meet you," Henry quipped. "What we just watched didn't paint you in the best light either."

"I'm disgusted with you. It was bad enough you married that bitch, but then you add that sad sack to the mix?" Riona said, gesturing at Laurel. "I wasn't enough for you? I let it go that you got married, but I'm certainly not going to allow you to continue on with that one."

"You're not in a position to say anything, Mina." Henry snapped. "And you, what were you thinking? Did you have cameras set up in the house?"

Gabriella stared at him; her face remained stoic. "You put cameras in my house, in my office? You fucking psychopath!"

Laurel began to cry at Henry's outburst. "Why the fuck are you crying?"

Laure looked to Gabriella. "I'm so sorry, Charlotte. I never meant for anything to happen. I don't know what came over me. You just have this perfect life, and I was jealous and…"

"And she could give me the one thing you can't." Henry said, which silenced everyone.

Gabriella slowly stood up and began to walk towards the outside lounge. "Charlotte, please," Laurel begged.

Gabriella turned abruptly to face the three of them. "Fuck you. Fuck all of you. None of you are worth it."

"What are you going to do Charlotte? Huh? You think you can take me down? You think you can break my empire. I'll destroy you. I will leave your ass with nothing, not even the clothes on your back." Henry shouted.

Gabriella began to walk away as he shouted. "You go public with any of this, you are as good as dead," he threatened. "You are nothing without me, you frigid bitch."

Gabriella about-faced, stomped over to Henry and smacked him across the face, which caused Laurel and Riona to gasp. Henry's face was sheer surprise as Gabriella leaned in and said, "We'll see about that."

She turned and walked to the back of the ship, then down the stairs as Henry called out the rest of his threatening lines.

"Cut! Oh wow, Gabby, what was that slap?" Don questioned.

"Sorry, Don, you told me to react, that's how I would do it." Gabriella responded.

"I fucking loved it! Wow! It was so unexpected. Alright, lets reset and go again." Don instructed.

Gabriella made her way back to the group and approached Henry. Henry jokingly put himself in a fighting stance. "I'm sorry I slapped you. I hope it wasn't too hard."

"No, it wasn't, but I was completely caught off guard."

"I promise I won't do it again in the next take." Gabriella said before walked back to her mark.

"It felt good to do that, didn't it?" Laurel asked as she approached Gabriella.

"It would have felt better if it was Riona."

***

Don finally called it quits near three in the morning. The group made their way to the entrance of the marina where cars waited to take them home. "How long are you guys here?" Jake asked as they walked.

"I'm only here until Saturday night, I'm back in Vancouver on Sunday," Laurel responded.

"Same for us, we fly out on Sunday," Gabriella answered for her and Liam.

"I'm off to Ireland on Monday for a new streaming series. Hopefully I'll get to rest after this project." Henry said.

"What about you, Ri?" Jake asked.

"I'm flying back with Henry. I'm in-between projects after we're done here, so I'll go home and spend some time with my family."

"Gabby, are you done filming?" Laurel asked.

"I am. Do you still have more to film?"

"Yep. Me, Henry, and Riona have to be back tomorrow to film some more. Don promised it shouldn't take too long."

"Well, while we're all together, why don't we do something tomorrow?" Jake suggested.

"Sure, after filming is done, I have nothing planned." Henry responded.

"I was planning on hanging out with Matt, but I'm sure he would be good with going out." Laurel chimed in.

"Well, I'm doing some house hunting tomorrow morning, but Liam and I were planning on going to the Disney parks during our last two days."

"Why don't you go to California Adventure tomorrow during the day, and then tomorrow night we'll all meet up for dinner and dancing or something. There is this great Cuban place in Hollywood that we can go to." Jake suggested.

Gabriella looked to Liam, who shrugged his shoulders in response. "I'm good with it if you are, goober. What is more Hollywood than hanging out with a bunch of stars?"

"Alright, we're in. Just let me know what time in advance so we have time to leave the park." Gabriella conceded

.

Eight

At seven-thirty in the evening, Gabriella and Liam found themselves exhausted in the back seat of a ride share in route to Hollywood. "I think we should bail," Gabriella said, her head pressed against the window.

"No way, I get to party with movie stars tonight. We can sleep on the flight home on Sunday."

"Ugh, I'm just so tired," Gabriella complained.

"No one said we had to go house hunting and to a park all in the same day."

"But I want to go to Disneyland tomorrow. I've never been to the California parks. Laurel is not a Disney fan. And you can't say you didn't enjoy looking at the way people live here."

"Yeah, some of those houses were amazing. I still can't believe you put an offer on one of the tiny ones."

"A three-bedroom cottage a block away from the ocean is more than enough for me and my parents. Plus, it's a great location to rent out while I'm not here."

"I'm not sure it is going to be enough room when we're all out here."

"All out here? Are you inviting yourself to stay with me and my parents?" Gabriella asked with a raised eyebrow.

"I think it's inevitable," Liam said with a smirk.

"How presumptuous of you," Gabriella said with a laugh.

Liam shook his head, with his smirk still intact, "tell me, goober, do you really want to go to a theme park tomorrow after the day we had today? And who knows how tonight is going to go."

"We're normally a very laid-back kind of crowd, but I will admit, Jake is a wild card. We don't have to go early. And the park is open late. And our flight isn't until four on Sunday, so we will have plenty of time to relax before we leave."

"We're here," the driver called out as he pulled in front a white and red nondescript building, save for the neon sign and the line that formed down the sidewalk.

"Wow, this must be some place to draw that crowd," Liam said as he got out of the car. "I guess we should see if anyone got here before us, they may have a spot in line already."

Gabriella nodded as they started to look at the people on the line. "I don't see them," Liam said as he quickened his pace to get in line before more people joined. Gabriella took out her phone and called Laurel.

"Hey, where are you?" She asked when she answered.

"We're outside, standing in line. Where are you?"

"We're at our table. What are you doing standing in line? Go to the door and say that you're with Jake," Laurel said over the background noise.

"Okay, stay on the phone with me," Gabriella said as she turned to Liam. "They are already in there. We need to go to the door."

Liam grabbed Gabriella's hand as they walked towards the door. The people waiting in line made comments amongst themselves about being cut and for them to wait their turn. The bouncer eyed them up and down before told them to go wait in line.

"I'm sorry to bother you, but we're here with Jake Wilson," Gabriella said with a smile as the bouncer looked at her. "Yeah, I'm sure you are. Get in line."

"No, you don't understand, we're here with him and Laurel Dolce. I'm actually on the phone with her right now, she can vouch for us."

"I don't have time for this. What is your name? I'll see if you're on the list."

"Gabriella DiStella and Liam Stewart."

The bounce eyed a clipboard that another gentleman beyond the doorway had in his hands. "Sorry, you're not here."

"Oh my god, Laurel, they won't let us in, they said we're not on the list." Gabriella said, her voice full of embarrassment.

"I need you to step into the line, miss." The bouncer instructed as he gestured to the end of the line with his hand.

Liam turned to walk away, "great, the line is even longer now. We'll never get in."

"Maybe you can facetime with me to prove to the guy that I'm here?" Laurel suggested.

"It might be worth a try," Gabriella said as she facetimed Laurel. Laurel answered, but it was too dark where she was sitting to see her.

"It's not going to work. I can hardly make you out."

"It's pretty dark in here."

"Can you tell Jake to let the bouncer know that we are here and to let us in?"

"Yeah, as soon as he gets back from the bar, I'll tell him."

"Okay. Just keep me posted." Gabriella sighed as she hung up, as the two of them made stood in place at the end of the line.

"So, now what?" Liam asked.

"I guess we just wait and see what happens."

Ten minutes passed and the line hardly moved. One of the bouncers walked down the length of the line for crowd control, when he paused in front of them. "I need you to come with me."

Gabriella and Liam shared a look and then followed the bouncer to the front of the line. Jake was in the vestibule of the club, out of sight from the crowd outside.

"Are these people a part of your party?" The bouncer asked Jake.

Jake took his time as he looked them over then shook his head. "No, I have no idea who they are."

"Jake! You have to be kidding me!" Gabriella shouted, unable to manage her anger.

"Alright, I think that's enough for the two of you tonight. I'm going to have to ask you to leave," the bouncer said as he held his arms up to barricade them from entering the building.

"Seriously Jake?" Gabriella said as she tried to look past the brawny chest and arms of the bouncer.

"Guys, I'm kidding. They are with me." Jake said with a laugh. "As a matter of fact, you should remember her name, I just wrapped up filming a movie with her."

The bouncer stepped aside and allowed Liam and Gabriella into the building. The second bouncer smiled as they walked past. He leaned and said to Gabriella, "for the record, if you weren't here with that guy, we would have let you in no problem. It's customary to let beautiful, single women into the club."

"Lovely," Gabriella said with a smirk as she continued up the stairs into the dark light club, then smacked Jake on the arm when she caught up to him. "You're such a jerk!"

"I don't know why you went to the front of the building. We all came through the back. They knew to look for you there." Jake said with a shrug.

"You failed to share that with me," Gabriella said with a huff.

"I guess you're not accustomed to rolling VIP." Jake said with a smirk as he followed a beautiful blonde to the bar.

"I see Laurel," Liam said as they headed towards a private corner table.

"I'm so glad you made it!" Laurel said as she jumped up to hug Gabriella. She held her at arms distance and looked her up and down. "Damn, girl, you look fire tonight!"

"We didn't pack club attire with us, so we went shopping before meeting Duke's daughter-in-law. Is it okay? Liam said to get it, but he's a guy."

"Um, you should take him shopping more often. The girls are tastefully on display, this fabric is hugging your curves, and those red heels are hot! I know you picked the color because you feel comfortable in black."

"This really isn't my comfort zone, even with the color." Gabriella said with a laugh. Matt approached them and pulled Gabriella into a tight hug.

"Wow, *mamacita*, someone is looking to blow Hank's balls off tonight," he said with a whistle and a laugh. Gabriella rolled her eyes. "Matt, this is Liam. Liam, this is Matt, Laurel's boyfriend and fitness extraordinaire."

"We met back in New York briefly. But it's pleasure to meet you officially," Liam said with a smile as he shook Matt's hand.

"We have table service. There isn't anything to eat here, but somehow Jake pulled strings and get a bunch of tacos delivered to us from next door. I think he know the owner or manager or something. I already have bottle service getting us their specialty rum drinks. Apparently, there are dancers up on the second floor. And I heard there is a cigar room here too." Laurel said as they sat down at their table.

"Really, a cigar room? I would love to check that out," Liam said as he sat next to Gabriella.

"Dude, I'll go with you at some point tonight. I want to get a few drinks in me first," Matt said, and Liam nodded in agreement.

A few minutes later, Jake approached the table with bags full of tacos, followed closely by a beautiful blonde with eyes the same green color as Jake's. "Alright, people. Courtesy of the best club manager, and second-best looking Wilson, I bring you grub."

"Oh, you poor thing, you're related to this jackass?" Laurel asked with a sympathetic smile as she reached for a taco.

"Yes, unfortunately, he's my annoying baby brother. I'm Madison. If you guys need anything while you are here, just let me know. The dancers should be starting in a few minutes. Enjoy!" Jake's sister said with a bright smile.

"No wonder you wanted to come here, family discount," Matt poked fun.

"Never mind that, if we did dinner first and then came here, we would never get in, even with my sister's pull." Jake said before devoured half a taco in one bite.

The table grew quiet as everyone dug into the food and imbibed in their rum drinks. The music started and dancers appeared on the next floor, which was open in the center and surrounded by a banister.

"Oh damn, it's burlesque!" Liam said with a smile, his eyes glued to the women.

Halfway through the ten-minute set, Henry and Riona appeared at the table. "Took you long enough," Jake said as they sat down.

Henry rolled his eyes. "Yeah, someone couldn't decide what dress to wear."

"You know we're going to be photographed here; I need to make sure I look my best." Riona said as her eyes fell to the bags of food on the table. "What is this?"

"Tacos," Jake said as his eyes returned to the dancers.

Riona scrunched her nose in disgust. "I'll just stick with drinking."

Gabriella and Laurel shared a look and an eye roll as they both reached for another taco. The crowd erupted into a cheer when the dancers finished their set. The music continued its Latin vibe, but it wasn't so loud that you couldn't hear a conversation.

"So, how did filming go?" Gabriella asked the table.

"I was wet half of the time I was on set," Laurel said.

"From the boat scene?" Gabriella asked.

Laurel shook her head. "No, and we're not allowed to share our parts that we filmed with one another. They really have a bug up their ass about keeping the ending a secret."

"How about the rest of you?" Jake inquired.

"Same for me. Ri?" Henry responded. Riona nodded her head in response.

"How was your day, Ella?" Henry asked.

"Busy and great. Put an offer on a house and spent the day at California Adventure." She responded.

"Oh! Where is the house? Is it by me?" Laurel asked.

Gabriella shook her head. "I'm not in Bel Air, Lau. It's a three-bedroom cottage in Santa Monica. You know I wanted to be by the beach."

"Eh, it's closer than being in New York," Laurel said with a wink and a nudge.

"True, hopefully they'll except my offer."

Once they ate, the drinks started flowing. There was another show by the dancers, followed by people who made their way into the open area of the bar to dance. Gabriella sat and sipped her rum punch and while she danced in her seat.

"Someone looks like she wants to boogie," Matt said with a laugh. Gabriella nodded in response.

"Go on, Liam, take her for a whirl," Matt encouraged.

Liam shook his head vigorously. "Oh, no way, I do not dance, ever. Maybe I can sway in one spot to a slow song. I've been known to do damage to women's feet." The table laughed in response.

"Come on, Gabby, I need to move too," Jake said as he stood up and extended his hand out to her. Gabriella raised her eyebrows in surprise, then finished her drink and stood up to join Jake.

"Is this seriously happening?" Laurel asked as she watched Gabriella walk around the table to join Jake.

"You wanna join them?" Matt asked. Laurel laughed and shook her head. "Mind if I do?" He asked.

"Go shake what your momma gave you, babe." Laurel encouraged him. He leaned down and gave her a kiss before he joined Jake and Gabriella on the dance floor.

Jake moved Gabriella around in Salsa-like dance moves, complete with twirls as they moved around the dance floor. Gabriella laughed and smiled the entire time he maneuvered her around. "Jake Wilson, you surprise me!"

"I know, blonde haired, green-eyed, all-American boy doesn't scream Latin dancer, but the truth is, my mother is half Colombian. And she always had us dancing at home or at parties. I guess some of it rubbed off on me," he said with a grin.

"Alright, you need to share. I'm not dancing by myself like an idiot. And I have moves too," Matt said as he approached them.

Jake offered Gabriella to Matt as he moved onto another woman who danced next to him. "Replaced so easily," Gabriella joked as she danced with Matt.

"Just a heads up, Henry has not taken his eyes off of you since you stood up from the table." Matt said as he twirled her. "He looks like one of those cartoon wolves whose tongue rolled out of his mouth and his eyes are fifteen-times the size they should be and are popping out of his sockets."

"Oh, well, that's his problem, not mine." Gabriella said with a shrug.

"Uh huh. I'm sure it has nothing to do with your outfit and the fact that you've been shaking your ass out here like you need to pay rent?" Matt quipped.

"I'm enjoying myself with my friends. I love dancing, it's freeing." Gabriella answered.

Jake came back, and grabbed Gabriella away from Matt. Matt danced by himself for a little bit until Liam approached him. "Dude, cigar room?" Matt nodded and waved to Gabriella and Jake as they headed off the dance floor.

"Not that it's any of my business, because I've tried to keep myself out of it, but are you going to do something about Henry and Riona?" Jake asked.

"Not at all," Gabriella said with her eyebrows furrowed. "Why would you even ask that?"

"No reason. I just feel like their relationship is a publicity stunt or something. He doesn't seem like a guy who is into Riona Murphy. Is she into him? Absolutely. But I don't think it's mutual." Jake said with a look back at the table, which was empty.

Gabriella shrugged her shoulders as they continued to dance. Jake spun her away from him, and she was caught by another pair of arms. She looked up to see Henry smile at her. "Can I take you for a spin?"

Gabriella hesitated to answer as she looked over her shoulder to see Laurel swoop in and dance with Jake. "It seems that my dance partner is otherwise occupied, so why not?"

The two of them began to dance, but their body language was completely different from when she danced with Jake and Matt. Henry held her closer, the movements softer. "How has your trip been?" He asked.

"Good. Very productive. I feel like I'm accomplishing everything I wanted to this week."

Henry nodded thoughtfully. "So, you're putting down roots here?"

"It makes sense to have a place of my own when I'm here."

"And Liam is okay with that? You living somewhere else a few months of the year?"

"I never really thought to ask. He knows it's part of my job."

Henry nodded again, but wanted to ask her exactly how their situation was different if they lived in two different places.

"Where is Riona?" Gabriella asked.

"Bathroom, I think. Maybe outside. I'm not sure."

He spun her out from his arms, then pulled her back tightly against his body. "You look phenomenal tonight."

"Thank you."

"It's driving me crazy. I don't know if you're dressed like that for him, or if you're dressed like that for me."

Gabriella looked up at him and asked, "why can't it just be for me?"

"You're right. But in my jealous mind, I only want you dressing like that for me."

"Yeah, well, I'm sure your girlfriend wouldn't be happy to hear that."

"What wouldn't I be happy to hear?" Riona asked, as she appeared out of nowhere. Henry and Gabriella froze, and Gabriella stepped away from Henry like he just caught on fire. "Did I interrupt something?" Riona asked innocently, but her eyes bore into Gabriella.

"Not at all, just keeping this one entertained with my fancy footwork until you got back," Gabriella said uncomfortably as she shrugged, her eyes downcast.

"Huh, you seem to be good at that." Riona said with a judgmental look, then intertwined her arm with Henry's. "I hope she didn't tucker you out with her fancy footwork."

Henry had the decency to look sheepish as Riona pulled him away, then suctioned her body against his as she began to dance. Gabriella tried to avoid them and turned to find Jake and Laurel watching. "Are you okay?" Laurel asked timidly.

Gabriella plastered a smile on her face as she responded, "yeah, of course. Why wouldn't I be?"

Jake and Laurel exchanged a concerned look, then pulled to Gabriella towards them. They tried to get her to dance with them, but the awkwardness of the moment was impossible to ignore. Gabriella's eyes remained downcast, her movement slow and somber as she tucked her hair behind her ears as she moved. "Hey, how about we go check out that cigar lounge? I think Matt and Liam are still in there," Laurel suggested, as she took Gabriella by the arm.

"That's a great idea. I can get more drinks sent in there for us," Jake agreed as he placed his hand on Gabriella's lower back to help Laurel navigate her to the room. The room was smaller than the one they left, thick with a cloud of smoke. They made their way to the back corner, where Liam and Matt chatted with some other men, with cigars in their mouths.

"Hey! Come sit down! Do you guys want a cigar?" Matt said as they came into view. Jake nodded and made himself comfortable and grabbed one from the humidor in front of Matt.

"Did my sister give these to you?" He asked as he cut the cigar.

"Yeah, as soon as she saw us head in here, she had someone bring it to us. Thank you," Liam said with a smile. Jake nodded in response and lit his cigar.

Jake looked at the other men at the booth. "Hey, are you Ethan James?"

"Yeah, man. You're Jake Wilson, right?" The guy responded.

"Yeah. Holy shit, I'm a huge fan!" Jake said as he shook his hand. "Likewise, bro."

"We've been talking about how insane they have been this season. I hope you guys take it all," Matt said as he raised his glass to them.

"Are you Laurel Dolce?" One of the other men asked, after he recognized her.

"Sure am. And I don't know a thing about sports," Laurel said with a laugh.

"These guys are football players, babe. Patriots. Ethan James is a tight end, Martin Jacobsen is a wide receiver, and Marcus Smith is a defensive tackle." Matt explained to Laurel.

"I'm not even going to pretend to understand any of that, but it's really nice to meet you."

"And who is this beautiful woman standing next to you?" Ethan asked as he eyed Gabriella. Laurel threw her arm around Gabriella and responded, "this is my best friend, manager, and up-and-coming actress Gabriella."

"It's a pleasure to meet you, Gabriella, I'm Ethan," he said as he offered his hand to her.

She shook it and responded, "I know who you are."

"You don't seem so happy about it," Matt said as he gave Gabriella a death stare.

"Forgive her," Laurel chimed in, "The only thing I know about football is that Gabriella bleeds blue. Giants all the way."

"Ah, I get it," Ethan said with a laugh. "My apologies for not being big blue. Maybe I could get you a drink to make it up to you?"

"I'm okay, but thanks for the offer," Gabriella said dismissively.

"Did you want to sit, Gabby?" Liam offered as slid out of the booth and allowed her to slide into the booth, then he sat down next to her, his arm casually settled on the booth behind her.

Ethan smiled and noticed Liam's possessiveness, and Gabriella's complete disregard. "So, Gabriella, are you from around here?"

Gabriella looked across the booth to Ethan, who smiled at her with straight white teeth. His face was covered in a trimmed beard, his dark hair tapered on the sides, but slightly longer and curled at the top. His honey eyes crinkled with his smile, and his light cocoa skin contrasted against the crisp white button-down shirt he was wearing. His extreme handsomeness was not lost on Gabriella, and she could feel Laurel watch her from a few seats down.

"No, you?"

"Nope, born in raised in Georgia, but I'm in Massachusetts now." He responded.

"New Yorker. Born and bred." Gabriella responded as Laurel and Liam raised their glasses in comradery.

"What brings you to L.A.?" Ethan inquired.

"They are filming a movie," said the mountain of a man, Marcus, his voice as deep as he was large. "Don't you pay attention?"

"Thank you, Marcus," Ethan said with a smile and a shake of his head, "but I was engaging Gabriella in a conversation."

"Well, he's right. I came out here to finish some scenes. Liam and I decided to stay for a few days to make a mini getaway out of it." Gabriella answered.

"Oh, pity," Ethan said as he took a drink, his eyes glued to Gabriella.

Liam cleared his throat. "When do you guys go back?" Matt asked to ease the tension.

"We were off for the holidays. We're back at it on Monday. Decided to get in a little boy's trip between family obligations and getting back for the post season," Martin answered.

The conversation carried on between Jake, Matt and the football players. After some time, the smell of the cigars made Gabriella sick. "Liam, would you excuse me? I need to get some fresh air. The smoke is a bit much for me."

Liam nodded and stood so Gabriella could leave the booth. "Are you okay, Gabs?" Laurel asked.

"Yeah, just need some air."

"We can go back to our table if you want," Laurel suggested.

Gabriella shook her head, "no need to rush on my account."

"Go to the back door if you leave the building. Just let the security guard know you're with me and that you'll be back." Jake called out as she began to walk away.

She made her way out of the lounge and back into the main room where the dance floor was packed and the dancers performed on the top floor. Gabriella quickly walked by their VIP table, where she took a double take, and couldn't believe her eyes when she saw Riona straddling Henry's lap as the two of them making out in front of everyone.

170

The queasiness from the cigar smoke intensified as she watched the two of them go at it. Her stomach dropped as her heart lodged in her throat simultaneously. She was a fool to listen to anything Henry said to her, he was obviously very involved with Riona. She barely held herself together as she made her way down the stairs and headed towards the back of the building. The security guard nodded as she gave him her information and opened the door and released her into the slightly cooler California air. She pressed herself against the wall of the building and doubled over with a sob, followed by a gasping, guttural cry. Although the tears didn't come, her body shook with emotion. She knew she lied to herself when she said that they could be friends. The illusion they had built for one another had just shattered before her eyes. She resolved that she would not let Henry know what she saw or let him know that he affected her so much. Her new year's resolution to focus on herself was her top priority, and she would not let any man interfere with her self journey.

A few moments later, the door opened again, and Gabriella straightened herself out and ensured she was completely composed. The door closed to reveal Ethan. "Hey. Getting some fresh air?" Gabriella asked as she attempted to quell the slight tremor in her voice.

"That's my excuse," Ethan said with a flirty smile. "I thought I would check on you, make sure you were okay. Plus, it would give me a chance to talk to you without your bodyguard hovering."

"Bodyguard?"

"Yeah, the guy sitting next to you. He looked like he was going to pee on you to mark his territory." Ethan said with a laugh.

Gabriella couldn't help but bark out a laugh at his comment. "Are you spoken for?" Ethan inquired.

Gabriella pursed her lips and shook her head. "No, Liam and I dated for a bit, but we work better as friends."

"Good to hear. You think I could get your number?" Ethan asked as he approached and leaned against the wall next to her.

"For what?" Gabriella asked, completely taken off-guard by his blunt question.

"For communication purposes?" Ethan responded with a smirk.

"I'm flattered, but I'm not really in a place for anything. I'm taking a break from the dating thing and focusing on myself."

"Are you taking a break from friends too?" He asked.

Gabriella looked up at him, her eyes wide with embarrassment. "Oh my god, I'm so embarrassed. I'm sorry, that was so presumptuous. I thought you were hitting on me."

"Oh, I totally am, but I can work the friend angle."

Gabriella scoffed and rolled her eyes. "What harm is it? I'm, like, two states away," he said with a laugh.

Gabriella laughed, then nodded as she took his phone and programmed her number into it. As she handed the phone back to him, the back door swung open to reveal Laurel with a crazy look in her eyes. "Gabby! Are you okay?"

172

Gabriella looked at Ethan, then back at Laurel. "Yeah, I'm fine. The cigar smell has dissipated enough that I don't feel sick."

"Oh, good. You didn't happen to go past our table, did you?" Laurel asked.

"Ah, that. Yeah, I did, but I'm still fine." Gabriella reassured Laurel.

"Did I miss something?" Ethan asked. The girls shook their heads in unison. Matt made his way outside in a rush, "Babe, we have a situation." He shut up when he saw Gabriella. "Oh, hey Gabby. It's nice out here."

"Relax, Matt, she already knows." Laurel said.

"You told her?" He asked.

Laurel shook her head. "I saw it myself, and I'm fine." Gabriella chimed in. She looked back at the door and inquired, "where is Liam?"

"Um, believe it or not, Jake, Martin, and Marcus got him on the dance floor." Matt said with a laugh.

"I kinda want to see that," Gabriella said as she began to make her way to the door before Matt put his hands out to block her.

"Maybe we should wait out here for a bit. Cool off?" Matt suggested.

"Okay, I really feel like I missing something," Ethan said.

"There is something I'm trying to protect Gabby from." Matt responded.

"I don't need protection." Gabriella said, as Ethan questioned, "from what?"

"Someone she's involved with is in there with another woman." Matt answered.

"What the fuck, Matt?" Gabriella yelled.

"Wait, I thought Liam was dancing with the guys," Ethan questioned.

"He is," Matt confirmed.

"There's another guy?" Ethan asked as he looked at Gabriella. She shook her head in response. "No, I don't know why you guys are making such a big deal out of this. Who cares if they are making out? They are together. Now, I don't know about all of you, but I'm going back in there to watch Liam make a fool of himself."

She entered the building and thanked the security guard as she made her way back to the staircase. By the time she reached them, the others followed. Gabriella returned to the main floor, where she was greeted by Jake, Martin, and Marcus who surrounded Liam as he danced in the center of the dancefloor, as the crowd cheered him on as he let loose. Laurel and Ethan flanked her to watch the show. "Yeah, get it Liam!" Laurel yelled out as she cheered.

"Well, that is some white boy dancing if I've ever seen it. But I gotta hand it to him, he's really getting into it." Ethan said with a laugh before he cheered.

Gabriella giggled in response and cheered as Liam made his way over to her, reached out, and yanked her into the circle with him. Liam swung her around with a smile on his face as a large smile overtook her face. "I'm having such a good time, Gabby. Thank you for bringing me," he said as he pulled her closer.

Gabriella smiled in return as Jake pulled Liam away from her and dragged him over to a bachelorette party on the other side of the dance floor. A hand latched onto her wrist and turned her around, and she found herself face-to-face with Ethan. "I would be remiss if I didn't get one dance with you tonight," he said with a smile as he lifted her hand and encouraged her to spin underneath. He then pulled her close, his hand splayed across her lower back as his hips swayed to the rhythm of the Latin music. He maintained eye contact as he pressed himself against her, his breath warm on her skin.

Gabriella fell into a trance as his smooth movements made her forget everything she saw at the table. Ethan's fingers danced across her hips as he manipulated her body on the dance floor. The heat that built in her body was different than what she had felt before, it was intoxicating without the familiarity of Liam or the intensity of Henry. Her eyes closed as she gave into the thrum of the crowd while the music wrapped around her as seductively as Ethan's body.

A commotion behind them caused Gabriella to shake the trance she was in, to find Laurel and Matt over at their table, Matt leaned over Henry, who was slumped over slightly in the booth, his eyes closing as Matt shouted and tapped the side of his face. Laurel pushed her way on to the dance floor, where she found Jake, and shouted at him to go get his sister.

"What is happening?" Gabriella asked, concern overtook her body, suddenly sober from the night's events. She disentangled herself from Ethan and made her way to the table, when she was pushed aside by Jake and Madison. Liam and the football players stood back and watched as Madison called over her headset. A few security guards made their way to block the view of the crowd. Gabriella approached and threaded her arm through Laurel's as they watched a guard flash a light into Henry's eyes.

"Madison, I think he's been drugged," the guard said, then instructed someone to get a medic to the club.

"How the hell did that happen?" Madison asked as she tugged her hands through her blonde hair. "Okay, let's not panic. Let's get Henry to the office and wait for the paramedics to get here." She looked up at the group that surrounded the table. "I would suggest you all head out, I don't think it's safe for you to be here."

"I'm staying with him," Matt said, as Laurel nodded in agreement.

"That's fine, but I think the rest of you should go." Madison said as she looked back at her brother.

"Yeah, okay, as long as Matt keeps us updated on him. I really don't like leaving him like this." Jake said.

"We will let you know," Laurel said with a nod as she rubbed her hand over Gabriella's arm. Matt and a guard both helped Henry stand up, their arms supported his upper body as they moved him toward a set of private stairs in the back of the room, which lead down to the private offices of the club.

Laurel hugged Gabriella goodbye before she followed them. Gabriella hugged herself as she watched them disappear into the doorway, her nerves alive with nervous energy as her eyes scanned the club. Someone in this room drugged Henry and they had no idea why.

"Has anyone seen Riona?" Jake asked as his eyes traced the walls of the club.

"No, do you think something happened to her too?" Liam asked as the severity of the situation penetrated the haze of booze.

"Shit. I'll go look for her," Gabriella said as she began to walk away from the group. Ethan was quick to follow her. "I don't think it's a good idea for you to wander off alone."

Gabriella looked back at him and nodded, then made her way through the main floor and searched everywhere. She noticed Jake and Liam head towards the cigar lounge, as Marcus and Martin stood by the table and kept an eye out for her return. Gabriella checked the women's room as Ethan took the men's room, but she was not in there. They made it down the stairs to the back entrance to see the paramedics enter the private office.

Gabriella walked through the door to the back patio area, where she found Riona with a cigarette in her hand, sitting in a chair and speaking to what looked like a reporter. A man with a camera was taking photos, indistinguishable if he was the press or a paparazzo.

"Riona! There you are! Are you okay?" Gabriella yelled out in relief.

"Yes, here I am. Why are you asking if I'm alright?" She asked, then took a long drag of her cigarette.

"Um, can I talk to you in private?" Gabriella asked as she eyed the reporter and the camera nervously.

"Anything you have to say can be said in front of my mate here," she said with a wink to the reporter.

Gabriella chewed on her lip and tucked her hair behind her ear. "Um, I think we should really talk in private."

Riona scoffed and waved her off as she turned her attention back to the man in front of her. She smiled and winked at him as she continued her conversation.

"When did you last see Henry?" Gabriella asked.

Riona raised an eyebrow at her, "I left my boyfriend at the table, enjoying a cocktail and speaking with a few people."

"How was he? Did he seem okay?" Gabriella asked.

Riona smirked. "I think it is sweet that you have a crush on him, I really do," she said as she stood up and smoothed out her crimson dress. "But really, I think it would be best if you just let the thoughts of him out of your little head."

Gabriella closed her eyes and pressed her lips together, then took a deep, calming breath as she prepped herself to respond. "I think you should come with us." Ethan said quietly as his hand gently touched Gabriella's forearm.

"And who are you?" Riona asked loudly, as she gained the attention of the few people outside. "Are you with her?" She chuckled without any humor, "really, Gabriella? Two men in one night? Honestly, I think you have your hands full; I don't think you need to mind Henry. I don't believe he is into sharing."

Riona tossed her blonde hair over her shoulder and sauntered away, then settled herself across from the reporter, who smiled like a Cheshire cat. Gabriella sighed and knew this interaction was going to be in the tabloids tomorrow. She stood there and watched as she resumed her conversation. The reporter's eyes continued to shift towards Gabriella and Ethan by the door. Mid-sentence, Riona followed the gaze of the reporter and rolled her eyes in response. "We're done here, Gabriella, you're dismissed."

Rage flared in Gabriella, and it took all the strength she had to turn around and enter the building. The undiluted anger radiated off her like heat and kept people around her at a distance as she barreled through the hallway. She paused by the office door and spotted Jake and Liam. "Did you find her?" Jake asked as she approached.

"Oh yeah, I found out. She's outside doing an interview and a photo shoot," Gabriella said as she crossed her arms.

"She's a real bitch," Ethan chimed in.

Jake shook his head in response. "Is he okay?" Gabriella asked.

"Yeah. It was like we thought, someone slipped him a roofie. Madison said she was going to check the cameras to see if they can find who did it. We're not sure if he was the target, or maybe someone else in the group. The good thing is since he's such a big dude, it won't affect him as badly as if it was a petite woman. The medic said he should be good in a couple of hours; he'll just feel hung over. Laurel and Matt took him back to their place."

"Did they already leave?"

Jake nodded in response. "Yeah, I think it's best if you head out. Madison got you and Liam a ride to take you back to the hotel. Just let me know when you get in. I can't help but feel responsible for what happened tonight."

"Jake, none of this is on you. Thank you for doing all of this. It was a lot of fun, until it wasn't," Gabriella said with a smile as she hugged Jake.

"Thanks, Gabby. Take care of yourself, okay? I'll see you at the premiere." Jake said, then kissed her on the cheek.

Jake then gave Liam a hand clap, half hug, back slap. "It was good to meet you, my dude. I hope you enjoyed your trip. Hopefully we'll see each other again."

"Thanks man, I hope so too." Liam said, then turned his attention to Gabriella. "You ready, Gabby?"

Gabriella nodded and started to head to the entrance with Liam. A hand on her shoulder stopped her. She turned to see Ethan, his face twisted unsurely. "Oh, I'm sorry. I don't know where my head is at," Gabriella said. "It was nice to meet you, Ethan. Good luck with the rest of the post season."

"Um, thanks." Ethan said, "so, I'll reach out to you, and we can get together when I'm in the city."

"Look, I had fun tonight, but I meant what I said earlier. And this night has been a complete clusterfuck. I just…" her voice trailed, unsure how to end the conversation.

Ethan flashed his pearly whites, "hey, I get it. It was nice to meet you too."

Gabriella nodded her head, then turned and joined Liam at the door, where their ride waited for them at the curb.

Nine

Three weeks later, Gabriella found herself decked out in her Giants jersey to watch the NFC Championship game at her parents' house, surrounded by booze, food, and her extended family in similar jerseys. Giuseppe, Gabriella, Marco, and Caroline sat in the living room; their eyes glued to the television as they watched the game. Maria sat in the kitchen with Sierra, Desmond, and Arnie, as they drank wine and commented when there were cheers and jeers that echoed from the living room.

Dino paced the living room, wearing a New York Jets jersey, and purposely stopped in front of the television to take a drink or scratch his ass. Giuseppe threw a pillow at Dino's head, "*Fanabla!* Sit your ass down, you sorry excuse for a football fan!"

Dino laughed, "what is your problem?"

"I should kick you out of my house for wearing that shitty green jersey." Giuseppe yelled.

"Wow, someone is in a bad mood." Dino said with a shake of his head.

"Dino, sit your ass down, or go sit inside with the women. I'll kill you in your sleep if you make me miss this game," Caroline said to her husband.

"Ooohhh…" Marco said with a laugh as he reached for a buffalo wing.

"You guys suck. I wish Matt was here," Dino said as he sat down with his arm crossed.

"Why, so you wouldn't be the only non-Giants fan? He'd be sitting here in a Chargers jersey, looking almost as sad as you do in the Jets one," Gabriella said with a smirk as her father clapped, then gave her a high five.

When the first half of the game was over, Desmond entered the living room, holding Gabriella's phone and a piece of paper as most of the parents made their way into the kitchen to refill snacks and drinks. He held out the paper to Gabriella. "Check my boxes. Did I win any money?"

Gabriella shook her head as she took the paper. "Why is it that you get into football pools when you don't care or understand the game."

"I don't need to care or understand the game to win some cash," he said with a scoff.

"Sorry, Des, nothing yet."

"By the way, your phone has been blowing up. Who do you know that has a 404-area code?" Desmond asked as he handed her the phone.

"You're checking my messages?"

"Naturally. Liam messaged a few times, why isn't he here?"

"Business trip." Gabriella responded as she opened her messages.

Unknown: No congrats?

Unknown: I know you hate my team but making it into the Superbowl is an accomplishment.

184

Unknown: I'm guessing your elbow deep watching the NFC. It's cool, I'll wait.

Unknown: Wow, you really take your football watching seriously.

"Who is it?" Desmond asked, reading over her shoulder.

"I think it's Ethan James, the football player I met in L.A.," Gabriella explained. Desmond googled his name on his phone and gasped when his image came up.

"Bitch, this man is sexy. Text him back immediately."

"You know I'm steering clear of the men for a while."

"You have not had this flavor of man before. Do not disappoint me."

"You're disgusting sometimes."

Gabby: I'm hoping this is Ethan and not some other random Patriot texting me

Unknown: I'd be insulted if one of my teammates were trying to slide into your dms

Gabby: not really a dm, it's a text. Congrats btw.

Ethan: Thanks, it means a lot coming from a Giants fan

Gabby: I've got five minutes before they have my full attention again

Ethan: Are you a betting woman?

Gabby: depends on the terms

Ethan: if the Giants lose, I get to take you on a date when I'm in the city

Gabby: Hm. And if they win?

Ethan: They aren't going to win. But if they do, your choice.

Gabby: ...hm...

Ethan: make it good, Gabby

Gabby: If they win, I want to see them in the Super Bowl

Ethan: really? You think I can make that happen?

Gabby: I think you're going to the Super Bowl, you can definitely make it happen.

Ethan: okay, they win, you come to the Super Bowl, as my guest.

Gabby: And my dad. He'd die if I didn't take him.

Ethan: deal. This date is going to be so much fun.

"Are you sexting?" Desmond asked with a wolfish grin.

"Oh my god, no!"

"You've got that look."

186

"This is the look of someone who's going to the Super Bowl."

Desmond cocked his eyebrow in response and waited for an explanation.

"Ethan just bet that if the Giants lose, he takes me out, but if they win, I get to go to the game."

"So, he wins either way, because he gets to see you?"

"Des, Super Bowl tickets. Could you imagine excited my dad would be?"

"Mhm, I'm sure it will just be an innocent game," Desmond said with a wink.

Arnie walked in with a tray of food and held it in front of Gabriella. "You haven't come into the kitchen since the game started. I need you to taste test for me. Mini meatball sliders, stuffed with sautéed mushrooms, onions, and smoked mozzarella."

Gabriella's stomach growled in response as she took one from the tray. She took a bite, the flavors exploded in her mouth and danced across her tastebuds. "Oh wow, Arnie, this is delicious. This might be the best meatball I've ever had in my life."

"I heard that," Marie yelled out from the kitchen.

"Sorry, ma."

Marie walked in and smiled. "You're right though, Arnie blows my cooking out of the water."

"That's not true, Marie. And I still need you to teach me some of those family secrets." Arnie said with a wink.

"Gabby can outcook me too, she's the one you need to butter up for my mother-in-law's recipes." Marie said with a smile.

"Seriously, Arnie, you're going to sell these at Dino's, right?" Gabriella asked.

"Yeah, we were thinking of making them as a hot food item, and then maybe making some grab and go in the freezer section. You think they will sell?" Arnie asked.

"I could punch you in the face, they are so good! Yeah, they will sell."

"Okay. That's quite the review. I've got some dips in the oven that I'm bringing out in a few." He said as he walked away.

Gabriella turned back to Desmond, who sat there and watched Maria and Arnie head back to the kitchen. "Penny for your thoughts?"

Desmond rolled his eyes, "worth more than a penny."

Gabriella face dropped into an unamused, blasé look. "Do you want to talk about it? The game is starting again."

"I'm proud of him for chasing his dream, but I feel like I'm an afterthought. And I know that he's putting a lot of effort into this, but between his new ambitions and my new role starting next month, it's like we're two ships passing in the night. And when I say passing, I mean passing out in bed, asleep, all night."

"It will be worth it, Des. He's one of the good ones. Just hang in there." Gabriella said with a smile as she patted Desmond's arm.

"Game's on!" Gabriella yelled out, which made Desmond jump up as the football fans crowded back into the living room.

The next forty-five minutes were passed in nail-biting intensity as the Giants held a three-point lead. The house was filled with anxiety as they groaned and yelled when flags were thrown in favor of the opposing team, and when the quarterback was tackled at the end of the third quarter.

The Giants were down by four with only five minutes left of the game, their defense was on the field trying their hardest to prevent more points. One defensive player intercepted the ball and ran it down the field for a seventy-yard touchdown. The room went nuts, popcorn flew in the air as they jumped up off the couch and screamed like maniacs. The Giants were able to keep the lead and eventually won the game.

Everyone celebrated and hugged when a high-pitched scream came from the kitchen. Everyone ran in there to see Desmond scream as he danced around the kitchen. "Desmond, what happened?" His father asked as he stood among everyone.

"I just won five grand!" He said as he waved around the paper with the football pool on it.

Everyone cheered again as they celebrated Desmond's big win. Gabriella's phone buzzed in her pocket. She checked it to find a message from Ethan.

Ethan: See you in Miami, beautiful.

"Hey Dad!" Gabriella said as she approached her father. "What are you doing in two weeks?"

Giuseppe looked at her. "Um, I'll be here, Super Bowl party?"

Gabriella smiled brightly, "how would you like to be in Miami? To watch the Super Bowl?"

***

The DiStellas touched down in Miami thirteen days later, and checked into a gorgeous, towering hotel on the beach. Maria joined them to thaw out from the New York winter in the sun while Giuseppe and Gabriella prepared to live out their football fan fantasy.

Gabby: We just checked into the hotel. Nervous about tomorrow?

Ethan: Nah, we'll kick their asses

Gabby: Those are fighting words

Ethan: we'll see. How long are you going to be in town?

Gabby: We're leaving Monday night. Mom couldn't get much time off on such short notice.

190

Ethan: Can I see you Monday before you leave? Maybe we can do lunch?

Gabby: it should be doable. Good luck tomorrow, not because I want you to win, because you're gonna need it.

Ethan: It's okay, I'll console you when your team loses.

Gabriella and her parents sat out by to pool when she put her phone away. "Can you explain to me again how we are here?" Giuseppe asked.

"I met guy who plays for the Patriots. He lost a bet he made with me on the last game, and I won two tickets."

"And you met this guy?"

"In L.A."

"*Bambolina,* this isn't the same guy the tabloids were talking about, is it? You know, *Henry's ex heartbroken by his new relationship, seeks comfort in the arms of two men* or *Football star snag's Henry's ex from him?*"

"Thanks for that reminder, mom. Yes, it's the same guy, but nothing happened with him. You know the tabloids are bullshit."

"But you were there with Liam," Maria pointed out.

"As a friend. Dear lord, don't read that trash." Gabriella huffed as she laid back on her lounge chair.

"Is it true what they said about Henry? Was he really drugged?" Maria asked.

191

"Yeah, that part was true."

"Is he okay?" Giuseppe asked.

"Yeah, Laurel and Matt took him to their house. He was fine, they even finished filming the next day. Laurel let me know how he was."

"Have you spoken to him?" Giuseppe inquired.

"Listen, guys, I know you love Henry. I get it, he's a great guy. There's a lot to like about him, but he's in a relationship, and I'm going to respect it and not reach out. We have a history, and it's not fair to anyone if we keep communicating. Okay?"

Giuseppe and Maria exchanged a look and then nodded. "Okay Gabby, we'll drop it. We just want you to be happy."

"I know, and I love you guys, but please, I'm focusing on me right now. We're in Miami, in the sunshine, we're going to watch the Giants kick ass tomorrow, and we're together. I'm happy, I swear."

***

Giuseppe and Gabriella had the time of their lives watching the game, and the experience was even sweeter when their team won. They danced around in their seats, and high-fived the fans around them, and enjoyed the once in a lifetime experience. They met Maria at the hotel restaurant for a late dinner and continued their celebration from the stadium.

Gabriella's phone began to blow up as people commented on her Instagram posts of her and her father at the game, and a video of them as they celebrated after the big win. Texts came in from Laurel, Matt, Desmond and Liam, excited for the win and that they got to experience it in person. Once in bed, Gabriella returned all of the messages, then sent one to Ethan.

Gabby: Hey, you played a really great game.

Ethan: Thanks, looking to gloat?

Gabby: not at all, I didn't play. You really did a great job.

Ethan: Not enough to win.

Gabby: I'm sorry. Are you okay?

Ethan: Not really. I've gotta go.

Gabriella stared at the messages, a little taken back by the response she received. She shook it off and fell asleep to the sounds of the ocean from the balcony in her room. The next morning, she woke up to find her parents still asleep in their room. She took her time to ready and soaked in the jetted tub in her bathroom. She sent Ethan a text to check on him.

Gabby: Hey Ethan, I hope you are feeling better.

She finished her bath and checked her phone to see no response. She called her parents and agreed to meet up for breakfast. After they ate Maria questioned her daughter. "*Bambolina*, what do you want to do before our flight home?"

Gabriella checked her phone again. Nothing.

Gabby: Hey Ethan. I'm sorry to bother you. I just wanted to see if you still wanted to get together for lunch.

"Um, I'm not sure. I thought I was supposed to meet up with a friend for lunch, but it looks like that isn't going to happen. Maybe we can just hang out in South Beach? We're going to back in the snow in a few hours."

***

Gabriella sat on her beach towel, unable to put her phone down. The silence from Ethan was deafening. Also deafening were the constant messages she received from her group chat with Desmond and Laurel. Desmond started the conversation by sending a few links from trashy tabloids.

Desmond: Henry's ex supporting new boyfriend, Patriot Ethan James at Super Bowl

Desmond: Boyfriends in two states, how Henry's ex juggles her new men

Desmond: Thruple alert: Ethan James in relationship with Henry Anderson's ex and another man

Gabby: Seriously Des? You're sending me this shit?

Desmond: It's insane how you are in the tabloids this morning. I thought things quieted down after you got home

Gabby: They did. This is ridiculous

194

Laurel: I don't know why they are bothering you. Why not go after Riona?

Gabby: Because she gives them what they want

Laurel: What did Ethan say?

Gabby: Dunno, he ghosted me

Desmond: WHAT?!

Gabby: texted last night about getting together today, then nothing. I've sent messages.

Laurel: Maybe he's bummed out about the loss?

Gabby: maybe

Desmond: maybe it is because of this.

Desmond sent a link to an interview with the team after their loss. During the press conference the players were interviewed by journalist, and a few were surrounding Ethan and asking his questions about the loss and what could have been done differently. As they typical questions were asked, Ethan's demeanor tensed and became uncomfortable as they continued to pepper him with questions about the team's struggle. Then one reporter asked him. "Ethan, do you think that all of the tabloid fodder about your new relationship messed with your head since she was in the stands watching the game?"

Ethan's nostrils flared as he looked to the journalist. "Excuse me?"

"Your personal life has been in the limelight recently; seems you're attached to an actress who dated Henry Anderson. Maybe all of that attention has taken your focus off of the game."

"Are you kidding me? I just lost the biggest game of my life, and you're all up in here asking about who's in my wheelhouse? Hell, no, man. Keep my name out your mouth. We're done here." Ethan responded, then stood up from the table and left the room.

Gabby: well, shit, that isn't good

Desmond: no, it really isn't

Gabby: now do you know why I want a break from men?

Laurel: yeah, I get it

Desmond: fuck them. You've got us

Gabby: thanks, I'm gonna hang with my parents, ttyl

Ten

New York City had finally thawed from the long winter, and entered the rainy period before the sweltering heat baked the sidewalks, and those who traveled them. True to her word, Gabriella spent four months focused on herself. After she found peace with the way life came at her, she decided to put her energy to something more conducive. She started her morning sat the local yoga studio, where she learned to calm her mind before she took on the day. Her daytime hours were consumed with work, she setup more endorsement deals for Laurel, while she worked with Desmond and his new advertising campaign to support the LGBTQ community.

Her evenings were filled with events for Desmond's campaign, dinners with Desmond, Arnie, and Liam, and kickboxing classes which she used as an outlet for her rage. She felt comfortable for the first time in a long time. The tabloids left her alone once they saw Ethan Jones out with Victoria's Secret model. Gabriella couldn't help but laugh to see how low he must have sunk to hit on her now that he was dating a model. They never even spoke after Miami.

Riona and Henry were still a mainstay in the tabloids, mostly due to Riona's social media, where she constantly posted throwback photos of them from the show the first worked on together, as well as mushy messages she posted about how amazing of a boyfriend he was. It was quiet on Henry's end, he only posted photos from the location of his Arthurian legend project in New Zealand, or photos of Leigh.

Weekends were spent with her family, she usually traveled to visit her parents or hosted them in Manhattan and took them to museums or art galleries. On the weekends she did not spend with them, she volunteered at the community center that Desmond campaigned for.

On a Friday night in early May, Gabriella hosted an intimate gathering at her apartment with her core group. She made Nonna Rosa's meat and cheese ravioli with her tomato sauce, along with prosciutto-wrapped asparagus, and bruschetta. The sound of her open front door as all her favorite men walked into the apartment made her look up as she set the plates up on her island.

"Hey Goober, I brought the wine. Dry white and a Chianti." Liam said as he walked over and placed a kiss on her cheek.

"Hey guys! Just put the stuff on the coffee table, I've got the food on the stove. I was just pulling out the plates and the silverware."

Arnie walked over with his arms full of aluminum foil covered trays. He placed a kiss on Gabby's cheek and nudged to the tray. "Your mom gave me her recipe for some of her cookies."

Gabriella's eyes lit up with delight as she asked, "pignoli or lace cookies?"

Arnie smiled, "both."

"You are rocketing to the top of my favorites."

"Hey, I'm right here," Desmond pouted.

"Yeah? What did you bring over?"

"My fabulous self. You know it's rare that I have a Friday night off." Desmond said as he grabbed a plate and started to scoop food onto it.

Gabriella rolled her eyes as she nodded her head to the others for them make a plate.

They all settled onto the couches, quiet apart from moans and grunts of appreciation for the food they consumed.

"Fuck, Gabby, this is way better than takeout," Liam said as he rolled his eyes back and happily chewed on a meat stuffed ravioli.

"Truly, it's like Rosa made this," Desmond said with a wink, which made a smile to break out onto Gabriella's face.

"Best compliment ever."

"I know you have your schedule full, but if you ever wanted to team up, we could sell your food at the deli. It really is delicious." Arnie said with a genuine smile.

"Thanks, Arnie. I appreciate it. Let's get through me being in L.A. this summer. Guarantee you are going to be a huge success on your own. You're an amazing chef."

Arnie smiled and nodded. "Deal, but I still think we could do an awesome limited time collaboration or something."

Grunts and moans filled the silence once the guys refilled their plates. "Alright guys, you need to stop with all of that, things may be on the up and up, but I am in a dry spell, and those noises are getting me all hot a bothered."

Desmond started to laugh, which stared a chain reaction of laughter to erupt in the room. Gabriella wiped the tears from her eyes as she reached for her wine, "I'm serious though. I know my plan was to focus on me, but it's been a long time since I was even kissed properly."

"Why not go back to the dating app? There's nothing wrong with getting a little something without anything serious," Arnie suggested.

Desmond shook his head violently while he mopped up tomato sauce with his bruschetta. "Uh-uh, no baby, Gabby doesn't do one-night stands. She needs to feel a connection to a person before she gets down and dirty."

"Ugh, Des, you're vile." Gabriella said with a look of disgust.

"I'm speaking the truth."

"Seriously? You don't need to be so repressed about your sexuality," Arnie said.

"It's not that, I just have issues," she said with a shrug.

"You know, I'm sitting right here." Liam said after he cleared his throat.

"What does that mean?" Arnie asked.

"It means that I'm available. We've been intimate before. I can scratch your itch, Gabs."

Gabriella studied him for a moment, as he waggled his thick, dark eyebrows at her. She laughed in response, "very funny."

"I'm not laughing." Liam said as he kept his gaze on Gabriella.

"Uh-huh, right. Are you guys done? I'll start cleaning up. Who's turn is it to pick the movie, and who wants coffee?" Gabriella asked as she stood up and collected the empty plates from the table.

"It's my turn to pick, and I will absolutely take a coffee," Arnie said with a smile as he handed his plate to Gabriella.

The others agreed to coffee as Gabriella made her way to the kitchen. After she put away the small amount of food that was left over, she started the coffee maker and turned the faucet on to wash the dishes. Desmond made his way next to her and threw the towel over his shoulder and waited for the wet dishes to dry.

"Is something wrong? You never help with cleanup duty."

"Shut up, bitch," he said with a smirk as he nudged his hip into hers.

"You know you should take Liam up on his offer, right?"

"Get the fuck out of here."

"I'm serious, Gabby. You've really hunkered down, sticking to your new year's resolution. Don't get me wrong, it's fantastic. Most people let that shit fly out the window January second. But no one said you needed to be celibate to achieve your goal."

"Pretty positive swearing off men means no sex."

"Have you given yourself carpel tunnel yet? Or got one of those sybians?"

"You have no filter, Des."

"I'm just saying, he is a perfect solution to your problem."

"He's my friend. That would be weird. It would be like fucking you."

"One, eww, no it wouldn't, I wouldn't get near your beave. Two, his p has already been in your v, multiple times. It's like two friends doing a favor for each other. Three, you wait any longer, your virginity is gonna grow back."

"You mean my hymen? That's a myth."

"You want to chance it?"

Gabriella rinsed off the last plate and turned off the water with a sigh. "Des."

"Don't Des me. I know, I know you've been burned by Henry. I know things didn't work out with Liam. But I'm not telling you to marry the guy. I'm telling you to get yours. You know him, he's safe. I don't have to worry about you meeting some weirdo on an app or out at a bar."

204

Gabriella reached into a cabinet to retrieve the coffee mugs, then began to prepare the beverages as Desmond leaned against the counter beside her. "It's not like I'm some nympho. I'm okay. It was a joke."

"It wasn't a joke, and it's okay to want some kind of affection. Gabby, it's totally normal. Don't be ashamed of it. And if you don't want to pursue anything with Liam, that's fine too. Do what makes you happy. But don't cut yourself off from something you want because it isn't in your comfort zone."

Gabriella rolled her eyes as she looked at Desmond, then placed the coffee on a tray and reached for the cookies.

"I'm not saying to join a bacchanalian orgy. A little out of your comfort zone."

Gabriella shook her head as she arranged the cookies on a plate and placed it onto the tray. She made her way to the living room as Desmond trailed behind. He sat on the loveseat next to Arnie and shook his head slightly as he silently communicated with his boyfriend.

Gabriella grabbed a cookie as she dropped back onto the couch and moaned when the pillowy confectionary melted in her mouth. "Oh, I love pignoli cookies. You really are my new favorite person, Arn."

Arnie laughed and raised his fist in victory, "all it took was some cookies to get to number one. No one else stands a chance now."

"So, what movie are we watching? Comedy? Maybe some Dodgeball or Wedding Crashers? You know I love me some Vince Vaughn." Gabriella asked as she reached for another cookie and her coffee mug.

"Unfaithful," Arnie said as he started the movie.

"Odd choice," Gabby said under her breath as she settled into the couch. Liam leaned over and asked quietly, "have you seen it before?"

"Maybe once when I was younger."

"You'll like it."

***

Gabriella got half-way through the movie and tried not to feel awkward or turned-on by the sex scenes. She tried to remind herself that it was all fake, Hollywood magic, but those thoughts brought her back to the very real sex she had with Henry on the set of their movie, which did nothing to help with the frustration she was feeling. She adjusted in her seat and reached for another cookie. When she leaned back, Liam gently rested his hand on her thigh.

Her eyes snapped to him, but his attention was still glued to the television. She stilled, like a deer in headlights, unsure of what to do. Liam noticed her gaze on him, so he turned and smiled, then raised an eyebrow when she didn't respond. He leaned into her, his breath tickled her ear as he asked, "is everything okay?"

Gabriella nodded in response and licked her dry lips as she turned her attention back to the film. They watched the scene where two of the leads had sex in the stairwell, and Liam's thumb began to rub slow circles on her leg. Gabriella's breath hitched slightly, which caused Liam to lean in again.

"Are you sure you're alright? Your breathing seems a little shallow."

206

"Yeah, I'm fine," she whispered back.

Liam nudged his nose behind her ear, inhaled her scent, then let his lips glide briefly against her skin. She sunk her teeth into her bottom lip in response, which made Liam smirk. "Am I turning you on?"

Gabriella nodded in response. Liam lightly grunted in response. "Do you want me to stay after the movie is over?" She nodded once again.

Gabriella rethought Desmond's advice; maybe he was right. Why was wrong to indulge her friend who offered his services to her. It would be mutually beneficial, and it didn't have to go too far. She was a mature, independent woman would take charge of her sexuality.

When the movie ended, Desmond stretched. "You guys want to watch another one?"

"No," Liam and Gabriella responded at the same time.

"Board game?"

"It's time to leave," Gabriella said as she stood up and prepared to walk them to the door.

"You're kicking us out? That's so rude!" Desmond said.

"Do you want me to help you clean up, Gabby?" Arnie asked.

"No, I'm good. It's just the coffee mugs, I'll let them soak overnight."

"Liam, you want to share a cab or take the train together?" Desmond asked.

Before Liam could respond, Gabriella shot daggers at Desmond and said through her clenched teeth, "go home."

Desmond threw his head back and laughed and he waved goodnight to Liam, then threaded his arm through Arnie's. "Love you, bitch."

They walked through the door, and as she closed it, she heard Arnie say to Desmond, "so, the movie worked?" To which Desmond responded, "fuck yeah it did."

She rolled her eyes and closed the door, then locked it. When she turned, she found Liam on the couch, his shirt gone and his toned body waited for her. She smiled, then ran over and pounced on top of him.

***

The rest of May and early June were spent the same way as it was in the winter and spring, with the exception that any free moment was spent with Liam in some sexual way. It was almost as if they picked up right before Christmas, but their relationship was more solid than ever. She wasn't sure what caused the change, maybe it was that they broke up and came back together. Maybe it was they knew each other better than they had in the past. Whatever the reason, Gabriella felt comfortable with him, like everything was right with the world.

Which is why it stressing her out to no end that she would leave for her time in California in a week. She knew that he knew her plans, she never kept them a secret. Hell, he was with her when she put the offer on the house. It was just that things changed over the past month, which scared her to ruin the good thing they had going on.

They watched reruns of The Office in her bed, with her head on his shoulder as he played with her hair. She had pepped some talking through the last episode but knew that she needed to rip the band-aid off and have the conversation.

"Liam?"

"Yeah, goober?"

"So, we haven't really talked about it, but I'm heading back to L.A. next week."

"Yeah, I know. I have it in my calendar."

"Oh. So, did you want to talk about it?"

"What about it?" He asked as he sat up. Gabriella lifted her head and looked at him.

"I dunno. I just thought maybe we can figure something out. I know I'm going to be busy with press for the movie for a while, but the premiere is twenty-first of July. I was thinking maybe you could fly out with Des and Arnie and my parents?"

"Oh, that would be awesome, but I'm away on business the last two weeks of July in London."

"Oh, okay. Well, maybe I can come back here in August, or you can come out to see me? I'm not due to come back here until a little before Thanksgiving."

"Don't worry about it. We'll just take it as it comes, okay? No need to stress. We'll see each other before November."

Gabriella gnawed on her bottom lip as she fidgeted with her fingers.

"What's wrong, Gabs?"

She shook her head slightly, "it's nothing really. You just seem so nonchalant about me leaving."

"I'm going to miss you like crazy, goober. You're going to leave me with Desmond and Arnie?" Gabriella giggled slightly. "Besides, we'll still talk and text and video chat. Maybe make some use of that video chat feature and have some phone sex?" He said as he waggled his thick eyebrows at her.

"Yeah, I guess that's all true. It's just a long time to be away from each other."

"It'll be fine, goober. You're worrying for nothing." He said and placed a kiss on her lips to silent her protest.

***

"*Bambolina*, are you sure you have everything you need? You're going to be gone for so long," Marie asked as her worried face took up Gabriella's phone screen.

"Yes, Mom. I have everything I need. You do realize that we own a house out there. We're going to need stuff there too."

"Don't you dare go shopping without me! We are decorating that place together!" Maria warned.

"I know, mom, but you know that I already ordered my bedroom furniture and Laurel was there to let the deliver guys in and set it up. I need somewhere to sleep when I get there."

"Fine, but nothing else!"

"I need to get some essentials, like towels, toiletries, a coffee maker, maybe a toaster."

"Ugh, enough! Why are you going there so much sooner than we are?"

"Because the school year hasn't ended for you? You're coming out next month. Speaking of which, you expect me to not have a couch or a kitchen table for a whole month?" Gabriella asked and raised her eyebrow at her mother.

"Fine, but either we shop online together, or you facetime me in the store." Maria conceded after she considered her daughter's logic.

"What time is your flight, Gabby?" Giuseppe asked, his face came partially into frame.

"Three o'clock. I'm taking the Airtrain to JFK."

"You're going to drag your luggage to the subway? We can take you!" Giuseppe insisted.

"Dad, by the time you get out here, it would be cutting it way too close. Besides, Arnie offered to go with me, which was super nice of him. He's gonna take the subway with me to Jamaica, then I'll hop on the Airtrain. It'll be fine."

"What about all of your luggage?" Maria asked.

"I have one piece of luggage, and one carry on."

"For six months?"

"Mom, I'm buying a lot of stuff to keep there. Relax. I'm not sure if you know this, but they have these things called stores in L.A."

"Smartass," Giuseppe said with a laugh.

"Hey, before I go, I wanted to ask you guys if you wanted to buy a car out there, so we have some form of transportation."

"What will happen to it while you're in New York? Do you trust a car to be left there if you are renting it out to vacationers?"

"I have it worked out with Laurel, Dad. She said we can leave it at her house when we aren't there, and we can store anything over by her too if we need to."

"Don't go looking for a car until we get there. I know what I want."

"Let me guess, something fast and topless?"

"We're still talking about cars, right?" Giuseppe asked while Maria rolled her eyes, "Thanks Gabriella, now we'll have to deal with two midlife crises."

Gabriella barked out a laugh and shook her head at the screen. "I love you guys. I'll let you know when I land, and I will see you in a month."

***

"Gabby, are you sure you packed enough?" Arnie asked as they waited for the arrival of the Airtrain.

Gabriella laughed and rolled her eyes, "have you been talking with my parents?"

Arnie laughed, "no, not at all. I just want to make sure you didn't forget anything."

Gabriella smiled warmly at her best friend's boyfriend, who had become like a brother to her over the past few months. "I promise, Arnie, I have everything I need. You guys have the key to my place just in case. I've got plenty of nesting to do when I land."

"Okay. If you need anything, you call me, you got it? I can always ship anything to you that you forgot."

"I know. Just take care of yourself and Desmond. I know he is busy, and as much of a diva as he is, he won't admit that he's upset that I'm leaving. Be extra nice to him."

"I'm upset that you're leaving too. It would be nice if you and Laurel and Matt could just live here."

Gabriella grabbed onto Arnie and squeezed him in a hug. "I know. I'm gonna miss you too. You'll come out for the premiere, right?"

"I'm planning on it. We'll see what life looks like in July." He said with another squeeze.

"Hey, Arn?"

"Yea, Gabs?"

"Can you do me a solid? Could you maybe check in with Liam once in a while?"

"Check in? We're still planning on our weekly dinners."

"Oh, I'm glad to hear that. That's good to hear."

"Gabby, what's wrong?" Arnie asked as he tilted his head down to make eye contact.

Gabriella sighed, "I don't know, I feel off leaving. Like he was so chill about the whole thing. We're not going to see each other for months. I know we haven't been back together for a long time, but things feel different this time. Better. More like a solid relationship, we're gelling together like we didn't the first time. Am I making a mistake splitting my time?"

"Gabby, you've had this plan for a long time, and Liam was aware of it. That guy is crazy about you. I can tell that you two are more into each other this time. The way he looks at you, and the way you guys keep finding ways to touch each other all the time, it's looking a lot like the beginning of love."

"So, I should stay?"

"No, doll, you go. A few months apart isn't going to end your relationship. If it makes you feel better, I can chat with him, casually, and see where he is. I'll give it a week or two, then I'll report back."

The train arrived at the station, and Gabriella threw her arms around Arnie one last time. "Thank you, Arnie. I love you!"

"I love you too, Gabs. Call me when you land." Arnie said as she got onto the train. She nodded in response as the doors closed and Arnie waved goodbye.

***

Gabriella arrived at her California home almost seven hours after leaving JFK. She could not keep the large smile from her face when the uber pulled up to her beach home. With her bags retrieved from the car, she made her way to the front door and smiled as she slipped the key into the lock. She opened the door and took in the view that she hadn't seen in over four months. As she closed the door behind her, something caught her eye in the corner of the living room.

Fear flowed through her body as she kept her hand clenched to the doorknob. The sound of water from the back of the house caused her to panic. She opened the door and began to run out as a scream came from inside the house, and then she was captured in someone's arms.

"Ahhhh! Omigod you're here!"

Gabriella screamed, then realized that she knew the voice. "What the mother fucking shit, Laurel? You scared the ever-living fuck out of me!"

"Wow, colorful," Laurel joked as she squeezed Gabriella.

Gabriella turned around to find her best friend wrapped around her like a snake around a mouse. Her attention shifted to the living room, where Matt sat on a papasan chair in the corner. "And what are you doing sitting in the corner like a creeper?"

Matt laughed as he stood up and lazily made his way over and encompassed both girls in his arms. "Welcome home, Gabby."

Once they disengaged, Gabriella looked around the house. "Where did the chair come from?"

"I bought it, it's got a beachy vibe," Laurel said with a smile.

"Is my mother aware of this? She said no furniture purchases without her approval."

"Yeah, she knows. She picked it out." Laurel responded as Matt carried the luggage to Gabriella's bedroom.

"I wasn't expecting anyone to be here," Gabriella said as she watched Matt make his way through the house.

"I would have met you at the airport, but you know, cameras and whatnot. Plus, we need to do some major shopping, you have nothing here. I did set up your bed though, so at least you'll have somewhere to sleep." Laurel said as she opened the front door.

"Can I at least unpack before we go out?"

"Why do you ask questions to things you already know the answer to?" Laurel asked with a smile as Matt walked out of the house with them.

Eleven

The first week in California was filled with shopping, FaceTime calls with Maria about furniture decisions, and time spent with Laurel, which included a sleepover in the new house. Maria stuck to her guns about Gabriella not making any large purchased without her but compromised on allowing a table set and some small appliances to be bought without her in the same state.

Gabriella made herself at home, and settled into the master bedroom, as her parents said since she was the main occupant of the house, she should have the room with the bathroom attached. They agreed that the smaller bedroom in the back would be set as a guest room, but also an office for when Gabriella needed to work. The light blue walls in the living room were an extension of the bright blue skies outside the large windows. The white cabinets and yellow subway tile backsplash in the kitchen felt like the sun was shining inside of the house.

The space was not the largest, but it was an accomplishment to have a place to call home while on the west coast. After she soaked in the full-sized claw-foot tub in the master bathroom, an amenity that she was extremely happy to indulge in since the shower in her apartment was the size of a tissue box, she took stock of the business attire she purchased with Laurel and settled on a Robin Egg blue sheathe dress and nude sling-back heels for her meeting with Laurel, Lily, and Nicole in the morning.

She allowed her hair to air-dry as she sat in her bed and flipped through Netflix on her iPad. An incoming FaceTime call interrupted her search, which she answered on her phone.

"Hey, beautiful. I've been missing your face. How's the first week been?"

Gabriella smiled at Liam's handsome face before she responded. "Has it only been a week? I don't think it's long enough to miss you yet." She winked as he shook his head. He pulled the phone further away, then pantomimed stabbing himself in the chest, and moved the knife around for added effect.

Gabriella laughed, "I'm only kidding. I've been beyond busy here, getting the house together, but I have missed you too."

"I didn't say anything about missing you, just your face," Liam joked as Gabriella scratched her cheek with her middle finger.

"Are you all settled?"

"Eh, my room is set. I have a small desk in the guest room. Mom allowed me to get a dining table and chairs without her. And I have one of those large basket-bowl looking chairs in the living room, courtesy of Laurel."

"I guess your mom doesn't trust your taste in furnishings" Liam joked.

"No, she's a bit of a control freak, but I love her. Plus, it will give her something to do when she comes out here next month. Any chance of your business trip being moved so you can come for the premiere?"

"Sorry, goober. There was talk of extending my travels. There is some big campaign my firm is trying to get for a company in Tokyo. They might want my team there to pitch."

"Oh, wow, that's awesome. You'll be a legit world traveler."

"Yeah, it's nice branching out from the North American scene."

Gabriella smiled and stared at Liam's brown eyes. "So, when does work start up for you again?" He asked.

"Tomorrow. I have a meeting with Laurel's team. The press tour for the movie starts in a week. We need to work out the schedule for the press interviews. There are some spots on morning shows and a few magazine interviews. Of course, we have to finalize the logistics of the premiere. It's going to be very time consuming."

"Are you ready to see the rest of the cast?"

"I won't see them until the premiere. I don't participate in the press stuff. All the leads do that. Bernie and Samantha might even get out of doing most of the stuff."

"I wouldn't be too sure about that, Goober. There was a lot of buzz about you during filming."

"Yeah, it was all trash. I'm back where I belong. Behind the scenes managing my best friends."

"What are you wearing?" Liam asked, one eyebrow raised with a smirk on his face.

Gabriella looked down at herself, then responded, "a tank top and shorts pajama set."

"That sounds like too much clothing to me."

Gabriella rolled her eyes and giggled as Liam removed his shirt. "Your turn."

***

Laurel sat with her back to the floor to ceiling windows in Lily's conference room. Her hair was swept up in a loose bun and she wore a backless, loose-fitted, blush-colored romper with sparkly gladiator sandals. She sipped on the cucumber infused water that one of the assistants handed them. Gabriella sat next to Laurel, her laptop opened to Laurel's calendar, prepped and ready for the meeting. She watched as condensation race down the side of the glass next to her computer and lifted the heavy braid off the back of her neck.

"Drink the water, it will help cool you off," Laurel suggested.

"It's not just me, right? It's hot in here."

"New assistant. Lily will fix it when she gets here."

Nicole walked into the room and visibly blanched at the temperature. "I already did my hot yoga today. What is this shit, a sauna? Are we getting facials during this meeting?"

Gabriella shrugged her shoulder as Laurel laughed. "Lil, are you turning into a sweat shop or something? How about a little air conditioning in here?" Nicole yelled out.

Lily walked in a few moments later and cringed. "Ugh, how long have you been in here? Let's go, we'll meet in my office, this is horrendous."

The girls followed Lily through the hall but stopped at the desk outside of her office. "Tasha, what is going on with the thermostat in the conference room? It's too hot in there. Get it fixed."

The women entered Lily's office and settled on the white leather chairs that surrounded a glass table. "Alright. Laurel my dear, you are going to be one busy bee. This movie is all the buzz, we're talking summer blockbuster, maybe some Oscar nominations. This is *THE* movie, and the studio is throwing beaucoup bucks at it. You guys are going to be at Comic-Con this year, it's happening two days after the premiere."

"Okay, sure, whatever we need to do. I'm pretty excited about this one," Laurel said with a head nod and a smile.

"What are we looking at schedule wise?" Gabriella asked as her fingers danced across the keyboard, the rhythmic keys filling the room like a tap solo in a Broadway show.

"We have a press meet scheduled next week here in L.A. There are a few interviews with some magazines, including photo shoots for each. There is going to be a few days in New York to film on The Today Show and Good Morning America, but we are going to split the cast for those. There is also

223

going to be a filming for Live, which will be done with the full cast." Lily explained.

"Do you know about tickets for the premiere?" Gabriella asked.

"The studio has been notified of who you all requested to be on the list. Gabby, I'm going to have Tasha send you everything in one email. We'll summarize everything and make sure we share the calendar."

"Okay, great. Are we going to discuss logistics today? Scheduling for each day, travel arrangements?" Gabriella asked.

"Actually, there is something that Nicole and I need to discuss with you," Lily said as Nicole nodded.

"Okay, shoot."

"Like I said, this movie is really causing a buzz. One of the interviews is with Vanity Fair."

"Whoa, that's awesome!" Laurel said happily.

"It is. They want to interview you, Riona, Henry, Jake, and... Gabby." Lily revealed.

"What?" Laurel and Gabriella asked at the same time.

"Oh my god, Gabby, that's amazing," Laurel said as Gabriella asked at the same time, "why me?"

"Most of the magazines and talk shows want to focus on the stars of the movie. But the writer at Vanity Fair said that she wanted to interview all of the characters involved with the love story." Lily explained.

"So, the interview only? Like to discuss the movie?"

"And the photo shoot," Nicole chimed in.

"No way." Gabriella said.

"Gabby, come on, this is Vanity Fair. Can you imagine what they are going to do for the photoshoot? This is a once in a lifetime opportunity. And we can experience it together! Please, Gabby! Don't say no." Laurel begged.

"It would be amazing for your image to do it," Nicole advised.

"What image? I'm a manager." Gabriella asked.

"You know that is bullshit. Don't you want to control your narrative? How much crap has been published about you since filming? People speculating about you, about your relationships. Do the interview, be the bigger person. Speak for yourself." Nicole said as she hit her hand against the arm of her chair as she spoke.

"This is about the movie, not my personal life," Gabriella retorted.

"You know that is not true. Personal questions are always asked. Imagine what a badass bitch you would be to sit in the same interview as the people who caused so much drama in the tabloids and speak your truth." Lily interjected.

"Plus, the article is going to come out before the premiere, so your story will be out there, in black and white," Nicole added.

Gabriella gnawed at her bottom lip and contemplated her options. As much as she wanted to set the record straight, the thought of being put out for public consumption terrified her. "I really don't want to be in the public eye."

"Gabby, you're in a movie, a big movie, that is not an option anymore. Control the narrative." Nicole said as she introduced a load of reality into the conversation. Gabriella sighed and typed a few notes into her calendar.

"Fine. Send me the schedule. Indicate what events I need to be there for as an actor versus a manager. I need a clear line on what my role is through the rest of this process."

***

Two days later, Gabriella and Laurel arrive at the studio where the Vanity Fair interview was being conducted. They entered a large warehouse, where a few stools were set up in front of a grey backdrop, and a camera was setup opposite the stools. On the opposite side of the large room were hair and makeup stations, as well as curtained off areas that served as a changing station.

"Welcome, Miss Dolce and Miss DiStella, I'm Jonathan, I will be assisting you all today. We are going to get you in hair and makeup. The first thing we will be doing is the interview, and then we will move into the photoshoot. Please follow me."

The girls were sat at stations near one another. There were five stations spread out, one for each of them, with a dedicated glam squad to adjust the hair and makeup as quickly as possible. As their makeup was being done, they could hear Jake on the other side cracking jokes. "Well, at least we'll be entertained by that jackass today," Laurel commented, which made Gabriella laugh and loosen up a bit.

Jonathan approached when they were done and walked them over to the stools. Laurel was instructed to sit on the middle stool, with Gabriella sitting to her right. Jake was next to join them and sat on the opposite side of Gabriella. "Hey, girls! How have you been?" He asked as he gave them both a brief hug before he sat down. Jonathan began to mic them up as Riona and Henry approached. Once the microphones were connected, Riona sat between Laurel and Henry.

Gabriella kept her eyes focused in front of her as Henry settled, the awkwardness on the set was palpable. "Still haven't spoken to him, huh?" Jake leaned in and asked. Gabriella shook her head slightly and Jake mimicked her motion.

"Hi everyone! I'm Annie Egerton, it's so nice to meet you all! I'm a huge fan of all of you, well, except you," she said with a point at Gabriella, "but I know I will be after I see the movie!"

Everyone chucked at her joke. She sat down on the stool next to the camera and pushed the frizzy auburn curls away from her face, then adjusted her black-framed glasses. "Alright, so we're going to film the interview. No worries, it will be a written article, but we will use some clips for promotional things, just an FYI."

"So, I understand that the movie is about a guy, who every time he gets killed, he wakes up in a new timeline. And in each timeline, there are the same characters, and it is all intertwined in a love triangle?"

"Yes, so I play Carson Young, who is partnered with Laurel's character, Abigail. Jake plays Chester Finn, who is my rival, and Riona is his wife, Wilhelmina. I get involved with Wilhelmina, and then I also fall for Charlotte, who is played by Gabriella." Henry explains. "Carson is not a good man. He is a womanizer and unfaithful and really is a rather despicable character."

"Laurel, what do you think of the film?" Annie asked.

"It's amazing. It was so much fun to do all the timelines. I can't wait to see the finished product. Do you know that they won't let us know the ending? We have no idea how it ends. It really was such a great project to work on, and the cast is amazing." Laurel answered.

"I found it interesting to not play the bad guy in this one. When you hear that you are the guy who constantly kills the main character, you think you're going to be playing the villain. But because Carson is such a prick, you kind of cheer for him to be killed." Jake said with a laugh.

"I understand there were some issues with filming at the beginning, and it delayed some of the actors. Riona, how was it for you joining the cast late?" Annie questioned

228

"Oh, it was fine. I wish I would have been there from the beginning, but I don't feel like I missed out too much. Everyone was so welcoming when I finally got there, like everything was finally right with the world because the final main cast member arrived. Plus, it was great reconnecting with Henry, I hadn't seen him in years from when we worked together last. I'd say this movie changed my life," she answered in a thick Irish brogue.

"Speaking of life changing, Gabriella, I understand you're not even an actor. How did you get caught up in all of this?" Annie asked.

"Yeah, that's correct. I was on set as Laurel's assistant," Gabriella started as Laurel interrupted. "My manager. Gabby is my manager."

Gabriella laughed and continued to speak, "manager, sure. Like you mentioned, the issue early on during filming was a huge storm. Many actors and extras couldn't make it to the set, and the studio was desperate. They asked me to be an extra."

"But you've become such an integral part of the storyline, how did that happen?"

"There was such a natural chemistry between Henry and Gabriella, it was impossible not to keep filming them. Wait until you seen their sex scenes. Wowza!" Jake volunteered.

"Really? I guess that was the spark that ignited all the tabloid fodder." Annie offered as an explanation.

"Perhaps, but you know all of that is so warped and full of lies. I will say that for someone who never had a desire to act, it was an honor and a privilege to work all these actors with me today. They were nothing short of professional and really helped me out when I had no idea what I was doing, which was all of the time." Gabriella responded.

Jonathan appeared with small whiteboards and markers and distributed it to the group. Everyone looked at one another, then back down at the items in their hands. "We're going to play a game of sorts. I'm going to ask some questions, and I want you to write one-word answers on them. Yes, no, a name, true or false. It's a fun way to get to know you guys and how life was on set." Annie explained. "Question one. Which cast member was the craziest on set?"

Everyone turned their boards around, and they all wrote Jake. Jake laughed the loudest of the group. "It's so true. I was always pranking everyone. I think Don Starr, the director, might have wanted to kill me at some point."

"Question two. Who was the most outgoing on the set?" Laurel wrote Jake, while Riona wrote Henry. The rest wrote Laurel. "Seems to be a difference of opinion."

"Me? Really?" Laurel asked.

"Absolutely, you were the one who always tried to get everyone together after filming. Between you and Patti, there was always something to do." Henry explained.

"Who is Patti?" Annie inquired.

230

"She was our set mother, but not really. She is an amazing chef, her and our other good friend, Joshua, were the talented people who kept us fed in South Dakota," Laurel answered.

"Question three, who was the most generous?" Annie asked.

Everyone wrote Henry, except Henry, who wrote Gabriella. "Henry always knows everyone's name on set. He helped plan out wrap party too." Riona said.

"He also threw a party for the staff before you got to set. And he flew out a bunch of us to see Gabriella graduate from grad school." Laurel added.

"Wow, that is very generous, Henry. Why do all of that?" Annie asked.

"I feel like it's important to appreciate everyone who is a part of the film. No part is too small. Also, we all became really close on that set, one of my people were celebrating a big moment in their life, and it was important for our extended family to be there." Henry replied.

"And why write Gabriella?" Annie asked.

"She cooked for the entire cast and crew for a party. She didn't have to do it; she wanted to help out the kitchen crew. I think it took her almost twenty-hour hours to prepare enough food for everyone, and it was delicious." Henry said with a smile.

"Question four, who is the most like their character in real life?"

Laurel and Gabriella looked at each other, then both glanced over at Riona, who happily wrote her answer. Gabriella looked back to Laurel, who raised her eyebrows and gave a quick nod, then returned her attention to the whiteboard. Everyone turned their board except Gabriella, and all of them had Riona's name.

Riona giggled in response as she flipped her blonde hair. "Riona across the board. Gabriella, no answer?" Annie questioned.

Gabriella gnawed on her bottom lip slightly. "Um, I don't think anyone was very much like their characters. Their personalities are so stylized to fit a stereotype. The Madonna, the whore, the defender, the guy who does whatever he wants to get his way, the idolization of someone you can't have. I would like to think that all of us have more substance than those characters."

Annie's eyebrows shot up in surprise. "Do you not like the characters in the movie?"

"No, it's not that at all. The characters are phenomenal and need to be who they are for their part in the movie. I feel like they start to develop more as the timeline moves on, but their purpose is to fit those stereotypes." Gabriella clarified.

"Right, so why Riona?" Annie asked the rest of them.

"I think it's because I had both male leads wanting me. It's not too far off from reality," Riona giggled.

Laurel rolled her eyes and said, "actually, she's the one most likely pursue someone already in a relationship, just like her character."

Jake started to laugh, then tried to cover it with a cough as Henry and Gabriella looked wide-eyed at Laurel. "That's not true, they just flock to me." Riona said with a sneer, then looked to Annie and smiled sweetly.

"Alright, last one of these superlative questions. Who changed the most during filming the movie?"

Gabriella wrote Riona. Riona wrote Jake, and the rest wrote Gabriella. "Another mixed bag. Riona, why Jake?"

"I just feel like he and I got closer working together, we became friends."

"Gabriella, why Riona?" Annie asked.

"I think it was because she wasn't there when I was there, and then I missed a bunch of when she arrived. I guess my expectations were different than what the reality was. It's more of a me thing than anything else." Gabriella tried to explain without flat-out calling her a bitch.

"And why Gabriella?" Annie asked.

"She was really shy and apprehensive at the beginning of filming," Laurel said, "but once she got into it, and she got more comfortable with everyone, she came out of her shell."

"Wonderful. Onto the next game. Since this movie is all about relationships and love triangles, and weird timelines, we're going to get into some personal questions. Are you currently in a relationship?" Annie asked.

Jake and Henry wrote no, while the women write yes. "Henry! Why would you write no?" Riona asked.

"Because I'm not in a relationship." He stated.

"Yes, you are, silly." Riona said with a giggle.

Henry shook his head as Jake, Laurel and Gabriella exchanged looks. Annie coughed, then asked, "Laurel, you said yes?"

"Yes, and I met him on the set of the movie." She said with a genuine smile.

Henry looked at Gabriella's board and shook his head. "And Gabriella? You also responded with a yes." Annie said.

Gabriella nodded her head as Henry scoffed. Gabriella looked to Henry and raised an eyebrow. "Must be that football player," he mumbled.

"Pardon?" Annie interjected.

"She was dating a football player." Henry said.

Gabriella shook her head. "I never dated a football player."

"Back to the dating app guy, then?" Henry asked sarcastically.

234

"If you must know, yes." Gabriella responded.

"Figures," Henry said with a roll of his eyes.

"What is that supposed to mean?" Gabriella asked.

"Guys, calm down. Let Annie ask her next question," Laurel said to quiet the two of them.

"Actually, Riona, you said yes as well." Annie said.

"Yes, Henry and I have been together for a few months now." Riona said with a smile as Henry shook his head.

"But Henry said he's not in a relationship," Annie pointed out.

"He just likes to say that so he can keep his heartthrob status." Riona said with a laugh. Henry exhaled deeply and then asked Annie, "can we move on please?"

"Sure. If you could pick any time to live from the periods your movie spanned, which would it be?"

Laurel and Gabriella responded with the 1950s, Riona responded with the modern day, and the boys responded with the wild west. "And why did you choose that, ladies?"

"The clothes," Laurel responded as Gabriella laughed and nodded.

"I'm too dependent on modern technology to leave this timeline," Riona said with a laugh.

"Gentleman?" Annie prodded.

At the same time, the boys said, "the guns." Everyone laughed, the staff on the other side of the room included, as they stood up at pretended to have a shootout.

"Okay, last question for this round. Did anyone fall in love during the movie?" Annie asked and raised a thin eyebrow.

Jake and Gabriella wrote no, while the rest wrote yes. "Aww, Henry," Riona cooed as Henry shook his head.

"Did the two of you fall in love on set?" Annie asked hopefully.

"No. I fell in love on set, but it wasn't with Riona." Henry answered, his eyes betrayed him as he looked at Gabriella.

Gabriella looked at him quickly, then down at her whiteboard. *'Maybe he didn't fall in love with her on set, but he's with her now'*, Gabriella thought to herself.

After they answered some more questions about the movie, Annie wrapped up the interview and informed them that Jonathan would direct them to their dressing stations. As everyone started to stand from their stools, Henry interrupted.

236

"Annie, can I just say one thing? And it could be on the record."

"Of course, Henry, whatever you want."

"I just need to say this here, in front of everyone," he said as he looked at Gabriella before he turned to Riona. "Riona and I are not in a relationship. The studio thought it would add to the appeal of the movie to let people think we are. But we aren't."

Gabriella and Laurel gasped, along with some others in the room. Riona's façade began to crack as she tried to maintain the smile on her face. "Henry, what are you talking about?"

"Enough, Riona. I know you like to ham it up for the press, but I can't do it anymore. We were never in a relationship," he said as he stared at Gabriella.

Laurel threaded her arm through Gabriella's as they stood there. Henry pleaded with his eyes for Gabriella to believe him, but Jonathan interrupted and brought everyone to their respective spots to prepare for the photo shoot.

***

The area where the interview was conducted was slightly transformed for the photo shoot. Gabriella approached the set, dressed in a white power suit, with no shirt underneath. Her hair was pulled back in a tight bun, and her shoes were nude pointed slingback heels. Laurel sat on a stool in a short, off the shoulder body-hugging lace dress, her nude stiletto heel hung over the bar of the stool, her highlighted chestnut hair fell in romantic waves down her back.

"White theme?" Gabriella asked as Jake walked over, wearing khaki-colored pants and a white dress shirt.

"Did we die and go to heaven?" Jake joked.

"Claude, our photographer, had a very specific vision for this shoot, I'm sure he'll explain it to you when everyone is here." Jonathan explained.

Henry arrived next, dressed in a white dress shirt with the top two buttons undone and untucked from a pair of white pants. Both he and Jake were barefoot. "Where's Riona?" Jake asked.

Henry shook his head. "Diva-ing out? Mad at what I said during the interview?"

"Maybe you shouldn't have said it like that, Hen," Laurel suggested.

"Well, it's not like she's ever listened to me any of the other times I've tried to talk to her about it." He replied with a sigh as he sank down on the stool next to Laurel.

"So, you guys were never actually dating?" Laurel asked quietly as Gabriella made it her business to stare at the lighting, as if it was the most fascinating thing she had ever seen, to remove herself from the conversation.

As Henry was about to respond, when Claude approached the group and clapped as Riona joined the group, dressed in a long, flowy white dress with a deep v-neckline with strappy nude heels. Her blonde hair was swept up halfway, with the rest flowed down her back.

238

"Belle, beau. This photoshoot will be magnifique. My name is Claude, I will be your photographer," the lanky man with the long sandy blond hair said with a thick French accent as he stood before his subjects. "I understand your film is about love, and I want to tell that story. We will have three stages of love, the innocence, the desire, the forbidden."

He explains as he starts to set the men on the two stools. Laurel is placed between Henry's legs and faced him, as Riona was placed behind Jake and draped herself around him. "I want you to feel like this is your first love, your crush perhaps. It is innocent and pure. I want loving touches, a hand hold, a brush of fingers against the cheek. Loving glances until I tell you to look at the camera."

Gabriella stood off to the side and watched the rest of them partner up. "You there, Gabriella, I need you to stand here, next to Jake, but slightly in front, oui. I want you to stand tall and strong, hands-on-hips in a power pose. I want no smile from you, just stare down the camera. You are too good for the innocence."

After he took multiple shots with everyone in different poses, except Gabriella, Claude asked for music. "Alright, I need you all to loosen up a bit, interact, dance, laugh." *Happy* by Pharrell blasted through the speakers, which made Jake jump up and swing Riona round, then bumped his hip into Gabriella's, which caused her to laugh. Laurel and Henry held hands, arms straight as they twirled around with each other.

Jake tangoed across the set with Riona, and hip checked Gabriella as he passed. "I need a little more from you, Gabriella, you still look stiff," Claude yelled out. Gabriella huffed, then started to do the Carlton dance, which made the rest of the cast to stop to laugh at her, then joined in.

"Alright, you sexy people, off with you for your outfit change," Claude called out as he looked through his photos on his laptop.

The next round of photos had them all dressed in bright red. This time, Riona was in the lace dress, Gabriella was in the flowing dress, and Laurel was in the power suit, their hair styles changed with the outfit and their makeup grew bolder with black eyeliner and red lips. Jake wore a red blazer with a tight black shirt and black pants, while Henry was dressed in a red button-down shirt, sleeves cuffed at the elbow, and black pants.

Claude posed the men in the same spots, but had them stand, with Gabriella between them, Riona next to Henry and Laurel beside Jake. "Riona, ma belle, I want you to lift the leg nearest me up onto Henry. Henry, I want you to grab onto her leg and hold it there. Jake, I need you to wrap your arm around Gabriella, your hand splayed across her stomach, oui, like that, then I need Laurel to have her back against Jake's side, and arch into him with your back arm draped over head, like so.

"I want the music on now. I want this one more passionate. Move with the music, touch each other." Claude instructed as Beyonce's *Naughty Girl* played.

"Good, good, Laurel, behind Jake, reach around and grab him, Riona, I need you down on one knee, reaching up Henry's body, look up at him, Henry, look at her, but I want your hand gripping Gabriella's thigh, same with you Jake. Gabriella, stand there in your power pose, but I want you to move your arms above your head with the music. Make is sexy."

240

As the photos were taken, Jake tried to sing the high parts in the song, which made Gabriella laugh so hard she snorted, which took everyone out of the sexy mood Claude tried to set. "Christ, mate, don't quit your day job," Henry said with a laugh as the music was cut.

"Sorry Claude, I couldn't help it, Beyonce is my jam," Jake said as he started to gyrate on Laurel.

"It is okay, I have enough to work with, please, go get changed into the next outfits." Claude said dismissively.

"Way to go, Jake," Gabriella joked as they headed back to the dressing area.

"Oh, come on, it was funny. And how can you not expect me to sing and dance to that?" Jake asked.

"The rest of us were able to do it," Riona joked.

"You wound me, Ri," Jake said as he pressed his hand to his heart.

"Do you think this is going to be the last outfit change?" Gabriella asked as she went to her curtain.

"It is, but I am not sure what Claude has in mind," Jonathan answered as he deposited her in her changing area.

As she walked in, Gabriella saw a very small black lace dress with long sleeves, and sky-high black patent leather heels. "Um, Jonathan, I think you left me the wrong outfit."

"Are you decent?"

"Yup."

Jonathan walked back behind the curtain and looked at the outfit. "No, that's it."

"It's small."

"It stretches." He responded as he walked away.

Gabriella took some deep breathes as she studied the dress that looked like it was Laurel sized. "We need you in makeup, Gabriella," Jonathan called out.

She sighed, then said a silent prayer that the tummy control undergarments they gave her would suck in her gut and not make the dress burst. After she poured herself into the dress, she walked out to the makeup area and pulled on the bottom of the sleeves, which caused the off the shoulder top to drop a little. After having her hair teased out and sultry eye makeup with a nude lip painted on her face, she met the rest of the cast.

Everyone's outfits had been sexed up, Laurel's black flowy dress was backless with a plunging neckline, Riona's power suit was swapped for tight satin pants and a tuxedo jacket, but the jacket was opened and taped to cover her chest. Jake wore an all-black suit with the top few buttons undone, and Henry wore black dress pants and a black button-down shirt with almost all of the buttons undone, the sleeves cuffed at his elbows.

"I am so uncomfortable in this," Gabriella whispered to Laurel, and she stood next to her and waited for Claude to place them.

"Hommes, to your spots. Please sit on the stools. Laurel and Riona, I want you two surrounding Jake, Gabriella, you are next to Henry. Now, I am going to do this one different, this is the forbidden love. I want you to feel the music, I want you to move organically. If I yell out to do something, you do it. Let's see how this goes."

Pony by Genuine starts to play, which made Laurel and Jake to yell out, "oh yeah!" The two of them started to grind on each other and pulled Riona into the mix. Gabriella looked over at Henry, who just sat there on the stool and stared back at her.

"You two need to do something. Dance in front of him, react to her dancing Henry." Claude yelled out.

Gabriella turned and faced away from Henry and started to sway. Henry stood up behind her, without touching her, but leaned in, "so are we just going to pretend that we haven't spoken in months?"

Gabriella nodded, "seems to have been working so far."

"I'm not with Riona," he said sternly.

"Well, I am with Liam," she responded.

"Less talking, more interacting. Touch each other," Claude yelled out.

"Well, I guess while he isn't here, I should enjoy what I can," Henry said and pulled her tightly against him, his hips swayed with hers, one hand on her stomach and the other on her thigh. "This is what we've been reduced to? Touching because we are directed to?"

"I guess so," Gabriella responded as Claude yelled out for them to move around more.

Henry grabbed Gabriella by the waist and turned her around to face him. "I guess it's a good thing I'm in my profession, acting out fantasies."

He pulled her against him, his hands gripped her ass as his nose and lips grazed down the side of her neck and lightly licked it. Her head arched back as he dragged his lips up her throat. He pulled away as she straightened her head and gazed into his blue eyes as her hands continued to grip his hair. She did not remember reaching out and gripping onto him, but she didn't let go until he straightened himself and stepped back slightly and put some distance between them.

"You may say that you're with him, but your body still wants me." He said with a smirk as Claude called out to place them in a few poses.

Gabriella reeled from what he said to her but kept her composure for the rest of the shoot, which mostly consisted of her being touched by Henry is some fashion. When Claude finally called it a day, Gabriella hustled over to her changing station where she quickly dressed in her own clothes, then arranged the car service to pick up Laurel.

"Gabs, are you okay?" Laurel asked as she poked her head around the curtain.

244

"Yeah, are you?"

"Of course, it's just, today was a lot. You know, with Henry."

Gabriella cut her off before she could fully finish his name. "Yeah, I don't know how you do this all of the time. The interviews and the photo shoots and the constant clothing changes. It's exhausting. We've been here for hours! I don't know about you, but I'm ready to go home and pass out."

"Um, yea, I guess. So, listen, Matt and I were planning on going out for a late dinner tonight before I have to start doing the rest of the press junket. Why don't you come with us? I'm not going to see you for a bit while we're away."

"I appreciate the invite, but really, I'm exhausted. Mom realized that by waiting to come here to get furniture, her and dad will have nowhere to sleep. So now I have to get a guest bed for my office so they can sleep somewhere, because she still needs to find their bedroom set in person. I have some meetings with the makeup brand you work with, and there is a workout gear company that wants to work with you to design clothes for women. I'm trying to work Matt into the deal as well. I have plenty to do while you are gone. Before you know it, it will be the premiere, and then my life can go back to normal."

Gabriella paused when she gets a text. "Oh, good, your car is here."

"You aren't coming with me?"

"No, I'm going to get another ride, stop off to get myself some Mexican food on the way home, then sack out for the night."

Laurel hugged Gabriella and shook her head slightly as she started to walk to the exit. Gabriella followed and made sure Laurel got into her car before she pulled out her phone to get an Uber.

"Still avoiding me?" A deep voice asked from behind her, which made her jump and almost drop her phone.

"Jesus, Henry. Give me a freaking heart attack, why don't you?" Gabriella said when she calmed down.

"It wasn't my intention. I just wanted to talk to you without a camera in our face, or our coworkers with us."

"My ride will be here in ten minutes."

"Fine, I'm not dating Riona."

"You've already said that." Gabriella said with a sigh as she crossed her arms.

"But you aren't listening."

"I hear you, Henry. You're not dating Riona. Congratulations."

"Are you really dating Liam? Or are you keeping it under the rug with the football player?"

Gabriella closed her eyes and shook her head. "I don't know why you have a bug up your ass about Ethan. We never dated. He invited me to the Super Bowl and then blew me off. Apparently, he's dating some supermodel."

246

"What about Liam?"

"What about Liam, Henry? Yes, he and I started dating again. Yes, we are currently dating."

"So then why is it that it's okay to have a long-distance relationship with him, but it was impossible for you to have one with me?" Henry asked, his hands flung out at his sides. "I need to know why. I need to l know why him and not me."

"Are you being serious right now? You're really comparing yourself to Liam?"

"Why is the distance not a problem with him?"

"It's easy with him, Henry. He's a nobody, like me. There aren't hordes of people constantly attacking me because I'm too hideous or too fat to be with him. No one cares about me when I'm with him. And yes, the distance is still an issue, but we're in the same city together at least half of the year."

"Do you love him?"

"What? Well, yeah, I mean, we've been friends for a while," Gabriella stammered out.

"Are you in love with him?" Henry asked as he moved closer and punctuated each word.

Gabriella stepped back and then shook her head. Henry paused, then nodded in return.

"I just wanted to know where I stand with you."

"What does me being in love with Liam have to do with you?" Gabriella asked, completely confused as her phone notified her that her ride had arrived.

"Everything. See you at the premiere." He said as he turned and walked away.

Twelve

Giuseppe and Maria arrived in California on the second of July, because they didn't want to miss out on the fourth of July celebration with their only child. Gabriella was happy for the early arrival, since her plans were non-existent. Although she had spent the past few weeks focused on Laurel's press tour, which to date had consisted of press interviews with newspapers and shows like Daily Entertainment, she didn't see her much.

The day her parents arrived, Maria dragged them to furniture stores, where she proceeded to buy a bedroom set, couches and tables, and an outdoor set complete with a firepit and an outdoor fridge and grill. Giuseppe agreed to go on the condition that the next day, he got to purchase all of the electronics for the house and got to get the car he wanted.

By July third, the house was occupied by delivery men as they set up the furniture. Gabriella was in charge of accepting the deliveries of the appliances while Maria instructed the movers where to place all of the furniture. Once the furniture was in place, Gabriella and Maria began to setup the appliances. After the television and the soundbar was setup in the living room, a honking horn from the garage pulled them away from their tasks.

They walked into the garage to find Giuseppe behind the wheel of a gunmetal grey Camaro with the top down. Maria laughed, then ran out to jump into the car with her husband, reached over and gave him a big kiss on the lips. Gabriella leaned against the wall and laughed at her parents' antics. She smiled and thought to herself how lucky she would be if she got half of what her parents had in their relationship. She pictured herself in the future, watching her significant other pull up into the garage in their car and honk to get her attention, but the person in the car was fuzzy. As much as she tried to picture it, Liam didn't seem to be the one sitting in that driver's seat.

"So, this is your topless midlife crisis?" Gabriella asked her dad as she approached the car.

"You know it. I always wanted a Camaro. It might not be an older version in a cherry red, but I think this new one is sexy. I'm good with looking sexy in this beauty." Giuseppe said with a smile. "Why don't you lock up. We can run up to the Whole Foods and get some food to grill for tomorrow night."

***

By the end of the first two weeks that her parents were there, the house finally felt like a home. There were mirrors and paintings hung on the walls, throw blankets and pillows on the couches, and vases and tchotchkes on the shelves and tables. Maria even brought a few family photos in frames to place around the house. She took the theme of the bright yellow tile in the kitchen and decorated everything with lemons, including the plates and glasses.

Giuseppe and Maria spent most of their days out at the beach or driving around town to familiarize themselves with the area and tried to keep out of Gabriella's way while she worked. As the movie premiere loomed around the corner, Gabriella was occupied with Laurel's schedule, which currently had her in New York to film the *Today Show* where she was with Riona. It was her understanding that Jake and Henry were on set at *Good Morning America*.

In the middle of the day, Nicole, Laurel's publicist, called. "Hey Nicole, is everything okay?"

250

"I can't just call to shoot this shit?"

"It's very out of character for you, but sure," Gabriella said with a laugh.

"Everything is fine with Laurel. I'm actually calling to check on you. The premiere is in two weeks."

"Yes, I am well aware. I have glam squads coming to Laurel's house to prep everyone. And when I say everyone, I'm talking Laurel, our mothers, Desmond and his mom, even our fathers are getting prepped and quaffed. I have so many schedules I'm juggling for that day. Trust me, I am aware of it coming up."

"You have yourself on that list, right?" Nicole asked.

"Yes, of course."

"What are you wearing?"

"I have some dresses that I've worn to other premieres that Laurel has had. I'm just going to wear one of those."

"Wrong! I knew it! This is why I called. I have a friend who has a connection with a new designer who is absolutely obsessed with you. She designed a dress with you in mind and wants to meet you."

"That's not creepy at all. Obsessed with me? And you want me to meet this person, Nicole? Are you serious?"

"Obsessed isn't the right word. She's inspired by you. You're an average woman, you have curves. You were thrown into the media in this whirlwind, and she was impressed by how you've handled it. I had a discussion with her the other day, and she brought up the dress. I'm going to pick you up in an hour." Nicole said before she hung up the phone.

Gabriella looked at the phone, then shook her head as she made her way to the bathroom to take a quick shower.

***

"Gabby, this is Izzy Knight, the designer who worked on the dress. Isabella, this is Gabriella DiStella," Nicole introduced them when Izzy met them in the lobby.

The petite five-foot-three woman with her red hair in a pixie cut approached and extended her hand out to Gabriella. "It's so nice to meet you, Gabriella. I was following your story since you first came out online. You have such a story!"

"It's not really that exciting, but thank you, it's really nice to meet you too."

"Please, follow me ladies, I'll take you up to where I have the dress." They followed Izzy into the elevator, then exited moments later and were taken to a private fitting room, where a dress in the most bright and beautiful shade of royal blue hung in a bag on the wall.

"That color is amazing," Gabriella said when she spotted it.

"Thank you. I thought the color would complement your skin tone and your hair. Is that all your hair, or do you have extensions?" Izzy asked.

"It's all mine." Gabriella said as she looked to Nicole, who shrugged her shoulders.

"Wow! It's beautiful. Now, before we get to you trying on the dress, I need to know. What really happened with you and Henry? There was so much crap out there, but I know it's not real. Please tell me it was a princess love story, like he swept you off your feet. How is it to be the mystery brunette?" Izzy said as she sat down on one of the plush chairs.

"Izzy, Gabby isn't really comfortable talking about any of this," Nicole interjected before Gabriella could respond.

Izzy looked slightly deflated. "Oh, sure. I shouldn't have asked."

"Listen, Izzy, all the stuff in the tabloids was really garbage. Henry and I became very good friends during filming. There is always speculation when a Hollywood heartthrob is seen with someone of the opposite sex. I was on the set as my best friend's assistant, you know Laurel Dolce?"

Izzy perked up and smiled as she nodded in response.

"Well, he saw me unpacking her trailer, and he thought I was there to help. We didn't really get along at first, but I became friends with his dog, and we got stuck together during a bad storm and we became friends. All the rest of it was really phony."

"But, what about the karaoke? He sang to you. And wasn't he at your graduation? Please tell me you guys at least kissed." Izzy whined.

Gabriella smiled at the designer. "I will tell you this, there was definitely an attraction, but nothing really ever happened."

"Not one kiss?" She asked.

Nicole knocked her arm into Gabriella's and nodded. "Yes, we kissed, but nothing ever came of it. We really are just friends. I have a boyfriend back in New York, and it's my understanding that he is dating Riona Murphy."

Izzy sighed in response. "Well, I guess it is what it is. Still, I think the two of you would make the best-looking couple. I made the dress for you, like a modern-day sexy princess. Come on, let's try it on."

Izzy helped Gabriella get into the dress, and Nicole gasped when she saw it. "Gabby, that dress is… wow. Izzy, it's stunning."

Gabriella smiled at Nicole and Izzy, then admired her reflection. The dress sat wide on her shoulders, then dipped low in the front, where a sheer mesh covered the exposed material, which looked sexy without much cleavage displayed. The dress narrowed at the waist, then came out in an A-line design, with a sheer layer filled with sparkling appliques, which started sparingly near her waist and increased the closer the dress got to the floor. There was a slit in the dress that you could only see if she moved the dress in a certain way, and there were a few small appliques on the top near her shoulders and dipped down her back. The dress sparkled and danced when the light hit in the right way.

"Izzy, I'm speechless, this dress is phenomenal." Gabriella said as she grabbed Izzy's hand.

"Do you love it? Do you think you would wear it?" Izzy asked.

"Absolutely. Can I buy it from you today?"

"I need to do some adjustments, but I promise that I will have it ready for you for the premiere."

"I'll tell you what, I may not have had a princess love story, but this dress is princess worthy." Gabriella said with a smile as she looked at the dress in the mirror one last time before went to get changed.

Once she returned to the fitting room, Izzy ran over and hugged Gabriella. "I know this is going to sound silly, but I just wanted to say thank you."

"You made a stunning dress Izzy; I should be the one thanking you." Gabriella said with a smile.

"No, it's not that. It's refreshing to see someone like you in the media. You're not a stick thin glamazon, you're a normal girl. And it seemed like you lived out this fantasy of having a handsome actor fall for you, even if you're just friends. It's just nice to have some real women be represented in Hollywood. All of us non beauty queens need our own queen to look up to." Izzy said with a smile.

Gabriella looked confused as Izzy stumbled over her words, "oh my god, I don't mean that you aren't beautiful. I'm such an ass; this is why I stick with designing clothes. I just mean—"

"Breathe, Izzy," Gabriella said with a chuckle, and interrupted her nervous mumblings. "I totally get what you are saying. And thank you. I never set out to do that, I didn't even want to do the movie because I am so self-conscious. I never had any type of person to look to and say it's okay to not fit a beauty standard. As much as I don't see myself the way you do, thank you. What you just said made being pushed out of my comfort zone worth it."

They bid farewell to one another, with a promise from Izzy to have the alterations done before the premiere. The sun shone down on Nicole and Gabriella when they exited the building and head to the parking garage down the block. After a few moments of silence, Nicole asked, "so, what did you think?"

"I think I'm overwhelmed. She's a brilliant designer, and she's going to blow up in the industry. But I'm completely humbled by what she said and why she wanted to design for me."

"Gabby, I know you aren't comfortable with all of this, and I know you shy away from the media, but don't you see what you are representing to people? Not only young girls, but women like Izzy? Laurel is one of the most down-to-earth and relatable people I've ever worked with, but she has that Hollywood look. People relate to you because they feel like they could be you or could be friends with you. That has some serious power to it."

"Nicole, I just want to be behind the scenes."

256

"Gabby, you are already strapped into the roller coaster. You've experienced the smaller drops, some of the fast turns, but hold on, babe, you're climbing up to the peak, and are about nosedive down the biggest drop and some loop-de-loops."

***

Four nights before the premiere, after a long day with her mother as she shopped for the perfect dress for the event, Gabriella received a panicked phone call at four in the morning.

"Gabby, oh my god, wake up, I need you, there is an emergency."

"Des?" Gabriella asked, still half asleep.

"Bitch, wake up! Emergency!"

Gabriella sprung out of bed, "I'm up, what's wrong Des?"

"There is a huge protest going on about diversity in Broadway, and I'm being contacted by journalist about being an affirmative action hire for my new role. There is talk of a possible strike."

"Okay, calm down. I'll speak with your publicist. Manny is great with this stuff."

"No, Gabby, you don't understand the severity of the situation. There was an article about the lack of diversity and some of us were called out in it, it's going viral."

Gabriella took a deep breath, then quietly made her way to her office, careful to not wake her parents in the process. She started up her laptop and went through her emails and searched around for the article. "Alright Des, I see what you are talking about. I will get it all under control."

She pulled up an airline site and booked the first ticket to New York that she could get, which would leave at seven in the morning. "I booked a flight; I will be with you around four. I want you to ignore all calls, except if Manny calls you."

Desmond continued to babble on the other end of the line as he freaked out about his situation. As Gabriella checked her email for the flight confirmation, she saw an email about a show Desmond had auditioned for. "Hey, Des, can you pause the meltdown for a sec?"

"Excuse you?"

"Do you remember that hosting gig you auditioned for? The one for the Christmas cake baking competition?"

"What does this have to do with anything Gabby? Can we focus? I'm in the middle of a crisis."

"Watch it, diva. The host had to cancel, something about breaking his leg. They want to know if you would be available to fill in."

"Is that even a good idea?"

"We'll discuss it when I see you. Try to calm down. Maybe try to get some more sleep?"

"Ha. I'm going to wake Arnie up and make him cook for me."

Gabriella shook her head as she hung up, then sent a message to Manny to notify him that she would be in town later in the day. She collected the items she needed from her office and went back to her bedroom, where she pulled out her carry-on bag and started to pack.

"Gabby?'' She heard her father call from her doorway.

"Sorry Dad, did I wake you?"

"I'm a light sleeper. What's going on?"

"Desmond called, he's having an emergency with his job and called me, I have a flight at seven to get over there."

"Gabby, the premiere is Thursday."

"I know, I'll be back in time. I should only be there a day or two." Gabby said as she picked out an outfit and headed to the bathroom.

"I'll get dressed and take you to the airport," Giuseppe called out.

"Dad, it's not necessary, I'll get an uber."

"I'm not going to take no for an answer. Plus, it gives me an excuse to take the car out."

***

It was after five by the time Gabriella reached Manny's office, who stayed late to meet with her. Desmond attended the meeting, where they decided that all the actors who were targeted by the article were going to do a joint press statement on their thoughts on the discrimination topic. It took an entire day to get all the actors on the same page, and another twenty-four hours to get the statement published. Gabriella and Manny were able to convince Desmond to take a few weeks off from the play, considering the current events, and take the hosting gig, which was scheduled to be filmed the last week of July for ten days in a studio in Chelsea.

Gabriella sat in her apartment, and fielded text messages from her parents and Laurel, who were freaked out about her not being able to return in time for the premiere. She was able to book a flight the day of, but it would get her in a two in the afternoon, which was three hours before the premiere started.

"Are you fucking crazy?" Laurel yelled into the phone as Gabriella laid on her couch.

"There is nothing I can do, Lau. Desmond and his parents already left tonight. I couldn't get an earlier flight. I'll be there in time."

"What about hair and makeup?"

"I'll be there. Just make sure everyone else is done before me. I'll rearrange the schedules tonight. I asked Izzy if she could have the dress delivered to your house. I'll be the last to get into glam. It's not a big deal, it's your big night, just relax and enjoy it. Don't you have an appointment at the spa with everyone?"

"Yes. Our mothers, Desmond and Sierra, and Jem and Patti are going to be there. I can't believe you are missing this, but freaking Desmond, who made you fly across country, is going to make it." Laurel vented.

"I'm sorry, Laurel. There was nothing I could do. It's my job, I had to help him. You know I would drop everything for you too."

"Whatever, Gabby. You're alone in New York right now, everyone else is here. Are you at least seeing Liam while you are there?"

"No, he's in London. I spoke with him earlier. He's jammed with meetings, but he says it's looking good, and his team might get picked for the Tokyo pitch."

"Good for him, I guess. There were seriously no earlier flights? Not something that was leaving tonight?"

"Laurel, I looked, I got the earliest flight possible. Why are you so concerned? I'm not."

"You're going to be a mess being stuck on a plane all day."

"I will shower before I leave, make sure I wear no makeup, and I'll keep my hair up. I will come straight to your house, where they can do my hair and makeup right away. I'll get in my dress, and we'll head straight to the premiere. My parents will be at your house with everyone else to get ready. The glam quad will be there at noon, and Matt said he would be home to let them in, in case your spa visit runs a little longer than planned."

"I know you have everything planned, you have backup plans for your backup plans, Gabs, it's just what you do. But I wanted this to be special for you. It's your movie premiere too, your first."

"And only. And I'm just an extra."

"Stop downplaying it. I know you watched all the interviews we did. Kelly Ripa couldn't stop asking questions about you."

"Tabloid fodder. Don't worry about anything. What are you up to right now?"

"Aside from creating a groove in my hallway because I'm pacing so much? I'm waiting for Jem and Patti to call when they are settled in their hotel. I'm meeting them in the hotel restaurant for dinner."

"No boys?"

"They are doing their own thing. Matt is meeting Desmond and Arnie at their hotel, then meeting with Joshua, Bob, Max, and Darius at some steakhouse."

"No Henry?" Gabriella asked.

"No, I think he's getting in tomorrow morning."

"Well, I hope everyone has fun. Maybe you could FaceTime me when you guys are at the restaurant?"

262

"Gabby, are we ever going to talk about it?"

"Talk about what?"

"Henry."

Gabriella sighed, "There isn't anything to talk about, Lau. We tried being together, we tried being friends, none of it worked. After tomorrow night, I probably won't ever be in the same room as him again."

"Are you sure you're happy?"

"I have a great career, an apartment in my favorite city in the world, a beach house in L.A., family and friends who people would kill to have, what is there to not be happy about?"

"What about love? Does Liam make you happy?"

"I love my friends, I love my family, I have love, Lau. Liam and I are good friends who are lucky enough to be compatible in a more than friendly way. I have no complaints."

"Alright, Gabby. If you say so. Try to get some sleep, you need to be refreshed for the flight and for the event tomorrow."

Thirteen

When Gabriella arrived at Laurel's house, it was controlled chaos. She walked into the door, and was crushed by Patti and Bob, who eagerly waited for her when she entered the gates.

"Gabby!" Patti yelled out as she danced around excitedly.

"Patti, you look amazing! I love what they did with your hair and makeup." Gabriella said as she hugged her.

"Who knew so much spackle could get this mug to look good!" Patti said with a laugh.

"Oh my god, Bob!" Gabriella exclaimed as she hugged him, shocked at how much broader and thicker he had gotten since she last saw him. "You're getting so big!"

"That's what she said!" Patti yelled out in response.

"Hey sis! I've missed you. Mom and dad are in the media room with the rest of the parents." Bob said with a smile.

"Is everyone else in there? Max and Jem and the others?" Gabriella asked as she started to pull away.

"Gabriella DiStella! It's about time you got your ass here!" Laurel shouted as she barreled down the hallway.

"Hey Lau, I told you I'd make it."

"You have less than two hours to get ready before we need to leave. Stop socializing and get your ass back there." She said as she pointed down the hallway to her bedroom.

"I guess I better head back before she decapitates me." Gabriella said with a shrug as Laurel grabbed her arm and dragged her into the master bathroom, where a hair stylist and makeup artist finished up Sierra.

"We'll see you at the premiere," Patti yelled out as they disappeared down the hallway.

"I thought there were multiple stations set up, that was what I had asked for," Gabriella said as she sat in the chair.

"We sent them home. We're all ready. Sierra was the last one. Most of them are heading back to the hotel to get dressed, since they are meeting us there. Only our parents are staying, as well as the Balvins and Matt." Laurel said as she hustled out of the room.

Gabriella slipped on the provided robe and answered emails from her phone and verified all the transportation to the event while her hair was styled in a deep side part with very loose waves. As the makeup artist worked on her bold smokey eye that accentuated her almond eye shape and a nude lip, the hair stylist lifted her hand and scoffed.

"You didn't get a manicure? You're going to be photographed!"

"Um, it was such a hectic week, I didn't have time." Gabriella mumbled.

"Go in my bag, I have the press-on nails in the emergency kit," the makeup artist said.

"Really? I hate fake nails," Gabriella complained as they handed her a pack of fake nails in the color of a nude dusty rose.

"You should have gotten a manicure then. Please tell me your toes are painted." The hairdresser said with a sigh.

Gabriella nodded her head. "Is this color going to go with my dress?"

"It's neutral enough, I always keep neutral shades on me."

A commotion down the hallway, complete with a shriek occurred half an hour after Gabriella was in the seat. Caroline and Laurel ran into the master bath in a panic. "Our faces are blotchy. What is happening?" Laurel freaked out.

"It looks like you are both having a reaction to something. Did you use something new on your faces today?" The makeup artist asked as he completed Gabriella's makeup.

"We went to a spa," Caroline offered.

"Okay, up you go. You two, sit. You're going to take half an allergy pill each, I have the non-drowsy kind, and we're going to coverup this blotchiness with my heavy-duty stage makeup. I tried to go natural, but looks like plans change. We're done here, go put on those nails and then get dressed." The makeup artist barked, which prompted Gabriella to take the box of fake nails and get out of the way.

"Gabby, your dress is in the guest room at the end of the hall. Your mom said she'll help you into it when you're ready." Laurel called out from her seat.

To get herself away from the chaos in the master bedroom, Gabriella wanted a quiet place to relax before the circus really began. The main part of the house was quiet, which indicated that their friends had left to change at the hotel. She could hear some sounds from the media room, so she tried to put the most distance between them and entered the kitchen, where she set herself up at the large marble island.

Frustrated from being rushed around the past few days, which included an uncomfortable plane ride in a middle seat and not much sleep from being worried about getting here on time, relaxation was a must. She poured herself a glass of water and settled at the corner of the island and set her music on shuffle. The audio level from her phone was enough to drown out some of the external noise, but not loud enough to draw attention to herself as she opened the package of fake nails and read how to put them on without nail glue.

***

Henry arrived at Laurel's house later than he expected to. Traffic had been heavy, and his tailor took a little longer than expected to adjust his suit jacket. He hadn't realized how much more muscle he had put on since he began to work on the King Arthur series. He spent hours in sword fighting training and chorography for the fight scenes almost daily.

After the car entered through the gate, his driver dropped him off at the front entrance, where he walked through, dressed in his custom steel grey three-piece suit with a black dress shirt, with the top button undone and no tie. His shoes reflected the lights in the house and clacked on the tile as he walked through the hallway. He could hear chatter from further into the house, but it was the dim sound of music that perked his ears. Rather than heading down the main corridor, he ventured to the left and stopped in the large archway that led to the kitchen, where he found the dark-haired beauty hunched over the kitchen island, her body swayed slightly as she quietly sang along to Madonna's *La Isla Bonita*.

Her hair cascaded down the shoulder of her robe and blocked her face from his sight. He heard her sing a line is Spanish, he laughed to himself, then said out loud, "I knew you could speak Spanish."

Gabriella gasped; her eyes wide with surprise when she looked up to see the source of the voice that proved that she wasn't as alone as she thought she was. Her breath caught in her throat as she took in the perfect male specimen who stood twenty feet away from her. The suit hugged his muscles like they were trying to contain them.

"Oh, wow," Henry said, as her face was finally revealed to him. Her brown eyes shined through the makeup, which just drew more attention to one of her best features. He stared at her as his hand involuntarily reached over his heart. Even in a fluffy white robe, she looked stunning.

"My singing isn't that bad," she responded with a slight shake of her head and the returned her focus back to the countertop but lowered the volume of her music.

"I wasn't commenting on your singing." He said as he remained in the archway.

269

Gabriella looked up at him, puzzled to his response. "What are you doing here?"

"Laurel asked me to meet here, we're all heading over together." He said as his attention drew to her hands. He walked closer but remained on the other side of the large island. "What are you doing?"

Gabriella sighed, then dropped onto a stool beside her. "Apparently I can't attend tonight without my nails done, which I didn't so, so I'm subjected to this crap." She gestured to the items in front of her.

"I have to peel these stupid super sticky sticker things off of this sheet at put them on my nails, but it gets harder to do the more I put on."

"Do you want me to peel off the stickers for you? Will that help?"

Gabriella pouted as she looked down at the sheet of stickers, then held the sheet out to Henry. "Please?"

He laughed and nodded, then took the sheet and removed the stickers so she could apply them. "I don't mind helping, but can we change the Madonna song?"

"No way, it's a great song," she said with a smirk, "plus, it's almost over."

Henry dutifully peeled off the stickers as she tried to fit them to her nails, the fake nails she would use were laid out across the island in order.

"How did you forget to get your nails done? Isn't that a part of the primping process?" Henry asked as he watched her press the thumb nail on her right hand and held it tight, so it adhered. The song changed in the background to Elton John's *Sacrifice*.

"I had to go to New York for an unplanned trip. I just landed a few hours ago and didn't have much time."

"You look really good for someone who was on a flight earlier today."

Gabriella smiled, then returned her attention to apply the next nail on her right hand. "What's with the depressing music? Shouldn't you be listening to something upbeat to pump yourself up for tonight?" Henry asked.

"It's not depressing, it's Elton John. And it's on random, I can't help what comes on next." They sat in a comfortable silence as she completed her right hand and did the thumb on the left one.

"Why not just put all of the stickers on the nails at one time so you don't have to keep stopping to fix them." Henry suggested.

A familiar baseline came from the speakers, which made Henry smile. He reached over to her phone and raised the volume all the way up. "See, this is what I'm talking about. I can get into the music."

He pushed away from the island and danced slightly to the Motown beat as he came in with lyrics. "I've got sunshine, on a cloudy day. When it's cold outside, I've got the month of May." He sang along and snapped his fingers and bopped, which made Gabriella laugh as she stopped the nail application to watch his performance.

When he got to the chorus, he reached his hand out and gestured for her to take it and join him. "I don't think so, Henry Anderson. I have no time for fun."

"Come on, how can you just sit there when The Temptations are playing? It's sacrilege." He said with a smirk and a wink.

Gabriella shook her head and smiled. Henry tipped his head, then walked around the island and pulled her by her hands to make her stand up. He twirled her around and kept two armlengths between them and he danced with her, then raised their arms up and down as he moved her around in circles. He sang as they danced, twirled her under his arm, then twirled her out from him, as he kept a hold of one hand, then bought her back in to him, their sides pressed against each other.

She laughed as the second chorus started, and he pulled her a little closer, his hands on her upper arms as he still swayed slightly. He stared deep into her bottomless brown eyes and sang the words *my girl* to her as his hand grazed her cheek, his index finger slid under her chin as his thumb rested on her chin and tilted her head up slightly.

Her laughter quieted as she tingled from his caress and the gentle pressure he placed with his thumb as he held her in place. Caught under the spell that was Henry Anderson, her hand gently ran up his arm as she returned his smoldering stare. The instrumental interlude crescendo choreographed their lips softly pressing together. A sweet, tender kiss filled with longing they both held for a while. They separated for a brief moment, then came back together, the kiss grew with the need they had denied themselves for months.

Their lips parted, and they gently massaged their tongues together, tentatively at first, as if they were afraid to wake up from the blissful dream they shared. The kiss grew urgent, desperate, a need to get their fill of each other while they could. Gabriella's fingers dug into Henry's back as he wrapped his arms around her waist as tightly as possible.

As gently as they had come together, they parted and inhaled each other as they stayed pressed together. Gabriella looked up into Henry's face, and the realization of what happened crashed into her. The man who she had denied herself since last summer was wrapped up in her arms. The one who she wanted above all others, the one who stole her heart and never returned it. As all of that remained, nothing had changed. He was still the Hollywood heartthrob that she would never be good enough for. The one who would destroy her if she allowed it, and boy, was she tempted to allow him.

"Ella," Henry whispered.

"I have to go." She said as she pulled herself away from him.

"What? No, Ella," he argued as he tried to keep her with him.

"I have to, um, get dressed. And probably touch-up my lipstick." She said as she slowly backed away from him.

"Come on, Ella."

"I'll see you on the red carpet," she said, her body in shock and her heart tried to leap out of her chest and cling to the man in front of her.

"*Bambolina*? Are you ready to get dressed?" Maria yelled out from down the hallway.

"Coming!" She responded as she stepped into the hallway backwards, her eyes never left Henry until she reached the archway. She took one last look at him and slipped away.

***

"*Bambolina*, you look stunning," Maria said with a smile after she zipped the back of the custom royal blue dress. Gabriella studied herself in the mirror and took in the sparkle of the silver jeweled sandals that peeked out from the slit in her dress as she shifted from one foot to the other. She made eye contact with her mother, who was standing behind her and futzed with the dress. Maria wore a fitted black evening gown with black heels and a sheer wrap around her arms.

"You look beautiful, Mom."

"I can't believe we are going to your movie premiere. I'm so proud of you, Gabriella. Your father and I are both so proud of you."

"Mom, I'm just an extra. It's Laurel's movie premiere."

"Stop it. I know this isn't what you wanted to do in life, but it is amazing that you took a chance and did it. You would have never stepped out of your comfort zone like this as a child. You've really grown into a beautiful person."

274

Gabriella felt overwhelmed by her mother's words. She turned around and squeezed Maria in a tight hug. When they pulled apart, Maria's wrap slid from her arms, attached to Gabriella's hand.

"Gabby, why are you taking my wrap?"

Gabriella looked down and realized the wrap was stuck to the stickers on her nails, of which two did not have the phony covers. "Oh no, Mom, I didn't finish putting on my nails. I have to go to the kitchen and put the last two on."

Maria laughed as she followed her daughter back downstairs to the kitchen.

"Oh, good, you're done, we have to go, the limos are here," Laurel said as Gabriella dashed across the hall to the kitchen. As she approached the island, she saw everything was gone.

"Shit!" she exclaimed as she looked around the floor and went to check the garbage. "What are you doing?"

Gabriella looked up to find Desmond staring at her, who looked dapper in a mustard yellow velvet jacket, white dress shirt, black bowtie and black pants.

"I can't find my nails."

"Did you check your hands?"

"Can it, wise ass. I had to put on these stupid phony nails, and I forgot to put on the last two before I went to get dressed, and now they are missing."

Desmond laughed and called Laurel into the kitchen. "We don't have time to fuck around, our parents and dates are all outside getting into the limo."

"Show her," Desmond said with a laugh as Gabriella huffed, then stuck her left hand out. Laurel tried to contain her laugh as she looked at the sad naked ring and pinky fingers.

"It's not funny. My nails are getting stuck to everything because the stupid sticky sticker things are on them. I left them on the counter, and they are gone. Did you touch them?"

"No, the makeup artist finished redoing my makeup and then I got dressed."

"Oh! She said she had emergency nails in her kit, maybe I can get them from her!"

"Oh, honey, she left like ten minutes ago," Desmond said with a pout.

"Fuck! What am I supposed to do? We're gonna be on the red carpet. I'm going to look like an asshole," Gabriella whined.

Desmond walked out to the foyer and came back with a silver clutch. "Here, I already transferred your essentials into it. Just hold it in your left hand with your fingers underneath, keeping them towards your body, but don't touch the dress otherwise it will get stuck."

"You're a genius. And you look amazing. And Lau, you are stunning."

Laurel looked down at herself and admired her pale pink dress which was embroidered with gold. The long sleeves and body-hugging design ended in a small train, but the front of the dress was a plunging neckline, which she informed everyone was taped to keep her boobs from escaping. Her hair was pulled back into a loose bun with tresses strategically falling to frame her face.

"Thank you, you're looking like quite the A-lister yourself," Laurel said with a wink. "Now let's move it."

"Ah, ah, ah, hold up, I'm definitely getting a selfie of us looking smoking hot and posting that shit everywhere," Desmond said before took a few pictures of them together.

"We're riding in separate limos. They have a certain order they want us to arrive in. Bernie, Samantha, Henry, Me, Riona, Jake, and Gabriella. My parents and Matt are going with me, the Balvins and your parents are with you, Gabby." Laurel explained as she rushed them out of the house.

Matt and Arnie waited for them outside of the limos. "You all look amazing," Matt said with a smile, dressed a navy-blue suit. "We need to get moving. I got a call from Henry; he heard that Bernie was about ten minutes out from arriving."

Matt directed Laurel to their limo as Arnie, who was wearing a tan suit with a brown bowtie and brown shoes, lead Desmond and Gabriella to the other limo. "Are you ready?"

Gabriella looked at Arnie and nodded slightly as he got in, which left her to sit near the door.

***

The limo pulled up to the theater twenty-five minutes later, and they were directed to wait in the limo until they were retrieved by staff. Gabriella swallowed deeply; her nerves got the best of her as she watched the crowds of fans by the entrance of the red carpet. The flash of lights brought back her previous experiences on the red carpet. A vibration from her clutch caused her to snap out of her worry and focused her attention back to the excited chatter in the limo.

"Are you okay, Gabs?" Desmond asked quietly.

"Yeah, just trying to mentally prep myself for all of that," she said with a gesture to the crowds ahead of the limo.

"Laurel and Matt just exited the limo," Sierra said from the opposite side of the car.

"You can see them?" Maria asked as she tried to look out of the window.

"No, this crazy woman has the live feed from the red carpet on her phone," Marco said as he rolled his eyes at his wife.

"At least you have more time before you have to go," Arnie said with a smile.

Gabriella pulled out her phone and saw a text from Liam.

Liam: Break a leg, goober.

"Hey, Gabs, do you want me to walk the carpet with you?" Desmond asked as the limo pulled a spot in line.

"What do you mean?"

"If you don't want to walk it alone, I can do it with you. I'm sure Arnie wouldn't mind."

"That's so sweet of you, Des, but I want you to experience this with your man. Plus, I don't need any rumors going around about what a whore I am that I have another guy with me. It will be a quick walk for me. A couple of pictures and I'll be inside with the rest of you."

"That blonde bitch with the accent just got out of her car," Sierra announced with a sneer.

"I guess your mom know about her?" Gabriella asked.

"You know she's a tabloid junkie. And maybe I filled her in on a few things."

"A few things?" Arnie scoffed, "this wash woman over here was on the phone with his mother giving her the dirt constantly."

Gabriella shook her head and bit her lip as she turned her attention back to the crowds. "Don't bite your lip, *Bambolina*, you'll ruin your makeup."

"Yes, mom."

"I've decided that I'm going to walk you, Gabby." Giuseppe announced as the limo moved up another spot.

"Don't you dare, Dad, you're walking with mom."

"You shouldn't have to walk it yourself. It's your big night," her father shot back.

"What is with you people? I'm a big girl; I can walk this myself. You guys are making a bigger deal out of this than it needs to be. I'll post for a few pictures and be on my merry way."

"Jake is out of his car." Sierra announced.

Gabriella took a deep breath as the limo pulled up to the final spot. She watched as Jake posed for photos and made his way down the carpet to where the reporters waited to interview him. She closed her eyes and tried to center herself, but the sounds of the crowds outside distracted her.

"Last chance, Gabby, do you want one of us to walk with you?" Desmond asked as all eyes watched for her response.

Gabriella shook her head and smiled as the door began to open and the sound of the cheers flowed into the limo. "I'll see you guys inside."

Fourteen

"Oh my god, it's the mystery brunette." "That's the girl!" "Why did Henry come without you?" "She's so much prettier in person." "Can you sign this for me?" "Can I get a selfie?" "That's Gabriella, right?"

It was difficult to focus on one thing that came from the crowd of people who stood behind the barricade. The paparazzi snapped photos as soon as the door opened. Gabriella made her way to the crowd and signed books and pictures and posed for photos with fans that asked.

She was then escorted to the backdrop where the name of the movie was printed in a futuristic gun metal font against a black backdrop. She posed in front of the sign and smiled as a million flashes blinded her. When she moved down the line, she started to head to the building but was stopped by a worker dressed in all black.

"This way, Miss DiStella."

"I'm sorry? I think you're mistaken."

"No, ma'am. You are to be interviewed by the press. Please follow me."

Gabriella looked back to the safety of the building entrance but reluctantly followed the man in black. "Please wait here, someone will get you when they are ready for you."

She stood off to the side and watched Jake shamelessly flirt with a reporter. She looked back down at her hand and hoped that she remembered to pose the way Desmond told her and hid her horrible nails.

"Fancy meeting you here," a deep voice snuck up on her, which caused her to jump. She looked up to see Henry's blue eyes sparkling with mischief.

"Christ on a cracker, Henry, you scared me."

"How are you holding up with the red carpet?"

"Fine, just waiting my turn."

"You look absolutely stunning, Ella. I thought you were breathtaking in the kitchen, but this gown is heavenly."

Gabriella smirked and averted her eyes. "Thanks, Henry. You look dashing yourself."

He smiled, then leaned in and whispered, "I have something for you."

Gabriella arched an eyebrow as he took her hand in his. His other hand removed something from his pants pocket, and he placed it in her open palm. Two small phony nails sat in her hand,

"You took them? I was looking around for them like a lunatic. And my nails were sticking to everything, and I had to pose to hide them!"

"May I?" Henry asked as he took the clutch from her and tucked it under his arm. He took her hand in his, then placed the two nails on her fingers and

282

gently pressed down on them, while his fingers gently caressed her hand. "That kiss meant something, Ella. I still feel it, that pull between us. I'm not giving up until I don't feel it anymore."

"Henry, now is not the time or the place to discuss this. Especially when we are surrounded by cameras and reporters."

He gave one last firm press on her two nails, then let go of her hand and stepped back. "You're right, we'll continue this later. I'll see you inside." He said with a smirk, then walked past the reporter, and gave her a wink.

"They are ready for you," the man in black said from behind her.

In a slight daze from what Henry just pulled on her, she approached Loretta Owens, the famous red-carpet reporter for Entertainment News. Her sharp features and former model physique were intimidating to say the least. Her jet-black hair fell like straightened silk to below her waist, and her brown eyes were piercing as she studied her subject.

"Gabriella? Loretta Owens, it's a pleasure to meet you. I understand this is your first red carpet."

"It's nice to meet you too. I feel like I've been watching you for years."

"Oh, you're a fan of the show?"

"Actually, I've watched you from the red carpet. I've been to a few before, with Laurel Dolce."

"I understand this is your first movie."

"That's correct."

"Your dress is beautiful. It looks like a night sky. Who are you wearing?"

"Oh, this is an Isadora Knight original design. And the shoes are Jimmy Choo."

"I'm not sure who Isadora Knight is, but I'm going to find out. Are you excited for tonight?"

"Absolutely. I'm looking forward to finding out what happens at the end. There was so much hard work put into this movie, and with the setback from the original release, I'm so happy to finally be here."

"I noticed you and Henry Anderson getting cozy before we spoke. Are you two together?"

"Oh, no, Henry is a good friend. We all became really close during filming."

"Is that all? Because Henry was singing your praises during our interview."

"He was?"

"Absolutely. He kept talking about how talented you are and how amazing you are in the film, and how beautiful you are."

Gabriella blushed and looked down. "Well, that is really nice of him to say. I think the world of him, he's such a nice and talented guy."

"What did I tell you, Loretta? Isn't she stunning?" Henry asked as he approached them.

Gabriella's head snapped up and looked at the gorgeous man standing next to her. Loretta smiled her pearly whites at Henry and nodded in agreement. "You are not a liar, Henry."

"Are you poaching my interview?" Gabriella asked.

"I finished mine; I figured I'd tag along." Henry said with a wink.

"It was lovely meeting you, Gabriella. Enjoy the rest of your night." Loretta said with a smile, then looked excitedly at the cameraman.

Henry escorted her over to the next report as Gabriella asked, "what are you doing?"

"Henry! Back so soon?"

"Come on, Spencer, you know I can't stay away from you," Henry joked with a stunning man in a sharp suit. He stood almost as tall as Henry with a slightly smaller frame and beautiful dark chocolate skin. His perfect teeth flashed as he looked to Gabriella.

"Gabriella, pleasure to meet you, I'm Spencer Johnson. You know my boy Henry here is one of our favorites at Access Hollywood. And he wouldn't stop telling me how much I needed to interview you."

"So, it's your fault that I had to do interview row?" Gabriella asked as she eyed Henry.

"On no, you were definitely on the list, but Henry wouldn't shut up about you."

"Thanks for blowing up my spot, Spencer," Henry said with a laugh.

"So, how was it working on this movie together?"

"It was a lot of fun. It's way different being behind the scenes than it is to be acting." Gabriella responded.

"Behind the scenes?" Spencer asked.

"I've been working with Laurel Dolce for years. I'm her assistant-turned-manager. I've been on set a bunch, but this is the first time in front of the cameras."

"And they love her," Henry said with a smile as he wrapped his arm around her waist. Spencer's eyebrows shot up in response.

"It seems like you two caused quite a stir during filming. People were on Henryella watch, scouring social media for anything related to you two. Tell us about it."

"Henryella?" Gabriella asked.

"Yeah, your couple name."

"Wow, do you guys do this for everyone?" Gabriella asked.

286

"Only the ones we're really into," Spencer said with a wink.

"We all became super close on the set. There was a core group of us, actors and staff, who would hang out all the time. We were just a typical group of friends sharing our antics on social media."

Henry began to laugh hysterically, which caused the other two to look at him. "I'm sorry, that name has me laughing. We sound like a demented Disney princess."

Gabriella and Spencer joined in the laughter. After she answered a few questions about who designed her dress, Spencer ended the interview.

"Okay, before I let you go, I have to ask, really, there is nothing going on with you two?"

Gabriella shook her head as Henry answered, "unfortunately for me, no. But it's not for a lack of trying on my part."

"He's incorrigible. Truly, we really are just friends. The women of the world can drop their pitchforks and relax." Gabriella said with a smile before she was directed to a woman who reminded her of Ariel from *The Little Mermaid*.

"Hi, Felicia Rhodes, The Hollywood Reporter. I understand that you weren't supposed to be in the movie, how did that happen?"

"Oh, um, there was a storm, and they needed actors because people couldn't reach the set, so they asked some staff members to fill in as extras."

"But how did you get such a big part?"

"It evolved. I really was just an extra."

"We had natural chemistry," Henry said as he approached from his conversation with Spencer.

"Welcome back, Henry," Felicia's demeanor changed from a rude bitch to a sweetheart.

"You're going to be blown away by her in this movie." Henry said with a smile as looked down at Gabriella.

"Henry, where did your date go? Did you ditch her?" Felicia asked as Gabriella's face froze.

"I guess I did kind of ditch her. I should go check on her. I'll leave you two to it," he said with a smile as he walked towards the theater.

"Are you looking to act in other movies?"

"Um, no. No, I'm not. I'm strictly back to managing my clients. This was a one-time thing."

Felicia continued her questions as Gabriella watched Henry approach a tall, slender woman with shiny brown hair in an updo and piercing blue eyes. She smiled when he kissed her cheek, then hit his arm as her lips formed into a pout on her delicate features.

Jealousy bloomed in her chest as she answered the interview questions. Felicia followed Gabriella's line of slight and smirked. "Don't they make a handsome couple?"

"I'm sorry, who?" Gabriella asked as she focused back on Felicia.

"I think she is a model. She is so suited for him. After that Riona fiasco, it's nice to see him with someone so attractive. And pleasant. She was a total peach during the interview."

"That's nice. Good for them. Will you excuse me?"

Gabriella walked to the next interview, which was a pretty standard cut and dry red-carpet interview. As she headed towards the theater, she watched as her family spoke and laughed with Henry and his date. "Hey there sexy lady!" Patti yelled as she grabbed Gabriella's arm.

"Hey! When did you get here?" Gabriella asked as she threw her arms around Patti in a big hug.

"About fifteen minutes ago. Got my red carpet walk on, they snapped some photos of me. Of all of us really. But I wanted to get a group shot of us in front of the backdrop. Desmond said he'd take it for us."

"You do realize there are photographers here that could do that?"

"Yeah, but I'm not giving my phone to just anyone."

Gabriella walked over to where Jem, Max, Darius, and Bob were, and hugged them all. Joshua appeared with Laurel and Matt in tow. "Alright people, get together," Patti yelled as she handed Desmond her phone.

"Hey, Hank! Stop flirting with Giuseppe and get in the picture!" Matt yelled out. Henry stopped his conversation and ran over, then threw his arm around Joshua at the end of the group.

Don Starr started to direct people for group photos, which included the cast members, the executive team, and other staff photos. When the photos Don mandated were done, Laurel approached a photographer she knew and asked for them to take some photos for her.

"Family group shots, people," Laurel said as she approached the extended family. They took photos of the individual families, all of them together, then Laurel requested photos of just her with Desmond and Gabriella.

"You know we could have done that at the afterparty," Gabriella said as they were finally allowed to head into the theater.

"Yeah, and we will, but I wanted them here too. It's a special night, and I get to celebrate it with everyone I love," Laurel said with a smile as she threaded her arm through Gabriella's.

They entered the theater, where people crowded in the lobby to get their free refreshments and then headed to their seats. Desmond, Arnie, and Matt approached them, their hands and pockets filled with treats. Desmond handed Gabriella a bag of popcorn and a water.

"You really are the best," she said with a smile as she happily took the food.

"I've got the Twizzlers in my pocket. I'll sit near you so I can share," Desmond said with a smile.

"Ella!" Henry yelled out as he made his way through the crowd. "Hey! There you are, I have someone I want you to meet."

Gabriella looked to Desmond, who shrugged and turned his attention back to Arnie. "Really?"

"Yeah, Ella, this is May. May, this is Gabriella." Henry said with a smile.

Gabriella looked to the beautiful woman on his arm, who smiled brightly and extended her hand. Gabriella looked down at her hands, which were currently filled with popcorn and water, with her clutch tucked firmly under her arm.

"Oh, your hands are full. It's so nice to meet you, finally! Henry has told me all about you," May said happily with a bounce in her stance.

'Of course, she's super nice and gorgeous. And super perky and happy. I guess I would be too if I was her,' Gabriella thought to herself.

"Nice to meet you too. Will you excuse me, I need to get to my seat."

"Ella, what the hell? Why are you being so bloody rude to my sister?" Henry asked as she tried to walk by.

Gabriella paused, then turned back. "Your sister?"

"Yeah, my sister."

"Oh my god, hi, May. It's nice to meet you too. Henry has told me about you too."

May smiled brightly and clapped a little. "I have been wanting to meet you for ages! Henry has always been so private, but he's spoken about you so much over the past year. Of course, I get to hear more than the rest of the fam because I get those little sister privileges."

Giuseppe and Maria approached the group, her father's hands filled with candy and soda. "Dad, you know there is an afterparty with food, right?"

"So? The after party isn't going to have Twizzlers and Raisinets. I even have bags of Sour Patch Kids in my pockets for later." Giuseppe said before he glanced around and whispered the last part.

"*Bambolina*, did you finally get to meet May? She's such a sweetheart," Maria asked as she balanced her popcorn and her purse in one arm.

"I did, but only just," Gabriella said with a smile.

May smiled at them, but her eyes kept darting over to the abundance of treats in Giuseppe's arms. Gabriella traced her stare and sighed. "Please, May, take something from him. It's embarrassing what he has in his arms right now."

May smiled as Giuseppe gestured with his head, "take whatever you'd like, dear."

May looked over at her brother, who smiled and nodded, as he accepted a bag of popcorn from Matt. "What is the yellow box? I don't think I've ever seen those."

"They're Dots. They are like a gum drop. Go on, take it. I have another one inside my suit jacket," Giuseppe said with a wink as May took the box from him with a giggle.

"Oh my god, Dad, I can't take you anywhere," Gabriella said with a smile and a roll of her eyes as she headed towards the theater.

The cast was led to their designated seats, where Laurel sat at the end of one row, Henry across the aisle from her, Bernie and Samantha were two rows in front of them, and Riona sat two rows behind Laurel, with Jake across from her. Family and friends filled the seats next to and behind the stars. Laurel asked Gabriella to sit close to her, so she sat between Matt and Caroline. Arnie sat behind Laurel, with Desmond next to him, and Maria and Giuseppe behind Gabriella. Patti, Bob, Joshua, Max, Jem and Darius all sat with Henry, since his sister was the only one in attendance.

Don Starr appeared on stage, followed by Lloyd, Gina, and April. "Welcome, everyone, to the premier of The Edge of Time. I'm Don Starr, director of this epic tale. I'd like to introduce you to a few of the people who made this film possible. Right here I have Lloyd Stevens and Gina Levine, our producers, and April Brown who wrote the script for this movie. This film is a labor of love for everyone involved. There have been a lot of challenges thrown at this film, starting off with a major storm that led to delays, re-writes, reshoots, and a delayed release date by about six months. But let me tell you, it is well worth the wait, ladies and gentlemen.

"There is some real star power in this film, including the legendary Bernie Renyold, the exquisite Samantha Pierce, Hollywood powerhouse Henry Anderson, America's sweetheart Laurel Dolce, the imported beauty from the emerald isle Riona Murphy, and an actor so good you love to hate him, Jake Wilson!" The crowd went crazy with applause after every name that was introduced, as the actors raised out of their seat to wave to the crowd. When everyone calmed down, Don continued his speech.

"Like I had said, this film really was a labor of love, and I can't explain the dedication of the staff and crew that we had working on the film. As most of you know, there was a huge storm that really put a delay on filming. Most of our extras couldn't make it to the set, and we were running out of scenes to film without them. So, as you watch tonight, you may notice some familiar faces that are sitting amongst you. I want to take a minute to acknowledge my crew members, and the staff members, especially my kitchen staff, who swung double duty performing their day jobs, then pitched in to be extras in their down time. Please stand up and take a bow!"

The theater cheered for the members of the team who stood up and smiled and waved, with Patti making the most fuss out of all of them. "And I'm not done. There was one reluctant person who put her concerns aside and really stepped up and helped us out. I want to thank our own lady of the night, you'll understand what I mean when you watch the movie, and the muse of our re-write. Without her, this movie would have taken an entirely different direction. Gabriella DiStella, ladies and gentlemen."

Gabriella was forced out of her seat by Matt and Caroline, where she awkwardly stood and waved at the patrons of the theater. She quickly sat down and tried to calm the redness that crept all over her face.

April took the microphone next. "Thank you, Don, for bringing this crazy idea to life, and doing such an amazing job with it. I wanted to echo Don's sentiments and really give a heartfelt thank you to the cast, crew, staff, and studio for making this movie. I started writing as a young girl, mostly jotting down crazy dreams that I would have, after one of my heroes, Stephen King. I had this strange idea, what would happen if someone had to relive their life, encountering the same people in different lives. Would they make better choices? Would they learn from their mistakes? Would anything change at all?

"I began working on this story fifteen years ago. I would go back and rewrite it, I wanted to publish it as a novel, but I kept seeing it played out in my mind like a movie. And I knew that's where it could really take shape. Don understood where I was going with this script, and took off with the idea, making it a thousand times better than I could have ever imagined. Then the cast blew me out of the water, to have such talented and amazing people telling my story on film. This really has been a dream come true. But I will say, what the actors brought to these characters helped to shape the story in a way that I didn't know was missing. From the chemistry of the cast to some of the outlandish things in the press, it inspired me, and I hope you see this as the triumph it is meant to be. Please, enjoy the show."

***

The movie was already a half an hour in, and Carson Young had just woken in the old west timeline. The audience was completely captivated by the screen, hardly anyone spoke. There were reactions from them when Carson and Charlotte screwed in the barn, and when Carson was killed by Chester. Gabriella nervously sipped her water and nibbled on her popcorn, as she awaited the sex scene. The first one she sat through was awkward enough, but they had argued when they filmed that one. But the next one, she squirmed in her seat as she thought about it.

Red licorice popped up between her and Matt, as Desmond held it from behind her. She took it and absentmindedly nibbled on the end. "Are you okay?"

Gabriella looked over her shoulder and Desmond and briefly nodded, then returned her attention back to the screen.

"The movie is phenomenal Gabs, and you are amazing in it." He whispered and he gave her shoulder a squeeze. The bar scene started, when Carson first sees Charlotte in this timeline. People sat with bated breath, as the emotion of longing and desire poured from the screen.

"*Bambolina*, you look amazing," Maria whispered to her daughter from behind. A semi-smile formed on her face, but she couldn't tear her eyes away from the screen. She watched as Charlotte led Carson up the stairs to the room. This was the moment she wanted to watch unabashedly and run away from in equal measure. She watched as Carson laid in the bed with just his shirt and underwear, and Charlotte made her way from behind the changing curtain and dropped her dress. A few wolf whistles came from the back of the audience as Charlotte undressed.

296

She turned beet red as Desmond squealed behind her and gripped her shoulders. Her eyes remained glued to the screen as Charlotte straddled Carson on the bed and unbuttoned his shirt as he tried to speak with her. Her eyes remained attached to the screen as she watched herself climax on film, which lead into a montage of Carson as he walked through town with Abigail on his arm, scenes of him secretly meeting with Wilhelmina for their dalliances, a scene of him at the saloon playing poker with Jake, and their remaining sex scenes peppered throughout. It really showed what a piece of garbage Carson was, but Gabriella couldn't calm her breathing as flashes of them actually having sex. A heated gaze from across the aisle pulled away her attention for a mere moment when she saw Henry stare at her. Her eyes jumped from his stare to the screen, and back again until the sex montage ended with Charlotte's breathy moan, and Carson whisper I love you. But it wasn't in Carson's twang, it was when Henry said it to Gabriella.

Panic rose in her chest as she started to lift out of her seat. Matt clamped his hand on her forearm and shook his head. "Don't do it, Gabby, you'll draw attention to yourself. Just sit here and watch the movie. It was an intense scene, but it was freaking amazing. Just calm down, it's only a movie."

Gabriella took a deep breath and nodded, as she composed herself and settled back into the seat. Matt handed her bottle of water to her and insisted she take a drink. The movie eventually came to the standoff between Carson and Chester. As Carson is shot, as his vision starts to fade and he hits the ground, he looks over Charlotte at the saloon, his memory fades in of the two of them in their post coital cuddle, while Carson runs his fingers through Charlotte's hair and tells her that he loves her. The mixing between his memory of Charlotte as she put on her robe and walked away from him in the bedroom, and her as she

297

walked away from him outside of the saloon drive the poignant point home that he was in love with her, and she did not feel the same way.

There were some sniffles from the audience as Carson died alone in the middle of the town, as the woman he loved walked away from him as if he were nothing. Just as the camera panned to his closed eyes in the dirt street, his eyes reopened as he woke up in an apartment building in New York City in the nineteen fifties. Peppered in between the transition scenes, there were flashes of Carson asleep, bathed in light.

The audience was captured by the scenes that played out and adored the innocence of Abigail and Charlotte in this timeline. The mafia vibe was a hit as well, and people cheered for Bernie as the mob boss. In the transition between the fifties and the modern timeline, there was a longer flash of Carson as he thrashed about in the light, his eyes squeezed shut as his head shook from side to side.

The modern scene started as Carson opened his eyes in his bed, then made his way into the bathroom of his swanky Manhattan penthouse apartment, with a gratuitous scene of him bare-assed in the shower. There were cheers from some of the women in the audience as the camera panned down the muscles of his back as he held himself up in the shower. Most of the modern timeline showed Carson in a very wolf of wall street existence. There were many women on his arm at a multitude of events. It showed his very single lifestyle, where he slept with his assistant and his co-worker's wife.

When Carson was killed in the modern timeline, the camera went out of focus, then focused in on an office, where there was a framed photo of Carson and

Charlotte on their wedding day, the two of them smiling at one another in a candid moment. The camera pans to a wall full of frames, there are framed degrees on the wall with the name Charlotte Smith. There are photos of the wedding party, and framed newspaper articles announcing the merger between Young Industries and Life Sciences, with a photo of Carson and Chester as they shook hands with Bernie's character. There is another framed newspaper article that announced the nuptials of CEO Carson Young to head scientist Charlotte Smith.

The camera panned to a few other photos of Carson and Charlotte, then one of Charlotte and Abigail when they were younger, which Gabriella was surprised to see a photo of them from high school was used. There was a photo of Carson and Charlotte with Chester and Wilhelmina at a black-tie event, which the art department seamlessly put together.

A phone ring broke the eerie silence of the room, and Chester's voice was heard muffled through the phone, "it's time." The camera cuts to an industrial hallway, and the noise of heels as they clicked against the linoleum tile is the only sound. The back of a woman fills the frame, which stared from the black heels and worked its way to her black pencil skirt and white lab coat, her dark hair pulled back in a tight bun, as she walks further away from the camera. She meets a secure door, where she punches in a code and waves her id in the scanner. The doors open, where Chester waits, dressed in a similar lab coat and khaki pants, his blonde hair gelled away from his face.

The woman follows Chester back to a workstation, where there are rows of large, clear coffin-like structures, some of which stood upright against the wall, and others laid down. Chester makes his way to the technician at the computer

299

and demanded a stack of reports, which he hands to the woman. From the back of the woman, you can see her study the file she was handed as Chester nervously looked on.

The camera returns to the office and picked up on the wall where the photos and articles were hung. The camera panned past a large bookshelf with awards and medical books, then focuses on the wall next to it, where there was an article about the fertility issues Charlotte and Carson faced, which caused Charlotte to dedicate her time to find new advancements in fertility treatments. There was an article about Young Industries dedication to a new department to support his wife's passion project. There were multiple articles about their donations to assist young couples afford treatments, as well as their work with adoption agencies to help infertile couples. There were photos from an award dinner where Charlotte was recognized for her bravery in telling her story and using her tragedy to help others. There are a few more photos of Charlotte and Carson posed at various dinners and with some of their friends.

The next article the camera focuses on is about a boat explosion, where three perished, and one survived. The photo showed the splintered remains of the luxury yacht in one frame and then yacht before the explosion in the other. The camera zoomed into the before photo, where the main characters were visible on the back deck of the yacht. The group of them celebrated and drank champagne.

Gabriella sat up straighter in her seat and was curious as to what was going to happen at the end of the movie. She noticed everyone around her were hypnotized by the movie, including all of her co-stars, since the studio kept everything locked down.

300

Chester announces that they are out of champagne and urged the group to watch the video. The movie focuses on Chester as he finds the captain and they head out to the mainland on the smaller boat. The focus returns to the others on the boat, where a video starts to play. It was security footage of a home office, where Carson sat behind a desk as Abigail enters the room with a tray of food and drinks. There is no audio on the video, but you see the two of them talk, then you see Abigail make her way around the desk, where Carson stands up and pushes her down onto the desk. The two begin to kiss, then it jumps forward to them having sex. The video then shows an outdoor view of a driveway, where Carson and Wilhelmina are engaged in sex in a car. There was footage of Abigail and Carson together in the home office a few times, and Carson and Wilhelmina in his office at work. The final bit of footage is Abigail in Carson's home office as she paced back and forth as Carson sat at his desk as he watched her. She finally paused and hands him something from her pocket, her mouth formed the words "I'm Pregnant."

Carson looks down at the pregnancy test, then back at Abigail and smiled as he jumped up from his desk and romantically kissed her. After the video stops and Carson begins to scream and Charlotte smacks him across the face, she made her way down the stairs and entered the master bedroom. From the outside of the boat, the view is through the portholes, where candles lit and rose petals were on the bed. The next scene shows Carson as he made his way down the stairs and slammed his hand on the door to the bedroom. After a few moments, he broke down the door, and from the outside of the porthole, he was visible as he trashed the room and screamed like a lunatic. The camera panned out to see Wilhelmina and Abigail on the deck, as the former ranted like a lunatic and threw pillows and bottles of liquor around the deck, and the latter sat on the couch and continued to sob. As the camera panned out further, there was a giant explosion, and the yacht was destroyed.

There are gasps and cries heard throughout the theater, as sirens wail in the background, the aftermath of the explosion showed on the screen. Next, there is a search and rescue boat, along with helicopters as it searched the area of the wreckage. In the dark, it was difficult to make out what was in the water, until someone on a boat started to shout that they found someone. Charlotte was found as she clung to a piece of wreckage, her eyes closed and her breath shallow as she floated in the water.

The next scene focused on Charlotte in a hospital bed, the beep of machines and the low chatter of people as the spoke in the room were heard as Charlotte began to awaken. Chester sat in the chair next to her bed, his face shadowed by grief and his eyes trimmed in red.

"Welcome back, Mrs. Young. I'm Kiesha, you're nurse. You gave us quite a scare. How are you feeling?"

Charlotte nodded her head slightly and gripped at her throat, which the nurse gave her water to drink. "There are some officers that need to speak with you. Are you feeling up to it?" Kiesha asked.

Charlotte nodded as the nurse left to fetch the cops. Carson gripped her hand as he choked out, "I thought I lost you. I thought you were gone. I'm so glad that you are here, Charlotte."

"Mrs. Young, Mr. Finn, I'm Detective Owens, this is Detective Stecher. I'm sorry that you were in such a terrible accident. I've been told that you are feeling better. I have some unfortunate news for you, if Mr. Finn didn't tell you already."

Charlotte looked from Chester to the detectives and shook her head. "Mrs. Young, I'm sorry to inform you, but you were the only survivor from the accident. It appears the other passengers on the boat have perished. We have divers searching the area, but the outlook is grim. I am sorry for your loss."

Charlotte looked to Chester, who slowly nodded his head and gripped her hand harder as she sobbed.

The camera focused back to the wall in the office, where a framed article announced the identities of the people on the yacht. The last article reads about how Carson Young's wife, head scientist Charlotte Young, and business partner Chester Finn, vowed to keep Young Industries alive, and dedicated their future endeavors to the memories of their beloved husband, wife, and best friend.

The focus returned to Carson as the woman in front of him snaps the folder shut. "Well, the readings show that the program has terminated. We can run another cycle, or we can have him come out of it. This is the first time after all the cycles that he's started to wake on his own."

The woman walked away from the workstation and made her way to the wall where the standup glass coffins stood. She pulled a file from one of them and looks at is as Chester continued to speak. "The second program is just about ready. I have really been giving it a lot of thought as to what I want her to experience. I'm thinking more of a hell landscape, but I haven't finished designing everything."

She placed the file back and walked on, where the camera focused on Wilhelmina in a glass surrounding, suspended in a liquid with a mask over her mouth and nose and her eyes closed with her hair floating about her face. "The fetus is still stable in the other one. Have you decided to keep the child once its born?"

The camera shows the woman as she stared at Abigail, suspended in the same way as Wilhelmina, with extra IVs and diodes connected to her body, her torso swollen with Carson's unborn child. Chester looked up at Abigail and stated, "it really is amazing, what you've done with gestational manipulation, that you were able to slow and control the development of the baby. This is Nobel prize winning stuff. We could really do something with all of this technology."

The two of them return to the glass coffin that laid horizontally on a table where Carson was, diodes connected to his bald head, and all over his body. There were massive amounts of wires that connected him to various computers, with IVs in his body to keep him alive.

Carson's head twitched back and forth; his eyes moved quickly below his closed eyelids. The monitors connected to him had spiked and beeped as the woman in the lab coat watched. The scene focused on Carson, the sound reflecting what he can hear, as the technicians spoke about his vitals. Something about a completed program. Another simulation. The sounds didn't make sense to him. The scene flashed from him in the glass coffin to his affair with Abigail, to his affair with Wilhelmina, to his friendship with Chester, to the first time he saw Charlotte in the lab. The vision went back to their wedding, flashes of them as they danced and laughed, to their kiss and as their cake cutting. There was a flash of him being devastated after he learned

Charlotte couldn't have children, and the joy when he learned he would to be a father because of Abigail.

The flashes then returned to the night of the yacht, where he lashed out at Charlotte because she learned the truth. It showed the anger he felt as he destroyed the room, then the look of defiance on Charlotte's face as she walked away from him. Which then flashed to her as she walked away from him when he died in the wild west. The flashes changed to someone as they jumped on his back while he destroyed the room on the boat. He was tackled down, and something was pushed into the side of his neck. Then everything went black.

The film picks up on the ship, as a man dressed in all black, complete with a ski mask approached on a small craft, made his way onboard the yacht. On the back deck, he quietly crept up to a sobbing Abigail and injected a tranquilizer into her neck. The man then crept up to Riona, who was distracted while she looked out to sea, and injected her as well. The noise from Carson as he thrashed about from below deck were heard as the masked man approached the room.

The man jumped on Carson's back, took him down to the floor and injected him. Once Carson was out, the man dragged him out to where the small craft waited, and he removed him from the yacht. The man in black then made his way back to the deck, where he lifted the women one at a time and laid them next to Carson, then placed a tarp over the bodies.

A sound as someone approached startled the masked man, which caused him to turn in a panic, where Charlotte stood as she watched in fear. The masked man straightened and made his way over to her. He looked down at her and studied her face before removed his mask. "It's done, Charlotte. Grab the wood and get in the water. I'll pull you to a safe distance."

Charlotte smiled as she took the piece of boat debris from Chester, then climbed down the ladder and jump into the water. Chester pulled the mask back on and threw a rope to Charlotte and he pulled her out to open water. Once the smaller vessel was gone, Charlotte gripped the sides of the debris, then took a deep breath and ducked under the water as the ship exploded in the distance.

The scene switched to Charlotte and Chester in her office, as she showed him the security footage she had of her husband's affairs with her best friend and his wife. Chester raged, and threatened to kick the shit out of Carson right then and there, but Charlotte shook her head no.

"You have something planned, don't you?" He asked as he watched a slow, evil smile splay across her face. "Whatever it is, I'm in."

The scene returns to the lab, where Chester is asked the woman what to do. She leans down, her face near the glass coffin, and hovered over Carson's. From the profile, it is obvious that Charlotte is the woman staring down at her husband. His eyes moved with more urgency below his eyelids as she watched.

"Dr. Young?" Chester asked and pulled Charlotte's attention away from Carson. "Do you want to start another simulation? See if he learns a lesson this time?"

"It seemed that this round, he was distancing himself from the temptation of the third woman in the later simulations, although he was still infatuated with her, but he still was not able to remain faithful to just one. It seems as though he may be heading on the right path," a technician said from her post.

Charlotte looked between Chester and the lab tech, then back down at Carson. Her eyes then scanned the wall and focused on Abigail and her swollen belly, and her eyes glossed over for a moment.

"Charlotte? Are we running another round of simulations?" Chester prodded.

Charlotte looked away from her former best friend, then looked back down at her beloved husband. A slow, evil smile spread across her face. She looked to Chester and gave one solid nod, then began to walk back to the exit, the click of her heels distanced as made her way through the security door. The camera panned down to Carson, a tear falling from his closed eye as the technician announced the next simulation began to load.

As the technician's hand hovered over the launch button, Carson's eyes opened, and the screen went black.

Fifteen

The theater erupted in applause and cheers as the credits rolled over a melancholic song about heartbreak. Gabriella and Laurel remained seated as others gave a standing ovation, the two shared a look of utter disbelief. Gabriella's heart raced in her chest as she struggled to understand what she watched now means for her. She couldn't understand how a non-speaking, do a favor for the studio role, turned into such a lynchpin for the movie. The complete genius of the script, along with the amazing directing and edits made the Oscar buzz about this movie a reality. How was it possible that this masterpiece came out of all the fun they had in South Dakota?

Laurel blinked a few times as she came out of her shock and reached past Matt and grabbed onto Gabriella's hand. Gabriella squeezed her hand back, and they shared a smile. Everything would change from this point, in her heart, Gabriella knew that Laurel would soon be known as academy award nominated actress Laurel Dolce. The two of them stood up, and grabbed a hold of one another, which forced Matt to move out into the aisle.

"I'm so fucking proud of you," Laurel said as she choked back a sob.

"Me? You were phenomenal, and you are so taking home some serious hardware for that," Gabriella retorted.

"We did that together, you know?" Laurel said with a smile. Gabriella nodded as she swallowed down a lump in her throat.

Don Starr was back on stage with the microphone and asked the crown to settle down. "I'm guessing you liked the movie?"

The theater erupted in cheers again as Don chuckled. "I wanted to get my stars up here, so they can get the proper credit they deserve. Bernie, Samantha, Laurel, Henry, Jake, Riona, and Gabriella, can you please join me on stage?"

Laurel pulled Gabriella out of their row as Henry made his way over to Samantha and offered his arm to escort her on stage. Gabriella followed suit, and approached Bernie and offered her arm to him, as Laurel took his other arm. Jake followed up the rear and escorted Riona. They made it to the stage, and Don walked over and hugged everyone as they approached him. "Now, as you all know, this is the first time our stars have seen the movie. Bernie, what did you think?"

"I think I've still got it. Did you see it, Don? I had two beautiful women escort me on stage," Bernie said with a smile. "I've been in this industry for over fifty years, and I've got to say, I was a concerned about not seeing the movie before all of this, but wow, you guys really pulled off something amazing. It was a pleasure to be a part of this."

The crowd cheered as Don approached Samantha. "The beautiful Ms. Pierce, what is your reaction to our film?"

"I'm in awe. The script had captivated my attention from the beginning, that multi-timeline had me hooked. But to see what was done with it. How it was weaved into this ultimate payback for betrayal? I'm floored. This cast made you invested in the characters, which is not an easy thing to do."

"Laurel, you seem to be very emotional, care to share?" Don asked.

"How did that," Laurel said as she pointed to the screen, "come from this?" She asked as she gestured to the others on stage. "I can't understand how it happened, but I'm happy it did. That is lighting captured in a bottle. And I'm really happy that I got to do it with my best friend," Laurel said as she threw her arm around Gabriella's shoulders. "So many amazing things have come out of this movie, including meeting my boyfriend," she paused to wink at Matt. "This really was a once in a lifetime opportunity, and I'm so happy to be a part of it."

"Ah, the best friend, Gabriella. I'm very curious to hear your reaction," Don said as he pointed the mic in her direction.

"I'm speechless," she responded.

Don let out a booming laugh, "how about that, the first time you get to hear her voice all night and she's speechless."

The crowd laughed along as Gabriella smiled. "It's surreal. I thought I was just going to be an extra. You guys really undersold my role. I'm just flabbergasted that Charlotte was so heartbroken that she sold her soul to seek revenge. It's so twisted, but it's amazing. I'm just nervous about the amount of hate I'm going to get now."

"Riona, how about you? What is your reaction to the film?" Don asked.

"Wilhelmina is a badass bitch. I hate her homewrecking ways, but I love that she's unapologetic about it. It's refreshing to play such a feminist part. She did what she had to do, and she owned it. Honestly. I'm going to echo some of my costar's remarks, this movie was mind blowing and I'm honored to be a part of it."

"Mr. Wilson? How did you feel about the twist?" Don asked.

"You know, Don, I thought for the first time I wasn't going to be the bad guy, even though I killed Carson a bunch of times, but then killing them on the boat. What?!" Jake mimicked his mind exploding. "You guys are sneaky with your secret footage and body doubles. I had no idea you were doing that. Such a bad ass movie!"

"Finally, the man of the hour, Mr. Carson Young himself, Henry Anderson. I need to know, what did you think?"

Henry approached Don and threw his arm around him. "Bloody brilliant."

Some women in audience started to cheer in response, a few yelling out their love for Henry.

"Truly, Don, you and the rest of the execs are mad, and I love you for it. This film exceeded my expectations in a way I didn't know was possible. There truly is no redeeming quality about Carson, yet, in that final scene, you feel sympathy for him. He's an absolute bastard, and it's sad that he couldn't love his wife in reality the way he loved her in the simulation, which just breaks your bloody heart for Charlotte, seeking the love of her husband in a sim. But even there, the bastard couldn't keep it in his pants. Just mind boggling."

"So, are you happy with it?" Don asked with a smile.

312

"Absolutely. And I'm hopping on Laurel's train, this movie really did change my life. I've met some amazing people during this film, some life-long mates, and although the road wasn't always smooth with filming, I wouldn't change one bit of it." Henry said with a smile, as he looked out to his row where his friends sat, then turned to Gabriella with a wink.

"Alright, everyone, I give you the cast of The Edge of Time. Thank you so much for coming, and I wish you all a good night." Don said over the thunderous applause of the crowd. Henry grabbed Samantha's hand, and led her over to Gabriella, and took Gabriella's in his other hand. Laurel, who caught on to what Henry did, held Gabriella's hand and took Riona's in her other. Riona grabbed onto Jake's and Samantha took hold of Bernie. Together, they took a bow, as the audience gave them a final standing ovation.

***

"Oh my god, *Bambolina*, that was unbelievable! I can't believe that was you!" Maria shrieked as they joined Gabriella in the ballroom for the afterparty. The actors were all escorted through another entrance from the rest of the guests.

Gabriella clung onto her mother as her father wrapped his arms around the both of them. "I'm so proud of you, Gabby. Maybe I could have lived without watching some of those scenes, but honey, you stole the whole show."

"Thanks, Dad. Trust me, those scenes were awkward enough without you and Mom seeing them." She said with a laugh.

"Biiiiiitchhhh!" Desmond yelled as he ran over and barreled his way through the DiStellas and he wrapped his arms around Gabriella. "You were so bomb.

Like hot fire all over that screen. Who knew my bestie was such a sex kitten, meow."

"That's enough, Des," Giuseppe said with a shake of his head.

"Thanks, Des." Gabriella said with a smile as Arnie, Sierra, and Marco approached. She hugged each of them and spoke briefly when Desmond interrupted again. "Where is Laurel?"

"She saw a few of her old co-stars on the way in, so she was chatting with them."

"How does it feel to be a bona fide actress?" Arnie asked as they made their way to the tables.

"Unreal, because I'm not an actress, Arnie. But really, I'm kinda scared."

Arnie arched his eyebrow as Desmond wrapped his arm around Gabriella's waist. "Scared? Why?"

"You saw how people were during filming. I'm afraid it's going to get worse before I'm forgotten again. I'm just not sure if I can deal with it."

"Well, you have me, and Arnie, and Liam," Desmond said with a smile. "We won't let anything happen."

"I know. I'm just going to take Nicole's advice and stay away from the internet. I'm still going to be out here for a few months, so I can just dive into work. Hopefully you and Laurel will keep me busy."

"Speaking of Liam, have you spoken to him yet?" Arnie asked.

Gabriella shook her head. "No, not yet. He did text me before I left the limo. I'm planning on calling him later. The time difference between here and London is no joke."

Laurel approached the group and kissed and hugged everyone while her parents followed her. "Gabs, you need to come with me. There are requests for pictures, and I want to get it out of the way before the party really starts."

Desmond blew them both a kiss and settled down at a table with Arnie and their parents as they made their way through the crowd. "Who wants pictures, Lau?"

"Listen, I know you feel comfortable with our family, but you need to be out and about, mingling and rubbing elbows. I know this is the part you can't stand, but trust me, so many doors have just opened for you."

"Lau, that's not what tonight is about. And if anything, I'm using the opportunities for you and Desmond. I should probably have him come and work the room with us."

Laurel rolled her eyes. "Gabby, I love you. You are an amazing friend and an amazing manager. Please remove the work hat and enjoy tonight. You are a hot topic, please embrace it. It's only for a few hours."

Laurel winked, then threw her arm around Gabriella and smiled for an Associated Press photographer. "I'll have Matt get Des and Arnie later, and I will walk them around and introduce them to people. Don't worry about being by yourself, trust me, people are going to flock to you."

Laurel kissed her on the cheek and made her way into the crowd, then stopped to say hello to a few people while the DJ announced that the party was ready to get started as music floated through the air at a reasonable level. A waitress approached Gabriella as she stood where Laurel left her.

"Can I get you something to drink? We have a few specials inspired by the movie. There is the patriot, a red, white and blue cocktail which is sparkling lemonade vodka. The wild west is a bourbon and schnapps cocktail, the mobster martini is rum and apple juice, and the time jump, which is an espresso martini. Or I can get you anything else."

"Oh, I think I'll take the mobster martini. Thank you."

"Gabriella! I'm so happy I found you. I've been wanting to talk to you for months! Be completely honest with me, what did you think of the movie?" April asked as she ran over and gave her a quick hug.

"It was phenomenal, April. You really are such a brilliant writer." Gabriella said with a genuine smile.

"I'll be honest, it was soul crushing when the studio wanted a new ending. I thought Carson being shown his mistakes and how he never could change himself despite all his chances was a decent ending. Having Charlotte be the desire that slipped further and further away from him the more corrupt he became was poetic. But after watching the footage, and then seeing what was happening off camera, I couldn't help but be inspired.

316

"You inspired me, Gabby. The obsession the public had with you and Henry during the shoot, and the way they attacked, and the way you handled it. It was exactly what I needed. I thought of what Charlotte would do in your position. Powerless in the public eye, thrusted into the spotlight with a well-known public figure. Wronged by people and the press. Would she take the high road, like you did, or would she seek revenge? And then I thought, why not do both? Be untouchable in the press, but secretly, dish out the appropriate punishment."

Gabriella was shocked by April's confession and slightly confused. "April, I'm flattered, but really, what happened was no big deal."

April shook her head and patted Gabriella on the arm. "It was. And I'm in no way saying you sought revenge or anything like that. You just inspired me. It was a shitty situation you were thrown into. It's nice that Henry is such a stand-up guy. Some of those other guys would have really fed into it, got all the publicity they could. I guess I just wanted to thank you for taking such an ancillary character and making her the vengeful protagonist that I didn't know we needed."

The waitress appeared with Gabriella's drink, along with a few others that she passed out through the crowd. April took a cocktail from the tray and clinked their glasses together. Gina stomped over, grabbed a cocktail before the waitress walked away, and sighed deeply and took a swig of her drink before she acknowledged the others.

"I swear, if I have to spend any more time with Lloyd and his boy wonder over there, I'm going to lose my shit."

April and Gabriella exchanged a look before they turned their attention back to Gina. "Sorry, I've been dealing with those two knuckleheads for far too long. I've never been so happy for a movie to premiere. By the way, congratulations ladies on a stellar film."

She paused for a moment while a photographer stopped to take a picture of the three of them with their drinks in their hands.

"Did you happen to see the spread they put out tonight. Spare no expense Lloyd really threw a hissy fit to the studio execs, and they gave him what he wanted like the fucking man-child he is. Everything is themed. The food, the drinks, the décor. It's insane. Anyway, I just wanted to stop by and say my hellos. I'm off to grab my sushi rolls, have a few more of these wild west drinks, and get myself a sexy, young man to have my way with tonight. Enjoy your evening ladies."

Like the hurricane she was, Gina blew right through and made her way to the sushi bar on the other side of the room.

"Wow," Gabriella said, then took a sip of her martini. "That was unexpected."

April rolled her eyes and sighed as she watched their personal hurricane walkway. "She slept with Lloyd. That's the rumor anyway. She may or may not have walked in on him dipping his pen in other pots of company ink. I think the two of them need to steer clear of one another."

Gabriella froze at the information, not sure what to say. April smiled widely as she murmured into her drink, "Hottie inbound. Time for me to mosey on. Enjoy your night." April winked and walked away as a heated stare singed her skin. Her eyes moved on their own accord and locked onto Henry has he made his way through the crowd; his eyes unwavering as he said pleasantries to the people in his wake.

He paused as a waitress approached with drinks and snagged two from the tray and continued on his mission. "It looks like you can use a refill."

Gabriella looked down at her empty glass and smiled. "I'm sure you have better things to do than making sure my glass is full."

"You would think so, but alas, my attention is focused on you. And I have noticed that you have not eaten anything yet." He said as he offered his arm up.

Gabriella slipped her hand through and rested it on his forearm as she smiled up at him. "Ever the observant one, Mr. Anderson."

"You know it, Miss DiStella." He said with a wink and a smirk.

"Henry, Gabriella, over here," one of the photographers called out for them pose for a photo. They acquiesced to the request, then kept moving.

"I have a feeling you are going to want the pizza."

"They have pizza here? Seriously. Gina said there was sushi too." Gabriella said as she carefully made their way to the tables and tried not to spill her drink.

"There are also sliders and barbecue chicken and ribs. I think I saw some chips too."

"Chips? As in Potato chips or French fries?"

"Fries, Ella."

"And you want to take me to pizza? Are you nuts?"

Henry laughed as he guided her to a table. She smiled at the others at the table, then placed her drink down. "Where is your sister?"

"Apparently your parents have a knack for picking up strays. She's sitting with them and Bob."

Once they filled up their plate with food, which Gabriella did wind up with pizza, along with everything else they had to offer, they rejoined the table. Henry made introductions, which included a few actors, a cinematographer, and two writers. "I feel bad," Gabriella said as she finished the last of her fries. "I haven't spent as much time with my family as I thought I would tonight. Not to mention our little rag-tag group of friends. I got to Laurel's so late; I missed hanging out with them."

"I understand. These parties are always more about rubbing elbows than enjoying yourself. Why don't we go gather the troops and make our way to the dance floor? Have a little Beer Garden reunion?"

Gabriella nodded and joined Henry in saying goodbye to their tablemates and made their way to where Patti and Jem were. "If it isn't two of the most beautiful women in the room," Henry said as he placed an arm around both of their shoulders.

"I'm not sure if you're a terrible liar, a good actor, or needing to get an eye exam," Patti said with a laugh.

"Come on, Patti melt, you know how much I love you girls. You know I'm not one to tell porkies."

"There he goes with that British shit." Jem said with a laugh as she checked her hip into his. "Notice he said two of the most beautiful, I guess that top title still belongs to this one over here," Jem said with a smile as she gestured her head toward Gabriella.

"Yeah, you're right, Jem. I'm sure our love and beauty fall in a different category than this one." Patti colluded with a similar smile.

"Alright, enough of that, you two. We want to dance. Where are the boys?" Gabriella asked as she looked around the room.

Patti pulled out her phone and sent a message, then put it back in her bag and grabbed a drink from the bar. "They will meet us in the middle of the dance floor. I sent out the bat signal."

Jem followed suit, grabbed drinks and handed them to Henry and Gabriella before she took one for herself and headed towards the dance floor.

"I have to ask," Patti said quietly as she pulled Gabriella aside. "Did I look okay in the movie? Like, do I have to worry about anyone making fat chick comments?"

Gabriella's head fell to the side in concern as she rubbed Patti's arm with her free hand. "Patti, you looked beautiful in the movie. Why would you say that?"

Patti's eye dodged away and studied the ceiling as she searched for the answer. "I know you don't like to read the gossip columns or read the comments on social media. But I saw what some people were saying about you when you were with Henry, and you are half my size. And you are beautiful. I would give my left arm to look like you. And I know I'm not a huge part or anything, but I'm just scared that I put myself out there like that."

"Oh, Patti. I get it, believe me. I'm sure there will be trolls out there who are going to make their asinine comments. I know I'm going to get a shit ton of them. Guarantee the back fat roll you saw when I was on top of Henry in the bed is going to be pointed out. But do you know how many people have praised the movie for having real-life women in it? And how many people are happy to see non-stick figures in the film. We're real women, Patti, and if people don't like it, they can just suck my left tit, you know?"

Patti couldn't contain her laughter and hugged Gabriella with her free arm. "You really are something else, Gabby. And I love you for it. Now, can I ask you one thing, and you won't get mad?"

"You're killing me, girl."

"What is going on with you and Henry? I was looking at some of the red-carpet stuff, and he was holding your hand and talking about you nonstop. There are some photos of the two of you canoodling on the carpet before your interview."

"Oh, no, it was nothing like it looks. He had my fake nails. It's a weird story, but he was giving me my nails."

"Okay, and is that why he's been staring at you all night?"

"Patti, stop it, please. I'm with Liam. We're friends. Let's just enjoy the night and hang out like we did last summer. Who knows the next time we'll all be together?"

***

Parched from dancing, and the laughter from the dance-off between Jake, Desmond, Giuseppe, Bob, and Max, Gabriella made her way to the bar to rehydrate. While she drank her second bottle of water, Don Starr approached her with a stunning woman. She wore a loose lavender dress with long sleeves and sequenced trim, with her natural hair tied back in braids, with the ends haloing her head in a gorgeous afro.

"Gabriella, I have someone who has been wanting to meet you. Gabriella, this is Veronica Edwards."

"Wow, Veronica Edwards, it's an honor to meet you. I am a huge fan of your work. Your films have such a unique style with their story telling. They are very empowering." Gabriella gushed as she shook her hand.

"Thank you, it's a pleasure to meet you too. I'm humbled that you know my work."

"Are you kidding? Starshine is one of my favorite movies. Maya Douglas is such an amazingly strong woman. Her story made me cry and stand up and cheer. It was so emotional."

Veronica smiled elegantly, then turned to Don. "Thank you so much for introducing us, Don. Would you mind if I had a moment alone with Gabriella?"

"Not at all. It was a pleasure, Ronnie. We'll talk soon. Enjoy the rest of the party." Don said with a brief kiss on her cheek. Once he was out of ear shot, Veronica continued her conversation.

"I understand that you have a unique experience with this film. Not even a cast member, yet you wound up stealing the spotlight."

Gabriella shook her head slightly. "That was not my intention at all. I really was there just to help. I'm not an actress. Not even close. It's why I had no lines in the movie."

"You say that as if it was a bad thing. And you say you're not an actress, but that's not what I saw. Acting is not only how you deliver lines; it's about how you can make the audience feel. You, my dear, made people feel."

"I appreciate that, Ms. Edwards, but really, I am a behind the scenes person. I work for Laurel Dolce and Desmond Balvin."

"You really aren't looking to pursue an acting career? I can tell you, Gabriella, people are going to be knocking down your door for their projects once they see this film. It's lucky for me that I saw it first."

Gabriella looked perplexed as Veronica continued to speak. "I am working on a film about the Amazons. The cast is going to be full of strong leading women. We are spanning generations of women for this film, and I think you would be perfect to be in it."

"Me? Seriously? I'm flattered, but really, I'm not an actress."

"I want you to think about it." Veronica said as she handed her a business card. "I think you are a perfect fit for this movie. You have the look and build of what I imagine the Amazons to be. Don't sell yourself short, Gabriella."

***

Henry watched Gabriella from the dance floor as she was approached by Don and Veronica Edwards. "If you stare any harder, your eyes are going to fall out of your bloody head," his sister said as she danced her way over with Desmond.

"Such a comedian, this one is," Henry said with a scoff as his eyes shifted over to May.

"Hank, I've never seen you so attentive to a woman before. And I am including your ex-fiancé in this observation. What is going on?"

"Nothing, yet. Well, that isn't entirely truthful, is it? We had a very brief thing, but it went all to pot when I didn't confess to something that upset her. We haven't had much luck, and I am not ready to give up yet. I really think we are meant to be together."

"That's terribly romantic, Hank. So, what are you thinking? Do we need a grand gesture?" May asked hopefully.

"Um, I'm going to have to interject." Desmond said and interrupted their conversation. "I'm not sure that is the best of ideas, Henry."

"Why, Desmond? Does she not have feelings for him? I would say they both look smitten with each other," May asked.

"It's not that. I mean, firstly, she is dating someone."

"Well, where is he? Is it serious?" May questioned.

"He is on a business trip in London. I'm not sure how serious it is, but she does seem content with their relationship. But my main concern is that I don't think this is the best timing."

"How so?" Henry asked.

"Look, man. This is all new to Gabby. Sure, she's been in the industry for a while, but she has never been thrown into the limelight. And let's be honest, things are going to blow up for her now. She already mentioned to me tonight how scared she is for what is coming next. She never wanted this. You know how she reacted when the tabloids were speculating about the two of you."

"I think it could be better for her to be with someone who know how to handle the press and the pressure of the industry. We could be a united front; we could face all of that head-on." Henry rationalized.

Desmond shook his head. "I've known Gabriella almost my whole life. What she needs now is normalcy. She needs the consistency of working and the life she had before this movie came out. You know she doesn't need the extra pressure from this."

Henry looked over and studied Gabriella as she spoke with famous director. Her deep brown almond eyes were wide with surprise as she animatedly spoke with a flush on her olive skin. Her hair, which was only a few shades darker than her eyes, softly swayed as she responded to her conversation. The blue dress complemented her voluptuous figure and made her look like an angel in the night sky. His heart ached as much as his loins when he looked at her. He wanted to wrap his arms around her to protect her from the world and hold her so close that she permanently became a part of him. He knew in the depth of his heart that they could be happy together. He looked at her and saw his future, happy and full of love.

On the other hand, he knew what this industry was like, and it was something he dealt with because it was his dream to be an actor. But there were times that even for him it was too much, and he had to take a step back to center himself. Fame was a fickle bitch. You played it up for the cameras, so the fans loved you, but then the fans loved you too much, and you had to shun the cameras away.

Desmond watched as the thoughts ran through Henry's mind, and he could see the battle rage within him. "Henry," he said softly, which snapped him out of his thoughts. Henry's eyes refocused onto Desmond as he continued to speak. "If you love her like you say you do, and I believe you do, you know that you need to give her time. You need to let her survive the next month or two on her own. Wait until the excitement of the film dies down. Then, see where she is and feel things out then."

Henry sighed as he listened to the unwanted but wise words of advice. "What if it's too late?"

Desmond shook his head, and patted Henry on the shoulder. "Then it wasn't meant to be. But Henry, as much as I like Liam as a person, I'm rooting for you."

May gestured for Desmond to leave as she hugged her brother. "What are you going to do?"

Henry shrugged, then kissed his sister on the top of her head. "What I have to. Give me a second, I need to make a call."

***

After she spoke with Veronica, Gabriella was pulled aside by Jake and his sister, Madison, who she hadn't seen since the fiasco at the club when Henry was drugged. After they spoke for a few minutes, she made her way to the bathroom, where she spotted Henry walk past while he tucked his phone into his breast pocket.

"Hey, Henry! Is everything okay?" She asked as she noticed the stern look on his face.

"Yeah, of course, why wouldn't it be?"

328

"I don't know, you look…angry?"

"Nope, I'm good, just got off the phone with my manager. Buttoning up some items. It's already seven in the morning over there, so he wanted to catch me before I went to sleep."

"Oh, okay. So, I have this super exciting news and I'm dying to tell you. Guess who I just had an insane conversation with. Veronica Edwards, as in award winning director Veronica Edwards." Gabriella gushed.

"I did see you having a conversation with her." Henry said with a slight smile.

"She told me that she wants me for a new movie that she's working on about the Amazons. She was saying that it is going to be a strong female cast with some Hollywood heavy hitters, and she actually wants me, non-actress Gabby, to be in the film. She said there is some part that I would be perfect for. I would have to audition, of course, but it's just so beyond flattering that she would even suggest that I do it. I almost want to ask you to pinch me because this can't be real!"

"Are you going to do it?" Henry asked with genuine curiosity.

"Oh, I don't know. I mean, I don't want to act. But I would be a moron to turn this down. I mean, I should at least try it. I might make an ass out of myself, and I most likely wouldn't get the part. But if someone like Veronica Edwards tells you to try out for a film, I feel like it would be insulting to her if I didn't."

Henry smiled as she watched her nervously babble on. She looked back at him with such wonder in her eyes, his heart skipped a beat. "What do you think I should do?"

Henry shook his head and grasped some of her silky hair between his fingers as if he were a blind man committing her features to his memory. "I would tell you to follow your heart. Don't listen to what other people tell you to do. Trust yourself enough to make the choice for yourself. Don't listen to the outside world, don't let anyone control you. You have the power to find your own happiness, Ella."

Gabriella stood there stared up at the most handsome man she had ever met in her life. He stood so close to her, she could feel the heat radiate from him, and she was surrounded by his uniquely masculine scent. An overwhelming feeling of desire and sadness overtook her as she stared into his blue eyes.

Henry let go of her hair, then slid his hand to her face, where he cupped her cheek and stroked it with his thumb. "I have to go," he said before leaning down and pressing his lips to her forehead. The sweet and heartbreaking kiss ended too soon as he pulled away and said, "goodbye, Ella."

She watched him as he turned away and headed back into the main room as she stood there, confused by their interaction. At one point she thought, and hoped if she was honest with herself, that he would pick up where they left off in Laurel's kitchen only hours ago. But instead, he chastely kissed her forehead and left.

While she stood at the vanity in the bathroom and retouched her lipstick, Gabriella pulled out her cellphone because Henry mentioned the time in

330

London. An overwhelming feeling of guilt came over her as she looked down at her phone, and she debated if she should call Liam. She couldn't pretend that she didn't kiss Henry in the kitchen, nor could she ignore the desire to continue their tryst and agonized over the strength she needed to pull herself away from him and get ready.

Even with their history, she couldn't deny the ache in her bones for Henry Anderson. It was biological, primordial, an undeniable part of her genetic makeup. Even though her conscious self-screamed out the sensical warnings of how much they did not belong together, how far above her he was, how much hurt she would set herself up for, she couldn't stomp out the subconscious flame her soul held for him.

She stared at her reflection for a few moments, her brain overruled her heart, and she cleared her throat, and knew that the prudent thing to do was to file Henry back into her fantasy file and accept her reality. She promised herself that she would come clean to Liam when he was back home, that she owed it to him to tell him what happened tonight to his face, and she would face the consequences she deserved. Liam had become a constant in her life, and she hoped that he would remain that way after her confession.

The phone rang a few times after she clicked Liam's name. As she prepared to leave a message, she was surprised when the call connected.

"Hello?" An unfamiliar female voice with a thick British accent answered.

"Oh," Gabriella looked at her phone to check she called Liam's cell. "Sorry, I um, must have the wrong number."

"Are you looking for Liam, yeah?"

"Um, yes."

"Hang on a tick." The woman responded, then called out, "Liam, call for you."

After a few moments of jostling to retrieve the phone, she heard Liam's voice, "hey, goober! How was last night? Was the movie what you expected? I'm sorry, I didn't check the internet to see any reviews."

"Hey, I'm actually still at the after party. I just wanted to give you a call. Who answered your phone?"

"Oh, that was Janet, she's one of my coworkers in the London branch."

"I'm sorry, I didn't realize you were at the office already. Do you need to go? Did I interrupt a meeting?"

"Oh, no, I just woke up a few minutes ago and was about to jump in the shower. I'll be heading into the office in an hour or so."

Gabriella paused as she realized why the woman answered his phone while he was still in his hotel room. A small piece of her heart began to tear, the feeling of betrayal began to flood her chest. The guilt she felt for the kiss she shared with Henry was washed away by the knowledge that her boyfriend had sex with a coworker.

"Oh." The one word she breathed out said more than she could express.

"Gabby, listen, it's not what you think," Liam began to say.

332

"So, you didn't sleep with your co-worker?"

"No, I mean, we never said we were exclusive. We've always been great friends, and that great friendship included us dating and having sex. But we were never in a committed relationship." Liam responded after he huffed, the sound as he rubbed his hand against his stubble muffled a few of his words.

"Oh, of course. My mistake." Gabriella said, as she tried to calm the tremor in her voice.

"Come on, Gabby, what did you expect? You're not even home half of the year. I'm supposed to just sit at home, twiddling my thumbs while you're off in California doing whatever it is you're doing?"

Gabriella swallowed the lump in her throat, the fear she had about a long-distance relationship with Henry was just shoved in her face by the person she thought understood. "I hear you loud and clear, Liam. Have fun in England. And when you get back to New York. I gotta go."

"Gabby, just wait, give me a minute. That didn't come out right." Liam said in a rush.

"No, it did. It was selfish of me to think otherwise. Have a good life, Liam. I hope you find what you're looking for." Gabriella said before she hung up.

And just like that, she was alone again, the way she always was, the way she felt the universe wanted her to be. Her phone began to ring again, Liam's face appeared on the screen. She ignored the call, but the phone rang again. After she declined the call, she blocked his number, cleaned off the minimal tear tracks on her cheeks, and made her way back to the party.

Sixteen

"There you are, I feel like I haven't spoken to you all night," Darius said as he placed his hand on Gabriella's arm as she walked from the bathroom towards the main room.

Gabriella looked up at the wardrobe guru from the film, his brown eyes sparkled behind black thin-framed glasses. His white suit and pale pink shirt contrasted beautifully against his dark skin. "Is everything okay?"

Gabriella nodded. "Yeah, I'm good. Just a bit of a misunderstanding with an ex. On my way to party with all my favorites, you included."

Darius laughed and placed his arm around Gabriella's shoulders. She raised her hear to look up at the man who towered over her. "Well, let's get in there before everyone else leaves."

"Who left?"

"Henry said his goodbyes and headed out. Joshua was complaining that he was jetlagged and headed back to the hotel. I think everyone was planning on ending the night soon, but May of all people convinced everyone to keep the party going and go to the bar in the hotel most of them are staying at."

"Oh. Henry left? But May is still here?" Gabriella asked before they entered the main room.

"Yeah, Henry said that the studio requested him to return to set in New Zealand. I think he said they were flying him back today. May was planning to go back to England in a few days, so she decided to stay here with the rest of them."

"I never even thought to ask how long Patti, Bob, and Joshua were planning on staying."

"It was a few days, maybe a week at the most. I think Patti is staying with Jem for a few days, and Max is hosting Bob and Joshua. I offered, especially since Samuel is with his sister in Italy looking at garment vendors, but since Max has his bachelor pad, they said they'd crash with him."

They stood on the precipice of the dance floor when Darius gently held onto Gabriella's arm. "Are you sure that you're alright?"

Gabriella smiled. "What is there not to be okay about? The party is amazing, the movie was a huge success, and we're all here together. It's been almost a year since that has happened."

"I'm just checking. It's okay to not be okay, you know."

Gabriella lifted up on her toes and placed a kiss to Darius's cheek. "I know and thank you."

After she danced for another hour with her friends and family and spoke to a few more people that Laurel introduced her to, Gabriella was ready to go home.

"Hey Mom, are you ready to leave?" Gabriella asked her mom, who was seated at a table with her shoes off.

"Hey, *Bambolina*, yes, I am ready to leave. But Dad and I aren't going home yet. Laurel offered for us to stay at her house tonight, so we're having a parental sleepover. I think we're all planning to have brunch at her house tomorrow afternoon. She said she's having caterers come, and your friends from the film are coming too."

"Okay, that sounds good. So, I'll meet you at Laurel's?"

"I'm so proud of you, Gabby," her mom said with a smile as she squeezed her hand. "Go have a good time with your friends. Don't worry about us old folks."

Gabriella kissed her mom, then made her way over to Desmond. "Are you going to the bar?"

"No, bitch, I'm tired. I need to get my beauty sleep. But I'll see you at brunch." Desmond said with a wink.

Gabriella retrieved her clutch and headed to the group of friends who waited to leave. "Are you ready to party?" Patti yelled out as she approached.

"Guys, I'm sorry to do this, but I'm exhausted. I think I'm going to go get a good night's sleep, and I'll meet you guys all bright-eyed and bushy-tailed tomorrow."

An eruption of boos was the response. "Are you sure, we won't keep you out too late," Jem asked as she used Patti to support herself.

Gabriella smiled at the drunken mess before her. "Yeah, remember, I'm the one who flew cross country and came to a premiere."

"Gabby, may I have a moment before you leave?" May asked as she headed towards the exit.

Gabriella nodded and followed her to the quieter hallway. "Look, it's not my place to butt in, but I'm going to, because little sister privilege. I'm not really sure what the story is with you and my brother, but I do know that I've never seen him look at someone the way he looks at you. I know you both say you are friends and all of that, but I think it's complete bollocks.

"He spoke about you non-stop when he was home for the holidays, nothing but positive things. I know that you're dating someone, and it may make me a complete bitch, but I think you're with the wrong person. I think you belong with my brother."

Gabriella looked at May as if she lost her mind. She knew this person for all of a few hours, and she has the nerve to tell her what she should do with her life. And what frustrated her most of all, was that May was spot on with her assessment. "We broke up."

"Yes, I am aware that you and my brother ended whatever brief thing you had."

"No, the person I'm dating, was dating, we broke up. Or we were never more than a friends with benefit thing. He just slept with his coworker on a business trip he's on." The words spilled from her mouth.

"Oh! Well, in that case, brilliant. Call my brother. He'll be over the moon to hear that you're single."

Gabriella shook her head. "May, I appreciate the unfiltered advice, but there is so much more to it than Liam. It was really nice to meet you, but I need to head home."

May's shoulders visibly lowered as her hope balloon deflated. "Okay. Just think about what I said, Gabby. I think the both of you deserve happiness, and you make each other happy."

"Thanks, May. Have a safe trip back home."

"Yeah, you too."

***

The hour-long drive home in the stretch limo was a lonely one. With her head against the window and her phone in her hand, she debated on if she should take May's advice and call Henry. It wasn't as if it would be strange for her to contact him, since they just spent time together. She could call and mention his sudden trip back to the set. She could talk to him about what a whirlwind tonight was. She could leave out the parts that threw her for a complete loop, like Liam cheated on her or the passionate kiss they shared.

Before she could second-guess herself, the phone connected to Henry's, which went directly to voicemail. "Hey, Henry, it's Gabriella. It's around one in the morning, L.A. time. I heard you were flying back to New Zealand, I guess that was the call with your manger, huh? It was really good to see you tonight. I wish we could have spent a little more time together. You're missing out on brunch at Laurel's tomorrow.

"I guess you're at the airport, or you could be in the air. I'm not sure what time your flight was. I guess I should stop rambling on your voicemail. Have a safe flight, Henry. Give me a call when you land, let me know you made it okay. Okay…bye."

She ended the call, then sighed deeply and opened a browser and looked up reviews on the movie. The reviews were all positive so far, and the reporters who attended the premiere were very complimentary in their write-ups. Some even speculated that the film would do well during awards season and named the cast as serious contenders as well as the film overall.

There were already a bunch of photos available, and she couldn't help but click through them, her eyes studied all of the photos of Henry. There was a photo of Henry's smoldering stare, which sent chills down her spine. She clicked on it, which took her to a blog, where it showed the image of Henry was zoomed in. She scrolled further down, where the original photo was, Henry was in the background of the red carpet as he spoke to a journalist, but his eyes were directed to further up on the red carpet, where she was surprised to see herself as she posed for the cameras.

Her heart began to slam in her chest as the caption read that Henry had his eyes on the prize, which is no other than the mystery brunette, co-star Gabriella DiStella.

The car came to a stop, and the door opened, the driver extended his hand to assist Gabriella out of the car. She quickly locked her phone and threw it into her clutch, then allowed the driver to help her. She thanked him and bid him a good night as she made her way to her front door. After she locked up, she made her way to her bedroom, removed her dress and laid it at the foot of her bed, pulled on a t-shirt, and collapsed onto the bed from the exhaustion of the day, surrendered to a dreamless sleep.

***

After she scrubbed her face free of the makeup she fell asleep in, Gabriella threw her hair up in a messy bun and took a quick shower, then threw on her two-piece bathing suit, a tank and shorts, and her flip flops, tossed a change of clothes into her bag, and jumped into her father's car to head over to brunch at Laurel's.

Once she made it past the gates and pulled into the driveway, she was met by a few rental cars, which she knew belonged to the parents and friends from out of town, and some cars she recognized as belonging to Jem and Max. She walked through the entrance, passed by the kitchen, where she paused to reminisce about last night, but was met by a few caterers as they carried trays of food out to the patio. Not to disturb them, she took the long way to the patio, walked through the den and out of the French doors.

"Oh my god, you're finally here!" Laurel yelled as she jumped up from the chair she was lounged in. "Everyone, Gabby's here! Okay, we can get started. Everyone, take a seat!"

Laurel ran over and captured Gabriella in a giant bear hug. After she sufficiently squeezed the life out of her, Laurel smiled and went back to the table, where Matt stood. He wrapped his arm around her and gave Gabriella a quick wave.

Gabriella walked to the table, kissed everyone hello as they took their seats as Desmond pulled out the chair next to him for her to sit in. "What is going on?" Gabriella whispered after she kissed him hello.

"I have no idea. She was adamant about waiting for you to get here before we could eat, but she didn't say anything about not drinking. I'm on my second mimosa." He said with a smile as he made his champagne glass dance a little.

Gabriella snorted in response as Laurel clinked her glass with her knife. "Okay people. I invited you here for a few reasons. One, I'm so happy to have all of our friends and family here together in one place. It's been way too long since we've all been together, and I hope we can remedy that with more get togethers. And that includes getting my Mid-Westerners here more often!"

A round of cheers came from Patti, Bob, and Joshua in response.

"I originally wanted to have everyone over to celebrate the successful premiere last night. I think it's safe to say that the movie was life changing, in hopefully all positive ways. It brought us all together, and despite some people on set being a bit of a pain in the ass, I will mention no names."

"Cough, cough, Riona, cough," Max said as Jem pretended to sneeze and said, "Irish bitch."

Laurel looked over at the two of them as everyone snickered. "Sorry, I had something in my throat," Max said as Jem said, "allergies."

"Alright, alright. Unfortunately, Henry couldn't be here to celebrate with us. But we have May as a fine substitution. And Jake said he will be stopping by at some point this afternoon and will be bringing Marissa. Now, as I was saying, this movie has been life changing. The reviews for the movie have been stellar, and the Oscar buzz is huge. I got to film this with my best friend," Laurel continued as Desmond interrupted.

"One of you best friends."

Laurel smiled and rolled her eyes, "yes, Des, one of my best friends. And I got to meet this handsome devil standing next to me. And I guess all I wanted to do was acknowledge how blessed we are, and WE GOT ENGAGED!!!" Laurel screamed, as she slipped the five-carat pink diamond with a halo of white diamond ring onto her finger, which was hidden in her pocket, and extended her hand out for everyone to see.

The table erupted into cheers and congratulatory sentiments. Gabriella's face split into a huge smile for her best friend, but a tinge of sadness circled her heart for the breakup she suffered hours before. Not that Laurel knew what happened. Desmond gripped Gabriella's knee under the table, and she turned her head towards him, and noted the smile he tried to keep plastered to his face. She patted his hand, then encouraged him to stand up and congratulate Laurel and Matt.

Gabriella threw her arms around Laurel and Matt and hugged them tightly. "I'm so excited for you guys. How did it happen. How didn't I know about this?" Gabriella asked as she smacked Matt in the chest with the back of her hand.

"He booked a suite at the hotel on the beach in Santa Monica. He had flower petals and candles all over the room. We took a long bath in the jetted tub when we first got there, then we had champagne and sat in front of the fireplace. He was talking about how amazing last night was and how thankful he was for the movie, because we would have never met. And he said how happy I have made him and Matty, and that Matty made me something for the movie. He took out an envelope, and it had my name written in Matty's handwriting. I opened it, and it was a drawing of the three of us, and it said Laurel, will you marry my daddy?

"I looked up and Matt was down on one knee holding this gorgeous ring. I don't know how long it took me to stop crying and fling myself into his arms, but I said yes."

"I did have to calm her down afterwards and told her that we don't need to set a date any time soon. I just want to make sure that no one tries to steal my girl and let them know that she is off the market," Matt said with a smile as he stared at Laurel, then gave her a quick kiss.

"Is Matty excited?" Gabriella asked.

Matt smiled broadly, "yeah, he really is. Helped me pick out the ring and everything. He's coming by with his mother and stepdad in a little while."

"That's really sweet. I'll let you guys talk to the others, I'm getting death stares from our mothers," Gabriella said with a laugh as she walked back over to the table with Desmond. "You and I will have a chat a little later, when we can break away from everyone."

Desmond nodded and sat down, and watched as the buffet was set up on the outdoor island. Once Matt's son and ex-wife and her husband showed up, the food was served. After sufficiently stuffing themselves, Jake entered the backyard with Marissa and brought a bunch of booze with them. It wasn't long until the music started playing from the hidden speakers, and people were in the pool with drinks.

"Babe, I'll be back in a bit. I need to speak with Dino about some vendor issues we're having for the upcoming fall menu," Arnie said as he placed a kiss on top of Desmond's head.

When he was out of hearing distance Desmond grabbed two hard seltzers and dragged Gabriella to the far side of the pool, where there were some lounge chairs available. "Does it make me a terrible person that I'm not over the moon happy for Laurel and Matt?"

Gabriella settled on the lounge chair and shook her head slightly as she opened the can. "No, because I feel the same way."

"Why, what happened with you?"

Gabriella shook her head as she swallowed her drink. "You first. Still upset about Arnie?"

Desmond sighed as he watched Arnie at the table with Laurel's parents. "The food is a hit at their stores. So much so that they've expanded how much he's producing. He quit the restaurant a few weeks ago and has been working solely on this food line. I'm kinda stressing out about it. I know I'm making way more money in this role, but I feel like it's all on me."

"Have you ever thought of proposing to him?" Gabriella asked.

Desmond looked as if she smacked him across the face. "Are you serious?"

"Are you? Why does he have to do it? If you want to get engaged, then you man up and ask him. I know you want the stupid ring, just buy one for yourself too."

"That's not the point. He should love me enough to want to marry me."

"Shouldn't you love him just as much?"

"I do, bitch."

"Okay, Des. You want to be asked. I get it, but you can't be mad if he doesn't do it right away. You know he has a lot going on. If it's that important to you, you should do it."

Desmond huffed, crossed his arms and looked away and pouted for a few minutes. Gabriella finished her drink when Desmond finally spoke up. "So, what happened to you that has you all twisted about the engagement news?"

Gabriella kept her eyes glued to the pool in front of her as she spoke, "Liam cheated on me. Slept with a girl he works with in London. We're done. I blocked him."

"That explains all the missed calls and texts I got from him last night. I just told him I was drunk, and I'd call him later. I think he was pinging Arnie too."

"He did what?" Laurel's voice broke through, which caused the two of them to jump and look between them. Laurel stood there with a few hard seltzers in a bucket of ice.

"How long have you been there?" Desmond asked.

"Long enough to hear that Gabby was cheated on." She said as she placed the bucket on the floor between the chairs and sat on the end of Gabriella's lounge chair.

"It's not a big deal. I called him last night during the party and a girl answered the phone. I thought he was in the office. He wasn't. He was about to take a shower in his hotel room. Informed me that we were never exclusive, and what did I expect when I'm gone for so long. Which, he wasn't wrong. We never had a convo about being exclusive, and I'm not around much. So, I told him to have fun, and I hope that he finds his happiness. And then I blocked him."

"Jesus, Gabby, and here I am throwing around my engagement news." Laurel said with a sigh.

"Stop that. I'm so fucking happy for you. And I'm happy to hear that you aren't rushing into marriage. You and Matt are a beautiful couple, and he's a really good guy, Lau. It's all I could want for you. He's so beyond what that douchebag was in college. You are still you with him."

Laurel teared up, then jumped on top of Gabriella and hugged her tight. "Thank you. It's all I want for you too. I was never a huge fan of Liam, but you deserve happiness to. Just remember that, no matter who you choose."

"Yeah, I agree. Things are going to be awkward back home with Liam though. I guess we can kiss that friendship goodbye." Desmond said with a sad smile, then perked up and said, "but I've always been team Henry."

Gabriella rolled her eyes. "He kissed me last night."

"What?" Laurel yelled as she jumped off of Gabriella and sat back down as Desmond started to clap. "When did this happen?"

"In your kitchen, while everyone was getting ready."

"So, what does that mean?" Laurel pressed.

"Nothing, I think. He said goodbye last night and left. I called and left him a voicemail, but he was probably on the plane, and I haven't heard back. Maybe he's still in flight." Gabriella said with a shrug of her shoulders, opening another can of seltzer.

"Didn't May say he landed? I thought she said he called her like an hour ago," Desmond asked.

Laurel nodded her head, "yeah, he FaceTimed Matt a few minutes ago to congratulate us on our engagement. He looked exhausted and said he was on his way to the set. I'm sure he'll give you a call when he's settled in."

"Yeah, you're probably right." Gabriella said with a small smile. "And Des, I know that you and Arnie have your own friendship with Liam. Don't feel like you have to cut him out because of me."

"You know you come before everyone else, right? Unless it was my own flesh and blood, which could prove to be a tough choice for me. You're my family, Gabs."

"I know, and I love you for it. But I know Liam doesn't have many people that he's close with. Just, don't let our breakup effect your friendship. I'll be here until probably November; it will give me plenty of time to adjust to things. And I won't block him forever. I just need some space."

Desmond shook his head. "You're too forgiving, Gabs."

"Nah, but what I am is too hot. I'm jumping into this pool." Gabriella stated as she stood up, removed her tank top and lounge shorts, and jumped into the pool, then swam over to Jem and Patti, who were seated on the stairs as they drank beer.

"Hey babe!" Patti said as Gabriella swam up and sat on the step next to her. "Hey yourself, what's going on?"

"You're not going to believe it, but Patti is getting some insta-fame." Jem said with a smile.

"Oh?" Gabriella asked.

"There were pics of the red carpet, and someone commented on a picture of all of us that Laurel made us take, and they tagged a plus-size clothing company. Said they should look into the movie because they had real women in it. I got a private message from someone from the company saying that they would love

349

to have us model for some of their clothes. I think they said they were going to try to reach out to you, but I said I would totally do it!"

"That's awesome, Patti, but are you sure it's legit? There is a lot of bullshit out there on the internet." Gabriella warned.

"I think it is. I wanted to bring it up to you because if it was legit, you could let me know. Maybe we could do it together? I mean, I could always use the money. Every little bit helps for the restaurant. Plus, could you imagine me being a model?"

"I've always told you, you're beautiful, but you have to hear it from some clothing store to believe me?" Jem said with a scoff.

"You're my friend, of course you have to say those things to me."

"Meh," Jem said with a bland face, then smiled.

"I promise, Patti, if I hear from them, and it's legit, I'll let you know. And of course, I will do it with you." Gabriella said with a smile.

Brunch at Laurel's turned into an all-day party, which prompted Arnie and Joshua to cook some food in the kitchen, while Jake and Matt manned the grill. Matty had water gun fights with Max and his stepdad, and Gabriella, Jem and Patti were on cleanup duty to clear out the mess on the table before dinner. Desmond taught Darius and May how to play Scopa, while the parents were actively playing the game.

Dinner was a delicious success, which got Arnie and Joshua to exchange numbers so they could talk recipes. Matty left with his mom and stepdad, and said he was looked forward to his vacation with Matt and Laurel next week. Somehow, the dads challenged the guys to a game of flip cup, which entertained everyone to say the least. Desmond and Arnie teamed up with the fathers, while the girls cheered on the different teams.

After they grew bored with the cheering, the girls decided to have their own games, and started a game of beer pong, which Bob watched with sad puppy eyes from his flip cup game. Eventually Bob abandoned his post and wandered over to the girls, where he took over for Caroline.

Gabriella noticed May wandered off to the far side of the pool where she was on the phone. She made her way back over to the crowd, with Henry's face on the screen looked a little worse for wear. She walked around the whole party and allowed everyone to say hello. She stopped when she was next to Giuseppe. "Are you taking care of my baby sister over there?"

Giuseppe laughed, "you know we are. I'm even going to bring her to the airport tomorrow night to make sure she gets home safely."

"I appreciate it, G."

"I got you, H. You know we help each other out. By the way, you look like shit."

"Yeah, thanks. It's about three in the afternoon here, I'm still jetlagged, and I've been filming for about three hours already."

351

"Take it easy, H. Make sure you take care of yourself over there."

"Will do, G. May, take me around, I've got a few more minutes before they need me back on set."

May made the rounds and paused at everyone for them to say hello. Just as she made her way to Gabriella, Henry stopped her. "Hey, May, I've got to get going, they are calling me to set. Enjoy the rest of your time there, and make sure you let me know before you get on the flight, and when you land, okay?"

"Got it. Love you, Hank." She said with a smile before they disconnected the call. Gabriella watched as May sat down across from her at the table with a smile as she settled down.

"It was so nice to hear from him, yeah?"

"Yeah, I'm sure who ever got to speak with him enjoyed it."

"Oh, did you not get to speak with him? I'm sorry, I thought I got to everyone."

"No, I think everyone but me," Gabriella said with a sad smile, then downed the rest of her drink.

"Did you want to talk to him? I can try calling him back, but he did say he was called to set."

Gabriella shook her head. "No, I called him yesterday and left a message."

"I'm sure he'll call you back when he gets a minute. Do you have anything you want me to tell him the next time I speak with him?"

"Thanks, May, but I'm good. It's nothing very important."

***

Two weeks had gone by since the premiere, and there was not one word from Henry. Everyone had gone home except for her parents, who planned to stay with her until late August when her mom had to get back for her job. Laurel and Matt took Matty to Florida for two weeks so he could do all of the theme parks. She received a communication from the same person who contacted Patti about a campaign for the plus-sized clothing brand. It was a legit offer, and they agreed to do a photo shoot in October for their Christmas campaign.

The buzz of the movie had not died down yet, and everywhere she turned, there were commercials and posters and magazine covers. The interview they had done for Vanity Fair was the subject of all the gossip columns and news shows. People were obsessed over the photo that was cropped from the shoot and used in the article, one of her and Henry, with her head thrown back and her hands gripped in his hair and the base of his neck, his open lips against her neck with the slightest glimpse of his tongue.

It was beyond erotic, and she was so turned on by it. It was by far her favorite picture. She was tagged in the photo everywhere on social media, which started a frenzy of rumors about them, which was supported by their photos and interactions at the premiere.

She also received a few emails from Liam, which asked her to speak with him. He said he was sorry, and didn't realize how much it would affect their friendship. He said he missed her, and that he wanted to commit to her, that he could handle the long distance because it was her.

Desmond had spoken to him while he was still in London, before he made the next leg of his business trip to Tokyo. Desmond told her that he told Liam to give her time, that she needs to process what happened, but not to get his hopes up for them to continue their romantic endeavors. That maybe, after some time, they could rekindle their friendship, but he needed to leave her alone, but that he was welcomed to still speak with him and Arnie.

***

Three weeks later, Gabriella's parents were headed back to New York. Children were due back at school the first week of September, and Maria needed to set up her classroom for their arrival. They took her out to their new favorite restaurant for an early birthday celebration, since they wouldn't be here for her actual birthday.

Laurel was on set in Germany, where she filmed the female serial killer series for next three months, with hopes that she would be back home with Matt in time for Thanksgiving. Gabriella was asked to be on a few podcasts, where they interviewed her about her experience as a first-time actress. People were obsessed with the movie, and equally as obsessed as how she came to be a part of it.

She was always very generous with her answers and tried to explain the experience as authentically as possible. Any time the topic of Henry came up, she always dispelled the rumors with the "we are good friends" statement. When Riona was mentioned, Gabriella perfected the response of everything was always blown out of proportion, nothing like that ever happened, Riona was a talented actress, and she was fortunate to have spent time on set with her.

Whenever she could, she would plug Patti and Joshua's restaurant, and Darius's partner's boutique. She always spoke about Laurel's latest project, and Desmond's run as Raoul on Broadway. She always spoke about her strong friendship with them, and when asked if she would to act in any other movies, she would say that she wasn't actively pursuing it, but if the right opportunity came along, she would consider it, but she was very happy with her current job.

The one question she could never get away from was asking her about her personal life, if she was in a relationship or had a love interest. She slowly changed her answer from I recently got out of a relationship to no, no relationship, to there is someone, but our timing never worked out, so I am just focusing on myself at the moment.

The days alone in her house went by the slowest. She tried to keep herself busy with work, but it wasn't enough to keep her occupied. She would sit out on her deck and try to enjoy the sunshine, but it grew old. She would take walks down to the beach, comb the surf for seashells and beach glass. The collection she amassed was saved in a large glass vase in the living room.

Her birthday was no different than the other days she spent alone. She received phone calls, video calls, and text messages from her family and friends, but it was still radio silence from Henry. She ordered fish tacos from her favorite place on the pier and sat in her backyard alone with a fire in the firepit with an open a bottle of pinot grigio that she drank without a glass. She took a picture of her feet in front of the fire, the container of tacos in her lap, and the half-full bottle of wine and posted it on her social media, with a caption of happy birthday to me #cheersto26years #HBD #drunkandalone.

After the tacos were long gone and the bottle was nearly empty, Gabriella curled into herself on the Adirondack chair, her arms hugging the bottle to her chest. She looked at her phone and could make out a bunch of notifications from her post, and a few text messages, but she was having trouble focusing. She proceeded to her contacts, where she selected Henry's name. She listened to the phone ring, then it dumped her into his voicemail.

"Hey Henry, it's Gabriella. I heard through the grapevine that you landed safely, congratulations. And thanks for the call back. It's been about two months, I guess they are keeping you super busy on the set though. No time to call me back. I don't know if you know this, but it's my birthday today. Well, I guess yesterday where you are. Yeah, I'm celebrating with fire and a bottle of wine and myself. I'm so pathetic, I'm talking to your voicemail. Top box office for the past six weeks, is it? Pretty good for the movie. Oh, Patti and I were asked to do a campaign for a clothing store. For us plus sized ladies. You know, the kind that aren't good enough for most people. Is that why you aren't calling me? Am I not good enough for you?

"Actually, I know the answer to that, I'm not. I just wanted to thank you for giving a girl like me the thrill of a lifetime. I'm sure when I'm old and in the nursing home, I'll recall my glory days talking about the movie star who slummed it with me for a bit. Did you know that Liam cheated on me? Yup, slept with a co-worker on his business trip. Told me I'm away too much. I'm not worth waiting around for. You know that. It's why you don't call me.

"This is a really long voicemail. Sorry. I'm sorry. I'm sorry I'm not good enough. I'm sorry you wasted your time with me. Bye, Henry. Happy Birthday."

356

***

A consistent buzz interrupted her sleep, which made Gabriella open one eye and find her cell phone dance in front of her on her patio. She reached down to stop the incessant annoyance.

"Gabby, are you okay?" A panicked Laurel yelled into the phone.

"What, yeah, I'm fine. Why?"

"Where are you?"

Gabriella opened both eyes to find herself on the outdoor couch, with the fire pit smoldering in front of her. "Um, in my back yard?"

"At five in the morning?"

"Uh, yeah. Why are you calling me so early?"

"What did you do last night, Gabs?"

"I had tacos and a bonfire. Maybe some wine too," she said as she sat up and held her palm to her throbbing temple.

"Mmmhmm, wanna check your call log and tell me what else you did?"

Gabriella looked down at her phone and navigated to her calls. "Oh no, did I call Henry?"

"Sure did. Left him a long ass message too. What is going on, Gabby?"

"Oh, I think I'm going to be sick."

"Nah-uh, you're not puking on the phone with me. Why did you call him?"

"I don't know, I was drunk. How do you even know that I called him?"

"He called me just before to tell me to check on you."

"He's not speaking to me anymore, Lau."

"What are you talking about."

The tears fell out without her knowledge until they fell onto her lap. "He hasn't spoken to me since the premiere. We had kissed that night, we danced and spent a bunch of time together, but then when he left, he said goodbye and kissed me on the forehead. I called him that night and asked him to call me whenever he got a chance, and I never heard from him.

"When we were at your house the next day and he was on the call with May, he said hi to everyone, but when she got near me, he ended the call. May said that she was sure he'd call me back and asked if I wanted her to relay a message. I didn't. I haven't heard from him, and I feel like I need to. It's breaking me. I see all of the stuff for the movie, it's a constant reminder of him, but he's not speaking to me."

"Gabby, I didn't know any of this was going on. It was late by him when he called, and I'm sure he could tell you were drunk. He cares, Gabby, he wouldn't have called me this early to check on you if he didn't."

358

"Or he just didn't want it on his conscious if something happened to me."

"You don't sound good, Gabs. Do you want to come here? You could spend some time with me in Germany."

"No, I'm okay. I was just feeling really lonely yesterday. I'm wondering if it was a mistake to be out here for months. Maybe I should just stay in New York."

"But then you would be dealing with Liam right now. I think you should stay where you are. Why don't you get together with Jem, or Max, or Darius?"

"They are all working. Everyone is working."

"So then go to Lily's. You know she would let you use an office there. Maybe you'd feel better being around people."

"Yeah, it's not a bad idea."

"Why don't you go in the house and sleep in your bed. I've gotta run, lunch is over. I'll call you later tonight when I'm done shooting."

"Yeah, okay, love you, Lau."

"Love you too, Gabby."

Seventeen

"I'm so happy you're here!" Gabriella shouted as Patti exited the airport and headed towards her car that waited in the pick-up zone.

"I'm beyond happy to be here too! Can you believe it, this ugly mug is going to be in a catalog, and an online campaign," Patti said as she vogued, then ran over and hugged Gabriella before they were told to move it along by an airport employee.

"Are you sure it's okay that I stay with you for the few days I'm here?" Patti asked as Gabriella navigated her way through LAX.

"Stop, of course I'm sure, my parents said that you better stay in their room, because it's nicer than my office with a guest bed."

"Your parents are the best. So, have I missed anything since we spoke last?" Patti asked.

"Nope, not one thing. I started using a spare office in Lily's building to get me out of the house for work. It's been nice having a space to have meetings in. Other than that, I've been working on getting Desmond some non-Broadway parts. He filmed the baking competition show last month, and they loved him. They want him to come back for another competition."

"That's amazing for him. Wouldn't it be something if his boyfriend wound up on that show."

Gabriella laughed as they pulled up to her house. "This place is precious, Gabby. I'm in love. And it's walking distance to the beach?"

"Yes ma'am. Let's get you set up and we can go take a walk if you're feeling up to it."

Twenty minutes later, the two of them walked up to the beach. "So, anything else new and exciting with you?"

Gabriella shook her head, "not really. Oh! I started to volunteer at one of the local soup kitchens. I wanted to do something helpful with my extra time. And they are really good about letting me stay in the back, so no one recognizes me."

"Are you sure that's safe to do? I mean, it's a wonderful cause, but you're pretty famous right now, maybe you should wait until all of the movie buzz dies down?"

"No, really, it's fine. I took a page out of Henry's book, I wear a hat and sunglasses all the time outside, and no one recognizes me.

"How is he doing on the set?"

"I have no idea. I haven't spoken to him since July."

"No, that can't be true,' Patti said taken aback.

362

"Yup. I made an ass of myself and drunk dialed him on my birthday. That was the last time I reached out. It was fun while it lasted, I guess," Gabriella said with a shrug.

"Wow, the beach really is beautiful," Patti said after a deep inhale of the sea breeze.

"Do you want to grab some dinner, there are some great places right on the beach that we can eat outside at." Gabriella suggested.

Patti agreed as they made their way to a small place on the beach. After they were seated outside and ordered a round of pina coladas, Patti blurted out, "I had sex with Joshua."

"I'm sorry, what?" Gabriella said in shock, the straw of her drink rested against her open mouth.

"Yeah, um, so we've been spending a lot of time together. Like a lot of time. We're always at the restaurant together, totally consumed with it. I mean, the business is phenomenal, we're always busy. One night we got to talking after we closed, and we were going over some of our inventory stuff in the back office. Joshua mentioned how long it's been since he's been out with a woman, because we're constantly at work.

"I commiserated with him, but lord knows it just isn't because of work for me. It's been a long time since I've had relations. He said he's had a hard go of it since his divorce a few years ago. Anyway, we were joking around about how long it had been since either of us had gotten laid. After going back to our work, he asked why we didn't just help each other out.

363

"We'd jokingly been referring to one another as work spouses for the longest time, and I can't say I've ever been super attracted to him, he was just always my buddy Joshua. Any who, one thing led to another, and we wound up having sex in our office."

"Oh, wow! When did this happen?"

"Back in August. And it's been happening since."

"What? Patti! How could you not tell me this happened? It's been going on for months!"

"I know, I know. At first, I thought it was a one-time thing. But then every time we closed together and did office work, we would 'work the office'. Then he asked me one day that we both had off if I wanted to go to dinner with him. I didn't think much of it at first, but then he took me back to my place and I invited him in, and well, you know."

"So, are you dating?"

"Do people call it that at my age?"

"You're not in your seventies, Patti. Yes, I believe forty-year-olds call it dating."

"Alright, then I guess we are. We never put a label on it. It just keeps happening."

"Can I offer you some advice? Have the discussion. Don't do what I did with Liam and just assume that you're in a relationship when you really aren't."

"I can do that."

"So, how is it? Is it weird, because you guys have been co-workers for so long?"

"Honey, he may not look like much, but he's definitely packing, and he knows exactly what to do with it," she said with a wink, and she sucked down her pina colada. "We're definitely going to need more of these."

***

After dinner, they made their way down the beach to the ale house, where they spent a few hours drinking their way through the menu. After they devoured a large plate of nachos, the girls stumbled out of the bar and headed back to Gabriella's house.

"Gabby, I've been dancing around the dead horse all night, but I've got my switch and I'm ready to beat it again. Why haven't you spoken to Henry in three months?"

"I think the real question, my dear, is why hasn't he spoken to me in three months. I tried calling, twice, and failed in a spectacular fashion in a drunken birthday tirade."

"I think I need to fix this."

"I think you need to fess up why you never told me you were sleeping with Joshua. You've been dodging that topic like it's a red rubber ball in gym class."

"Oooh! Look whose got her funny drunk girl going tonight."

Gabriella laughed as they made it to her front door. She missed placing the key in the lock three times, until she finally got it with the help of her phone's flashlight. As they stumbled through the door, Gabriella announced, "I gotta pee like a freaking racehorse. Lock the door behind you."

She took a little longer than usual during her impaired state, then left the bathroom to find Patti out on her patio, mid laughter. She headed into her kitchen to grab some water bottles when she heard Patti begin to talk.

"Helloooooo handsome!"

Gabriella laughed to herself as she took some ibuprofen out of her cabinet and headed towards the patio door and thought how cute Patti was with Joshua.

"Do you know where I am right now? No. Guess again."

Gabriella rounded the outdoor sofa and dropped the water bottle in Patti's lap, which caused her to groan. "Oh, wait, let me put it on speaker, you can guess who it is."

Patti put the phone on speaker and nudged Gabriella in the arm. "Say hello."

"Hello person I'm supposed to be thinking is a random stranger but it really Patti's lover. Hi Joshua! I miss you!" Gabriella shouted out on the phone.

"Oh my god, it's not Joshua!" Patti yelled out in her loud drunk voice.

"Sure, it isn't. I have to say, Joshua, I never saw it coming. But I'm pleasantly surprised and completely support your love affair. Just treat my girl well, or I'm coming to South D and kicking some ass." Gabriella said with a wink and a giggle.

"Um, Patti, can you take me off of speaker?" A deep voice with a British accent commanded through the phone.

Gabriella's face turned ashen when she realized Patti didn't lie. The smile that was splayed across her face suddenly dropped and Patti's eyes went wide as she complied with what Henry asked of her.

She held the phone to her ear as she listed to him speak, her head nodded slightly in response. "Yeah, I'm out here to do a photo shoot in a day and a half with Gabby. Yeah, we're safe. We just got back from the bar by her house."

She paused as Henry spoke some more, and Gabriella watched on in horror, the numb feeling seeped into her chest and slowly made its way through her limbs. "Yes, I really am with Joshua now. Thanks, Henry, that means a lot." She stood up from the couch and made her way to the door. "Yeah, I can go somewhere to talk in private."

Gabriella watched as Patti walked into the house and closed the sliding door behind her. It was obvious now that Henry was avoiding her. As if she walked through a tunnel, she got up and went into the house, Patti's hushed voice in the living room stopped as she went to her room, pulled out a joint from her stash, and returned to the patio. She laid across the outdoor sofa and tried to smoke her way through the tears. She just wanted to be numb and forget everything to do with Henry Anderson.

Patti stood at the patio door and watched Gabriella as she wrapped up her phone call. "What is she doing right now?" Henry asked.

"She's laying outside, smoking weed and crying."

"What? Since when does she do that?"

"I don't know, Henry. Why don't you just talk to her and ask her yourself."

"I can't do that. Can you let Laurel know what she's doing?"

"Jesus, Henry. What is going on? Why haven't you spoken to her since the premiere? We've all been in touch with you. I had no idea until I asked her how you were doing on set. She tried to answer nonchalantly, but I could see it in her eyes. She's hurting don't 'cha know."

"It just has to be this way, Patti. Just make sure she's okay while you're there. And let Laurel know. Good luck with your photo shoot. Give me a ring when you're back home."

Patti looked down at the disconnected call and shook her head and gave Gabriella a few more moments to herself before she made her way out.

"Hey, girl, keeping the party going without me?"

Gabriella looked up through damp lashes and sat up, then tucked her legs to her chest and hugged herself and she took another hit. Patti took a seat next to her and opened a bottle of water. "Since when do you do that?"

Gabriella shrugged. "It calms me, and it's legal here."

"Do you feel like you need to be calmed?

"I feel like I need to go to bed. Feel free to hang out as long as you want. I'll see you in the morning."

Gabriella stubbed out the joint and carried it in with her and placed it back with her stash. She changed into her pajamas and turned out the lights. As she laid in the dark, she let the tears drip down her face and promised herself that this was the last time she would ever shed a tear over any man, especially Henry Anderson.

***

Gabriella hid away in her office for most of the next day, which was already her plan since she had meetings she couldn't cancel. Jem had picked Patti up to spend the day together and agreed that Gabriella would meet them out for dinner.

She met them at a pub in Hollywood, since Patti was still determined to play tourist. To her pleasant surprise, Max, Matt, and Darius sat at the high top with the girls. "Hey! You made it," Matt said as she said her hellos to the group.

"Yeah, sorry, my last meeting ran late, but fabulous news for Desmond. I got him an audition for a streaming service show. Fingers crossed it works out."

"We already ordered. Do you want me to get you anything?" Max asked as she sat down next to him.

"No, I'll go up to the bar and get something," she said with a smile, then made her way to put in a food order. She returned to the table with two glasses in her hand.

"Double fisting tonight, Gabby?" Matt asked with a smile.

"Oh yeah, I'm going hard. Nothing gets the night going like some ginger ale and some sweet H2O." She said with a laugh as she settled into her seat.

"No drinking for you?" Jem asked with her eyebrows raised.

"No, Patti and I get to pretend to be cover girls tomorrow. Plus, I had my fill of booze last night to keep me away from it for the rest of the week."

The conversation flowed as the food was brought to the table. Max told them about his adventures of becoming a cat dad, and how they have acclimated to each other. "Do you know how much money I spent on this cat? I bought him a bed, a bunch of stimulating toys, one of those damn tower things that takes up a corner of my living room. Does he use any of it? No. He likes the damn carboard box the toys were delivered in." Max complained.

Matt slid around to the spot next to Gabriella and sat down. "So, how's it going?"

"Let me guess, I was the topic of conversation before my arrival and this is an intervention?"

Matt laughed. "Well, something like that. You have been the topic of conversation with a few conversations I've been having. But this is not an intervention."

"Matt, I'm fine. And not the fine a woman says when she isn't. It's been a bit of an adjustment, but I'm good."

"You know I'm here for you if you need anything, right? I know I'm not Laurel or Desmond, but I am here. We just care about you, and we want to make sure you're okay. I may or may not have been tapped to be on Gabby watch while Laurel is away."

"I know, Matt, and I appreciate it. Actually, if you aren't busy this weekend, I was thinking of going to the shelter and adopting a dog."

"Really? Are you sure that's a good idea? You're always so busy."

"I know, but I have the flexibility to work from home, and I think it would be good to have a companion. I think it would help with the loneliness."

"Alright, Gabby, I'll go with you. Sounds like fun."

***

The next day, Gabriella and Patti went to the photo shoot, where they were titled as brand ambassadors for the winter line. Some photos they had the girls dress in the same outfit, to show what it would look like on different body types. Other photos of them together were in different outfits, and other photos were of them individually.

During their photo shoot, a body-positive blogger was on site to ask them questions and cover the shoot. "Hi ladies, I hope you don't mind that I'm covering the shoot. I'm Shelly, and I have a blog, Un-Shelled, and I cover everything body positive. I'm always invited here to review the new fashion line that they put out, but when they said you two would be here, I freaked. I saw The Edge of Time three times already. I'm obsessed! It's so nice to meet you!"

"I know your blog!" Patti yelled out in excitement. "I love your stuff! It's so nice to meet ya!"

Shelley laughed and tucked her shoulder-length blonde hair behind her ear. "Wow, it's so nice to meet a fan. I'm a huge fan of you too. You're an inspiration to us big girls. I'm not sure if ladies like us would really be at a brothel, but it was nice to see the inclusion in the film. I wish you had more screen time."

Patti laughed, "I was in the background of a few other scenes, I think I may have been in the market during the colonial time. But my real job was feeding all of the cast and crew."

"I just love your accent. Where are you from?"

"South Dakota, born and raised. I feel like a fish out of water out here in California, but I love to visit my friends here." Patti said with a smile as she nudged her elbow into Gabriella's side. The awkwardness from the first night had melted away after the outing with the group.

"Oh my gosh, I'm so sorry, I'm being so rude. I'm a huge fan of you too, Gabriella."

"It's okay. I'm thoroughly enjoying the attention being focused on someone else. Patti is an amazing chef. Did you know that she opened a new restaurant about a year ago? She quit her job, partnered with her co-worker, and took a chance. And it's been really successful." Gabriella gushed about her friend.

"No kidding? Patti, I would love to feature you in the blog. Maybe you could share some of your favorite recipes?" Shelly suggested.

"I'd just love that, don't 'cha know." Patti said with a huge smile.

"Awesome! So, I was wondering if I could ask you guys some questions. Maybe we could grab a coffee or something when the shoot is done?"

The girls agreed, then continued their shoot. The clothing company offered them to take home an outfit they modeled. Patti opted for a red lace dress, black blazer, and a pair of black heels. Gabriella selected a pair of faux leather leggings, black booties, and an off the shoulder fuzzy white tunic. After saying their goodbyes to the photographer and staff, they headed to a nearby coffee shop with the blogger.

"So, I always ask my subjects, have you ever felt uncomfortable with your body?" Shelly asked as she sipped her Americano.

"Well, I'd say it's a mixed bag. My momma always told me that beauty is subjective, and that only a real man could handle a real woman. I think that painted a nice picture for me growing up. My whole family is on the larger size, big bones and all that. But when I was in my twenties, I realized there were no real men. They all wanted to skinny-minnies. I think it did some damage to my self-esteem. I did have a few boyfriends, but no one stayed around. But I learned to love myself, and now things are looking up." Patti answered.

Shelly smiled and looked to Gabriella.

"Oh, I'm always uncomfortable. I'm sure people don't want to hear it, but it's true. No matter what size I've been, there have always been comments about my weight. It's always been you should lose weight, or then when I was so busy that I didn't eat, it was you look sick, you need to gain weight. I've never been thin. The smallest size I've ever been was a ten, and that was for a few months in college. It's very soul-crushing to only be recognized for how you look. I'd gotten past it for a while, but now being thrown into the public eye just makes it worse. People are cruel. And when you hear enough of how disgusting you are, or how you don't belong with certain people, and all the ways you should crawl under the rock you came from and die, you start to believe it."

"Wow. That's so insightful. A lot of my readers feel the same way. I can't even imagine hearing that in the public."

"You'll have the people who say that if you don't want to hear it, then don't put yourself out there. I don't think that should be the case. People should be able to do what they desire, regardless of what public opinion would be. For me, I didn't seek this out. I know Patti didn't seek this out. We were doing another job and helped out because that is the kind of people we are. For those who think otherwise, and this is a direct quote and feel free to use it, you can go fuck yourself. Seriously, I don't know where you come off thinking you have the right to cast judgement on me, or anyone, sitting at home on your throne with your Cheetos-dusted fingers. You need to take a good, hard look in the mirror and find what makes you so hateful that you feel the need to put others down for your own enjoyment."

Patti began to clap in response as Shelly smiled and nodded along. "Seems like you've been holding some animosity towards the public and their opinions."

"Well, aren't you? Isn't that why you started the blog? I know it's to celebrate life and different shapes and sizes and abilities, but wasn't that birthed from the negativity that we all receive? To make something positive?" Gabby questioned.

"You aren't wrong," Shelley said with a smile. "I would love to do a follow-up with you both."

"I'm not sure if I want to do that, but I know Patti would be amazing to interview. Aside from my opinions, I'm a rather boring person."

"Oh, okay. Can I at least get a selfie with you guys for the blog?"

"Of course."

***

"Have you given any more thought about joining the Ortera Descent cast?" Veronica asked from the laptop screen.

Gabriella gnawed on her lip as Scampi, her six-month-old Yorkie laid by her feet in his dog bed, as he happily chewed on a rubber bone. "I am still on the fence about it. I know I will have to audition, but could you tell me more about it. Will it be another non-speaking role?"

"There are plenty of non-speaking roles, but that's not what I envisioned for you. The film is about Ortera, the queen of the Amazons, and her lineage. I was thinking you would be one of the daughters. Since it's about the Amazons, there is going to be a lot of physical training needed. There are going to be battle scenes, and if I get to cast you in the role I want, you'll be killed by Achilles in the Trojan War."

Gabriella's cellphone buzzed for the third time in the past few minutes, her mother's face showing on the screen. "Sorry, Veronica, I have to take this, my mother has been calling non-stop. Just give me a second."

"Yeah, of course," Veronica said as she continued to type.

"Hey Mom, can I call you back, I'm in a meeting?"

"Gabby, it's your father," Maria said between sobs on the phone.

"Oh my god, Mom, what happened?"

Veronica's eyes lifted to the camera and watched as Gabriella took the call. Maria continued to sob as she tried to choke out the words.

376

"Mom, you have to calm down, I can't understand you."

Is everything all right? Veronica typed into the messenger part of their call. Gabriella shook her head in response.

"Your father was outside raking. He fell to the floor. We're in the ambulance. They think it's his heart."

"Oh my god! Is he okay? Is he breathing?"

"They brought him back, but he's not awake. I don't know what is going to happen." Maria cried.

"Okay, Mom, I need you to breathe. I can't have you winding up like dad. I'm going to book a flight as soon as I can. Can you let me know which hospital they are taking him to?"

"South Shore."

"Okay, did you call anyone else?"

"No." Maria sobbed.

"Mom, listen to me, I'm going to call Sierra. I'll have her meet you at the hospital, so you aren't alone. I will be there as soon as I can. Keep me updated on dad's condition, okay?"

"Okay. We just got to the hospital. I love you."

"I love you too, Mom."

"What is going on, Gabriella? It sounds important." Veronica asked.

"I'm so sorry, Veronica, can we do this at a later date? My father is being rushed to the hospital."

"Of course. Forgive my ignorance, but where is South Shore hospital? Is it near San Diego?"

"No, it's in New York. Long Island. I have to get a flight."

"Let me take care of that for you. My production company has a private plane, I'll get it ready for you. How soon can you be at Van Nuys?"

"I'll get a car service to take me over. Probably an hour?"

"I'll handle it all. Just send me your address and I'll get the driver to get you in twenty minutes. Go get yourself ready and make whatever phone call you need to."

"You are a god sent, Veronica. I can't thank you enough for this."

"It's my pleasure. Just make sure your dad is okay. And don't forget to bring your pup. You can pay me back by agreeing to do the film." Veronica gave a wink, then ended the call.

Gabriella jumped up and packed a weekender bag and included her electronics and anything she would need for the puppy. She dialed Sierra as she dashed around the house and gathered her belongings and made sure everything was locked and turned off.

"Hey, Gabby! What's up?"

"Sierra, I need you to go to South Shore Hospital. Dad was taken in an ambulance. Mom called and what I made out was it was something with his heart. She went in the ambulance with him and she's by herself."

"Christ, Gabby. I'll head over right now. Is there anything I can do for you?" Sierra asked as she gathered her keys and coat.

"No, I'm flying out in an hour. I'll meet you at the hospital. Thank you for doing this, Sierra."

"No thanks needed. I'll let everyone know, and I'll get Des or Arnie to pick you up from the airport."

"Okay, I'll get them to land at Republic. It's going to be the closest to the hospital."

"Have a safe trip, Gabby. I'll keep Maria safe."

***

When the plane touched down on Long Island, Gabriella's phone exploded with text messages from all of her friends. She gathered her bag and the pet carrier and headed down to the tarmac to where Desmond was waited for her.

He threw his arms around her and squeezed her tight. "Come on, let's get over there. Giuseppe was still in surgery the last I heard, which was a few minutes ago."

Scampi cried from his carrier, so Gabriella opened it and held him in her lap as they made their way to the hospital.

"Look at this little fluff ball! Let me call Arnie and tell him to meet us outside so he can take care of this little guy. I doubt they will let him into the hospital."

Gabriella nodded her head in agreement as she sat in silence, her nerves frayed at this point. Scampi gnawed on her fingers and then licked them as Desmond made the call.

They arrived at the hospital twenty minutes later and met Arnie at the front entrance, where Gabriella handed him Scampi and ran into the hospital and left her belongings in the car. After she checked in with security, they instructed her where the cardiac wing was and where she could find her mother.

"Mom!" Gabriella called out as she rounded the corner to the waiting room.

"Gabby!" Maria cried as she ran over and flung her arms around her daughter. "I'm so happy you are here."

"How's Dad? Any updates? Des said he was in surgery."

"He's out. The doctor came by about fifteen minutes ago. They said he's in recovery, and we can see him in about an hour. How was your flight?"

Gabriella let out a huge sigh of relief. "I'm so glad he's okay. I've been a nervous wreck. The flight was good. I was able to get over here on a private jet, so it took less time than I expected."

"Private jet? How did you do that?"

"I was in a meeting with a director when you called. She set it up. Looks like I'm going to be in another film to thank her for her generosity."

"I heard he's out of surgery," Dino said as he carried in a cardboard box full of food, followed by Caroline with a small cooler. "You guys must be starving, we brought food."

"Thank you, guys. I've been too nervous to eat," Caroline said as she greeted them. Sierra helped Caroline distribute the food as Marco entered the waiting room.

"Sorry, I just got out of work and came straight here. I saw Desmond downstairs. He said he was going to take Arnie back to your house, Maria. The dog was not happy being in the car with them. He said he'd be back after they get him settled in."

An hour and a half later, Maria and Gabriella were allowed to visit Giuseppe briefly. They entered the recovery room, where he was asleep.

"Honey, we're here." Maria said softly which made Giuseppe open his eyes.

"Hey," he said with a small smile.

"Gabby is here too," Maria said with a smile.

"Hey, Gabby. Is this all it takes to get you home sooner?" He said with a small chuckle.

"You scared the shit out of me, Dad! I'm so glad you are okay."

"How are you feeling?" Maria asked as she gently caressed his hair.

"Tired. Very tired."

"We'll let you get your rest, Dad. We'll be back when you're in your own room. I'm glad you're okay," she said before she kissed her father on his cheek.

"Gabby, give me a minute with your dad?" Maria asked as she held his hand.

Gabriella nodded, then slowly made her way out of the room. Rather than go back to the waiting room, she wandered over a stairwell and descended the stairs, then settled down at the bottom of one set. She tried to stifle a sob, but it broke through, and the tears escaped the prison of her eyes. She rocked herself on the step as she released all the stress and nerves she carried since her mother called her that morning.

She looked at her phone and saw that it was already after ten at night. She scrolled through all of the messages that she ignored, and saw messages from Laurel, Matt, Patti, Bob, Lily, Veronica, and Max. There were missed calls from Laurel, Darius, and Matt. In her despair, there was only one person she wanted to reach out to.

The phone rang a few times, then the familiar voice mail picked up. Her sobs were recorded before she was able to stop them. "My dad is in the hospital. He had a heart attack. They operated on him. He's out now." She hung up and sighed, then pulled herself together and made her way to the waiting room, where Desmond waited to take her and her mother home.

Eighteen

Over the next two days, Gabriella and Maria took shifts in the hospital. Gabriella covered the day shift when Maria was at work, they overlapped around four in the afternoon, and then Gabriella went back to her parents to work. Sierra was nice enough to watch Scampi during the day and amazingly started to train him.

On the third day of Giuseppe's hospital stay, Maria had meetings after school, so Gabriella spent the whole day. Her father fell asleep around noon, so she took the opportunity to work on her laptop in the guest chair. She popped her headphones in when Lily called later that evening for a quick meeting.

"It looks like Laurel is off for the next two months from filming. She has a photo shoot scheduled with the makeup line for their Valentine campaign. That is in the first week of December. The next thing is in mid-January, which is the promotion of the project she did in Vancouver. After that, it looks like her next project starts production in March." Gabriella reviewed.

"Okay, did I tell you that a few radio shows reached out? They want to interview her. One is in L.A.; the other is in New York. Can we work those in? They both said she didn't necessarily need to be in the studio, she could call in." Lily requested.

"I know she'll want to do the New York one in person. She used to listen to them when she would get ready for school. When is that one?"

"December or January. I guess the sooner the better."

"She is planning to be back in New York the second week of December. See if they can do it then. And the L.A. one?"

"I think they want her in November."

"That's in a week. She isn't getting home from Germany until the fifth. They will let her do it via the phone?"

"Yes, that's what they said."

"Can give her a week or two to unwind? Maybe do it for the week of the fifteenth?"

"Got it. Shit, Gabby, I gotta run. One of my new clients is here and causing a commotion, and Tasha looks like she might cry or beat this shit out of him."

Gabriella laughed as Lily disconnected the call, the name Ella was called out as a question from within the room.

Her heart started a stampede in her chest as the butterflies exploded in her stomach. She caught her breath and tried to calm herself and looked down at her computer. She couldn't believe that he had finally showed up, she had hoped for a phone call, or maybe a text message, but for him to show up in person, it made her instantly forgive him for the past three months.

She looked up from her computer and anticipated his broad shoulders and dark hair, his sparkling blue eyes and his million-dollar, panty-dropping smile. Instead, she was met by a tall man with a firm build and dirty blonde hair, with a pair of glasses covering hazel eyes.

"Gabriella? Is that you?"

"Brad?"

"Yes, or Doctor Westerberg as I'm know around here. I can't believe you're here. I was shocked when I saw your dad's name in my case load. I've been checking on him since he was out of recovery, but I've always just seen your mom."

Gabriella was in shock as she watched the boy who started it all walk into the room, donned in a lab coat and scrubs. He picked up the chart from the end of Giuseppe's bed and flipped through it as he checked all the monitors as he went along.

"Your dad is healing nicely. I think we can release him in another day or two." Brad said with a smile as he wrote some notes in the chart.

"What are you doing here?" Gabriella asked, still in shock.

"I'm doing my residency here." He said with a smile as he closed the file and placed it back on the end of the bed. He stood there and studied her as he maintained the smile, the shook his head slightly. "It's really nice to see you again, Gabriella."

Gabriella just sat there, unable to speak. Brad chuckled to himself as he began to walk out of the room. "Listen, my shift is ending now, I'm not sure if maybe you'd want to get a cup of coffee, or maybe dinner? Maybe we could catch up? Maybe you could let me grovel for your forgiveness properly?"

"She would love to," Giuseppe said from the bed.

"Dad, what the hell?"

"Go, you've been here all day. It's already after dinner. Besides, Doctor Westerberg over here is an okay guy, even though he's still a Tom Brady fan."

"Dad, no. Someone needs to stay with you."

"Don't make me get out of this bed, Gabby. You've been here all day while I've slept. Stop working and go out."

"Yeah, but you're up now."

"And I'd like some time to myself to watch the game. Go."

"I'll just go to my locker and change. There is a nice restaurant right up the block we could walk to." Brad said with a hopeful tone.

Gabriella looked at her father, then at Brad, and back to her father. "Fine. I'll pack up my stuff and meet you down at the main entrance."

Brad nodded and left the room as Gabriella turned to her father. "What the fuck was that, Dad?"

"Watch it. I know you two had a falling out, but it was almost a decade ago. Bury the hatchet. Life's too short for these kinds of things."

"What are you, some Zen buddha master now?"

"Confucius say man who have heart attack have new view on life. Just go an enjoy yourself tonight. No one says you ever have to see him again. Maybe you'll get whatever closure you've needed."

***

Gabriella made it to the main floor to find Brad in a pair of jeans and sneakers with a sweatshirt and a jacket. "Thanks for coming. I wouldn't have blamed you if you stood me up. I'm sorry that I'm not dressed nicer."

Gabriella eyed him, then gestured her hand to herself as she pointed out the leggings, boots, and sweatshirt she was wearing, along with her hair thrown up in a messy bun, without a trace of makeup on her face. Brad laughed and let her pass through the automatic doors before him.

"I promise, the place we're going to isn't too fancy. Some of us go here after a long shift. Sorry, I'm talking a lot. I'm just really nervous and can't believe you're actually here."

"Brad, seriously, relax. I'm here. My dad is in the hospital and I'm here. It's not a big thing. Aside from his heart attack."

Brad shoved his hands into his jacket pockets. "Are you okay with walking? It's like a five-minute walk. Or I can get my car?"

"I can handle the walk. I live in the city, I walk everywhere."

Brad laughed, "Do you? That's nice. I thought you were in California now."

"Part time. But my primary residence in Manhattan."

"Wow, bi-coastal, that has to be nice. At least you can escape the winters for warmer weather."

"I stay here in the winter. Summers in the city are too brutal."

"It sounds nice to get away from here. I'm still at my parents. I know, super lame. But my mom was diagnosed with MS a few years back, and my dad is still working as a financial advisor, and he's trying to get my older brother up to speed so he can retire someday, so I stay with them when I'm not working crazy shifts myself."

They made it to the restaurant and Brad waved to the bartender and pointed to a small booth in the back. The bartender acknowledged him and turned her attention to the patrons at the bar. They settled into the booth, studied the menu on the table, then placed their order with the waitress.

"So, how have you been?" Brad asked with a smile.

Gabriella shrugged her shoulder, "okay, I guess. I've just been working. I manage Laurel and Desmond. I spend half of my time in New York and half in L.A. I somehow got conned into being an extra for a movie last year and somehow it became a bigger role than it was supposed to be. Oh, and I just got a dog a few weeks ago."

"What kind of dog?"

"A Yorkie named Scampi."

390

"That's adorable. I would love to have a pet, but unfortunately my hours won't allow it. My hours don't really allow for anything, but it will be worth it."

"Have you kept in touch with anyone from high school?" Gabriella asked as she sipped on her ginger ale.

"I've kept in touch with Steve somewhat. He moved upstate. Met a girl in college and got married right away. They already have two kids. He's up near Buffalo. I've seen Evelyn around. She lives in Nassau County, but she visits her parents every other weekend."

"Ever hear from Jordan?"

Brad shook his head. "No, I see her post online. Looks like she's trying to get famous posing for pictures. Not really sure what she is up to, I think she moved down to Florida. How about you? You talk to anyone from then?"

"Laurel and Desmond. I keep my circle small."

"You must have more friends than that." He said with a smile.

"Sure, but no one from school. I became very close with some of the staff from the movie."

"Does that include a famous actor?"

Gabriella rolled her eyes. "Please, not you, too."

"Look, I know what I said to you when we chatted online was out of line. But really, I'm not stupid."

"Your track record proves otherwise."

"Still so snarky," Brad said with a laugh. Gabriella shrugged her shoulder, a small smile formed on her face.

Their food was delivered, and they ate in a comfortable silence. Brad laughed when he realized what she ordered.

"What's so funny?"

"You. Nothing has changed. You got chicken fingers and a side salad."

"So?"

"It's like a classier version of the nuggets and side salad I use to bring you on your breaks at work."

Gabriella laughed for the first time that night. "Maybe my choice of food hasn't changed, but that might be it."

***

Brad insisted he pay the check, then the two of them headed back to the hospital. "Okay, so I'm going to take a chance at ruining this whole night and bring up the elephant in the room."

Gabriella looked at him and cocked an eyebrow, "is that a weight joke?"

392

His hand covered his face as she shook his head. "Wow, I'm really screwing this up."

"I'm just fucking with you, go ahead."

He eyeballed her to judge her reaction. She gestured with her hand to continue. "Alright. I was a complete asshole in high school. You were completely right, I had feelings for you, but didn't want to act on them because I was afraid of what people thought. And it was so wrong of me, and you really deserved better. It is true, I did have a crush on Laurel, and it was honestly the reason I started talking to you. But that was it. Our friendship was real. And those kisses were real. And what we did on the boat, however unsatisfactory for you it was because I was an inexperienced and selfish asshole, was real. And I'm so incredibly sorry, from the bottom of my heart, that I made you feel like it wasn't, or that you were less than what you really were to me. You were everything, and I was a fool to mess it up the way I did.

"I also had no right to talk about what we could have been if I hadn't fucked up. There is no way of knowing that, and it wasn't right for me to even bring that up. I know that we aren't who we were in high school."

Gabriella stood there on the sidewalk of Main Street near midnight on an October night in the middle of the week, and heard the words that should have brought her comfort and closure. Instead, it made her shut down more. "If it makes you feel any better, you were just the first in a line of men who thought I wasn't good enough."

She started to walk towards the entrance of the hospital as Brad reached out and held onto her arm. "That doesn't make me feel better at all. Damn it, Gabby. I don't even know what to do with that."

Gabriella shrugged. "There isn't anything for you to do with it. It's just a fact. I need to get home, it's been a long day, and have an early meeting with Desmond and a charity he works with. It was nice seeing you again, Brad. Thank you for dinner and thank you for taking care of my father."

Gabriella smiled, then headed to the parking lot where she left her car that morning. "For what it's worth, I appreciate your apology. But we shouldn't dwell in the past. Have a good night."

***

"You had dinner with Brad Westerberg last night?" Desmond asked as they spoke on the computer.

"How do you even know that?"

"There was a post online. One of his doctor friends was at the bar and took a picture of the two of you and posted it on his social media to bust his balls about finally being on a date. Then our former bestie Evelyn commented on it that it was you and tagged you in the comment. Of course, that got attention, and now people are speculating that you have a new man in your life."

"Lovely."

"Even better? Jordan, that sewer rat, started posting throwback photos of us from high school, tagging everyone in them. I guess she's trying to get her fifteen minutes of fame in."

Gabriella sighed and rubbed her face. "Wonderful. Can we talk about the charity work before we have to get on the phone with them?"

"Nice try, bitch. What happened last night?"

"Nothing. He's my father's doctor. Or one of them. He came in the room when I was there and asked to go out to catch up and my dad answered for me. We talked about how our lives are, and he apologized for everything that happened in high school. Said that he had feelings, and he didn't want people to judge him, so that's it. I thanked him for the apology and went home."

"Will you talk to him again?"

"No. My dad said to go and get the closure I needed. Was it nice to hear the truth? Sure, but it doesn't change anything."

"So, what happens if you run into him again?"

"I say hello and be cordial, like a normal human being?"

"Since when have you been categorized as that?"

Gabriella stuck out her tongue and gave the middle finger to the camera, which prompted Desmond to blow a kiss back.

"Seriously though, you are cool with him now?"

"Define cool."

"Not wanting to castrate him? Can be in the same vicinity as him for longer than five minutes?"

"I think I proved that last night. Are you wanting to hang out with him or something?"

"I've always been team Gabby, you know that. And I was disgusted by the way he treated you. But I was good friends with him at one point. We all lost a friend when he pulled that shit. It was the equivalent of your middle school fall out with Laurel."

"Des, I would have never held it against you if you wanted to be friends with him."

"You are such a liar. And I didn't want to be friends with the person he was at prom. But it sounds like maybe he's come to terms with his doucheness. Maybe that's someone I could reconnect with."

"Des, you have my blessing, reconnect with him. It might be good to have another friend who knew you before you became mister Broadway. Now, can we focus on the call?"

"Yes ma'am. But one last thing, I am going to reach out to him."

"Have at it, doll."

***

"Looking good, dad! You ready to get out of here?" Gabriella asked as she walked into his hospital room. She kissed him and her mother hello, then settled in one of the guest chairs.

"That I am. After the doctor goes over my chart with primary doctor, and they agree on my release, I should be out of here. The nurse told me hopefully tonight, but tomorrow morning the latest."

"How was you call this morning?" Maria asked.

"It was good. We've got some events planned for the holidays, so Desmond and I will be helping with those. We're also going to try to rope Laurel into it too, it will help the community center, and the PR can't hurt, so it's a win-win."

Gabriella turned her attention to a white takeout bag on the tray next to her father's hospital food. "Mom, did you bring dad fast food?"

"No, I didn't. It has your name on it." Maria said as she reached for the bag and gave it to her daughter.

Gabriella arched an eyebrow as she looked at her name scrawled in unfamiliar handwriting. She opened the bag and let out a laugh as she saw chicken nuggets and a side salad. "Doctor Westerberg had that delivered by one of the nurses when she reported to her shift not too long ago."

"And how did he know what time I was coming, Dad?"

Giuseppe shrugged his shoulders in response as Gabriella shook her head at her father. "Stop meddling."

"What? I heard that you and that idiot broke up."

"So? I don't need to be in a relationship. Give me a break."

"He means well, *Bambolina*. We just want you to be happy."

"I know, Mom. And I am. Just let me be."

"Knock-knock," a voice said from the doorway. Desmond walked in with a large pink squishy pillow in the shape of a pig, which was half the size of him.

"What the hell is that?" Giuseppe asked as Desmond brought it closer. "How the hell did you get here?" Gabriella asked.

"It's a giant mushy pillow to cuddle with and remind you to stay away from bacon." Desmond said with a laugh as he dropped it on the bed. "And I was on the train out here when we got on the call with the charity."

Maria and Gabriella laughed as Desmond made the little legs dance for Giuseppe.

"Sounds like someone is having a good time in here. Does that mean we want to stay until tomorrow?" Brad asked as he walked into the room.

"Absolutely not, Doctor Westerberg. The sooner I can get out of here the better."

Desmond turned around to see Brad standing by the door. "Oh, shit, hey Desmond. Good to see you," Brad let slip in surprise as he walked over to shake his hand. Desmond took it and pulled him into a hug.

"It's good to see you, Brad. Or should I say Doctor Westerberg."

"Only in the hospital," Brad joked, a huge smile across his face. "It's so good to see you. I have to tell you; I saw you in Hamilton. You were phenomenal."

"No kidding? You should have reached out to me. I could have gotten you better seats or backstage or something."

"Eh, I didn't want to do that. We didn't really leave off in the best place, and I didn't want to be one of those people. But I have to tell you man, I'm really proud of you. You really made your dreams come true."

"Me? Look at you mister M.D. You're a freaking doctor."

"I'd love to stay and catch up, but I have to make my rounds. I'll reach out to you on social media, we can get together maybe."

"That sounds like a plan. I look forward to it."

"So, Giuseppe, your cardiologist spoke with your primary and with our staff. We are discharging you today, but before you get excited, it takes some time to get it done. They are going to send your scripts to the pharmacy, and we'll have you out of here hopefully before dinner. I'm going to give you my cell number. I want you to call me if you ever need anything. Something doesn't feel right or whatever, let me know, I have no problem swinging by when I'm not here."

"Thanks, Doctor Westerberg. I appreciate your help." Giuseppe said as he shook his hand.

He turned to Gabriella and smiled when he saw the bag in her lap. "I see you got my apology lunch."

"Apology lunch? For what?"

"I saw the social media crap this morning."

"Oh, don't worry about that. I've been through much worse on the internet. But thank you, it was sweet of you. And you almost got it perfect."

"Almost?"

"You forgot my sauce."

Brad smiled and pulled out two containers of honey mustard from him lab coat pocket. "Did I? I know you can't eat your nugs without the sauce."

Gabriella busted into laughter as she took the containers from him. "Touché, Dr. Brad, touché."

***

Later that night, when Giuseppe was settled in his recliner at home, the Balvins and the Dolces came over with dinner in tow, so Maria didn't have to cook. They all sat in the den and ate the salmon and cous cous salad that Arnie had prepared, along with berry parfaits made by Elise.

400

"I got Brad's number from you dad," Desmond said to Gabriella as they sat at the kitchen island, away from the group. "I texted him and told him to stop by. Your dad said it was okay too."

"Oh, okay. What time is he coming?"

"When he gets off from his shift. I think he said he'd be here around seven or eight."

"You seemed pretty happy to see him again."

"Yeah, I guess I missed him. I didn't really think much of it, but now that he's back in the picture, I think I would like to be friends with him again."

"Good, Des. I hope you guys can do that. I completely support you. Who knows, maybe I can be friends with him again at some point too."

"Do you think that maybe it would ever be more? I mean, I know you guys have a pretty messed up past, and I'm not pushing it. I was just wondering if it was in the realm of possibility."

"No, Des. I should have stuck to my guns when I said that I was steering clear of relationships in the beginning of the year. I realized that Liam was just good to scratch the itch. It wasn't a real relationship. And I almost fell into the Henry trap again. I've been single for a few months, and it feels good to just focus on me. And look at this little mush I got out of it." Gabriella said as she picked up Scampi and snuggled him as he licked her nose.

"Are you guys going to be anti-social and hide in here all night? I'd like some quality Gabby time too." Elise asked as she threw her paper plate in the trash.

Gabriella reached her arm out to give Elise a hug. Scampi took it as a chance to lick a new face. "I can't believe you got a dog. How do you think he'll do with the traveling?"

"He was good on the flight here. It's not like I go back and forth too often. I think he'll be fine. It's just going to be a challenge potty training him in the city. He's used to going in the yard in L.A., and here. We'll see how that goes. So, tell me, how's the job going?"

"It's good. I like this place way better than the old one. I feel like they are taking me more seriously here. The commute sucks, though. I'm thinking of getting a place near the city."

"Well, I'm back home now, so I could help you find a place." Gabriella suggested.

"That would be amazing. This diva over here is too busy to help me at all." Elise said as she pointed at her brother.

"Are you guys coming in here? The movie is starting," Arnie called out from the den.

They joined the rest of the family, parfaits in hand, and started the new Jake Wilson action movie. Just before the credits were about to roll, the doorbell rang. Gabriella went to answer the door and was greeted by a giant gift basket.

"Oh, wow, let me get that from you."

"Gabby, it's me. I'll carry it in."

"You bought this?"

"No," Brad said as he walked into the house as Gabriella lead him into the kitchen to place it on the counter. "The delivery guy just left it on the porch as I was parking."

"Everyone, Doctor Brad is here," Gabriella yelled out and directed him back to the den. As he made his way in and said his hellos, Gabriella looked at the basket.

"Damn, that basket is huge! Giuseppe, did you see what is in here for you?" Desmond said as he entered the kitchen.

"What makes you think it's for me?" Giuseppe asked as he slowly made his way out of the recliner.

"There's a big ass get well soon balloon attached to it," Desmond responded. "Who is it from?"

"I have no idea. There is a card, but it's on the inside." Gabriella said as her dad walked in.

He began to tear the colored cellophane from the basket and started to laugh when he saw one of the gifts. He opened the card and smiled when he read it.

"Take care of your ticker, G. You need to be around so we can help each other out. Be well, mate. Cheers, H."

Giuseppe laughed as he removed a large England Rugby fleece blanket from the basket, along with some protein shake mixes, heart-healthy supplements, a guided meditation kit, a pair of fleece-lined slippers, and a shirt that said I was fighting a bear. "Oh, he has a great sense of humor. I'll have to send him a picture of me wearing this shirt."

"You and Henry talk?" Gabriella asked as she tried to mask her confusion.

"Oh yeah, we text. Someone needs to bust his balls when the Cowboys lose." Giuseppe said with a laugh as he grabbed the blanket. "*Cara mia*, grab my phone. I'm gonna send him a picture of me holding the blanket over the garbage."

Giuseppe took out the kitchen garbage from under the kitchen island and held the blanket over the top, with a thumb down on the other hand and his tongue out. Maria laughed and shook her head as she took the photo. "I'm sure Henry will get a kick out of that one."

Giuseppe took the phone back and typed out a message. Moments later, his phone pinged with a response, which made him laugh. "He said they should have fixed my sense of humor when I was still in the hospital. Got anything for that, doc?"

"I think your sense of humor is just fine, Mr. DiStella," Brad said with a laugh as Caroline made him a plate of food.

"Here, you must be hungry."

"Thank you, Mrs. Dolce."

Brad settled down at the kitchen island, where Gabriella had sat down in disbelief as she watched her father carry on his text conversation.

"What is Henry saying?" Arnie asked as he passed Giuseppe as he entered the kitchen.

"He's on lunch. Just shooting the shit. Let me get back to my recliner before one of those idiots take it."

"I think you might have recliner entitlements while you're healing," Arnie said with a laugh. He walked up to the island and stuck his hand out to Brad. "Hey, I'm Arnie Burns."

"Brad Westerberg, nice to meet you."

"You too. I hear your Giuseppe's doctor."

"I'm only a resident; I'm helping on his case."

"Babe, this is Brad that lives across the street from my parents. We grew up together. Brad, Arnie is my boyfriend."

"Congrats, guys. That's awesome. How long have you been together?"

"It will be three years in February," Arnie said with a smile.

"Wow, that's impressive. I hit the year mark once. I don't really know how to pick them." Brad said with a chuckle.

"You guys can't keep leaving me with them, I'm not the little tag-a-long anymore," Elise complained as she joined them at the island. "Hey Brad."

"Hey Elise."

"What's with the face, Gabs?" Elise asked as she pulled up a stool and sat next to her.

"Oh, um," she began to say as Desmond jumped in. "Henry is texting with her father but hasn't spoken to her since the night of the premiere."

"Seriously? Why?" Elise asked.

"Fuck if I know," Gabriella said with a sigh and rested her chin in both of her hands. "Are you guys talking to him too?"

Desmond shook his head. "No, but I hear from Laurel that he keeps in touch with them."

"That doesn't sound like him. He's always been really caring," Arnie said.

"Yeah, well, apparently he still is," she said as she gestured to the gift basket.

"Sorry, I don't mean to interject, but who is Henry and what is going on?" Brad asked.

"You wanna take this one?" Gabriella asked with a glance at Desmond.

406

"Alright, so we're talking about Henry Anderson, the movie star." Desmond explained.

"I got it." Brad confirmed.

"They had this whole friendship turned will-they-won't-they turned romance that crashed and burned before it really got going. Went back to the friend thing where things got weird when they dated other people, then they were cool at the premiere until they weren't apparently. Good summary?"

Gabriella nodded, "not bad."

"So now he isn't speaking to you, but is still speaking to your friends and your father?" Brad asked.

"Yup."

"Did you do something to upset him?" Elise asked.

"I have no idea. I think it makes it that much worse that I don't know what I did. There's no way to change it. And I'm okay with not talking to him anymore. Our friendship was based on the movie, and that's over. And he had his own friendships with Laurel and Matt and the others. But I'm not cool with him sending gift baskets and texting my dad like they are besties."

"It sounds to me like he's keeping tabs on you while keeping his distance," Brad said as he chewed on his salmon. "If I had the ability to do that back in the day, I totally would have."

Gabriella arched an eyebrow at him. He flushed slightly. "I guess I kinda did through social media. Sometimes circumstances keep you away from the people you care about and want to be with, but it doesn't mean that you stop caring. It doesn't mean that you don't think about them and wonder what they are doing or hope that life is going well for them."

"Wow," Desmond said with an exhaled breath.

"Hey, I made my bed, and I laid in it. It was lonely and stunk like shit. And I'm not saying it to earn brownie points or anything, it's just the truth." Brad said with a shrug before he cleared his plate. Gabriella took the paper plate and threw it in the garbage, then handed him one of the parfaits.

"Thanks for saying that."

"It's the truth. Maybe the best thing for you is to try to separate yourself from it. You're back home now, right? So, you don't have to worry about your L.A. friends mentioning him all of the time. And just tell your dad that you'd rather if he kept his friendship with Henry to himself. I think he would."

"Wow, you really are different now. You remind me of the guy I grew up with," Desmond said with a smile. "I liked that guy, a lot. Prom Brad could take a leap."

Recognition lit up Arnie's eyes when he realized who Brad was. "Oh! You're *that* Brad."

"Yup," Brad said, his lips pressed into a tight line.

"No judgement, I've just heard the stories. I agree with Desmond, I couldn't picture you like that. You seem like a nice guy." Arnie said with a smile.

"So, change of topic. Brad, tell us about you. Any relationships or love interest?" Desmond asked.

"There isn't much to tell. I dated a bit in college, the typical bimbo type. Dated one girl pretty seriously my senior year of college, but I was off to med school, and she wanted to move back home and start a family. That didn't work out. I pretty much threw myself into my studies, then I started my residency at South Shore this year."

"No current ladies?" Elise asked as she batted her eyes at him.

"I wouldn't say that. There is a nurse at the hospital who I get along with well. We've hung out in a group a few times, and we text a bunch. She's the one who got your food for you, Gabby. She thought it was an awesome idea and wanted to help."

"Why not ask her out?" Arnie asked.

"I don't know. Things are good and I really don't want to ruin anything. Plus, we work together, and I still have the rest of my residency to get through."

"How long is that?" Elise asked.

"Five years."

"You are going to wait for five years before asking that girl out? She could be married with two children by then!" Elise exclaimed.

Brad shrugged. "I'm not in a rush. If it happens, it happens. Maybe something else will come along when I lease expect it."

Desmond stared at Gabriella, who rolled her eyes in response.

"What about you, Elise? Any suitors?"

"What is it, the eighteen hundreds?" She asked with a laugh. "I was seeing this guy for a while, but he was one of those serial daters. Constantly on the lookout for someone better than the last."

"Oh, no, I thought we liked Jeremy," Gabriella said.

"We did, until we didn't. So, I was thinking, since you're back, and I'm planning to move closer to you, and we're both single, maybe we can go out together? Maybe find some hotties in the city?" Elise asked hopefully.

"I'm not really in the market for a boyfriend. I'm enjoying being single. But I can absolutely be your wing-woman. And if you can't find a place right away, and the commute is getting to be too much, you can come crash on my couch for a few weeks." Gabriella said which made Elise squeal and throw her arms around her in a tight hug.

"Best older sister ever!" She chanted. "I'll start looking for apartments!"

After she ran off, Arnie and Desmond said their goodbyes and headed back into the city. The parents were next to leave, everyone made sure to say goodbye to Brad before they left. Brad suggested that Giuseppe get settled into bed, then went upstairs to check his vitals and make sure everything was looking good.

"It's nice having a doctor around," Maria commented when the guys were upstairs.

"Don't start, Mom." Gabriella warned.

"I'm not starting. I'm just saying, you two were close when you were younger. I know the whole he asked Laurel to prom thing, but he was just a kid. It would be nice for you two to reconnect, as friends only."

Maria quieted down as Brad came back down the stairs. "Everything looks good, Mrs. DiStella. Just make sure he takes his medicine, and don't hesitate to call or page me if something happens. He has a follow-up with his cardiologist scheduled, right?"

"Yes, thank you so much for everything, Brad. We really do appreciate it. I'm going to go head up and make sure the patient is comfortable. Stay as long as you'd like."

Gabriella kissed her mother goodnight, Brad accepted a warm hug, and then Maria headed upstairs. Brad turned back and smiled at Gabriella as he lifted the plastic dish. "Elise did a really good job on these."

"You want another? There are plenty in the fridge."

"No, I don't want to overdo it. I've got to be on my feet again tomorrow."

"What time is your shift?"

"Oh no, I'm off. Tomorrow I'll be doing housework, raking the yard and making sure the Halloween decorations are to my mother's liking."

"Oh! Sounds like a fun problem."

"Yeah, it is. So, I wanted to ask, and feel free not to answer, but you seem to not have too much luck in the relationship department. What's going on?"

Gabriella laughed. "Yeah, relationships have never been my strong suit. Liam, my latest ex, was a red flag when we started dating, but we were friends for a while and then made the switch. Before that was a guy in college who wouldn't even kiss me. And then there was Jason, which never really went anywhere, sadly."

"You dated Jason? I didn't know that."

"We didn't really date. We hung out. He asked me on a date, and I had said yes. But he never showed up to the restaurant. He was on his way to meet me when he was killed."

"Holy shit, I didn't know that. I'm so sorry. He really was such a great guy. It was so tragic."

"Yeah, he really was. I still cry when I see his pictures."

"So, you really haven't had the best luck."

412

"Nope."

"And then there was the movie star."

"That there was, and he is in a league of his own."

Brad laughed and shook his head. "Sometimes, I wish I could go back and make a different choice. Just one. I wonder how different things would be. But then again, had that happened, we wouldn't be where we are now. Maybe you wouldn't have ever left, maybe I wouldn't be practicing medicine. But maybe if I did get to make that choice, we wouldn't be sitting here right now, and that would be sad."

Gabriella looked at him with a smile and finally saw him as the best friend she had before everything got twisted, and not the asshole at prom, or the doctor who helped her father. "As shitty as the road may have been, you're right, it led us here. Maybe we are exactly where we are supposed to be."

Nineteen

The three nights before Christmas, Gabriella found herself on the couch with Scampi in her lap as she sipped hot cocoa and watched *It's a Wonderful Life*. After Halloween, she moved back to her apartment, and Elise crashed on her couch for a few weeks. Desmond and Arnie helped move Elise into her apartment a few blocks south of where Gabriella lived. As nice as it was to have someone to talk to every night, she was glad to have the place back to herself.

She kept in touch with Brad, and even met up with Evelyn for dinner, which Desmond also attended. She had felt a little more at peace with life now that she had spoken with some of her other friends from high school. She kept her word to Elise and went out with her to bars, where she became friendly with some of Elise's co-workers. They would get together once a week for happy hour, and always included Gabriella, which she was grateful for. They made a bit of a fuss when they first met her because of the movie, but after the initial excitement, they treated her like another member of the group. She finally felt like a normal New Yorker in their mid-twenties.

Another thing she started to do when she returned to the city was talk to a therapist. She was recommended to her by Arnie, who had been a regular patient for years. He convinced her that it could help to have an outside, non-biased, professional opinion guide her through her problems. She spoke through many of her feelings, the ones she delt with because of the movie's popularity, and others that stemmed from back in junior high.

Of all the advice the therapist had given her, one of the most important lessons was to let go that which you can't control. Gabriella was a planner and a control freak; the fact that she still carried around her large purse with a first aid kit, snacks, and a change of clothes everywhere she went proved it, and although she could control her actions, she couldn't control the actions of others. Slowly, she learned to let go of the feelings she tried to keep under control, which included a deep conversation with Laurel to explain how she felt when they were younger, and how much she appreciates and values their friendship now. She had one with Brad, which took a lot of courage for her to sit down and tell him how she felt when everything happened, and how much it affected her throughout her life. He cried when she told him the truth, and she forgave him for what happened in the past. She informed him that she no longer held anything against him and how he had proven himself to be a dependable friend since they reconnected. She even had a conversation with Desmond about how much he meant to her because he threw a hissy fit when he wasn't included.

There was still one person who she had not been able to have the conversation with, and it ate her up. Although he wasn't around nearly as long as the others, she couldn't deny that Henry had a significant impact on her life. As much as she tried to avoid it, she compared people or situations to him or what he would do. She was in no place to start a new relationship with anyone, and she was okay with that, she had to work on herself first. But she did think that she needed to get over Henry and let go of him before she would ever feel ready to fully invest in someone else.

She muted the television and dialed a number she had avoided for months. Her heartbeat rapidly in her chest as the phone started to ring. As all her experiences had gone over the last six months, his voicemail answered. She mentally sighed, but she didn't have time to discern if it was from frustration or relief. "Hi, Henry, it's Gabriella," she paused to collect her thoughts. She would only get one chance to say what she needed to say, and since there was no chance of a dialogue, she needed to convey her sentiments as clearly as possible. "I was hoping to have this conversation with you in person, but it seems like this might be the only way I'll get to do this. I wanted to say thank you for coming into my life. You entered for a reason, and although I am still trying to understand what that reason is, there is a reason. I appreciated the time we spent together, and I hope you will do the same.

"I fear that I may have done something to upset you, or to cause this rift between us, and I am truly sorry for whatever it is I did. You really are an amazing person, and I really hope you are happy, because you are someone who deserves it.

"I just wanted to say that I'm letting you go. I've been holding onto you for all these months, and it's not fair to do to myself. I really hope that you have an amazing life. I hope it is full of love and joy, because that's what you bring to others. If our paths ever cross again, I hope we will both be in a place to greet each other with a smile. Because what we had, however brief and undefined, it was real. Take care, Henry."

She ended the call as sadness and calmness overtook her, she felt as though she finally said goodbye and could move forward. Scampi sat up and cried, which prompted Gabriella to pick him up. He began to lick her face, which made her notice the tears that fell during that call. She kissed Scampi on the head, then unmuted the television, and snuggled into the couch, and felt at peace that she finally got the closure she needed.

***

Maria knocked on her daughter's door around noon on Christmas Eve eve. Gabriella opened the door in the middle of her phone conversation and gestured to her mother to come in. "Patti, I think we are going to be fine having the virtual party like last year. I think everyone had a good time. I agree that all of the gifts were too much last year. No, I think the secret Santa idea was the right move. Yes, I did get my gift in the mail. I have it under my little two-foot tree."

Gabriella kissed her mother hello as Scampi jumped into Maria's lap when she sat in the living room. Maria smiled as she watched her daughter try to wrap up her phone conversation. "Yes, I got the food you guys sent us. I put it straight into the fridge so it would thaw out. I'll heat it up before the party. I think moving it to six was a good move. Yes, I sent all the cookies I made to everyone. If you don't get it today, then you should definitely get it tomorrow. Hey, Patti, my mom is here, I have to run. Yes, I will be continuing my bake-a-thon over there. Okay, I will tell her. Bye."

"I'm surprised you got off the phone so quickly," Maria said with a laugh as she played with Scampi.

"Yeah, you know how much Patti loves to talk. She tweaked the virtual party and was freaking out, I had to talk her off the ledge. Kinda like you with Christmas Eve."

"Yeah, don't be so sure you won't be doing it later tonight. Although, it was helpful that we set up most of the house last weekend."

418

"I don't want Dad doing anything, and I'm sorry if it was awkward having the tables and chairs set up for the past couple of days, but at least now we can focus on the food prep." Gabriella said as she retrieved her overnight bag from her room. "Should I pack food for Scampi?"

"No, your father insisted that we have everything at our house that he would need. He wants to spoil his grandpuppy."

"This coming from the guy who didn't want pets when I was a kid," Gabriella laughed.

"What do you need to bring out to the car?" Maria asked.

"Take your pick. Overnight bag, gifts in the large shopping bag by the kitchen, and I have three cakes in the fridge."

Maria grabbed the overnight bag and two of the cakes while Gabriella put a leash on Scampi and got the rest. She locked up the apartment and they made their way to the street, where Maria had parked her SUV halfway down the block.

"Why did you bring the big car?" Gabriella asked as they loaded the trunk.

"I was supposed to pick up Elise, Desmond, and Arnie, but Arnie called this morning and said they had a change of plans and were going to take the train tomorrow morning."

"Good timing! I was afraid I wasn't going to make it before you left to get me," Elise called out as she approached the truck.

"Why didn't you wait at your apartment? I was coming you." Maria asked.

Elise waved her hand as she put her overnight bag in the trunk. "It's silly to try to find parking again. It's not like I'm not walking distance."

"What's up with your brother and Arnie cancelling last minute?" Gabriella asked as she hugged Elise.

"Who knows, does that mean we get ladies night in the a.m.? Am I hearing brunch?" Elise said with a smile as she climbed into the back seat.

"Do you know how much trouble we'd get in if your mom or Caroline find out?" Gabriella asked as she buckled her seatbelt.

"I think what they don't know won't hurt them. But let's go closer to home," Maria said with a wink as she pulled into the street.

***

A full twenty-four hours later, Gabriella and Maria had baked three more cakes, sugar cookies, and a bunch of side dishes. The ladies woke-up around ten in the morning to see Giuseppe sneak into the house with breakfast from the local diner.

"Giuseppe, there better be healthy food in there," Maria scolded as she made her way into the kitchen.

"There is, *cara mia*, egg white veggie omelets, turkey bacon and turkey sausage, and fresh fruit."

420

"Ugh, seriously? It's Christmas eve," Gabriella complained. She looked into the bag and smiled at the everything bagel with cream cheese.

"You're the best, Dad," she said with a wink and sunk her teeth into the bagel.

"Are we expecting anyone new this year? Or anyone not coming this year?" Giuseppe asked as he cut into his omelet.

"Nick is going to his fiancé's side this year," Maria said.

"Brad said he was going to stop by for a little."

"No work?" Giuseppe asked.

"Not tonight, but he's working all day tomorrow. Worked out a deal to cover for a resident who has children. Plus, Chanukah was last week. What else is on the to-do list, mom? Do you want me to run to the store for anything?"

"No, *Bambolina*, Dino and Caroline decided to take care of four of the fish this year. Maybe you can man the grill to get the salmon cooked. And maybe take care of the food that we reheat on the grill? I'll get everything going in the kitchen. I don't want your father to do anything."

"I still need to make my cocktails. It isn't Christmas eve without it. I can handle the drinks. I promise, no heavy lifting. I'll have Marco deal with the ice."

"They are all coming early to help us out. Dino is bringing the sternos. They should all be here around two. It should give us plenty of time to get everything ready for when everyone gets here at five. So, eat up, we're going to need our energy." Maria said with a smile.

Gabriella found herself outside cooking on the large grill, bundled in her winter coat, with a scarf and knit hat. Matt walked out with two mugs in his hands. "Hey Gabby!"

"Matt! When did you get here?" She asked after she kissed him on the cheek.

"About fifteen minutes ago. Laurel and I went up to your room but found it empty. Your dad thought we went up there for some privacy. He let me know you were taking over some of his responsibilities and told me to bring you this."

Gabriella smiled and took the mug full of spiked hot chocolate. "You can always count on dad for the booze."

"Elise also told me to tell you to come in. Apparently, Desmond is in rare form and is demanding for everyone to be together when he gets here."

"Dear lord, what does that diva have planned now? Let's do it. I'm still waiting for the charcoal grill to get ready, and the trays will be okay on the other grill."

They entered the house, and Laurel grabbed onto Gabriella before she could get her coat off. "I'm happy to see you too, Lau."

"I missed you so much! I've got some good news. I'm planning on staying here for January. Matt is heading back after the two weeks, so I'm thinking I can stay with you when he's gone, relive our roommate days?"

422

"Sounds like a plan to me. Just be prepared to share my bed," Gabriella said with a laugh as she finally pried herself away from Laurel and removed her coat. "Any idea what Desmond's deal is today?"

"No clue," Laurel responded as she snatched the hot cocoa from Gabriella and sipped it.

"That's cool, I wasn't drinking that or anything."

Laurel winked at Gabriella as the front door swung open. Everyone was gathered in the kitchen as Arnie and Desmond walked in with cases of champagne. "Wow, what's with all of the champagne?" Marco asked as he took the case from Desmond and put it on the counter.

Desmond shook his head as Arnie took out the plastic flutes and set them out. They continued to work as a team and fill the flutes and hand them out. Once everyone had a glass in hand, Desmond cleared his throat. "I would like to propose a toast."

"Okay, go for it," Elise said after a few moments.

Desmond stood there as his hand still held up his glass. Suddenly, Sierra screamed. "You boys got engaged!"

Everyone finally focused on the ring sitting on Desmond's left hand, which was holding up the champagne glass. The thick platinum band had a single diamond embedded in the center. The room erupted in cheers and excitement as they all bombarded Arnie and Desmond with love and congratulations.

Gabriella got her chance to congratulate the boys. "Arnie, you sweet, sweet man. I could never have asked for anyone better to love my best friend. I'm so happy that we have you in this family for life," she said as she wrapped her arms around Arnie and kissed his cheek.

"Thanks, Gabby. You've already been like a sister to me."

Gabriella turned and enveloped Desmond into a hug. "You got your Christmas wish. You're gonna have to think of another one for this year. I'm so happy for you, Des."

"Thanks, baby doll. Maybe you're Christmas wish will come true too."

"It already did. My best friends are happy and in love, my family is healthy, and we're all together. I don't want anything more than this." She said as she squeezed him tight. "Now, how did he ask?"

"Oh, I want to know too!" Laurel yelled out.

"Well, we were supposed to head home yesterday with Maria, but Arnie said that we had to come here today instead, that he had an emergency at the café in Nassau that he had to take care of. He told me to go use part of my Christmas present, so I went to the spa. When I got home, our apartment was transformed into a winter wonderland, and this handsome sneak was dressed in a suit, down on one knee when I walked in."

"I told him that I had been really good this year, and all I asked Santa for was for him to be my husband," Arnie filled in.

"Of course, I said yes. We celebrated, then both got dressed up and he took me out to dinner at Jean-Georges. We were so giddy afterwards; we went to Rockefeller Center and ice skated."

"Was there anything special about the date that made you ask, Arnie?" Sierra asked.

"No. I was going to wait until our third anniversary, but I decided that I didn't want to wait anymore. He supported me this year while I changed my profession, and I wanted to make sure he knew how much I appreciated his support and how much I want to support him for the rest of our lives."

Gabriella swooned at Arnie's response, a huge smile on her face as she looked over at Desmond, who stared at Arnie as if he hung the moon and the stars in the sky.

Slowly, everyone got back into party-planning mode and divided up to get everything set up. Matt joined Gabriella outside and helped to grill the fish and heat some food, with as Arnie brought the food back inside and brought out anything else that needed to be grilled.

Once everything was ready to go and the first of the family members started to arrive, Gabriella and Matt made their way inside to defrost and mingle. It took nearly a half an hour for Gabriella to say hello to all of her family members before she was finally able to get to the bar setup in the kitchen and get a drink.

"What's your poison?" Marco asked as he made himself a drink.

"I'd say shots of one-fifty-one after getting through the DiStella/Lorenzo gauntlet back there, but I'll stick to my dad's Christmas martinis. I'm pretty positive he filled the drink dispenser cooler with it."

Marco laughed, then grabbed a red solo cup and poured the drink from the cooler. "Wow, he really didn't mess around this year."

Gabriella laughed and took the cup from Marco. "Thanks. And no, he didn't. Forward planning at its finest over there."

The doorbell rang, and Maria shouted out from center of the kitchen, "Gabby, can you get the door please?"

"On it!" She responded. "Duty calls. Thanks for the drink."

Marco laughed, "I'm sure I'll meet you here frequently tonight."

They clinked their cups together, then Gabriella made her way to the hall, where she spotted Laurel and Desmond come down the stairs.

"Where were you two?"

"Nothing. Nowhere," Desmond responded with a smirk.

"We were up in your room, just making sure we have reinforcements for tonight." Laurel explained.

"I always have the sangria stashed for Christmas eve."

"Well, we added some champagne and a few folding chairs," Desmond explained.

"Okay, weirdos," Gabriella said with a smile as she went to the front door. "Who the hell rings the bell for this party," she said before answering it.

"Merry Christmas, Gabby!" Brad said with a smile as he scooped her up into a hug.

"Hey, Brad! Merry Christmas. I'm glad you could make it," Gabriella said with a smile as she let him into the house and closed the door behind her.

"I brought cannoli and some other pastries from that bakery you like," he said as Desmond grabbed the box from him.

"We need to hide this. Gabby, I'm putting it up in your room. We'll keep the good stuff for later. Hey Brad."

They watched as Desmond ran back up the stairs. Laurel approached as their eyes were focused on the stairs. "Well, well, well, if it isn't Doctor Bradley Westerberg."

Brad looked over at Laurel and his smile faltered slightly. "Hi, Laurel. It's nice to see you again."

"Mmhm." Laurel said as she looked him up and down.

He nervously shifted his weight from one foot to the other and glanced quickly at Gabriella. "Laurel, I know we haven't talked in years, but I'm really sorry for everything that happened in senior year."

"Save it, we're cool. I've been hearing from Gabby and Des about you. I'm glad you pulled your head out of your ass." Laurel said before pulled him into a hug.

Brad laughed as Desmond joined them. "Why don't you let him take his coat off, cling-on?"

Laurel rolled her eyes and smacked Desmond in the arm as Gabriella took the coat from Brad. "What time are you going to see Kristie tonight?"

"I'm only going to hang out here until maybe seven or eight. Her shift ends at nine and I told her I would pick her up and take her over to her aunt's house."

"I'm so glad you finally asked her out. She's such a sweetheart. I'm going to just hang your coat in the closet here so you can grab it when you need to leave instead of having to dig for it on my parents' bed later."

Matt and Arnie joined them at the door. "Matt, this is Brad, we went to school together. Brad, this is my fiancé, Matt."

"Good to meet you."

"You too. Hey Arnie," Brad said as he shook Arnie's hand next.

"Hi Brad. Did Desmond tell you the good news?"

428

Brad shook his head as he looked to Desmond. "I'm shocked he didn't scream it in your face when you walked through the door," Elise said with a laugh as she approached.

"We got engaged last night," Desmond said with a smile.

"That's fantastic. Congratulations, guys!" Brad said before he hugged them. "Hey, Elise, how's the big city treating you?"

"Can't complain. I'm absolutely loving it out there."

"We can move it further into the house if you want, no need to hang out by the door," Gabriella said with a laugh as Scampi ran through the hallway to greet everyone.

***

After the first round of food, Laurel nudged Gabriella. "I think we should start our tradition."

"Alright, I'll go up and get the blankets. Do you want to grab the booze? What are we doing this year?"

"I think we should do the champagne that Des brought."

"I hid most of it up in Gabby's room. I didn't want her cousins taking it," Desmond said as he took their paper plates and went to throw them out.

"Wanna come help me?" Gabriella asked as she got up from her chair.

"Yeah. We're gonna go get the stuff for the tradition," Laurel explained to the rest of them.

"Tradition?" Brad asked.

Matt groaned as Arnie laughed. "Get ready to freeze your ass off. These three make us go sit on the porch and drink and say what we want Santa to bring us for Christmas."

"Yeah, but I think it's supposed to be a pervy answer," Arnie added.

"Wow, you guys are weird," Brad said with a smile as he looked at the girls.

"Whatever. We'll come get you when we're ready. Make sure Elise is ready too." Gabriella said as the two of them headed up to her room.

"How many bottles do you think I should bring out?" Laurel asked as she looked under the bed where Desmond stashed the champagne.

"I don't know, maybe three?" Gabriella responded from her closet. "Shit. I thought I left the blankets up here."

"Didn't you mention that you were putting them in the closet by the door last week so we could just grab them and walk out?"

"What would I do without you?" Gabriella said with a smile.

"Hey, Gabby, you need to come down here," Desmond yelled from the stairs.

"Yeah, we're coming." Gabriella yelled back. "Are you ready?"

430

"Right behind you," Laurel said with a smile as she grabbed the champagne.

Gabriella started to walk down the stairs when the sound of barking erupted from below. Suddenly a chocolate-colored lab sprinted up the stairs at her and jumped on her and licked her hands and her face.

"Whose dog is that?" Laurel asked in shock.

"It looks like Leigh," Gabriella said, and the dog barked excitedly. She looked down the stairs unable to see anything. She patted the dog on the head, which slightly calmed it until Scampi bounded up the stairs and barked and sniffed the other dog. She took advantage of the distraction and slowly made her way down the stairs, her heart lodged in her throat. *"That can't be Leigh. If that is Leigh, that means that Henry is here. And that is impossible,"* she thought to herself.

As she finally reached the landing, the group of people by the door blurred, her eyes focusing on the overwhelming force that stood in the foyer. His chiseled face turned in her direction, his hair peppered with the moisture of the fresh snowflakes slowly melted into his brown locks. His piercing blue eyes made a connection with her own, and his full lips pulled into a half of a smile.

"Ella."

Twenty

Gabriella stood still on the stairs; a full panic broke out inside as she stared straight-faced at the ghost by the front door. Matt and Desmond stepped aside to create an open path between the two of them. The dogs continued to bark at each other as they ran around the upstairs, and Laurel slowly made her way back to the bedroom to put the bottles down.

"Hola senorita," Henry said with a smile.

Gabriella blinked and responded, "asshole."

"*Bambolina*!" Maria scolded from the hallway.

"It's okay, Maria, it's our thing," Henry said, his gaze concentrated on Gabriella.

There was a pause where the sounds from inside the house overtook the silence of the foyer. Matt and Desmond quietly took in the scene, their eyes focused on the people in front of them. Giuseppe and Maria anxiously stood by, prepared to divert the guest away from the area if necessary.

Gabriella took a deep, cleansing breath before she asked, "what are you doing here, Henry?"

Henry nervously rubbed the back of his neck and gave a slight side smile. "Isn't it obvious?"

"Actually, it isn't," she replied as she crossed her arms and leaned against the banister.

Henry looked up at Gabriella, his arms dropped down to his sides and his palms faced out. He stared at the face he hadn't looked upon in six excruciating months. His heart beat rapidly as he responded, "I'm here for you, Ella."

Gabriella inhaled deeply, surprised by the words he uttered. Words that she so desperately wanted to hear months ago. Elation and anger intertwined to create a hurricane of emotion that rotated in her chest, "I haven't heard from you since July."

Brad and Arnie nudged past Giuseppe and Maria as they made their way into the hallway. "Hey Gabby, are we ready?"

Gabriella and Henry turned their heads to look at Brad, who unknowingly walked into a very awkward interchange. Matt shook his head at Brad while Desmond dragged a finger across the front of his neck. Brad's face was full of confusion as he looked at the people in front of him. Arnie walked up behind him and stopped short when he saw Henry by the door.

"Oh wow, Henry! I didn't know you were coming." Arnie said with a small nervous chuckle.

"Hi Arnie, nice to see you again," Henry said as he reached out and shook his hand, then he extended his hand to Brad. "Hey mate, good to meet you, I'm Henry."

Brad smiled and took his hand, "Brad, it's really nice to meet you, I'm a big fan."

"Thank you," Henry responded.

434

Laurel made her way down the stairs as the dogs followed behind. "Hey guys, I think maybe we should head back into the party and let these two chat without an audience." She rubbed Gabriella's arm in support as she moved past her. When she got to the landing, she made her way to Henry and gave him a kiss on the cheek. "Hey Hen, Merry Christmas."

"Merry Christmas, Laurel. Wish me luck?"

Laurel looked back and studied her best friend scowl on the staircase. "You're gonna need it, big guy," she said with a smirk as she patted his arm. Slowly, the rest of the crowd followed Laurel into the kitchen.

Once they were out of earshot, Henry looked up at Gabriella. "Can we talk?"

Gabriella rolled her eyes and turned as she gestured for him to follow her, then made her way back up to the second floor.

"Leigh, come," Henry yelled out to his dog.

Maria poked her head out from the living room, "she's fine, Henry. You go on up, she's exploring."

Henry nodded and started up the steps where he found Gabriella by a door. As he started to enter the room, Leigh ran up the stairs and into the room, where she jumped on Gabriella's bed and curled up. Henry followed behind and shook his head at his dog's antics, then looked at his surroundings.

Gabriella closed the door behind her and watched as Henry slowly circled her childhood bedroom. She settled on the bed next to Leigh and pet her head while Henry walked the cream carpet and looked at the white furniture set against the pale pink walls. He studied the old high school photos that hung on the walls with thumbtacks and the awards she had won from her childhood. He stopped at the bookshelf that held her yearbook and reached out to take it.

"Before you start delving further into my past, you need to explain yourself. Because for the life of me, I cannot even fathom why you are in my house right now."

Henry stiffened and replaced the yearbook on the shelf. He turned sheepishly to face her and leaned against the wall before he spoke.

"Ella, I- "

"Six months, Henry. You blew me off for six months. What did I do to make you cut me out of your life like that?" She yelled out.

Henry paused and looked down to compose his response. He pulled the desk chair out and sat down, his forearms on his knees as he chewed on the inside of his lip. His leg began to bounce nervously as he said, "I had to."

"You had to? Right. Care to explain? Or am I supposed to just accept that answer and pretend that it's normal for you to be here?"

Henry dragged his hand through his hair and expelled a deep breath. "I did it for you."

Gabriella pursed her lips and didn't accept his response.

"Think about it, Ella. The movie just came out, and things got out of control. People were obsessed with the movie. I know how much you want to stay out of the limelight. I wanted to give you time to adjust to this new life you were in."

"That makes no sense. Why would adjusting to life after the movie have any effect on our relationship?"

"Because being with me would only fuel the rumor mill, bringing more unwanted attention to you. I wanted you to be able to navigate this without added scrutiny."

"You're telling me that you didn't talk to me for half a year because you thought I needed to adjust to life after the movie? Did it ever cross your mind that maybe I needed you to help me adjust to life after the movie? And who the hell are you to make that decision without talking to me about it first?"

"Trust me, you were better off with me keeping my distance."

"How? How would us speaking after the movie affect me in some significant way? I thought we were friends."

"Bloody hell, Ella, I want more than that! If we'd carried on after the film, it would not have been as friends. I want to be with you, but the press would have been too much for you to handle."

Henry jumped up from the chair and approached Gabriella in three strides. She looked up with him and frowned. "I wanted to be with you too, but you ghosted me. You wouldn't return my calls. You purposely ignored me."

"It killed me to not answer your calls. I wanted to speak with you so badly, but I thought I was doing the right thing." He said as he sat down next to her.

"That's pretty fucking ballsy to assume you know what's best for me. You could have talked to me about it."

Henry sighed. "Desmond said–"

"Desmond? Desmond said what?"

"He said to give you some space. I wanted you that night at the premiere. May tried to formulate a way to get us together, but Desmond said you were scared about what was going to happen after the movie and he said it wasn't the right time."

"That didn't mean that you needed to pretend like I didn't exist!" Gabriella shouted exasperatedly. "In what world does it seem like a good idea to cut someone out of your life without an explanation and think it's in their best interest?"

A scratch at the door and a whimper made Leigh lift her head and bark. Gabriella removed herself from the bed and opened her door to find Scampi beg to be let in. He squeezed through as soon as the door opened enough for him to fit, then he jumped onto the bed and headed straight for Leigh and sniffed her, before he turned to Henry and sniffed him. Once he approved of Henry's scent, he jumped onto his lap and stood up and reached to lick his face.

Henry chuckled in response to the little pink tongue that lapped at his chin. "Well, aren't you a tidy little pup. What's your name, mate?"

438

"His name is Scampi." Gabriella responded, her back against the door of the room and her arms across her chest.

"It's a pleasure to meet you, Scampi. I'm Henry. I'm the sod who cocked-up things with your mum. Do you think if I tell her how sorry I am that she'll give me another chance?"

Gabriella sighed as she watched Scampi interact with Henry. If she had thought Henry was panty-melting with Leigh, her ovaries now exploded. Henry took her sigh as a negative and asked, "unless I'm too late?"

Gabriella shook herself from her momentary lapse of Henry and Scampi, "huh? Too late?"

"You said you let me go. It is because of that bloke downstairs? The blond that followed Arnie?"

"Brad? No, I'm not with Brad. That's *the* Brad, Henry. The guy from high school."

"Why is he here?"

"He was doing rounds at the hospital and my dad was one of his patients. We reconnected, but only as friends."

"And what about Liam? Is he still around?"

Gabriella shook her head. "We ended the night of the premiere. I've spoken with him a handful of times since. He's moved on." Henry placed Scampi onto the bed, then swiftly stood up and stalked over to Gabriella. He stopped in front of her, his eyes studied her face as leaned close, his hands pressed against the door on either side of her head.

His scent assaulted her senses as she studied the penetrating gaze that came from his blue eyes. She studied the way the hue of his eyes shifted from an intense blue to an almost light green near his pupil, with threads of blue and silver weaving in between.

"Is there anyone else? Some new bloke who I don't know about who weaseled his way into your heart?"

She shook her head ever so slightly in response, her pulse pounded, and her throat dried at his proximity. Her heart and body had betrayed her mind. As much as she wanted to remain aloof to the man who stood before her, the man who made her question her worth for months, her body and heart sung in harmony that he was in her parents' house. The longer she was near him, the more her brain started to pick up the tune that the rest her body sung.

"Gabriella DiStella, please forgive me for being an utter fool. I truly stayed away to protect you, and I apologize for doing it in such a wonky way. Be mine, Ella. You've been mine since the first time I saw you coming out the trailer, you just didn't know it yet." He softly pressed his lips against hers and waited for permission to continue.

She stood still, the song of her heart and traitorous body began to crescendo and chanted to give into him. But still, her brain, as catchy as the song was, was unable to move past how he handled everything. "Please, Ella. Be mine," he whispered against her lips, her resolve melted away a little more.

440

Slowly, she placed her hands on his broad chest, his heat warmed her fingertips. She gently pushed against him and caused him to move away slightly. Gabriella maintained eye contact with him while she spoke. "What does that entail, being yours?"

Henry's eyes traced the curves of her face and moved from her high cheekbones to her plump lips, up her slender nose and back to her almond eyes, fringed with long, dark lashes. His hand cupped the side of her face as he said, "it means we do this for real. You and me, together. No hiding. I'm one hundred percent in, Ella."

"And what about thinking you know what is best for me?"

"I'll never presume to know better again. I will talk to you about everything, and I won't take the advice of others. It's you and me."

"What about the press?"

"What about it? I'll follow your lead. We can protect our life from it, or we can let the world know and face it together."

"But what about where we live?"

"What about it? Ella, do you want to be with me?"

Gabriella bit on her lower lip, which made Henry groan and pull at her lip with his thumb. "It's a yes or no answer, Ella. Do you want to be with me?"

Gabriella's brain finally joined in on the chorus and made her slightly nod her head. "I need you to say it, Ella."

She swallowed the mix of nerves and desire that clogged her throat before she whispered a yes. Henry's mouth was on hers before she finished the word, his tongue probed her mouth as he pressed himself against her. She surrendered to him and fell under the spell he wove. The kiss grew desperate, as they pawed at one another. Gabriella's hands roamed down his cowl-neck sweater to the edge, her fingers gripping the edge and raised it to expose his abdomen.

Henry pulled her away from the door, his hands cupped her bottom and squeezed as he turned her and pushed her back to the bed, where she landed next to the dogs. The dogs jumped up and licked and pushed on the two of them because they thought that they were playing.

Henry and Gabriella broke away from one another and laughed as the two dogs barked and pounced on one another, then onto them. "Alright, you two monsters, calm down. Off the bed," Henry said as the dogs jumped down.

"Henry, we really do need to discuss our situation," Gabriella said as she sat up and adjusted her slouchy red sweater.

"Okay, I'm listening, tell me what your concerns are."

"We live on two different continents. How is that going to work?"

"Ella, we will figure it out. When I'm in between projects, and I can stay with you. When I'm on location, you could come with me if you want. We have

442

flexibility with our careers. You could come stay with me in England for a chunk of time if you want."

"I tried that with Liam, he said it was too much to expect him to wait around for me."

"Liam is a bloody idiot and obviously wasn't in love with you. I love you, Gabriella. We will make it work."

Gabriella looked up at Henry and smiled, then cupped his face and placed a sweet kiss on his lips. "I love you too, Henry."

Henry smiled, then grabbed her and pulled her down onto the bed, where he began to make out with her again. The dogs started to bark and jumped onto the bed, which made them to break away from each other.

"Okay, I think we need to get downstairs before people get the wrong idea," Gabriella said with a smile as she opened the bedroom door and let the dogs run out and down the stairs.

"We can get back to the bed now that the dogs are gone," Henry suggested with a waggle of his eyebrows. Gabriella shook her head and headed down the stairs.

She led them into the kitchen, where she directed his attention to the food spread out on every surface. "I'm not sure if you've eaten, but it's tradition to eat seven fish on Christmas Eve for us. Of course, there is a whole bunch of other food here to eat. It pretty much stays out all night and you can come back and gorge yourself."

"I'm famished. What did you make, beautiful?"

Gabriella smiled. "The seafood manicotti, the salmon, the linguine with clams, and the focaccia. Pretty much everything is made from scratch. Laurel's parents made the stuffed clams, the flounder, the shrimp scampi, and the calamari. Mom grilled the octopus and made her pasta salad."

"Is that sushi?"

Gabriella rolled her eyes and nodded, "yes, my cousin Frankie decided to bring it one year. Doesn't really fit with the Italian theme, but he argued that it was fish and has been bringing it ever since. I think people don't eat it because it annoys them, but I'm never one to turn down sushi."

Henry laughed as he grabbed a plate and piled food onto it. Gabriella joined him and made her second plate as she heard hushed whispers from her family who sat in the dining room and stared at Henry. She let her head fall back as she sighed. "Do you mind if we make a pit stop in there before we go find a place to sit?"

Henry shook his head as he followed her lead. The room quieted down as they entered. "Everyone, this is Henry. Henry, this is most of my family. Before you guys start in with the questions that I know you'll ask. Yes, this is Henry Anderson, the actor. Yes, he is celebrating Christmas Eve with us. The lab who has teamed up with Scampi is Leigh, and she belongs to Henry. Yes, you can talk to him, but can you please let the guy eat his food first? He just got here and he's hungry."

"It's nice to meet all of you. I will be back later to speak with all of you," Henry said with a smile as the family responded.

"Follow me, I've got one more room to get you through before we can sit and eat."

"Henry! You're alive!" Giuseppe shouted as they entered the den.

"Barely," Henry joked as Giuseppe approached them. Maria intercepted her husband and took the plate of food from Henry. "Give me this, I'll go put it on the table in the sunroom. What can I get you to drink?"

"I'll take whatever beer is easiest for you."

"Giuseppe bought Guinness for you; I'll grab it. It's really good to see you again, Henry," Maria said with a warm smile before she kissed him on the cheek. He returned the gesture before she headed through the sliding doors.

Giuseppe went in and enveloped Henry in a bear hug. "It's good to see you, kid."

"You too. You gave me quite the scare."

"You and me both," Giuseppe said with a smile. "I put all of your stuff in the guest room upstairs."

"Everything arrived alright?"

"Yes, got it yesterday. Snuck it in while this one was elbow deep in flour," he said with a gesture to his daughter.

"Wait a minute, you knew he was coming?" Gabriella asked her father.

"Who do you think invited him?"

Gabriella's mouth fell open in response. "We'll talk about it later, Ella." Henry said with a soft smile as he placed his hand on the small of her back and steered her towards the door. "Let me say hi to your friends' parents and I'll meet you in the room."

She nodded and headed into the sunroom with her plate in hand, where her friends sat at the table in wait for her. Shell shocked, she sat down in the chair next to Laurel, who handed her a red solo cup. Without even looking at its contents, she drank the entire cup in one go.

"It's a good thing you filled that with the Christmas punch and not the martini," Matt said with a wince as she placed the cup down on the table.

"Are you okay?" Brad asked.

Gabriella looked at all of them as Arnie got up and exited the room. "Um, yeah, I'm okay. I'm just really confused."

"About which part?" Brad asked.

"I mean, Henry is here. Apparently, my father knew about it. Already had his things in the spare room for him. Henry shipped his things here before he arrived."

"What?" Laurel asked as Demond's eyebrows twisted in concern.

"I don't know. They said we'd talk about it later. He's out there talking with our parents."

Arnie entered the room with a cup in his hand. "Here, don't drink it all at one time, Gabby. It's the martini. You look like you need it."

Gabriella smiled up at Arnie as she took the drink from him. "Thanks."

"Gabby, are you okay? Really?" Desmond asked as he threaded his hand through Arnie's as he sat down next to him.

"I'm really overwhelmed."

"In a good way?"

Henry walked in with a pint glass in his hand as he approached the table. A giant smiled formed on his face as he looked at Gabriella. Gabriella returned his smile as sat down next to her and placed a gentle kiss on her lips. Desmond smiled at the interaction and Laurel cleared her throat.

"You better shovel that food into your mouth, Hen. You interrupted our Christmas tradition with your arrival."

Henry's eyebrows raised as he looked at Laurel. "Is that so?"

"I say we go for round two, then we can do your torturous tradition," Matt said with a smile before he headed into the kitchen to grab another plate of food.

***

"It's fucking freezing out here," Matt complained as he claimed one of the rocking chairs.

Desmond and Arnie took two seats on the sofa. Henry and Brad followed them out as the newbies, both looked at the two remaining spots. Desmond patted the spot next to him on the couch and gestured to Henry. Brad headed to the other rocking chair next to Arnie as Henry squeezed in next to Desmond.

"Why are we out here exactly?" Brad asked as they settled in.

Gabriella and Elise came out with blankets as Laurel followed them with bottles of champagne. Gabriella looked at the seating situation. "I didn't realize our group grew so much. Let me go grab a few folding chairs."

Laurel handed a bottle to Matt, Brad, Arnie, and Henry before she settled down on Matt's lap. As soon as she was situated, Matt covered them with a blanket. "Just make it two," Laurel called out.

"I've got a perfectly good lap for you to sit on, Ella," Henry said with a wink.

Gabriella smiled and shook her head. "Okay, one seat then."

"Elise, you can sit with me if you want," Brad offered.

448

"Sure, Gabby, don't worry about the seat," Elise said as she perched herself on Brad's legs.

The guys opened the champagne while Gabriella settled onto Henry's lap. He wrapped his arms around her waist and placed a kiss on the side of her neck. "I'm so happy to be here with you right now," he whispered into her ear.

She looked at him over her shoulder and smiled, then leaned in and pressed a soft kiss on his lips. "I'm happy you're here too."

Elise cleared her throat, which brought Gabriella and Henry attention back to their friends, who were sat there and stared at them. Matt reached out his hand and hit his knuckles against Henry's. Gabriella shook her head as she smiled.

"So, what are we doing out here?" Brad asked again.

"One year, Gabby, Laurel, and I were sitting out here to escape the party when we were in college, and we were broke, so we said no exchanging gifts." Desmond explained.

"It was the first year we were invited for Christmas eve too," Laurel added in.

"It was also our first year of college," Gabriella chimed in.

"Yeah, yeah. Anyway, since we were poor freshman, we decided to share what we would ask Santa for Christmas. We were all single, so we said we wanted dick for Christmas." Desmond continued his explanation.

"Are you still wanting dick for Christmas?" Henry whispered which caused Gabriella to blush.

"Then Nonna Rosa came out and said she wanted dick for Christmas too," Laurel chimed in.

Henry and Brad laughed at the story as the rest chuckled at the story of what they already knew.

"How old was she?" Brad asked.

"I think she was eighty-five at the time," Gabriella responded.

"Your Nonna was a cheeky one," Henry said with a chuckle.

"Oh, you have no idea. Did you hear about the time Gabby walked in on her grandmother making out with Uncle George?" Desmond asked.

"Ugh, Des, shut up. We do not need to relive that one," Gabriella said after she smacked him on his arm.

"How about we start with what we want Santa to bring us for Christmas this year," Laurel suggested, "Henry and Brad have to go first because they are the newbies."

"Are Jewish guys allowed to ask Santa for something for Christmas?" Brad asked.

"This Jew does it every year," Matt said with a smirk as he lifted the bottle of champagne towards Brad is comradery, then took a swig from the bottle.

450

"Start us off, Dr. Brad," Gabriella said with a smile.

"Okay. Well, I don't want any dick for Christmas. I'd like Santa to bring me a good night tonight when I meet Kristie's family for the first time."

"Not too bad," Desmond said with a smile. "Henry, it's your turn."

"I don't need to ask Santa for anything, I already got what I wanted for Christmas in my arms right now."

Gabriella turned to jelly in his arms and sunk into the warmth of his embrace.

"Smooth, dude," Matt commented.

"It's the truth. I've made a mess of things, and all I wanted was another chance." Henry said before he placed a kiss in Gabriella's neck.

"Alright, I want Santa to bring me that Bugatti Divo I saw cruising around Bel Air. It was beautiful." Matt said dreamily.

"I don't think Santa brings multi-million-dollar sportscars, mate," Henry said with a laugh.

"I want Santa to bring us a bigger apartment, maybe closer to my job," Arnie shared.

"Really? You want to leave Manhattan?" Elise asked.

"Not really, but the commute sucks and it would be nice to have a bigger place," Arnie said with a shrug.

"I'm not opposed to moving out to where Nonna Rosa lived. The commute wasn't terrible, and you'd be closer to work," Desmond suggested.

Arnie smiled and squeezed his hand. "Thanks, babe. We can figure it out later."

"My turn?" Elise asked. Laurel nodded her head. "Earmuffs, big brother. I want Santa to bring me some dick."

The group began to laugh as Desmond squirmed in his seat. "Nah-uh. Santa is gonna bring your ass a chastity belt!"

"I thought you were cleaning up in the big city," Brad said with a raised eyebrow.

"Yeah, but there's no such thing as too much dick," Elise replied.

"Yes, there is, you whore," Desmond shrieked, which caused everyone to laugh more.

"I have a feeling that I've lost my wing woman," Elise said as she eyeballed Gabriella and Henry.

"Were you out hunting for dick, Ella?" Henry asked.

"No, no. I was purely her wing woman. I was on a no-dick kick."

"I hope you're still not on it," Henry prodded.

Gabriella's eyes roamed over Henry, and she shrugged, "that remains to be seen."

452

"Pssh, I'll take him if you don't want him, Gabby. That man is too sexy for his own good," Elise said while she shook her head.

"Can someone hose her down with holy water or something?" Desmond asked as he stared at his little sister in disbelief.

"Can you do something about that, Doctor Brad," Matt asked. "Spay her or something."

"I'm not an animal, Matthew," Elise said with eyes narrowed.

"You're definitely acting like you're in heat," Arnie said with a laugh.

Elise rolled her eyes and pushed her future brother-in-law. "Very funny, jerk."

"So, we're down to the original three. Baby, why don't you go first?" Matt said to Laurel.

"Honestly, Santa brought me what I asked for last year. I'm thinking I'll go easy on him this year. I want Santa to bring me an Academy Award."

"That's going easy on him?" Brad asked.

"It's practically in the bag for these two," Desmond said with a nudge of his head at Laurel and Henry.

"What about you, Des?" Laurel asked.

Desmond sighed, then lifted his left hand up and admired his ring. "Santa already brought me what I wanted. I don't want to be selfish."

Laurel and Elise rolled their eyes. "Gabby, what would you like Santa to bring you this year?" Laurel asked.

"Peace. I want Santa to bring me peace. Peace of mind, peace in life, peace for all my family and friends. This past year has been a rollercoaster." Gabriella said, then took her obligatory gulp of champagne. Her eyebrows furrowed as she struggled to swallow the mouthful of bubbly liquid.

"Champagne is a terrible choice for this type of thing," she commented.

"Yeah, I've been burping up a storm over here," Matt agreed.

"And that's different how?" Henry asked as he kicked his foot into Matt's.

"Yeah, I've missed you, buddy," Matt said as he patted Laurel on her hip to stand. "Can we please bring the Californian back into the house so I can thaw?"

"Actually, I need to head out. Kristie is expecting me in half an hour," Brad said as he got up, and pulled Elise into a hug. He made his way around and said his goodbyes to everyone. He hugged Gabriella tightly, "are you sure you're okay with him being here?"

Gabriella nodded in response. "Okay. Call me if you need anything. And thank you again for inviting me. I really feel like I'm part of the family."

"Any time, Brad. Be careful driving and wish Kristie a Merry Christmas."

"I will. I'm just gonna say goodbye to your parents. I'll text you."

Brad walked into the house, followed quickly by Matt, who ran to the kitchen to get himself a hot chocolate. The rest of them piled into the foyer and removed their coats, hats, and gloves. "Now, Henry," Arnie said as he threw his arm around Henry's shoulders, "this the part of the evening when these three sneak upstairs to Gabby's room and drink their sangria and talk about us. We usually give them about half an hour before we join them."

"I guess now is as good of a time as any to go speak to Ella's family. She rescued me from their questions so I could eat, but it's time to pay the piper." Henry said with a smile and let Arnie lead the way.

"I'll come with, you'll need as much of a buffer as possible," Elise said.

"Don't try anything with Gabby's man, Elise," Desmond warned.

Elise gave him the middle finger and followed the guys into the living room, where questions were directed at Henry as soon as they walked in.

"Just wait until Roberto gets his hands on Matt again. He thinks he's gonna one-up Giuseppe with the exercising," Desmond said to the girls as they headed towards the stairs.

"Well, that's not fair, Dad is still recovering," Gabriella responded.

"Did you know that all of them, including Roberto, are following Matt on social media now?" Laurel said as she walked into the room and made herself comfortable on the bed. "I swear they are children."

Gabriella went to her closet to take out the stash of sangria and handed out one bottle to each. Desmond looked at the bottle, then back at his friend. "Are we going to have a discussion that is going to cause us to get through three bottles?"

"What? No. You know they are all coming up here anyway. We can just start with one. It's called forward planning, Des."

"Okay, bitch, I was just checking."

"So, how excited were you when Arnie proposed?" Gabriella asked as she opened one bottle.

"I was beside myself, like on one hand I thought it was never gonna happen, but on the other hand, I was like bitch it's about time!"

"Did you pick a date yet?"

"Jesus, Gabby, he just got engaged, he doesn't have a date picked yet," Laurel said after she took a drink from her bottle.

"I was thinking next winter. Maybe on our anniversary. I think that would be romantic," Desmond answered. "And why wouldn't I have a date? I've had this whole thing planned for years. I'm thinking of black and silver as my colors."

"Are you okay, Lau?" Gabriella asked.

"Yeah, I'm fine."

"You seem a little edgy," Desmond observed.

456

"How the hell can you already be picking a date? You haven't even been engaged for twenty-four hours. I've been engaged for almost half a year and the thought gives me hives." Laurel said, then took a swig from her bottle.

"Not everyone has to rush into things. For all of the things you two have in common, you are both extremely different people. Just because someone got engaged first doesn't mean they have to get married first." Gabriella said to calm Laurel.

"Yeah, okay. So, Des, what have you planned so far?" Laurel asked.

"Well, you two and Elise will definitely be in my bridal party. Maybe Brad too, have my oldest friends up there with me. Not sure who Arnie would have, since he's an only child and has like one cousin who he barely speaks to."

"Maybe he can have Dino and Caroline since he works with them," Gabriella joked.

Desmond rolled his eyes. "I'm thinking black satin dresses with silver accessories. Black tuxedos with silver vests for groomsmen and Arnie and I in silver tuxedos. I'm thinking red flowers. I'm thinking rooftop with views of the city."

"I'm thinking we're gonna freeze our satin-clad asses on a rooftop in the winter," Laurel countered.

"Alright, I've got time to plan. But be available next winter. I'm talking to you, bitch," Desmond said as he eyeballed Laurel.

"Talk to my manager," Laurel said with a smirk.

"Easy you two, I'll take care of it. However, and this goes for both of you, I don't plan weddings. They have wedding planners for that shit." Gabriella said as she pointed her finger at her two friends.

"Can we please talk about that bomb that dropped on the DiStella's front porch this evening?" Laurel asked as she changed the topic.

"Yeah, did you have any idea he was coming?" Desmond asked Laurel.

"No, not a clue. Last I spoke with him, he was home with his family. He never once mentioned coming to the U.S., never mind seeing Gabby. Any time we spoke, he always asked about her, but that was it. Did he ever say anything to you?"

"To me? The last time I spoke to him was at the movie premiere," Desmond said before her took a drink.

"Des, he mentioned that you told him to leave me alone that night," Gabby mentioned.

"Yea, him and his sister were plotting on getting you two together, but I told him it wasn't the right time. You were so stressed about the movie and the public; I said to let you breathe for a bit."

"That's why he hasn't spoken to me since that night."

"Are you serious?" Laurel yelled. "I don't know if I'm angrier at Henry or you right now," she said as she gestured to Desmond.

"What did I do? I didn't tell him to ghost her for half a year. I told him to let the buzz about the movie die down a bit before pursuing her. Like give her some space for a month or so. I never said not to speak with her or stay away from her."

"He's such an ass. How did he think completely staying away was going to help anything?" Laurel asked.

Gabriella shrugged. "I'm not sure, you'd have to ask him. I mean, I get that he was coming from a good place, but I told him that he should have spoken to me. If I had known what was going on in his head, I would have been able to deal with the separation. I told him he went about it all wrong."

"So, now what?" Desmond asked.

"He wants to be with me. Officially."

"Are you ready for that?" Laurel asked.

"I think so?"

"Gabby, this is a huge decision. Everything that you were worried about before hasn't gone away," Desmond warned.

"I know that. But I don't think I should allow people I don't even know, dictate how to live my life. I compare every man to Henry. Everything that happens, I think of what his reaction would be. I like what we are when we are together. I know this isn't a normal relationship that I'm embarking on. But I've been miserable without him. Shouldn't I give myself a chance to be happy with him?"

"Holy shit. I'm gonna kiss your therapist on the mouth," Desmond said with a smile.

"Gabby, we're right here with you. And if you want to talk to someone, talk to Matt. He's been through it with me. Granted, people don't seem to be as ruthless with a man and actress than they are with a woman and an actor. You're not alone in this. And I know that Henry will do anything to keep you protected." Laurel said before the knock on the door stopped them from speaking.

"Knock knock, your time is up!" Elise yelled through the door.

Desmond opened the door and grabbed his sister into a headlock. "You're such an ass, Desmond," she complained as the guys walked past them.

"Did you save us some wine?" Matt asked as he sat in the desk chair.

"That bad down there?" Laurel asked.

"Henry might need his own bottle," Matt responded after he took a swig from Laurel's bottle.

Gabriella held out her bottle to Henry, who took it and drank deeply from it. "Ah, this reminds me of being in the trailer with you during the storm."

Gabriella smiled and knew exactly what he referred to.

"Will you two knock it off already?" Arnie said from the doorway. A shuffle could be heard over the noise that came from downstairs. Moments later, Elise dragged Desmond into the room with his head locked under her arm.

"He thinks because he's older he can take me. Such a joke."

***

It was after two in the morning when the last of the guest left the house. Henry was shocked at how long the party lasted, and was surprised at how little food was left over. Gabriella helped her mother put whatever food was left into containers to place in the refrigerator. Henry helped carry the leftover desserts down to the basement to store in another refrigerator.

"Leave everything else out, we'll get to it tomorrow," Maria said once Henry came back upstairs.

"Do the parties always go that long?" Henry asked as he tried to hide his yawn.

"Not this late. But it's not every year we have two celebrities in this house. I think you were the main attraction, Hank." Giuseppe said as he turned off the lights in the den.

"You must be exhausted, honey. Didn't you come here straight from the airport?" Maria asked.

"I did, but luckily, I got some sleep on the plane. I had a feeling it was going to be a long day." Henry answered. Gabriella walked to the French doors in the dining room and opened one to let the dogs in from relieving themselves outside.

"I've got the guest room set up for you, Hank, let me show you to it," Giuseppe offered as he made his way to the stairs and turned off the lights as he went through the house.

They all followed as the dogs ran up the stairs alongside them. Giuseppe opened the door to the guest room, which had a suitcase and a large duffle bag next to the bed. "Sleep in tomorrow. Our Christmas Day is lazy. Have a good night."

Maria wished them both a good night and followed her husband into their bedroom across the hall. Henry and Gabriella stood outside of their rooms while the dogs sat in the hallway and waited on their owners. "Well, I guess I'll see you in the morning," Gabriella said with a shrug as she stepped halfway into her room.

"I will see you in the morning," Henry confirmed, then gestured to Leigh to go into the bedroom. Leigh followed his command, and Scampi began to follow.

"Scampi, where do you think you're going?" Gabriella asked her dog.

"It's okay, I don't mind if he stays in here." Henry assured.

"Um, okay. Good night."

"Hey, Ella?" Henry asked and Gabriella to pause and look back out of the doorway.

"Yeah?"

Henry quickly made his way to her; his hands grasped her hair as he brought his lips down to hers. A bolt of electricity shocked through her body as his tongue made its way into her mouth. She clung onto his chest and deepened the kiss as if it was their last. Henry was the first to tear himself away, his breath heavy as he rested his forehead against hers.

"I'm going to hit the pause button on this. I can't do anything under your parents' roof, and I'm bloody exhausted. I'm so happy that I'm here, Ella. You have no idea."

"I'm happy you're here too, Henry." She said as she rubbed her hands against his biceps.

Henry gave her a soft kiss before he turned away and walked to his room. "Goodnight, Ella."

"Goodnight, Henry."

Twenty-One

It was near noon when Gabriella woke up and quietly slipped down the stairs to not wake her parents. Her hair was a pile on the top of her head, and whatever was left of her makeup from last night was smudged on her face. She wore her hooded onesie fleece Christmas pajamas, covered in gingerbread men with the words bite me on it.

The sight of broad shoulders clad in a tight black thermal shirt at the stove stopped her when she entered the kitchen. The smell of cinnamon, sugar, and eggs floated in the air as she stared at the intruder. She blinked away the sleepiness from her eyes as memories of last night returned.

"Good morning, gorgeous," Henry said when he spotted her in the doorway.

"I almost forgot you were here."

"Well, then I obviously did not make a good enough impression on you," he said as he stepped away from the counter. His eyes remained focused on her as he approached, the thermal shirt clung to his muscles and the black and blue plaid pajama pants gripped onto his hips and backside.

Without a word, he lifted her up and placed her onto the kitchen island, then wrapped his arms around her and leaned in for a kiss. Gabriella pressed herself into him, and the kiss quickly heated. Her hands roamed against his angular jaw and cheek bones, and up into his soft, slightly curled hair. Her breathy moans encouraged him to let his hands wander down her back and grip onto her full bottom.

She let one hand journey down his muscle clad torso, until she reached his thigh, and felt his hard length against her wrist. She slowly moved her hand over him and gripped his fullness.

"Fuck, Ella," he groaned as he tore his lips away from hers. "We need to stop."

Gabriella did not let go as she sucked on his neck. "Ella, please."

The sound of the front door as it opened was a bucket of cold water on Gabriella's head. Henry pulled back and tucked his erection into the top of his pajama pants and turned his attention back to the stove. The dogs barked happily in the foyer as her parents removed their leashes.

"It smells wonderful in here, Henry," Maria said with a smile as she hung her winter coat in the closet.

"Thanks, Maria. It's just about done." Henry responded, as he placed turkey sausage on the grill pan.

"What are you guys doing up already?" Gabriella asked as she hopped down from the countertop.

"We took the dogs for a walk, your father has his routine, and he didn't want to skip his daily walk," Maria said as she entered the kitchen and kissed her daughter on the cheek.

"I think we should get ourselves a dog," Giuseppe said as he entered the kitchen. "It will be an incentive to keep walking every day."

466

"It's not a bad idea," Henry chimed in as he took a casserole dish out of the oven.

"You guys are never up and ready to go this early on Christmas," Gabriella commented as her father started the coffee.

"Don't worry, Gabby. I intend to be just as lazy as I always am," Giuseppe said with a smile.

"*Bambolina*, can you get the orange juice and champagne flutes? Desmond left some champagne, and I think we need mimosas," Maria said as she grabbed plates to set the kitchen table.

The four of them worked together to get the food on the table and the dogs settled before they took their seats. "Henry, this looks divine," Maria said with a warm smile while serving everyone.

"Thank you, it's my mother's traditional Christmas day breakfast. She puts a twist on it every year, sometimes it is sweet, sometimes it is savory. I used Ella's focaccia bread to make it. It is a simple sweet French toast bake, and I made some turkey sausage on the side."

"It's delicious," Giuseppe said with a smile as he dug into his food. "You really didn't have to do this, Hank."

"It was the least I could do for everything you did for me," Henry said with a smile before gave Gabriella a small wink.

"Speaking of," Gabriella said after she took a healthy gulp of her mimosa, "what exactly did you do for him, Dad?"

Maria smirked at her husband, eager to hear his explanation to their daughter.

"We're friends, Gabby. That's all," Giuseppe said before took a sip of his coffee. "This coffee is so good. Did you try it? It's a Christmas blend. Dino is carrying it at his shops."

"Cut the crap, Dad. I need to know what is going on."

Giuseppe and Henry shared a look. "Ella, back when I first met your parents, your father and I had a discussion. He wanted to make sure you were safe."

Gabriella's eyebrows furrowed as she stared at the two men.

"I was just concerned for you, Gabby. I knew you were in this new part of your life, and you were so far away from us. I wanted to know you were okay. And I saw the way Henry was with you, and I knew if anyone cared about you as much as I did, it was him. I asked him to look out for you."

"So, you were keeping tabs on me for my dad?" Gabriella asked Henry.

"No. Not at all. I just promised that I would keep you safe. Not because he asked, but because I felt compelled to."

"Henry and I kept in touch. I always asked how you were. Then when you were back here, he would ask me the same. It just became our thing, to let the other person know that you were okay."

468

"Did you do that this past year? Since the movie came out?"

"Not at first. But Henry reached out after my heart attack. He just asked how you were doing."

"You didn't know that we weren't speaking?"

Giuseppe shook his head. "No, it wasn't until a few weeks ago that Henry said he wanted to surprise you and come visit. I told him that he could come for Christmas, but he wasn't sure if he'd be able to make it. He planned to send some stuff here so he could come by when he had availability."

"You planned to come here?" Gabriella asked Henry.

"I did. But then I heard that message and I thought I was too late. I got on the earliest flight I could to get here."

"What about Christmas with your family?" She asked.

Henry smiled and shrugged a shoulder. "They understand. Especially since May hasn't stopped trying to convince me that it was time to try with you since September. Mum has been ganging up with her and my sisters-in-law for me to come to my senses."

Gabriella looked from Henry to her father, then over to her mother, who quietly ate her breakfast. "Did you know anything?"

Maria shook her head. "Just that your father and Henry kept in touch. I told your father to not say anything to you about their friendship because I knew he was a sore subject. I didn't want anything to stop the progress you were making on your own."

"I'll be honest. I'm not sure how I feel about the two of you conspiring behind my back," Gabriella said as she pointed her fork between the two men, then stabbed a piece of the breakfast bake and shoveled it into her mouth.

"Was there more to that sentence?" Henry asked.

"Shh," she said before shoved another forkful of food into her mouth. "I'm eating."

***

Henry and Giuseppe cleaned the kitchen as Maria and Gabriella set the gifts under the Christmas tree in the living room. "I feel like we're doing everything out of order today," Gabriella said as she pulled the Christmas gifts out of the bags she brought from home.

"We'll get back to our pastries and binge watching after we open the gifts. I guess Henry's presence has thrown things a little off their regular schedule."

Gabriella laughed and settled onto the couch.

"Are you okay with everything?" Maria asked as she sat on the other couch.

"It's a lot to take in."

Maria nodded her head thoughtfully. "I want you to be happy, *Bambolina*. Are you okay with him being here? If not, we can tell him to go to the hotel that he had booked."

"No, that's not necessary. But thanks for asking."

"I know that it can't be easy to overlook everything that happened with the two of you. But I will say that the man in there is in love with you."

"How do you know that?"

"I can see it in the way he looks at you. It's not the grand gestures. It's not showing up here on Christmas eve to surprise you. It's not him bringing your friends to see you graduate. It's not him speaking about you on the red carpet. It's the way his eyes light up when he sees you in a room. It's the smile that he isn't aware that is on his face when you are near him. It's how no matter where you are, his sight is always on you, even if it's in his periphery. You can't fake that."

Gabriella swallowed as she stared at the lit Christmas tree, the twinkling lights began to blur as tears collected in her eyes. "There are still so many obstacles, mom. It can't be that easy."

"No one ever said that anything worthwhile is easy. You need to look past the excuses and the what ifs. If you keep focusing on those, you'll just keep going around in circles, never making any progress. You need to decide if he is worth it, and you need to decide if you're worth it.

"Relationships aren't easy, *Bambolina*. They take work and trust. I'm not going to say that your particular situation doesn't have its own unique issues to overcome. But there is no such thing as a fairy tale and a happily ever after. Is he worth the effort?"

Maria's words hung in the air as Giuseppe walked into the room with a tray of hot chocolate and a bottle of marshmallow vodka. Henry followed in with a few small gift bags that he stuck under the tree. His eyes connected with Gabriella's like magnets, and a large smile appeared on his face.

"Yeah, Mom. He is."

Henry sat beside Gabriella on the couch as Giuseppe planted himself next to Maria. Leigh and Scampi followed along and laid on the floor next to the tree. "Don't get too comfortable," Giuseppe warned. "We're only in here for gifts. We'll get back to our regularly scheduled program of laziness in the den after this."

They exchanged gifts and Scampi received the most gifts out of everyone. Since Leigh was an unexpected guest, they shared Scampi's treats with her. Gabriella gifted her parents with a work order from a local construction company to expand the sunroom that they always wanted to do. Gabriella received a beautiful new set of luggage for all of her work travel.

Giuseppe handed a large giftbox to Henry, who was surprised by the gesture. "You didn't need to get me anything," he said with a smile as he took the box, hardly able to see over the top of it.

"Oh, trust me, I did," Giuseppe said with a smirk.

Henry opened the top of the box and began to laugh as he took out item after item of New York Giants paraphernalia. He lifted a full fleece blanket, hat, scarf, football, Christmas stocking with his name on it, and a jersey with his last name on the back.

"Ah, for the get-well gift, I presume?"

Giuseppe nodded and gave Henry a hug. "Merry Christmas, Hank."

"Thanks, G. Merry Christmas."

Gabriella looked at Henry and bit her lip as his eyes zeroed in on the act. "I didn't get you anything."

Henry leaned over her and planted a soft kiss on her cheek. "You're my gift."

Henry stood, then walked over to the tree and grabbed three small gift bags. He handed one to Giuseppe, one to Maria, and one to Gabriella.

Maria opened her gift first, and gasped when she opened the envelope tucked inside the bag. "Henry, we can't accept this. It's too generous."

The attention of the room was focused on Maria, who held a brochure for Hawaii with the name of a travel agent connected to it. "He got us a trip to Hawaii."

"You said you've never been, and you always wanted to go. I have a friend over there who knows all of the best places and he hooked up the packages for me. I swear, it wasn't as much as you think."

Maria jumped up and threw her arms around Henry. "Thank you so much, Henry. This really is too much."

"I just want you to have a good time. You've always been so welcoming to me, and you made this beautiful woman. There isn't enough to thank you for her." Henry said with a smile.

Giuseppe took his turn next and opened his gift, which also contained an envelope. "Absolutely not, Hank," he said when he opened the envelope.

"What is it, honey?" Maria asked.

"A voucher for flights to England."

Maria smacked Henry on the arm in protest. "You don't need to spend your money on us, Henry."

"I got those for you in hopes that you would use them to come visit me sometime and maybe meet my family. You don't have to; you could visit whenever you'd like. But my hope is for there to be a reason for you all to meet one day."

Gabriella wanted to pounce on Henry and not let him up until she had her wicked way with him, but she kept herself in her seat for the sake of her parents. The fact that he bought tickets in hope for their families to meet meant that he was serious about the two of them being together.

"Ella, you want to open your gift next?" Henry asked as he sat down next to her. She nodded as she reached for the small giftbag. She pulled out a shirt,

474

which when she unfolded it was a black tank top with the word hola written in gold script.

Her face split into a smile as she shook her head and looked at Henry. "What? I couldn't write senorita on it, you're my senorita."

"You're an asshole." She said, before she quickly kissed him. "Thank you. I kind of love it oddly enough."

"There is more in the bag, Ella."

Gabriella looked in and found a small turquoise box at the bottom of the bag. She looked at him when she tipped the bag into her open hand. It screamed jewelry as she studied the box.

"Henry, I don't know what is in this, but it's already too much. I know this color."

"Just open it, beautiful."

Gabriella opened the Tiffany's box to reveal cluster diamond earrings. "These are beautiful, Henry."

"I wanted to get you something that you could wear every day. Something that will make you think of me when you see it."

Gabriella placed the box down, then captured his strong jaw with her hands and pressed her lips against his. It was a sweet kiss that lingered. There was no urgency, no tongue. Just a pure kiss full of thanks. When they broke, she looked over at her parents.

"Sorry guys."

They laughed in response as Henry urged her to put them in her ears. "I figured I'd start out with the basics. For every milestone we reach, I can build onto it."

"Why are you so freaking romantic?" She said as she stared up into hie eyes.

"It's you, Ella. You bring it out in me."

***

The rest of the day was spent in the den as they picked on leftovers and ate their weight in the cake.

"Oh wow, now I know what I was missing out on last year when Matt talked about how amazing your baking is." Henry said as he rubbed his hand over the washboard stomach hidden under his thermal shirt.

"You're not giving up already, are you Hank?" Giuseppe asked from his recliner.

"Absolutely not. Just need a moment to digest." Henry responded and put his arm around Gabriella and pulled her against his side. She snuggled into his body and sighed contently.

"Which was the favorite cake?" Maria asked.

476

"I hate to agree with Matt, but that German chocolate cake might be the winner." Henry said with a smile.

A Christmas Story had just ended on the television, and Giuseppe picked up the remote to find something else to watch. "I have to ask, G, since I'm here. Do you have any videos of Ella when she was little? She wouldn't let me look at her yearbook last night and I would love to see some home movies."

"Don't you dare, Dad," Gabriella warned as her father laughed.

"I absolutely do, and lucky for you, I had them all digitalized, and I can access them through the cloud," he said as he navigated through his smart television.

Just then, Henry's phone rang. "Oh, I have to take this, it's my mum."

He answered the FaceTime call, and a beautiful woman with light brown hair and delicate lines around her blue eyes was on the screen.

"Hey Mum! Merry Christmas!" Henry said as he answered the call.

"Merry Christmas, Henry. I didn't want to call too soon; did everything work out alright?" His mother asked.

"Yes, Mum, everything worked out fine. Say hello to Ella," Henry said as he angled the phone to include Gabriella, whose head was against his shoulder.

"Oh no, Henry, don't put me on camera, I look hideous," Gabriella squealed as she tried to cover her face with her hands.

"Nonsense, I've seen so many pictures of you, I know how beautiful you are," his mother said.

"You don't understand, I'm in pajamas and have yesterday's makeup on my face," Gabriella mumbled behind her hand.

"I get it. I'm in my robe myself," Henry's mother said with a laugh.

Gabriella removed her hand and smiled at the phone. "It's not ideal, but it is nice to meet you, Mrs. Anderson."

"It's a pleasure to meet you too, Gabriella. And please, call me Betty. None of that Mrs. Anderson stuff, that' my mother-in-law."

"Did you have a nice Christmas?" Henry asked.

"It was the typical hell it usually is. I'm getting too old for this nonsense," Betty said with a smile. "Nathan and Millie left after dinner; the poor thing is so exhausted from her pregnancy. Andrew left with Becca not long after, she got called into work for an emergency. Johnny and Shannon left about an hour ago. And you know your sister and Gerald are still here. Enough of that, tell me, were you able to grovel and get Gabriella to forgive you?"

"Yes, Mum. She had me on my hands and knees apologizing and kissing her feet."

Gabriella shook her head. "That's a terrible lie; I gave in far too easily. But I can't help it," she said as she pinched his cheek.

478

"Well, it makes me happy to hear it. He's quite smitten with you," Betty said with a wink.

Gabriella smiled as Henry looked at her. "It's mutual."

Betty's face lit up with a smile as she called her husband over. A man with graying hair at his temples who looked similar to Henry, but with dark eyes, came into the frame. "Hey Dad, Merry Christmas."

"Henry, Merry Christmas. And you must be Gabriella. It's nice to meet you. Merry Christmas."

"It's nice to meet you too, Mr. Anderson. Merry Christmas."

"Please, call me James. Mr. Anderson makes me feel old." He said with a smile that looked similar to his son's.

"So, tell us, what is the plan? Are you staying there?" Betty asked.

"Um," Henry said as he glanced down at Gabriella, "we really haven't discussed it yet. We're currently at Gabriella's parent's house."

"But we're heading back to my apartment tomorrow. We have a virtual Christmas party with our friends from the movie," Gabriella explained.

"Oh, well, I'm sure you'll figure it out," Betty said, her blue eyes twinkling with excitement.

"What are you plans for the rest of the night?" James asked.

"I convinced Giuseppe to show me old home movies of Ella," Henry said with a smile. "We're also gorging ourselves on Ella's baking. Her cakes are amazing."

"That sounds like fun," James said with a smile. "Don't worry, Gabriella, I have plenty of embarrassing things to show you of Henry when he was little," Betty responded.

"I look forward to seeing that," Gabriella said with a smile.

The dogs began to whine by the back door. Maria started to get up to let them out. "No, Mom, I've got it. Excuse me," Gabriella said as she got up from the couch to let the dogs outside.

"You guys want to meet Ella's parents? You will get along brilliantly," Henry asked as he shifted the phone to include her parents in the background.

Gabriella smiled as she watched her parents speak on the phone while she waited for the dogs to do their business. After the dogs frolicked in the snow for a few minutes, Gabriella called them back in and shook a bag of treats to get their attention.

The dogs bounded back into the house and jumped up on Gabriella with excitement for their treats. She gave them each a treat, which they took into the dining room and curled up under the table to eat. She entered the den to hear May's voice speaking to her parents.

"It's so nice to see you again," she exclaimed from the phone. "I was worried that my brother messed stuff up too much. Gabby is there, right? You didn't just take pity on him and let him stay?"

Giuseppe and Maria laughed as Betty told her daughter, "We were just speaking to her, she let Leigh out."

"You better not screw this up, H. I'm warning you," May threatened.

"Don't worry, May, I can handle him," Gabriella said with a smile as she poked her head between her parents.

May yelled with delight when she saw her. "I know you can. He's a bit of a handful, but I'm sure you can keep him in his place."

"How was the wedding?" Gabriella asked.

"It was amazing! I'll have to send you pictures. I'll follow you on insta. It was so perfect, right mum?" May said excitedly.

Betty nodded in response. "It was beautiful, and expensive, and I'm glad it is over," she said with a smile.

"Oh, it's almost eleven. I didn't realize it was that late. Gerald and I should go home. He has work in the morning." May said to her mother.

"Okay, I guess that's my cue to hang up. It was lovely meeting all of you. I hope we get to meet sooner rather than later," Betty said with a warm smile.

"Agreed. It was so nice to meet you too. And don't worry, we'll make sure Henry is plenty fed while he's with us," Maria said with a smile.

"And Gabriella," Betty said, "be sure to take care of each other."

"We will, Betty. Merry Christmas."

"Merry Christmas, I love you, Henry," his mom said as she blew a kiss to the phone.

"I love you too, Mum. I'll give you a ring soon." Henry said before he hung up. He looked to Giuseppe and said, "I believe we have some home movies to watch."

***

After three hours of home movies, her parents shared tales of Gabriella's childhood and ate more leftovers. Maria was ready to go to sleep after the long day. "What time are you planning on leaving tomorrow?" She asked as she fought a yawn.

"The party is at six, and I have to heat up the food before it. As long as we're at the apartment by four, it should give me plenty of time to get ready. Maybe we'll take the two-twenty out of Babylon."

"You're going to take Henry on the Long Island Railroad?" Maria asked.

"Why not?" Gabriella asked.

"Take the Corolla, Gabby. That might be a bit much for him to the on the train. Someone is going to bother him," Giuseppe suggested.

"There is no need for that, G. We can take the train; it's no big deal. I'd like to see what her commute is." Henry said reassuringly.

"What about the dogs?" Maria asked.

"Oh, I didn't think about that. Leigh is too big for a carrier," Gabriella said.

"Take the car, Gabby. I can bring it home next week after New Year's. You going to bed, *cara mia*?"

"I'm exhausted. Are you coming up?" Maria asked.

"Can I watch *Die Hard* while you're sleeping?" Giuseppe asked with a smile. Maria rolled her eyes and nodded as she kissed Gabriella and Henry good night. Giuseppe wished them a good night as well and followed his wife upstairs.

"So, did you want anything to eat?" Gabriella asked once they were alone.

"No, Ella, I don't think I could eat any more if I wanted to. I'm stuffed."

"Okay. Did you want to watch a movie or something?"

"Why are you acting so nervous?"

"I'm not nervous."

Henry put his arm around her shoulders and rubbed her upper arm. He looked at the two dogs curled up together on the floor and smiled. "At least the two of them are getting along."

Gabriella smiled and nodded. "Yeah. They are both so loveable, I'd be surprised if they didn't."

"Do you want to go inside and look at the tree?" Henry asked.

Gabriella shook her head. Her hand rested on his stomach, which she started to rub. He looked down at her hand, raised his eyebrows, then shifted his eyes to her. "Ella?"

"Mmm?" She responded as her eyes focused her hand.

"What are you doing?"

"Nothing," she said, her hand made its way under his shirt to graze her fingers against his skin. His abdomen clenched in response.

"Ella, you need to stop." He warned, but it fell on deaf ears. He exhaled as he tried to keep control. "Ella, please."

She looked up at him with hooded eyes and bit her lip. He growled slightly, then pushed her down on the couch and hovered over her. "You're playing with fire, Ella."

She lifted her hips up to his in response, which caused him to slam his mouth against hers. He stifled a moan that erupted from her throat as he ground

484

himself against her. Their tongues tangled as he unzipped the top of her onesie, his hand reached in and cupped her breast.

A slight bark from Leigh was enough to pull him out from what his was doing. "Bloody hell, Ella. We can't do this here. Not in your parents' house."

Gabriella sat up as she zipped her pajamas. "You're right. I'm sorry. You're just really irresistible."

Henry looked up at the ceiling as he covered his face with his hand and wiped down his jaw. "Yeah, Ella, I understand completely. How about you show me your yearbook, then we go to sleep, separately. That way tomorrow comes sooner, and I can fuck you like I'm dying to once we're at your apartment."

Gabriella nodded in agreement, then turned off the television and lights in the den and headed up the stairs. Henry called for the dogs, who lazily got up and followed to Gabriella's bedroom.

Henry found Gabriella on her bed with her yearbook in her hands. He snuggled up next to her and took the book from her. "Okay, I want to see what you, Laurel, and Desmond were up to in here."

He opened the yearbook where a few photos fell out. Gabriella explained who everyone was, which included Brad and Jason. Henry listened as she shared some stories and smiled when he saw the photos in the yearbook. She was embarrassed for him to see her at her heaviest, but he just told her that he thought she was beautiful.

He stood up and looked around her room, then pointed at things and asked to hear the story behind it. Around midnight, Gabriella began to fall asleep with Henry next to her. When she was finally asleep, Henry kissed her on the top of her head and made his way to the bedroom next door.

Twenty-Two

After they walked half a block and wrangled two dogs on leashes, and carried bags and containers, Gabriella was elated to be on the other side of her apartment door. Henry let the two dogs off their leashes and watched Leigh take in her new surroundings and followed Scampi through the one-bedroom apartment. Henry removed his coat and hung it on the coat rack as Gabriella placed the bags on the small dining table and went into the kitchen.

"What are you doing?" Henry asked as he watched her move in her small galley kitchen.

"I have to get the food Joshua sent into the oven to heat up. Could you give me that tan tote my dad gave us?"

Henry grabbed the tote and left it on the peninsula counter. He removed containers of food and a large thermos. Under the food was a six pack of Guinness. "I really love your father. He thinks of everything."

"I know. I'm sure the thermos is filled with his holiday martini. And he packed up some pastries and the German chocolate cake you liked."

"Looks like there is some focaccia in here too," Henry said with a smile when he removed an item wrapped in tinfoil.

"Between all of that and the food that Joshua sent; we could be fed through the new year. Oh, and I have the cookies I baked that I sent to everyone too."

Once the oven was preheated, Gabriella took out the trays of food and put them in the oven. "Do you know what they sent?" Henry asked.

Gabriella shook her head. "Patti told me no peeking. Just said to set the oven to three-seventy-five and let it heat for about an hour."

"Did you forget a tray in the refrigerator?"

"No, one was labeled to keep cold."

"So, are you done setting up for the party?"

"Once I put everything away that my dad gave us, yes. Did you want to go put your stuff in my room? The bathroom is right behind the kitchen, and my room is across the hall, you can't miss it."

"Put the food away, Ella." Henry commanded as he gestured to the containers on the counter. Gabriella gave him a strange look as she rearranged some items in the refrigerator to fit the rest of the containers. When she closed the door, Henry lifted her up and threw her over his shoulder.

"Your room is across the hall, right?" He said as he headed out of the kitchen.

"Put me down, Henry, I'm going to compact your discs!"

Henry playfully smacked her behind for her comment.

The dogs looked up from the couch in the living room as Henry strode by, then entered the bedroom and shut the door behind him. Gabriella giggled as he tossed her onto the bed. He pounced on top of her and only paused the kisses to remove their articles of clothing.

"This isn't going to last too long, Ella. It's been too long and I'm a very selfish man," he said as he made his way down her body, his mouth fitting against her lower lips. Gabriella moaned his name as he made her quickly fall apart.

As she came down from her sudden orgasm, she smirked as Henry's face approached hers. "I guess you aren't the only one not lasting too long."

Henry kissed her as he slipped on a condom and eased his way into her. "I guess that is what two days of foreplay will do to a person," he said as he filled her to the hilt.

"Fuck, Ella. I know it's been a while, and we haven't done this much, but you feel like home. I'm meant to fill you."

Gabriella looked up at Henry in wonder, her hands roamed down his back. "I know what you mean. But if you don't start moving soon, I'm going to scream."

***

They laid entangled in each other's arms, naked underneath the pale gray sheets. Henry took in his surroundings and studied the adult version of Gabriella's room. The stark white walls were covered in a painting and a few photo frames. The headboard was a tufted dark gray, and the comforter and pillows were a navy blue, which matched the drapes on the wall of windows.

The furniture was a rustic gray, and there was a fluffy white area rug that covered most of the room.

The sound of the timer on the stove made Gabriella start to move. Henry smiled as he looked at her as she began to sit up, her breast partially covered by her hair. "What?" She asked.

"I was thinking about how drastically different your bedroom is here to the bedroom at your parents'."

"You should see the one in California. It's all beachy and white and turquoise." She said as she stood up and reached for her clothes that were strewn across the floor.

"I would love to see the one in California," he said as he wrapped his arms around her naked torso.

"Then you will. If you'll excuse me, I need to get dressed and take the food out of the oven."

He batted her hands away as she tried to put her bra on, then gently cupped her breasts. "You don't need that. I'll keep them supported."

"Henry, I don't want you to do that," she said with a smile.

"It doesn't feel like you don't want me to do this." He said as he fondled her. "As a matter of fact, it feels like they want me to do this," he said as he turned her around and then captured a nipple in his mouth.

490

Her fingers threaded through his hair as she sighed and enjoyed the sensation of his suction. "Henry, seriously, we're going to be late for the party."

He continued, and moved from one breast to the other, his hand drifted down her stomach and into the underwear she recently donned. "Damn it, Henry, the food..."

"Will be fine. You're so wet, Ella."

Gabriella shoved him back onto the bed, then opened her nightstand and threw a condom at him. He looked at it and smiled as she pulled off her underwear and climbed on top of him. "Make it quick, Henry, I don't want the fire alarm to go off.

***

Twenty minutes later, Gabriella was dressed and had the food out of the oven, overjoyed that nothing burned. She checked the clock and realized they were almost ten minutes late for the party. Henry was in the shower, so she rushed to the living room to boot up her laptop, then rushed back over to the kitchen to get the thermos with the martini mixture. She pulled out two glasses from the cabinet and set them on the counter before she ran back to the computer to join the virtual party.

"Well, it's about time you joined the party, don't 'cha know," Patti said when Gabriella's face appeared on the screen.

"Sorry, guys. I lost track of time," Gabriella said with a smile.

"You're always the first one on these calls," Patti commented.

"She seems out of breath," Max said as he looked at Jem and Darius, who were all together.

"And a little flush," Darius chimed in.

"I was running around, I had to pull the food out of the oven, and I didn't realize the time."

Laurel and Matt smiled at her response, aware of what caused her to be late. The dogs barked at Henry when he walked out of the bedroom in gray sweatpants and a white thermal shirt. Gabriella's eyes followed him as he entered the kitchen.

"What's with the barking?" Joshua asked from the same screen as Patti.

"Oh, it's my dog, Scampi. You guys never met him. Come here, Scampi," Gabriella called the dog as he jumped onto her lap and licked her chin. The party cooed over how adorable he was when Leigh barked again.

"That was definitely not that dog." Joshua commented.

Bob poked his head up behind Joshua and said, "that sounds like Leigh."

Patti looked at the list of attendees and shook her head. "No, Henry isn't on. He told me he wasn't sure if he'd make it this year."

Leigh made her way over to the table where Henry had placed a plate of sugar cookies, her head in the frame of the camera. "That looks like Leigh," Bob commented.

Henry poured the martinis and handed Gabriella a glass. She smiled in response, then moved over for Henry to sit. Once he settled into the frame everyone on the call, aside from Laurel and Matt, began to scream and cheer. Henry took a sip of the martini before he placed it on the table, then put his arm around Gabriella.

"Hey everyone. Happy Christmas." Henry said with a chuckle.

It took a while for everyone to calm down at the sight of Henry in Gabriella's apartment. "Wait, wait, wait. Before we get all crazy. I need to know," Darius said as everyone settled down. "Are the two of you together? Like officially together, or is this some 'we're friends' bullshit?"

Everyone quietly awaited the response. Henry and Gabriella looked at one another and had a silent conversation. Henry raised his eyebrows and gestured towards the screen, which made Gabriella smile. She turned and faced the computer and nodded her head. "Yes, we're together. Officially."

Patti screamed the loudest of everyone as she started to dance in her seat. "It's about fucking time," Jem said with a shake of her head.

"I'm glad you approve," Gabriella said with a smirk.

Once everyone settled down, Patti took over. "Does everyone have their food prepared?"

Everyone nodded as Patti continued. "Okay, we have some South Dakota staples for ya'll tonight. Some of these are featured at the restaurant. There is hand pies stuffed with bison and beer battered walleye in one tray. There is chili in another tray, cinnamon rolls that need to be eaten with the chili, and in the cold tray are kolache and kuchen. We would have sent fry bread and chislic, but we didn't think they would travel well since they are deep fried."

"I'm sorry, did you say to eat chili with cinnamon rolls?" Max asked.

"Sure did."

"That sounds disgusting." Max replied.

"Don't knock it until you try it. It's amazing," Bob commented.

"Patti, I swear I can feed an army with what you send," Gabriella commented.

"Well, I was hoping that Henry would be there." Patti replied.

Gabriella tilted her head as she looked at Patti, then turned her attention to Henry. "Did Patti know you were going to be here?"

Henry shook his head. "No, I mentioned to her like I did to your father that I wanted to see you soon."

Patti waved her hand toward the camera. "He's such a romantic at heart, I knew he wouldn't make it to the new year without seeing you. Any who," she continued, "We switched up the party this year. Everyone is eating the same food, so no one is jealous of whatever desserts Gabby is moaning over. We

494

also did secret Santa, so only one gift per person. And we're gonna play Naughty or Nice, a holiday version of never have I ever."

"Let's start with eating. Everyone, get your food." Joshua announced.

Gabriella made two plates of food as she overheard a conversation. "Darius, why are you staring at me like that?" Henry asked.

"How do you know I'm staring at you; I could be looking at Bob, or Matt."

"That super villain arched eyebrow is directed at me and we all know it."

"What's with the sudden romantic gesture? We've been telling you for months to talk to her. Why the change of heart?"

"Darius, leave him alone," Matt warned.

"No, I won't leave him alone. We all saw what she went through this year. She tried to hide it from us the best she could, but we know it tore her up." Darius replied.

Henry's eyes shifted towards the kitchen before he turned his attention back to the computer. "She said she was moving on. I knew that I stayed away from her for too long at that point, and I did what needed to be done to not lose her forever."

"You're being selfish, Hank," Darius responded with a roll of his eyes. "If she said she was moving on, you should have let her."

Gabriella stood in the kitchen as she unknowingly held her breath as she listed. Darius did have a point, and maybe she was too forgiving to just let Henry back in.

"Hush your mouth, Darius," Patti scolded, "he's in love with her. He made a mistake, but it came from a good place."

"I think you're just a hopeless romantic, Patti," Darius clapped back, "but this isn't a movie. You can't just sweep in like some prince charming and then disappear again when things get real."

"Who ever said I was going to disappear? Not that I should need to explain myself to you, Darius, but I'm in love with her, and I'm in this for the long haul."

Before Darius could respond, Gabriella walked into the living room with the plates of food. She handed one to Henry before settling back onto the couch. "Guys, this food looks amazing. You really outdid yourselves."

"It does look yummy," Laurel corroborated as she attempted to clear the tension on the call.

"Thanks, ya'll. I've been dying for ya to try some of our personal favorites. We'd love it one day if you'd all come back to South Dakota and come to the restaurant, don't 'cha know." Patti said with a smile.

The party ate in silence, except to complement the food or ask what was in it. "Patti, why don't we start the game?" Joshua suggested.

"Good idea, love. Everybody needs a drink, because all we know how to play is drinking games. Remember, it's never have I ever but with holiday questions. I guess I'll start. Never have I been kissed under mistletoe."

Everyone but Gabriella and Bob took a drink. Henry glanced over as he took his drink. "Ella, seriously?"

Gabriella shook her head. "Nope. Not once."

"Let's go by party," Patti said, "Joshua, you're next."

"Alright, never have I ever dressed up as Santa Clause." Max was the only person to drink. "Really? No one else? I have a bunch of nieces and nephews that I dress up for on Christmas and I hand out presents to them."

"That's actually really sweet, Max," Jem said with a smile. "I never met a Latin Santa."

"You're not hanging out at the right places, mija." Max said with a wink.

"Never have I ever sung Christmas songs," Bob said with a smile because he knew that everyone would drink.

"Nice one," Matt said with a laugh.

"Why doesn't our next big group go? Jem, want to go next?" Patti suggested.

"Sure. Never have I ever worn an ugly Christmas sweater." Jem said proudly, which made Bob laugh. "Everyone has to drink to that one too, it was our theme last year. Two in a row for everyone to drink," Bob exclaimed.

"My turn," Darius said. "Never have I ever ghosted someone."

"Jesus Christ," Laurel mumbled as she rolled her eyes. Jem smacked Darius on the arm and Patti sighed.

"Wrong holiday, mate," Henry said coolly.

"Why aren't you drinking, Henry?" Darius challenged.

"Oh my god, enough!" Gabriella shouted. "I get it. We all get it. I appreciate the concern, Darius, but we don't need the snark. Yes, Henry ghosted me, yes, he came here on Christmas eve and apologized and explained himself. I get that you are looking out for me, but that's no better than the press trying to get into our business. Do we have some things to work out, yes? But it's between me and Henry.

"Please stop with the passive aggressiveness. It's supposed to be a fun holiday celebration with our friends. If I need help, I'll ask for it. But I'm a grown woman, and I can make my own decisions. I love you all, but can we please just get back to the game and have some fun?"

Darius stood up and walked out of the room, which made everyone call him back. Max excused himself as he chased after him.

"That's seemed a bit dramatic," Matt said before drinking his beer.

498

"I'm sorry, guys. I didn't mean to do that," Gabriella offered.

"You didn't do anything wrong. This is all on Darius," Jem responded as she looked over her shoulder to where the guys walked out. There was a bit of shouting in the background, but the words were muffled. Jem's shoulders sagged, then turned her attention back to the computer. "I'm going to sign off and deal with the drama queen over here. I'll come back on when everything is okay."

"Keep me in the loop, Jem," Patti requested before Jem signed off.

"Well, that sucked." Bob said after he took a bite of his chili-dipped cinnamon roll.

"I'm so grossed out by that," Laurel said as she looked at Bob's food.

"Well, what do we now? Do we continue without them?" Joshua asked.

Patti shook her head. "Jem is calling me, let me take this." She excused herself and left the room.

"So, this went to the shitter pretty quickly," Joshua said to the rest of them.

"I don't know what Darius' problem is," Laurel chimed in. "That was very unlike him."

"Agreed, but it's really none of his business," Bob responded.

"Should I have not said anything?" Gabriella asked.

"No, you were right to speak up. It's between you and Hen. It's nobody else's business. If you needed us, you would have said something. He's just stirring up trouble." Laurel replied.

"How's the restaurant going, Joshua?" Henry asked to change the subject.

"Really well. We're busy, which is always a good thing. We might have to expand the footprint, but we'll have to figure out if we can do it financially." Joshua replied.

"I'm willing to invest if you're looking for help," Henry offered.

"I totally would too," Laurel added.

"Really guys? That's incredibly generous. I'll have to discuss it with Patti of course." Joshua responded.

"We believe in you, mate. The food is incredible. You could even open another location if you wanted," Henry encouraged.

Just as Joshua was about to speak, he paused as he listened to Patti in the background. Bob shook his head at whatever happened, "Excuse me, everyone, I need to go check on Patti."

"What is going on, Bob?" Gabriella asked.

"Darius is having a breakdown. Apparently, he suspects his husband or whatever is cheating on him. So, he lashed out. I don't think it has anything to do with you guys. But it sounds like Jem is giving Patti the play-by-play, and Max is trying to calm Darius down. Sounds like a real shit show."

"Maybe we should just sign off?" Laurel suggested.

"Nah, not yet. Hang on, I'm going to go listen in and see what else I can find out," Bob said before he left the room.

"Maybe you guys should have just come here, and we could have had our own party," Gabriella suggested to Laurel and Matt.

"Hell no, I'm not going to be stuck in a one-bedroom apartment while the two of you get reacquainted," Matt said with a shiver.

"Besides, I'll be there in two weeks to spend time with you," Laurel said with a smile. "Unless I'm going to be cramping your style now that Henry is here."

"Oh, um, I didn't even think about it." Gabriella said as she looked to Henry.

"Well, we didn't really discuss how long I would be here. I have to be back in England for filming the next superhero movie in January." Henry answered.

"When in January?" Gabriella asked as her heart sunk into her stomach. The thought of him leaving her so soon after coming back made her feel sick.

"I have to be there by the fifth. I'm sorry, Ella, I know it's soon, but I really wanted to see you, and this was the only time I had available. I didn't want to wait until March or April to see you, and I didn't want to do this over the phone."

Gabriella nodded her head and swallowed down her feelings. "I get it. It's okay. You'll be here for new year's?"

Henry nodded. "Awesome, so then when one guest leaves, the other one will come stay! Just make sure you wash the sheets before I get there," Laurel joked.

"Um, there is something I didn't mention to anyone yet. I'm going to be heading to Greece in February to film the Amazon movie. Veronica had me cast in her movie. I'll be there for the spring."

"Gabby, that is amazing!" Laurel shouted.

"I promise, it won't change anything for you and Des, I'll still be managing your stuff from there."

"Who cares about that, Gabby, this is such an amazing opportunity for you," Laurel said with a genuine smile. Matt raised his beer in the air and toasted, "To Gabby and her new venture. Looks like this new year is going to bring some major changes for you."

Laurel and Henry joined the toast, as Bob came back into view. "Hey guys, it looks like they calmed Darius down. Jem and Max are planning to help him find out if Samuel is cheating on him. Kinda put a damper on whole party. I think Patti is upset that it was a bust, and Joshua is trying to cheer her up. I'm thinking we all bail."

"Hey Bob, you're planning on coming with me to England for the next movie, right?" Henry asked.

502

"Sure am, I'm looking forward to it."

"How would you feel about extending in a bit and helping Ella out in Greece with Scampi when you're done with me?"

"That would be awesome. Why are you going to be in Greece, Gabs?"

"She's a legit Hollywood movie star, Bob," Laurel said with a wink.

***

The week between Christmas and New Year's Day past quickly. Gabriella and Henry spent time together in the city, they took their dogs for walks, visited the tree in Rockefeller center, hung out with Desmond and Arnie, went out to dinner at five-star restaurants and dive bars, and visited museums that Henry never went to. Any time they weren't in public, they were naked in Gabriella's apartment to make up for lost time.

On New Year's Eve, they prepared to attend a party hosted at the Dolce's house. While Gabriella showered, Henry was on his phone and surfed through his social media accounts when he was inundated with alerts. He scrolled through the feed and saw multiple photos of him in New York with Gabriella. He received a text from his publicist to warn him that it's known that he is in the city with Gabriella, and to be on alert.

"Ella?" He called from the bedroom.

"Yeah?" She asked as she walked into the bedroom with one towel wrapped around her body and the other wrapped around her head.

"Don't distract me walking in here looking like a gift I need to unwrap." Henry said as he watched her search through her undergarment drawer.

"We have no time for that, Mr. Anderson. Did you want something? You called me before."

"Oh, right. Um, there are photos of us this week online, Ella."

Gabriella paused, then pulled her underwear on underneath her towel. "Well, that didn't take long."

"What do you want to do about it?"

Gabriella shook her head, then removed the towel from her hair. "Nothing, its already out there. I said I wasn't going to let it affect my life."

"Do you want us to put something up ourselves to shut the rumors up?"

Gabriella shrugged. "I don't think it matters what we do, they will post what they want to. You need to start getting ready, we have to leave here in an hour. We're taking the car back to my parents tonight, and Arnie is giving us a ride back tomorrow."

"Ella, are you positive you don't want to post something?"

"Yes, Henry, I'm positive." She confirmed before she gave him a quick kiss and went back to the bathroom to blow dry her hair.

Forty minutes later, Gabriella was dressed in a long-sleeved emerald-green sequenced dress that fell to her lower thigh. Her hair was loosely pinned up,

504

and her makeup was neutral with heavy mascara. She threw on her coat and slipped her feet into crushed black velvet heels as Henry, dressed in dark jeans, a white t-shirt, and a black velvet blazer, wrangled the dogs and put their leashes on them.

She grabbed the tote full of champagne cupcakes, strawberry and champagne cake pops, and chocolate-covered strawberries that she had made earlier in the day. After she locked up, they walked the half of a block to where the car was parked. Henry loaded the dogs into the back seat as Gabriella placed the baked goods in the trunk.

"Henry, what bag is back here in the trunk?"

"I packed us a change of clothes for tomorrow. Is that okay?"

"Of course, it is, I figured we'd just find something in my old bedroom, but this works way better."

***

They took the hour and a half drive to discuss their future together while the dogs rode comfortably in the back.

"So, I was thinking," Henry said as held Gabriella's hand, his thumb rubbed across the top of her hand, "when I'm done filming in March, I could come stay with you in Greece while you're on set. And since we're only three hours away from each other, maybe I can fly in to see you on my days off. I can get Bob to come and watch the pups so we can have time to ourselves."

Gabriella smiled at Henry. "That sounds really nice, Henry. But let's not get too crazy. I know how it is on set. I'm on board for you staying with me when you're done filming. The rest we'll play be ear."

"After you're done filming, would you want to stay with me in England for a while? You can experience where I live, meet my family?"

"See embarrassing home movies of you during your awkward phase? Sign me up! Payback is going to be a bitch." Gabriella said with a laugh.

Henry laughed along. "But really, Ella, would you come stay with me in England? You wouldn't have to bring much; we can get you what you need while you're there and you keep your things at my house."

"Have you left anything in my apartment?" Gabriella asked with a raised eyebrow.

"I'll leave everything I have with me. And Desmond was nice enough to run to the shop for me to get this outfit today. So, I have more that I arrived with."

"I guess I can clear out a drawer for you. And maybe some room in my closet."

"Deal. Now, how long are you willing to stay with me?"

"I'm not sure. I guess I have to check my calendar. I haven't looked much at my own schedule post filming. I'm assuming you'll have to come back here for the academy awards."

"Sure, if I'm nominated. But that isn't too long of an event."

"We could stay at my place in Venice Beach."

"Okay. Even if we stay there for a week or two, then what?"

"I'm not sure, but like you said, I have a very flexible job that can really be done from anywhere. We can go wherever. Just let me know when you get sick of me. I still have my own place I can escape to and give you your space."

"I don't think I'll ever get sick of you, Ella."

"You say that now, but you have no idea how annoying I can be," Gabriella warned with a smile.

"I'll take my chances. I have a feeling that all of your good will overcompensate for any annoying."

Gabriella pulled up to her parents' house and Giuseppe greeted them at the door as the dog jumped around excitedly at the attention. "Are you sure it's okay to leave them here while we're at the party?" Henry asked.

"Oh, it's fine, honey. We'll let them run around in the back. Giuseppe set up bowls of food and water, he got them chew toys and those huge bones to chew on. They'll have more of a new year's party than we will." Maria said with a laugh, then kissed Henry hello.

"Getting some use out of those shoes from last Christmas, huh Mom?" Gabriella said with a smile when she spotted the red bottoms.

"Yes, well, I don't get the excuse to dress up too often. And who am I to not wear these babies as often as possible."

Once the dogs were settled, they locked up the house and headed to the car. "Why don't I drive, Gabby?" Giuseppe offered.

"I have a bunch of stuff in the trunk that I'm bringing."

"That's fine. I'll drive the Corolla." Giuseppe said as he took the keys from his daughter. Gabriella and Henry sat in the back seat as Giuseppe drove them a few blocks over to the Dolce's house. Henry typed away on his phone on the way there.

"Who are you texting?" Gabriella asked, eyeing his phone.

"No one. I just posted something online," he responded with a smile. He held up his phone to show a picture Leigh and Scampi together on the dog bed with the large bones and chew toys next to them. The photo was captioned *New Year's puppy party*.

"That's pretty adorable." Gabriella said with a smile as Henry pocketed his phone.

"Did Gabby prepare you for this party, Hank?" Giuseppe asked as he parked on the street.

"No, should she have?"

Maria laughed. "If you think we had a lot of food on Christmas eve, just you wait. Dino goes nuts. It might not be huge trays of food like we do, but you will be stuffed. It's all hors d'oeuvres and he has servers here passing out the food all night. There will be bartenders set up. He usually has the patio open with heaters all over the place. He said something about getting a DJ this year too."

"He's really going the extra mile this year, huh?" Gabriella asked.

"Should we be concerned about the people working the event posting things, Ella?" Henry asked, looking up at the house.

"I'm not worried about it. Let's just have a good time."

***

After they greeted the parents and Laurel's family, Gabriella and Henry found Laurel and Matt seated outside in the tent-covered patio. "Wow, Dino went all out this year," Gabriella said when she greeted Laurel.

"I know. I sprung for the wait staff. I want my parents to enjoy the party. You know how much work these things are to set up. We had people setup the tent and all the tables and chairs. They even brought the bars with them. There is one out here and one in the kitchen."

"Bar?" Matt asked as he looked at Henry. Henry smiled and nodded as the two of them walked off together.

"This was really nice for you to do, Lau."

"Yeah, I kinda hoped it would soften the blow of me not wanting to actually plan a wedding anytime soon."

"Sneaky, sneaky," Gabriella said with a laugh.

"Hey, it's a reason for my dad to show off and have a good time, you know what a ham he really is. Loves the spotlight."

"I get it. Any word from Darius?"

Laurel shook her head. "I heard from Jem that they are trying to figure out what is going on. I feel terrible for him, I really hope his husband isn't cheating."

"I know. And I feel bad that Patti's party didn't work out because of it."

"Yeah. I love this dress by the way," Laurel said as she looked Gabriella up and down.

"Thanks. Believe it or not, Desmond picked it out."

"Oh, I believe it. That is not a dress you would ever pick for yourself. But it looks amazing on you."

"What about you, sexy bitch? This slinky rose gold shimmer number is doing wonders for you."

Laurel laughed, "it better. Matt has me strength training now. Might as well show it off while I've got it. You know how much I hate to exercise."

"At least you get a break while you stay with me."

"I do? You have no idea how happy that makes me. I thought you were going to make me go to yoga with you."

"No, I haven't gone since Henry got here. I started doing kickboxing a few months ago, they both really help me with stress. But, no, I won't make you work out with me."

"Will you make me cookies? Maybe some pasta?"

"Are you trying to carb load?"

"I won't tell if you won't," Laurel said with a smile.

"Oh, secrets! My favorite!" Desmond exclaimed when he approached them.

"I'm begging Gabby to bake me treats and pasta when I stay with her this month." Laurel explained.

"Oh, that is totally happening. And I'm staying with you guys. I already told Arnie that I'm planning on sleeping over at least a few nights a week."

"Seriously? I'm going to have two of you in my apartment. My bed isn't that big."

"Meh, Laurel and I together are about the same size as Henry. I'm sure you've been having no problem with him in your bed all week." Desmond said with a smirk.

"Why do I always walk over during the sex talk?" Arnie asked with a sigh as he greeted the girls.

"Blame your perverted fiancé. He's the one who brought it up," Gabriella said.

"Why am I not surprised. And he wonders where his sister got it from." Arnie replied.

"Where is Elise?" Laurel asked.

"Partying it up like a single New Yorker. Her co-workers were going to one of the rooftop parties," Gabriella explained.

"Sounds like fun," Laurel said wistfully.

"Stop it, you did a great job here. And you got a DJ. That's a first for a party here," Gabriella said.

"You're right. Besides, that couldn't be my scene anymore. Not without some sort of security detail."

Henry and Matt approached with beers in hand. Henry handed Gabriella cocktail as Matt handed one to Laurel. "What is it?"

"They called it giggle juice." Matt said with a shrug of his shoulder.

"Sounds good to me. I'm going to get one, what do you want, Arnie?" Desmond asked.

"I'll go grab it, stay with your girls." Arnie said as he walked off to the bar.

512

"Hey, everyone. I'm glad I found you. It's starting to get crowded," Brad said as he approached the group with a petite blonde on his arm.

"Doctor Brad!" They all shouted in greeting.

"Hey! I wanted to introduce everyone to Kristie, my girlfriend. Kristie, this is Desmond, Gabriella, and Laurel. I went to high school with them. And this is Matt, Laurel's fiancé, and Henry, Gabriella's... boyfriend?"

Gabriella laughed and nodded her head. "Oh, and this is Arnie, Desmond's fiancé. Hey Arnie!"

"Doctor Brad, pleasure to see you," Arnie said as he handed Desmond his drink.

Kristie stood there, shellshocked at the people who stood in front of her. "Did you not warn Kristie about who your friends from high school are?" Gabriella asked.

"Oh, wow, you're Laurel Dolce. And you're Henry Anderson. Holy shit. Wait a minute," Kristie said as she looked at Gabriella and then at Brad. "Gabriella is the mystery brunette from Edge of Time? Are you serious? How could you not tell me?"

"Sorry, Kristie. I didn't think of it. I wasn't sure if Henry was going to be here. I was in awe when I met him on Christmas eve." Brad apologized.

"You met him Christmas eve and didn't tell me?" She asked.

"Sorry, I was so nervous to meet your family it slipped my mind."

"It's okay, Kristie. I totally get it. We're normal people, I swear. It's so incredibly nice to meet you. Brad hasn't stopped gushing about you since we started talking again." Gabriella said with a warm smile.

"Thanks, it's so nice to meet you too. Brad did tell me about you guys but failed to share last names or current careers when he shared his stories."

"Dude, go get her a drink, I think she needs it," Matt side barred to Brad.

"Good idea. Get her a giggle juice. It's awesome," Laurel called out as Brad headed to the bar.

The group sat together at a table chatted while food was passed around. While they were enjoyed their food, Gabriella noticed a woman with a camera taking photos of them. "Lau, what's with the photographer?"

"Oh, that's my cousin, Anna. Don't you remember her?"

"Wow, that's Anna banana?" Desmond asked.

"Yeah, crazy, right. She's applying to college next year and she wants to be a photographer. Her stuff is amazing. She always has her camera around her neck. I told her that I'd hire her to take pictures tonight, but that she could use them for her college applications. She's so talented."

"She's not going to sell them to the press, is she?" Henry asked wearily.

"No, I told her it was for her portfolio only." Laurel confirmed.

514

"So, you're pimping out your famous friends for your cousin's portfolios," Desmond said with a smirk.

"Maybe," Laurel said with a wink, then stood up as the DJ started to play upbeat dance music. "Come on people, let's close out this year with a good time."

Hours were spent on the makeshift patio dance floor, with multiple cocktails consumed. It neared midnight and Henry walked around with his cellphone and filmed them all having a good time. "It's almost midnight here in New York. Technically, it's already the new year where I'm from, so hello from the past, mates! I'm here celebrating with some of my extended family. I'm here with Laurel Dolce and Matt Trammel, Broadway star Desmond Balvin and his fiancé and chef extraordinaire Arnie Burns, Doctor Brad and nurse Kristie, and this stunning beauty, Gabriella DiStella. Say hi Ella."

Ella smiled and waved as Henry continued. "Now, I know there have been some photos of us in Manhattan. Lots of speculation," he said as he wrapped his arm around Gabriella's waist. "I'm here to set the record straight. And if any of you have a problem with it, you can kiss my bloody backside."

The countdown began, and they all shouted out as they counted from ten to one, then yelled happy new year. Henry kept the camera on them during the entire countdown, then leaned in and gave her a toe-curling, passionate kiss. He dropped the phone down to his hip as he dove deeper into the kiss. Matt noticed and grabbed the phone out of his hand and turned the camera on them as Henry wrapped himself around Gabriella.

Matt looked into the camera and said, "oh, shit, this is live." He looked around and laughed, then turned back to the camera, "well, I guess you now know. Happy new year!"

Twenty-Three

February was one of the most grueling months Gabriella had ever experienced. After the influx of followers everyone received after Henry's new year's video went viral, things never really settled. Arnie had received requests for his food from Henry's friends and followers, which spurred discussions about a possible expansion of their production of take-home meals. Brad and Kristie received followers, which made life at the hospital a little hectic for a while, but it brought more attention to the hospital itself, which benefited.

Desmond was approached for a role in a Lifetime movie, which he was ecstatic about. Gabriella managed to negotiate the schedule so production would start over the summer, around the time his contract for Phantom of the Opera was fulfilled. He stepped up his contribution to the LGBTQ volunteer center since Gabriella could no longer fulfill her in-person duties.

Although Laurel wasn't scheduled to start a new project until March, she was approached to be the face of a new clothing line made with sustainable fabrics like recycled plastic and bamboo. Gabriella had organized the schedule for shoots, the campaigns she would take part in, and set up the mailing for products to be shipped so Laurel could be seen in the clothes at some upcoming events in Los Angeles.

With all of that, Gabriella worked twelve-to-sixteen-hour of filming at all different times through the week. Some hours of her day were dedicated to fight training and choreography, others were spent with a personal trainer and was on a limited caloric diet. With her workload, she was burning the candle at both ends. She hardly got a chance to speak with Henry, and she was so grateful to her assistant on the set who took care of Scampi for her.

It was nearing the end of February when Gabriella was able to get a few days off from the shoot. They were filming scenes after her character was killed by Achilles. She sat in her bathrobe after she indulged in a hot shower and worked on some of Laurel's commitments at the small desk in her hotel room when there was a knock at her door. Scampi barked at the sudden noise, which echoed from outside the door. Gabriella nervously fingered the diamond pendant Henry gave her on New Year's Day to celebrate their start of the year together, which matched the earrings he gifted her for Christmas.

Another knock at the door made Gabriella looked through the peep hole and was shocked to see Henry, Bob, and Leigh in the hallway. She unbolted the door and threw herself at Henry. Henry let go of his suitcase and wrapped his arms around Gabriella. "Oh my god, I can't believe you are here!" Gabriella cried tears of joy as she clung to her boyfriend.

"Bloody hell, Ella, I've fucking missed you." He said into her hair that was pressed against his face. He pulled back and kissed the life out of her.

Bob had made his way into the hotel room with Leigh, who sniffed Scampi and then played with him. After a few heated moments making out in the hallway, Henry pulled back. "I just want to be inside you."

Gabriella looked into his lust-filled eyes and shivered. All the pent-up frustration of not touching each other for over a month was overwhelming. She bit her lip slightly as her desire matched his. "What's stopping you?"

"The hallway, Bob in the room with the dogs."

518

Gabriella felt like a bucket of cold water was dumped on her head. "Oh, right. I should really say hi to Bob, that was pretty rude of me."

They walked into the room to find Bob on the couch with the television on as the dogs chased each other around. "Hey Bob!" Gabriella said as she greeted her friend.

"Hey sis. Ya'll done mauling each other?"

"Hardly," Henry murmured.

"Are you guys both staying here?"

"No, I got a room here. I was thinking maybe Bob could take the dogs tonight and we could spend some much-needed time together," Henry suggested.

"Bob, are you okay with that?" Gabriella asked.

"Hank pays me, I do what he asks. I'll take the dogs tonight. But I need some quality time with you while I'm here."

"Deal. I'm not filming for the next three days. When do you have to be back on set?" Gabriella asked.

"Not until Wednesday. We've got four days together."

"Tomorrow, maybe we can go walking around? Get lunch? Be tourist? I haven't had much down time while I've been here."

"Alright then, let me just get Scampi's leash and I will be out of your hair until tomorrow." Bob said as he grabbed Scampi's little supply bag and leash.

Gabriella picked Scampi up to give him a kiss goodbye before she handed him over the Bob. "We'll be two floors below you. I've never been so happy to not be on the same floor as someone before. See ya'll tomorrow."

Gabriella walked Bob to the door and said goodnight them. When the door shut, she turned to find Henry naked from the waist up. She drank in his sculpted body as she approached him.

"No fair, you skipped my favorite part," she complained as she ran her hands over his pecs.

"What's that?"

"Undressing you. It's like I get to open my very own present." She said as her hands moved up his neck and into his hair. "Your hair is longer. Curlier."

"They want it that way for the role so they can style it appropriately."

"I swear, you've gotten bigger since the last time I saw you."

"It's all the training they've got me doing. I also eat almost nothing but protein."

Her nails scraped along the sharp edge of his jaw. "I'm liking the little bit of scruff you have going on."

"I need to keep my face shaved every day; I finally get a break from doing it."

520

"I think it's sexy. I can't wait to feel it between my legs."

Henry groaned as her nails lightly dragged down his torso to the top of his jeans. "I left the best part for you to unwrap."

Gabriella bit her lip slightly as she moved to undo his belt. "You're right. It must me my birthday or something."

She unbuckled the belt, undid his fly, then pulled down the denim and black boxer briefs to expose his member that pulsed at attention. She dragged the clothing to the floor, then fell to her knees and pulled it from his body once Henry kicked his shoes off. She dragged her nails up his legs and caressed his thighs before reached for him and took him into her mouth.

He gasped at the sensation then groaned as she licked the underside of his shaft and then worked her tongue on his tip. "Ella, bloody... fuck, you need to... mmm."

Gabriella ignored his pathetic protest and worked him harder. Suddenly, she was lifted by her shoulder and pulled away. Henry forced her to her feet, a look of punishment burned in his eyes. Without a word, he pulled at the belt of the robe she was had on and caused Henry to groan in appreciation at the site of her naked body.

"Ella, what happened to your body?"

Suddenly nervous, she grabbed the edges of the robe and pulled it closed. "No, no, no, don't cover up. I don't think I've ever seen so much definition on you. I'm shocked."

"Is it a bad thing?"

"Nothing about you is ever a bad thing. You look amazing. But I also think you look bloody beautiful when you're soft and curvy."

"Do I look too much like a man for you now?" She asked self-consciously.

Henry looked down at his erection and looked back at her. "Does it look like I think you look manly? Ella, you're stunning. And I want you as much now as I always had. Now remove that robe before I tear it off of you and let me get a look at my woman who I want to devour."

Gabriella blushed and dropped the robe. Henry smiled, then wrapped his arms around her. "This is what I like to see. You, wearing only the jewelry I gave you. There is nothing hotter than that."

"I always wear it when I'm not on set."

"Good girl, Ella. Now, lay down on the bed so you can feel just how rough my beard will feel between your legs."

***

The next day was spent with Henry, Bob, and the dogs as they walked through some of the sights in Greece. They went to a local market where Henry purchased spices and other treats to send back to Patti and Arnie. The dogs ran through open patches of grass as they made their way through the countryside. After they dropped the dogs back at the hotel. Gabriella, Henry, and Bob took a taxi to a restaurant with an amazing view of the sea from the cliffs above.

522

"So, Bob, you've become quite the world traveler. What do you think you're going to do with your life?" Gabriella asked while drank a local wine.

"I absolutely want to work with animals. I've had great experiences on the ranch back home. And I love watching after Leigh. But I think I might want to become a veterinarian. Or even a technician that helps at animal hospitals."

"That's a noble career, mate. Have you given much thought to when you want to go to school?"

"I was thinking of applying this summer for the fall semester. But I don't want to mess up your plans with Leigh. I know you have some projects that you'll need me on."

"Bob, I appreciate everything you do for me and Leigh. You're like a little brother to me. And that means I want the best for you, mate. Don't worry about me and Leigh. I've been around the block a few times to know how to handle her. And if I have a project that happens to be when you are off, then I'd love for you to join me."

"Thanks, Hank, I really appreciate that. It's funny how life turns out sometimes. Who would have thought that me getting a job watching a dog would turn into all of this?" Bob said as he gestured with his hands around him.

"I agree, Bob. Never in my life did I think I'd be here," Gabriella said wistfully.

***

The next day, Bob and Henry took the dogs for a walk in the early afternoon while Gabriella got some work done. An email sent from Lily the night before reminded Gabriella to watch for the academy award announcements that afternoon. She ran to the restaurant next door to the hotel and purchased her favorite tiropita and spanakopita and an order of Greek donuts and settled herself down in front of the computer to live stream the announcements.

Henry and Bob entered the room just as the broadcast began. The president of the academy began his introduction and Gabriella looked up at Henry. Bob followed the dogs around the room as he recorded their antics on his phone. "Gabby, these dogs are cracking me up. People are eating up the videos of them. I think part of my new thing here is going to be recording them."

"What's wrong, Ella, you look so nervous?" Henry asked as he sat down next to her on the couch.

"I just really hope that you and Laurel get nominated. You guys deserve it so much. I want to call her screaming and wake her up to tell her that she was nominated."

"Baby, your heart is too big for its own good. It will be okay. We don't even know if the movie will be nominated for anything. There is always a lot of talk about the Oscars, but it's not set in stone." Henry said as he rubbed her arms.

He focused on the screen, "the announcements are starting babe. Supporting Actress."

Gabriella nodded and turned her attention to screen and wanted to cheer and cringe when Riona's name was announced for a nomination. "That's really

524

good…" Gabriella began to say as Henry grabbed her face and turned her attention to the screen where her name was announced and appeared on the graphic, two names below Riona.

Gabriella stared, her mouth impersonating a fish out of water. Her eyes were huge as she tried to grasp onto any thread of reality. Bob screamed out a cheer, which caused the dogs to bark. Gabriella looked at Bob, then back to the screen. "Ella, baby, you were nominated for an Oscar," Henry said calmly with a giant smile on his face.

"I was nominated for an Oscar? Seriously?" Gabriella asked, as she tried to comprehend the information.

"Yes! Ella! You were nominated!" Henry shouted, then pulled her face into his and kissed her on the mouth.

"Holy shit!" Bob yelled out, "Darius was nominated for costume design."

Gabriella's eyes widened even more. "Oh my god. Henry, this movie is going to dominate the nominations."

"Yeah, and you are one of them. Your first role, and you are nominated for an award," Henry said with a proud smile.

Gabriella grasped onto Henry's hand; the food completely ignored as they watched the announcements. Bob settled onto the arm of the couch as his phone continued to record. After a few categories passed, The Edge of Time was mentioned again for category of original screenplay. Gabriella shouted again as Henry cheered when Jake and Bernie were both nominated for supporting actor. The movie was also nominated for editing, cinematography, and makeup and hairstyling.

When the category for actor in a leading role appeared on the screen, Gabriella began to nervously rock in her seat and bite at the inside of her lip. Henry sat still and watched the nominees' names appear on the screen. When Henry's name was announced, Gabriella screamed at the top of her lungs and pounced at Henry, who captured her in his arms and gave her a deep kiss. Bob cheered as he continued to film their reaction.

"Oh god, oh god, oh god," Gabriella chanted as she jumped up and paced the floor when the actress in a leading role was announced next. Henry watched her carefully as she gnawed on her thumb. "I can't watch," she said as she walked over to the window.

When Laurel's name was announced, Gabriella began to cry. Henry jumped up and held her. "Baby, why are you crying?"

"I'm just so happy for her. She's worked so hard for this, and she deserves this more than anyone I know."

"Even me?" Henry asked with a smirk.

She pushed her hand into his chest and laughed. "You know what I mean."

"I do, Ella. Now you get to wake her up and tell her the great news. And the bonus? You get to wake Matt up too."

"Hey guys," Bob called out. The two of them turned their full attention on him. "Don was nominated for best director."

The announcement for the best picture was made, and the announcer began to talk about how the nominees were picked. The three of them stood still as the movies were announced and let out a huge cry of excitement when The Edge of Time was named.

Henry's phone rang right away, "it's mum." He said and answered the phone. Gabriella watched as Henry's face became sheepish as his parents praised him for his accomplishment. She took her phone off the end table and went to dial Laurel when Henry's phone went on speaker. "Yes, mum, she's right here."

"Gabriella! Congratulations you beautiful girl!" Henry's mom shouted.

"Thank you, Betty. I appreciate it," Gabriella responded.

"We saw the movie multiple times," James commented, "you absolutely deserve that nomination. We were flabbergasted when Hank told us it was your first role."

"Thank you, James. I'm not sure I fully agree with you, but I appreciate it just the same."

"What time is it where your parents are, dear? You must be dying to talk to them." Betty asked.

"It's around nine there. But I have to call Laurel and tell her the good news."

"Go on then, don't let us hold you up. We're looking forward to meeting you dear." Betty said before told her son to take them off speaker phone.

Gabriella dialed Laurel's number, even though she knew that it was six in the morning, and she was never one to be an early riser. Gabriella reached her voice mail twice before she finally answered the phone.

"You better need bail money or something to be calling me this early," Laurel mumbled into the phone.

"I need you to wake up, Lau, because what I'm about to tell you is really important and I need your full attention."

"Oh my god, are you pregnant?" Laurel asked as she sounded a little more awake.

"Seriously? Don't you know what today is?"

"No."

"Laurel, it was the Oscar nominations."

"Oh."

"You were nominated for best actress."

A blood-curdled scream erupted the phone, followed by a bunch of curses from Matt. Laurel informed him of the news, which was met with another scream. "Who else was nominated," Laurel asked.

"Henry, Bernie and Jake. There was wardrobe, best picture, best director, original screenplay, costume, hair and makeup, maybe editing." Gabriella listed off.

"Laurel, Gabby was nominated," Matt said in the background.

"What?" Laurel asked.

"Supporting actress. Gabby, Samantha, and Riona were nominated."

"Gabby? You were nominated?" Laurel asked, her voice wobbly.

"Yeah."

Laurel began to sob, which made Gabriella to join her. "My best friend was nominated for an Oscar," Laurel sobbed.

"My best friend was nominated for an Oscar," Gabriella countered.

"I wish I was with you to give you a giant hug," Laurel cried.

"Me too. I'm so proud of you. You deserve this so much, Lau."

"I'm proud of you too."

"Shit, should we call Desmond? He's gonna be so mad if we don't tell him."

Laurel agreed, so Gabriella added him to the call.

"Yes, my manager. What do you need of me today?" Desmond answered.

"Des?" Gabriella asked, her tears audible.

"Why are you crying? What happened? Is it Henry? Do I have to cut a bitch?" Desmond asked.

Gabriella and Laurel laughed. "No, Des, Laurel was nominated for an Oscar."

"What? Oh my god!" Desmond gasped.

"Des, Gabby was nominated for one too," Laurel choked out.

Desmond sucked in a deep breath. "Are you for real right now? You're not fucking with me, right?" His voice cracked.

"We're not that big of assholes, Des," Laurel flat panned.

Desmond began to cry as he croaked out, "oh my god, my girls! I'm so proud of you both!"

After a few moments passed to absorb the emotion, Desmond sniffled and cleared his throat. "So, the most important thing, who is taking me as their date?"

"Seriously?" Laurel breathed out.

"What? This is a huge deal. How many people can you bring?" Desmond asked.

"Three," Henry responded when Gabriella put the call on speaker phone.

"Well, that counts me out. I have to bring Matt and my parents." Laurel replied.

"Well, I have to bring my parents," Gabriella said looking at Henry. "But I guess since my date is nominated, you can come with me."

"Who are you going to bring, Henry?" Desmond asked.

"My mum and dad, definitely."

"How about that third ticket?" Desmond asked.

"Are you seriously trying to score yourself two tickets?" Laurel chastised.

"What? I'm supposed to leave my fiancé home?"

"I'm sure Arnie would understand and allow you to come here alone," Gabriella replied. "Besides, Henry has a huge family, I'm sure one of his siblings would want to go with him."

"Can we stop talking about the event and just appreciate this phone call? Who would have thought this would ever happen?" Laurel exclaimed.

Gabriella laughed. "I always knew you'd get this call, Lau. And I know you are going to win."

"I know Henry is going to win too," Laurel responded.

"I think Gabriella is going to take home the award," Henry said with a smile as he wrapped his arms around her and pulled her back into his chest.

531

"She's already going to put out, Henry, no need to kiss ass," Desmond said with a laugh. "By the way, congratulations."

"Thank you, Desmond. But no need to kiss her arse. She really is a talent." Henry said before he pressed a kiss to her cheek. "But, speaking of putting out, I think it's time that Ella ends this call, calls her parents, and then as Desmond so eloquently put it, put out, because we don't have much more time together."

"Oh my god, Gabby, call your parents!" Laurel yelled. "I'll talk to you all soon. Love you guys."

Gabriella hung up, then dialed her parent's house, who answered the phone as they shouted congratulations to both nominees. After an hour-long conversation where she discussed wardrobe for the ceremony with her mother, Gabriella collapsed on the couch and squeezed herself between Henry and Bob.

"Mom sounded super excited," Bob said with a laugh.

"Yeah. This is unexpected. I should check my emails to see if any information came through." Gabriella said as she reached for the phone she dropped on the table.

"No, I already heard from my manager. There is a luncheon in the end of March. The ceremony is in mid-April."

"But I don't think I'll be done filming in time for the luncheon."

"Don't worry about it, Ella, it's not important."

"But what about prepping for the awards? What if there are interviews? What do I have to do, I have no idea what I have to do?" Gabriella said in a panic.

"Gabby, it's going to be okay," Bob said with a smile as he placed his hand on top of hers.

"It's not going to be okay. You guys are leaving tomorrow, and I'm going to be alone again. And I'll have to deal with filming, and then I'll have to manage Desmond and Laurel. And then I have to manage myself because I have no one to help me with me."

"Ella, baby, just breathe. It's going to be okay. You are going to focus on finishing the film. You're not going to worry about anything with the awards. It's something far in the future. And all it is going to be is a small ceremony that we'll get dressed up for. And we'll have a great time with our families and friends." Henry consoled as he gently patted her hair in comforting strokes.

"I don't want you to leave, Henry. I want you to stay with me. Or I want to go with you. Don't leave me here alone. I'm panicking."

"I'm going to take the dogs out for a bit," Bob said with a smile, before he patted Gabriella's knee.

Once Bob got the dogs together and left the room, Henry gathered Gabriella up into his lap. "Talk to me. What's going on?"

Gabriella shook her head. "I'm not even sure. I just really missed you. And you're leaving. And now I know we're going to have to be back in the U.S. next month. And then after that you're probably going to be on set somewhere in the world, and I'll be back at home alone. And you're going to realize that I'm not worth a long-distance relationship. And then It's going to be all over the news that you're in a relationship with some sexy new co-star and I'm alone, adopting a bunch of cats."

"Whoa, where is that coming from?"

Gabriella started to sob as Henry consoled her. "I'm setting myself up for heartbreak."

Henry's face contorted into confusion and anger. "I don't know what I've done to make you think that. I've missed you too, which is why I came here to visit you. I meant what I said before, I'm in this for real. But if you really feel like this isn't worth it, just let me know. I'm not holding you to anything you don't want, Gabriella."

He slid her from his lap to the couch and stood up. He walked into the bedroom and picked up his bag. He took a quick glance around to check that he left nothing and made his way back out to the door. Gabriella remained on the couch and stared at the floor. She looked up as Henry crossed the room, his eyes straight on the door he was headed towards.

"No, Henry, please don't leave," she said as she jumped up and grasped onto his forearm. He looked down at her hand and then back up at her.

"Really think before you speak, Gabriella." He said sternly.

Gabriella looked up at him as she spoke. "I'm scared. But not because of you. I'm scared about what this nomination means."

534

"Explain." Henry demanded.

"I feel like this whole nomination is going to bring another level of scrutiny. I just don't know if I can handle negative attention. I just know that I'm going to be a basket case, like I am now, and I'm going to push you away with my brand of crazy. I'm already doing it. I'm sorry. I don't want you to go. I love you. But I get it if this is too much for you." She said as she wildly gestured around.

Henry dropped his bag to the floor, then dragged his hands through his hair as he watched her freak out. "Say it again."

She looked up at him and repeated. "I get it if this is too much for you."

Henry shook his head. "Not that part."

"I don't want you to go."

"Not that part either."

Gabriella took a deep breath. "I love you."

"That's all that matters, Ella. I love you. You love me. That's all we need."

"Really?"

Henry opened his arms and Gabriella to ran into them and wrap her arms tightly around his torso. "Don't push me away," he mumbled into the top of her head as he pressed his lips into it her hair.

"I'm sorry, Henry. I get like this sometimes. I hope you can put up with me."

"I told you that all of your good outweighs whatever you think your bad is. Don't push me away. Give me more credit than that."

"I'm sorry. This morning was really unexpected. And you're leaving. I thought I would be able to handle this better."

"I know, love. When you are done filming, I think you should come stay with me. Just the two of us and the dogs at my house in Chelsea. You'll love it. It's right on the river Thames; there's a yard for the dogs to run in. I think it would be good for us to have a month together. We can go back for the awards ceremony together."

"That would be really nice. I can't wait for this movie to be over so I can be with you full time." Gabriella said with a teary smile, then stretched her head up and pressed her lips against his.

"Looks like we've got something to look forward to."

Twenty-Four

Gabby: Hey, I just landed.

Henry: I can't wait to see you. I'm sorry I can't be there to get you.

Gabby: It's okay. Scampi and I are just excited to get to you.

Henry: May is already there to get you. She's by the luggage.

Gabby: Great! See you soon XOXO

"Gabby!" Her name rang out through the baggage claim as she approached the carousel. May bolted from where she was waited and threw her arms around Gabriella, which made Scampi to jump around excitedly and bark in response.

"Hi May, it's so good to see you!"

"I am so happy you're here! I've been dying for you to meet everyone. You have no idea how happy I am that you and Henry are together. I'm sure the long distance has to be difficult, but you two were destined for each other." May said without a breath. "Let's get your bags. Gerald is in the car waiting for us."

The girls grabbed the luggage and made their way to the curb where May's husband idled. As they approached, he jumped out of the car to take the luggage from Gabriella. "Hey there, I'm Gerald, pleasure to meet you." He said as he shook her hand and placed her bags in the trunk.

Gabriella smiled warmly at the redheaded man with sparkling green eyes and a short, kempt beard. "Nice to meet you too. I'm Gabriella."

"Oh, trust me, the whole family is very well aware of who you are." He said with a laugh as he opened the back door to allow Scampi and Gabriella into the car. Gabriella got settled and found it odd that the steering wheel was on the right side of the car.

"Are we heading to Henry's house?" Gabriella asked as they left Heathrow Airport.

"Yes, we were given strict instructions to bring you straight to Henry's. We were told to leave you alone for a week, and then he's bringing you to mum's and dad's for dinner next weekend. But be prepared, the entire family will be there."

"No pressure or anything," Gabriella laughed nervously.

"Don't worry much, they are a good lot. It is a bit intimidating at first because there are so many of them, but they are really nice," Gerald said sympathetically.

"I appreciate it, Gerald," Gabriella said with a smile.

The thirty-minute trip went by quickly, filled with small talk. When they pulled up to the house, May exited the car with Gabriella and Scampi.

"Hank wasn't sure if he would be back by the time you arrived. He told me to let you in and to give you a key. He should be here soon." She explained as she

538

unlocked the door and led them into the house. Gabriella was stunned by the beauty of the clean, masculine decor and high ceilings.

"I know, his house is amazing. It's six floors. This floor has the kitchen and dining room, upstairs is the reception room and sitting room. The next two floors are all bedrooms, the principal bedroom is on the fourth. The upper level are bedrooms remodeled to his study. The basement has his gym. There is a small wine cellar down there too. Out back is the garage and guest space above it." May explained as they walked through the main floor and ended in the chef's kitchen.

"Feel free to explore and make yourself comfortable. You can take any of the bedrooms upstairs, but I'm sure you'll be spending your time in the principal bedroom with him," she said with a smirk as she wagged her eyebrows.

Gabriella laughed as she took the key that May held in her outstretched hand. "This is for you. Henry made it and said for you to keep it. Must be serious if you have a key."

Gabriella smiled and shook her head as she added his key to hers. "It could be because I'm going to be here for a while."

"Maybe. I will let you settle in. I've left all our numbers on the counter. You've been added to the family chat, so be prepared for that. We were instructed to leave you alone for the week, but you'll be bombarded by Andersons right quick."

"Thanks, May. I appreciate all your help and for picking me up."

"Anything for family," she said with a wink and a brief hug. "Until next week," she yelled out from the front door as she waved her fingers in a goodbye before she closed the door.

Gabriella stood in the kitchen and looked out at the garage and garden laid out beyond the full-length folding glass doors. Scampi made his way to the door and whimpered as he pawed towards the lush green lawn. With Scampi still attached to his leash, she opened one of the doors and led them out beyond the large patio covered with plush outdoor furniture. She let the dog off of his leash, then made her way around patch of land sandwiched between the two buildings and the stone wall topped with a privacy fence and paused at the fireplace built into the stone wall and observed the rustic wood seating nestled into the grass.

When Scampi finished his business, they re-entered the house. She gathered two pieces of luggage and made her way up the three flights of stairs, as she skipped the over the living area and the spare bedrooms. She entered the open door to the master bedroom and was met by Leigh in her bed as her tail wagged.

Scampi jumped into the room and barked excitedly as he made his way to Leigh. They sniffed one another and barked playfully until Gabriella said Leigh's name, which pulled her attention away from Scampi.

"Leigh! Hey girl! It's so good to see you," Gabriella greeted the dog as she met Leigh halfway across the room and dropped to her knees to pet the dog and accept wet kisses all over her face. Once the dogs settled, Gabriella took another trip down to the main entrance to get the larger pieces of luggage. Once everything was settled in the room, the view of the River Thames lured Gabriella to look through the floor-to-ceiling windows and doors that led to the balcony. She absorbed the soothing view of the river, as boats passed under the Chelsea bridge. People walked along the path that followed alongside the flow of water. The crisp day looked comfortable as the sunlight glittered from the surface of the water.

Henry entered his home with a smile on his face, as he knew that his girlfriend was on the inside. After he surveyed the first floor, he made his way upstairs and checked every floor until he landed at the primary bedroom. He poked his head into the doorway, which made Leigh and Scampi bark a greeting. He held his hand out to quiet the dogs, then turned his attention to the silhouette that stood in front of the balcony.

Gabriella's head turned to see what caused the commotion for the dogs and sucked in a sharp breath when she saw Henry in the bedroom, mere feet away from her. A smile spread across her face as Henry leaned against the doorframe and crossed his arms and legs. "You are such a sight for sore eyes," he said with a smile.

Gabriella vaulted herself from the view beyond the windows and into Henry's arms, which wrapped around her tightly. She pulled her face away from the warmth and scent that enveloped her when she embedded her face into his neck, and looked up into his eyes for a moment, then pressed her lips against his.

The kiss turned heated, as Henry walked Gabriella backwards until the back of her legs hit the bed. She giggled as she pulled him down with her. "I've missed you so much," she said as she lifted his shirt up from his waist.

Once his shirt was removed, her hands automatically dove down to release his belt and unzip his fly. He chuckled as she tugged down his pants and underwear and released him from his constraints.

"Do you miss me, or do you miss him?" Henry asked with a laugh.

"Yes. Both. No talking," she said breathlessly as she yanked off her own clothes.

***

Satiated and sore, Gabriella stretched in the bed, her eyes drifted to the sunset as the pinks and purples filled the sky. She looked around the room and realized that she was the sole occupant. She threw on her discarded leggings and loose yoga shirt and made her way back to the first floor, where she found Henry cooking at the professional grade range, as the dogs ran around in the yard in the distance. A smile stitched across her face, a sense of feeling complete fell over her as she watched a version of her future unfold before her eyes. She could almost hear the laughter and footsteps of children stampede down the stairs she had exited from.

"Hey, beautiful. Dinner should be done in about an hour." Henry said with a smile as he approached her and pulled her into a mind-melting kiss.

"Where are your bags? I'll bring them upstairs for you."

"Oh, I already did that. I left them in your room, if that's okay."

"Of course. Did you think I was going to let you out of my arm reach while you are here? How many bags did you bring up?"

"Um, like 5?"

"You used the elevator, right?"

Gabriella's shoulders fell as she shook her head. "You have an elevator?"

"You dragged all of your luggage up the stairs yourself?"

She nodded as he barked out a laugh, then squeezed her biceps. "Must be all that training, you Amazon warrior. So, did you poke around my home? Check all the drawers? Try to find all my secrets?"

"No, I wasn't here for too long before you got home."

"So, what did you see?"

"This floor, outside. Nature called Scampi when we got here. Then I dragged myself and that luggage up to your room. May told me what was on each floor. How in the world do you have so many floors?"

Henry shrugged with a smile. "That's how it is in jolly-ole England. Sounds like you're in need of the full-service, Henry Anderson tour special."

"What does that include? Full-service sounds fancy."

"Oh, it is. I plan on showing you every meter of this home. And I plan on exploring ever meter of you as I do it. Before we return to the States, I fully intend on not being able to look at any room or surface in this place without seeing you naked and writhing."

"Well, that sounds pretty freaking phenomenal."

"We should get started after we eat. I must get you acquainted with proper fare. I've made Yorkshire pudding with roast beef. I need to pay you back for all the treats you've fattened me up with."

"I don't know," she said with a coy smile, "I'm really looking forward to the tour."

"I'm sure you are. But you'll need your energy for what I have planned. As it is, I've already knocked you out from our first encounter today. Don't be greedy."

Henry pulled Gabriella into him as his hands gripped her bottom and he slammed his lips against hers. She melted into him, but he pulled away soon after her started. "Now, I think you should sit down at the counter while I make sure our dinner is still cooking. But first, I'll pour you some wine. Follow me, I'll let you choose."

Henry led her down to the basement to show her the wine cellar and home gym, which included a sauna and a small massage studio. He pointed out a hallway that led underground to the garage beyond the backyard. When they went to select a bottle for dinner, Henry placed her on the countertop in the center of the room and ravaged her, then claimed that the wine cellar was checked off his list.

They ate dinner together while the dogs ate their food. Henry bought Scampi his very own food dish in preparation for their arrival. After Gabriella helped to clean up the kitchen, Henry took her upstairs to the living area. Gabriella took in the warm beige walls, accented with deep mahogany furniture and cream fabrics on the couches. The centerpiece of the room was a dark marble fireplace. Beyond that was a more relaxed version of the first room, with cashmere throws and large pillows on the overstuffed mocha-colored couches. A large flat screen television hung on the wall; the media stand below covered in framed family photos. The floor-to-ceiling windows gave a picturesque view of the River Thames, and led to another balcony, like the setup in Henry's bedroom.

"It's so cozy in here," Gabriella said with a smile as Henry gestured to the couch in front of the television.

"Thank you. It's where I come to relax. I need to be able to be myself somewhere." Henry said with a wink as he turned on the television.

Leigh entered the room with Scampi hot on her tail. When Scampi spotted Gabriella, he yipped and then made a running leap onto the couch next to her. "No, Scampi," Gabriella yelled out.

"It's okay, Ella, Leigh is on these couches all the time. I want Scampi to feel comfortable here." He said with a smile as Scampi walked across Gabriella to make himself comfortable in Henry's lap. Gabriella shook her head at her dog but threw her arm around Leigh when she settled onto the couch and rested her head in Gabriella's lap.

After they watched the evening news, Henry looked down Gabriella, whose head was nuzzled into his chest. "I could really get used to this, Ella. Having you in this house, doing mundane things like eating dinner and watching the telly."

"It's only the first day, Henry. Don't get too comfortable. You might want to strangle me by next week," she said with a smile.

"I highly doubt that, but I'll take it one day at a time, love."

"Do we have anything we need to do while I'm here? I know you are notoriously busy."

"Asides from dinner with my family next weekend, I am completely available to you. Are you still sure you don't want to attend the luncheon for the ceremony?"

She nodded in response as she snuggled into Henry. "Is there anything you wanted to do on your month-long holiday?"

"If it isn't too much of a pain in the ass, I would really love to play tourist. I've never been here before, and I really want to see Big Ben and the London Bridge and Buckingham palace. "

"I can manage that for you. But we'll have to wear my fool-proof disguises if you don't want the cameras following us."

"Oh! Can we see Stonehenge? And the Globe theater?"

"Ella, I'll take you all over England if you want. I'll take you to Scotland, Wales, and Ireland if you want."

Gabriella smiled and squealed in delight, which disturbed the dogs from their spots. "That would be amazing!"

***

True to his word, Henry took her all over the surrounding areas of his London home. They were settled in for the night after her first week in England. Snuggled up on one of the overstuffed mocha couches and tucked under a cashmere blanket as Henry surfed through the channels to find something to watch.

"Oh! Stop! That one, I want to watch that one," Gabriella shouted.

Henry rolled his eyes as he turned the channel back and looked over at her. "Are you taking a piss?"

"Nope, I haven't peed my pants in a very long time," she responded with a smirk.

"Cheeky bird. I mean are you kidding?"

"I don't kid or piss when it comes to watching your movies."

"Ella, you can't be serious."

"Oh, I totally am. You are very shirtless in this one. It's one of my favorites."

"Don't be daft. You want to see that," he nodded towards the movie, "you just have to ask." He winked, then took off his shirt, which pulled Gabriella's eyes from the screen to the topless man next to her.

"You're right, this does seem much better," she said with a smile as she climbed on top of him and dipped her head down to run her tongue from his belly button through the crevices of his abdomen and up between his pectoral muscles before roving over his Adam's apple and landed on his lips.

Henry growled as he unzipped the lounge jacket she had on and peeled it from her body before he reached to unhook her bra.

"I think we've fully covered the rooms on this floor in terms of making our way through your house. Should we take this to the next floor? I don't think we've violated any surfaces in the spare bedrooms," Gabriella suggested with a moan.

A look of pure desire shook her as Henry inhaled deeply. "You are absolutely right. I like the way you think, you dirty bird."

Gabriella giggled as Henry smacked her behind as she lifted herself off from him. The sound of sudden and continuous vibration paused their departure from the couch. "What is that?" Gabriella asked.

"Did you bring one of your masturbatory friends with you? I could have a lot of fun with that." Henry said as he wagged his thick eyebrows at her.

"Really, Henry? No, of course not. Why would I have that in your living room?"

"Maybe you were feeling randy down here?"

"Okay, one, we haven't really been apart from each other this week, so when would I have time to whip out a vibrator. Two, you have me fully satisfied in that department."

A wolfish smile overtook Henry's face. "Bloody right, I have."

The vibration continued as they looked around the room, and moved pillows and blankets from the couch until a dim light was seen from the crack between the cushions.

"I found the culprit," Henry said when he dug his phone from the couch.

Gabriella walked back into the room form the formal living room, her lit-up phone in her hand. "Yeah, mine was on the charger inside. I have thirty-five unread messages, and I don't know one number."

Henry looked at his phone and shook his head. "Ugh," he signed as his head forward in defeat. "Let me see, Ella."

He took her phone and shook his head and smirked as he looked through the messages. After he added information into her phone, he handed it back to her. "Congrats, you are officially being harassed by the entire Anderson clan."

Gabriella looked down at the group chat and her eyes widened. She couldn't keep up with the pace at which they appeared on the screen. She scrolled her way to the start and began to read the message thread.

May: It's been a week. Private time is over.

Johnny: Did you time it to the minute?

Gerald: She had a reminder set on her phone.

May: I gave them a few extra hours.

Andrew: Bloody Hell, May, don't be a git. Let them shag.

May: Piss off, tosser. I gave them a week.

Nathan: It's the honeymoon phase. Aren't you supposed to be in that too, May?

May: Says the one doing bugger all at home

Nathan: Are you daft? I've been helping Millie with Emma

May: Sure you have

Johnny: You'd think H would have responded by now

Andrew: Hey, Hank, get off her, mate

Johnny: You might snap it off if you use it too much

550

Andrew: She needs to breathe

Nathan: Keep her hydrated, mate. She'll be looking like Becca's roast

Becca: Sod off, Nath. Had to bring up that cock-up

Andrew: I love you, Bec, but you can't cook for shite

Gerald: Has Hank responded?

Johnny: No, go keep your wife occupied

Andrew: If May was being serviced like Hank's girlfriend, she wouldn't be bothering us

Millie: what have I missed?

Johnny: Gerald isn't shagging May so she's trying to interrupt Hank

May: he's a twit, don't listen to him. How are you feeling Mil?

Millie: Knackered, but looking forward to Saturday

Andrew: Think Hank will put it away long enough for them to show up?

Nathan: I've got a tenner that says Hank will shag his girlfriend in his bedroom.

Andrew: Top bunk or bottom bunk?

Johnny: Piss off, the top bunk was mine

Betty: My word, you boys are right foul

Andrew: Mum! I didn't know you were on this thread

James: We both are

Johnny: Oh... shite. Hey mum, hey dad

James: leave your brother alone, all of you

May: Dad, we gave Hank his week

Betty: I want you all here no later than 2 on Saturday. And be on your best behavior, we don't want to scare Gabriella off

Becca: I'm right chuffed to meet Henry's girlfriend. It's been ages since a new one of us has been around.

Betty: I think you will all love her, she seems like a lovely girl

May: She's the best. Her parents are brilliant too. Don't cock it up

Andrew: You're being a bit of a nutter about all this, May

May: You'll see, she's brilliant for Hank

Henry: All right, are you done slagging me off

Johnny: H, did we interrupt you?

Henry: piss off, Johnny

Johnny: we did, ha ha

Andrew: taking a break, Hank?

Nathan: drink some Lucozade so you don't cramp

Johnny: it's a good thing he's in such good shape.

Andrew: maybe not so good for his woman. She might not be able to walk properly

Nathan: he's got endurance

Johnny: can't say I blame him, she's a peng thing

Shannon: I'm on this text, nitwit

Betty: As am I

Henry: Ella is on this chat too. Say hi to my wonderful family, love

"Henry, I don't even know what half of the stuff they are saying is," Gabriella admitted.

"They were saying that we've been doing nothing but having sex. And apparently Johnny thinks you are very attractive."

"Oh my god, that's not humiliating at all."

"Ella, this is how my family is. We poke fun at each other. It's all in fun. You'll grow accustomed to it. You're a little spit fire; you can give as good as you get." Henry said before he placed a kiss to the side of her head.

"Henry, your parents are in this chat group."

Henry smiled and shook his head as he nudged his head to her phone. "Go on."

Gabby: Hello Andersons.

Nathan: She lives!

Millie: you are so embarrassing. We are excited to meet you Gabby

Becca: yes, please ignore these children that we married.

Shannon: I am a huge fan of yours, Gabby

Gabby: OMG, thank you, Shannon. You made my night!

Johnny: Hear that, H? My girl made Gabby's night. Looks like you're losing your touch.

Gabby: The night's young, Johnny, and Henry has never disappointed

Henry: That's my girl!

James: Ha! Good form Gabby!

Henry: mind your business about my stamina, brothers

May: I told you she was brilliant!

Andrew: As much as I am looking forward to meeting you, Gabby, I'm more interested in your baking skills

Nathan: yeah, his wife can't cook to save her life

Becca: tossers! The lot of you!

Henry: She's on holiday, Andy, she doesn't need to be making anything for you sorry sods

Gabby: I wouldn't mind baking. Betty, would it be okay for me to bring something on Saturday?

Betty: of course, dear, if you'd like. Don't let my son put you on the spot.

Gabby: Not at all, it would be my pleasure

Henry: you are all in for a treat

Andrew: May seems to have quieted down

Johnny: Maybe Gerald took our advice

James: You all better stop with this nonsense

Betty: I think it's time we all end this. See you all on Saturday. And I expect my children on their best behavior.

Henry laughed as he turned off his phone and looked over to Gabriella who had suddenly disappeared down the stairs.

"Ella?" Henry called out, then turned off the television and turned out the lights before he headed to the staircase. He found her in the kitchen as she opened cabinets and furiously typed into her phone. The dogs whined at the back door, so Henry let them out before he approached the frantic woman who had torn apart his kitchen.

"Everything okay, love?"

"I'm just taking stock of what you have in the house, so I know what I need to get at the market."

"We could just do this in the morning."

"Actually, I was hoping you would go with me tonight so I could start baking first thing."

"Make the list, I will put an order online and have it here as soon as possible."

"I don't think I'll have enough time to make everything if I don't start tonight," Gabriella whined as she began to pace the length of the island.

Henry placed his hands on her shoulders and put a stop to her motion. "All right then, love. Make your list, I'll ring my assistant and have him run to the grocer's and get everything you need. There really is no need for you to make anything for Saturday, but I know you have your heart set on it, yeah?"

Gabriella nodded in response. "Right, then take a deep breath, make the list, and then I'll be your sous chef and help you with whatever you need."

A smile formed on her face as she thought of Henry in a little chef's hat and white apron. Then the thought of him in only the chef's hat and apron creeped in. "Behave yourself, Ella. Make the list. Then we will pass the time waiting on our supplies. I don't believe I've had you on the dining table yet."

Twenty-Five

"Will you stop fussing?" Henry asked with a sigh as his eyes quickly drifted from the road to the passenger seat, where Gabriella performed an interpretive dance of ants in her pants.

"I'm not fussing."

"You are going to tear the hem of your dress if you don't stop yanking on the bloody thing."

"I think it is too short, your parents are going to think I'm a slut coming to their house in a short dress."

"You're wearing leggings and boots to the top of your knees. What are you showing?"

"I can't believe you let me leave the house in this."

"My lord, woman, you're driving me mad. You look beautiful. Please relax."

"Oh my god, did I bring the cannoli? I think I left them in the fridge."

"You're off your trolley today, Ella. They are in the boot, along with the two cakes and cookies you made."

"Did I make too much? Are they going to think I'm showing off? I'm such an idiot!"

Henry sighed, then pulled the car to the shoulder of the M11. "What are you doing?" Gabriella asked, her eyes as wide as dinner plates.

"Okay Ella, I need you to breathe. I know you are nervous to meet my family. I understand, they are a lot, but they are nitwits, at least my brothers are. My parents love you, and you know May is completely chuffed that we are together, so there is nothing to worry about. We triple-checked that we brought everything with us, including suitcases so we can continue our exploration of the country, yea? The dogs are safe in the back, and you look absolutely stunning. Nothing that happens today will change anything for us, yea? We're a team, Ella. You and me."

Gabriella looked down at their intertwined hands and took a deep breath, then slowly released it along with some of the nervous energy that had taken up residence inside. After two more breaths, she squeezed Henry's hand and smiled. "You're right. We're a team. Everything will be fine."

Henry smiled, then pulled back onto the road and continued to head towards Norwich. "I know you like to be prepared; do you feel like you forgot something?"

"No, you don't want to know what I packed in my luggage," she said with a laugh, "I also checked in with Laurel and Desmond while I was waiting for things to cool yesterday. I have my laptop with me so I can do work on the road when needed. I feel good about that."

"Right. Anything else that you need to discuss before we get there?"

"Are you sure they are okay with us bringing Scampi?"

560

Henry's deep laugh echoed in the cab of the car in response. "Oh, Ella, you have no idea what you are in for."

***

An hour later they arrived in a beautiful residential community, one where you can feel the history of the land and the people who walked the grounds centuries before. Henry slowed his Audi Q7 and signaled that he would make a right turn into a paved path hugged by brick pillars, the number twenty prominent on each side. As they drove down the pathway, beautiful greenery surrounded them on both sides until the landscape cleared to a large grassy lot with a large brick Tudor-style home stood in the near distance.

"Oh, wow. Henry, this house is gorgeous."

"Thank you. Welcome to my childhood home. Prepare yourself."

The car came to a stop on the grass, next to the paved pathway, where four cars were parked away from the two closest to the house. As the car was shifted to park, Henry quietly counted down, "three, two, one."

At that moment, the front door was thrown open, and four people rushed out of the door, slowly followed by another six. May reached the car first and threw the passenger side door open before Gabriella could remove her seatbelt. Not only was she shell-shocked by the amount of people who surrounded the car, but the parade of dogs that followed the humans.

"It's about time!" May shouted excitedly as she let Gabriella out of the car and ignored the symphony of barking that came from the back seat. Once Gabriella stood, May threw her arms around her in a tight hug.

"Oh! Wow. It's good to see you, May." Gabriella muffled.

"Don't worry, I'll protect you from the knobs," she chuckled as her brothers began to swarm.

"I think she is going to need protection from you, prat," a man with a similar bone structure to Henry, but a bit smaller in stature with hazel eyes and longer hair said with a smile as he put May in a headlock and rubbed his knuckles on her hear. "Don't listen to this one, she's a nutter. I'm Johnny."

Gabriella went to shake his hand, but he let go of his sister and pulled her into a bear hug.

"Hey, hands off, that one is mine," Henry said with a laugh as he opened the back door to unbuckle the dogs from their harnesses.

"Piss off, I don't see a ring on her finger," Johnny said with a laugh.

"Does that mean that Shannon is fair game?" A taller man with a slightly receded hairline and a large grin approached. His dark brown hair was short and tidy, and he had a large dimple on one side of his face.

"Not for an old bloke like you," Johnny snapped back.

562

"Let go of the girl, mate," the shortest of the men said, his eyes the same color as Henry's but they were smaller and squinty. "Apologies for this one, Gabriella, he was dropped on his head by the rest of us. I'm Andrew, it's nice to meet you."

"Nice to meet you too," Gabriella said as she offered her hand, but was pulled into another hug.

"I'm Nathan, pleasure to meet you." Gabriella smiled as Andrew released her from his hug. She went to hug Nathan, but he pulled away as if she had cooties and extended his hand out.

"Oh, I'm so embarrassed. I just assumed since the other two…" Gabriella explained as she reached out to shake his hand, the three brother began to laugh.

"Ah, we're just taking a piss, love, come here," Nathan said as he pulled her into a hug.

"They are rotten, I tell you," May said as she pushed her brothers away.

"Don't listen to that tart, Gabby, she's a known fibber," Johnny said with a laugh as he lifted his sister off the ground in a bear hug, which caused May to squeal.

"Well, now that is out of the way, you can meet the normal ones here," a beautiful blonde with a sheik chin-length bob that perfectly framed her heart-shaped face with sparkling green eyes said as she circumvented the rowdy siblings.

"I'm not so sure we're the normal once since we willingly married into this family," a willowy blonde with hair so light it was almost white said as she approached with a shorter, curvier woman with fiery red curls.

"Speak for yourselves, I didn't marry into it," the red head said with an Irish brogue.

"Please, you've been around longer than me," the blonde with the short hair retorted.

The willowy blonde extended her slender hand to Gabriella and smiled brightly, "I'm Millie, Nathan's wife. It's so nice to finally meet you."

"It's nice to meet you too," Gabriella said as she returned the smile.

"This is Becca, Andrew's wife," Millie explained with a gesture toward the other blonde, "and this is Shannon, Johnny's life partner."

"It's so nice to meet you both," Gabriella said with a smile as she shook both of their hands.

"Sorry for those prats. They can't help but show off in front of new people," Becca said with a roll of her eyes.

"That, and they love to torture Hank. It's been a long time since he's brought a girl to meet the family," Shannon explained. "But I'm so glad it's you. I really am such a fan of yours."

Gabriella began to blush, "thank you, Shannon. The whole acting thing was just a fluke."

"Nonsense, you were brilliant," Millie chimed in.

"But it's not just the acting, it was your whole situation and how you handled it," Shannon explained.

"It's how we knew you'd fit right in and be a great match for Hank. Taking no shite and standing up for yourself." Becca said with a smile.

"But we'll help you with that with this lot. Poor May was fending for herself before we came into the picture. Us girls need to stick together," Millie explained.

"Oh, I'm so glad you've finally arrived," Betty said as she made it through the crowd and pulled Gabriella into a tight hug. "It's so nice to finally meet you in person. You are more stunning than in your photos, and that says something."

"It's nice to meet you officially, Gabby," James said from behind his wife. "I would apologize for our children, but there aren't enough apologies in the world for that lot."

Gabriella laughed as she greeted Henry's parents. From around them, she spotted Scampi and Leigh chase around seven other dogs. "Hank, my boy, it's good to see you," James said as he embraced his youngest son, "need help with bringing anything in?"

"Hey Dad, yes, we can leave the luggage in the car, but Ella channeled her inner Paul Hollywood and baked herself silly yesterday. You are all in for a treat," Henry said with a smile as he put his arm around Gabriella.

"Rubbish, bring the luggage. We insist you spend the night. You can continue your trip north, yeah?" Betty said with a shake of her head.

"Where are the cakes, Hank? We'll help bring them in," Shannon asked as she made her way closer to the car.

"In the boot," Henry called over his shoulder. He placed a kiss to Gabriella's head and followed Shannon, as James and Becca followed. May ran over to join them as the door opened.

"Oh, wow! Gabby, this all looks so scrummy!" May shouted as she grabbed one of the cakes. "Stay back, you heathens, I have homemade pastry in my hands, and I don't want anyone to hurt it."

May led the precession into the house as various members of the family carried in bags and boxes from the car. Henry closed the trunk and locked the car, then winked at Gabriella and his mother and followed the rest of the family into the house.

Betty hooked her arm with Gabriella's, an action that made Gabriella smile and think of Laurel and headed to the house with her. "I hope my family doesn't scare you off. They are a cheeky bunch, but they mean well. The teasing just means they like you," Betty said as they approached the front door. She turned before she opened the door and slipped her fingers into her mouth and let out a loud whistle, which got the attention of the dogs. She called them in, and all nine dogs, Scampi included, followed her instructions and went into the house.

Gabriella watched on in awe as the dogs made their way into the house. "Wow, that was really impressive."

"Stick with me, Gabby, I'll teach you a thing or two, especially how to deal with my son," she said with a smile as they trailed the dogs inside.

The entrance was grand, the floors tiled in earth tones with light tan that matched on the walls. The staircase stood in the center of the hallway and doorways flocked either side. "I'll give you the grand tour while everyone settles into the conservatory. We always start the day off in there with some cocktails before we eat." Betty explained as Gabriella watched the dogs head in the direction she gestured to.

The first stop on the tour was a large drawing room, with cream carpets and green damask wallpaper. Large windows lined the wall facing the front and side of the house, which made it airy and bright. The next room was across the hall, a dining room with pale grey walls, original hardwood floors, and navy-blue drapes that dressed the large windows that faced the front yard. A large dining table sat in the center of the room with place settings for twelve, surrounded by server stations and a beautiful fireplace. "Dinner will be in here," Betty explained before taking her into the kitchen, which was cozy and well used. A small table sat on the opposite side of the room from where the wall of cabinets and appliance were stationed.

They made their way past the bathroom and the study behind the staircase and went to the second floor, where Betty pointed out each of the bedrooms, which included Henry's childhood bedroom that he shared with Johnny. Gabriella looked around the room and smiled, seeing proof of Henry's nerdy past and his love of dungeons and dragons. "Are we staying in here tonight?"

Betty laughed. "No, I wouldn't make you sleep in bunk beds. There are two apartments attached to the house. I'm sure centuries ago it was staff quarters. May and Gerald live on the first level. You and Henry will be staying on the second."

"Wow, this house is amazing. There must be so much history in these walls."

"Oh, yes. I wish it were nicer out; I would take you out into the gardens. Our grounds are large and beautiful to sit in during the warmer months. "

They made their way back to main floor, and Betty led Gabriella through what she called a morning room, which Gabriella thought was a den, which was decorated modernly, which was a stark contrast to the rest of the very traditional house. The family was in the connected room, which reminded Gabriella of a rounded sunroom. Everyone sat around the wicker furniture with martinis in their hands as they lively spoke over one another, with many jests thrown around at others expense.

Henry was in the middle of an exchange with his brothers when they entered the room. "You all better bugger off, my lady is in the room," Henry said as he stood and kissed his mother, then took Gabriella by the hand and led her to an empty wicker rocking chair next to Becca.

"Trust me, you are going to need this," Shannon said with a laugh as she handed her a martini. Gabriella eyeballed the glass as Henry informed her, "it's a dirty martini, an Anderson family tradition. We always have at least one of these before we eat to start the night off right."

Gabriella sipped the drink as Andrew looked at her. "Hank just wants you off your face, so you don't remember anything we say about him."

Henry rolled his eyes, "piss off, wanker."

"See? I bet he never spoke like this in front of you. He probably did his posh British bloke routine in front of you," Andrew retorted.

Gabriella laughed and looked around the room. "How many of these have you all had?"

"We're on our second round, except Millie who is breastfeeding," Becca offered.

"Speak for yourself," Johnny said, "I'm on three."

Gabriella arched her eyebrow and finished her drink in one large gulp. "Seems like I have some catching up to do."

The boys cheered her on as the girls giggled. James shook his head and looked from his wife to Henry and said, "yeah, she will have no problem fitting in."

***

After a delicious dinner prepared by Betty, the family sat around the table and chatted. Johnny seemed intent to get the ladies intoxicated as he continuously filled their wine glasses. Henry sat next to Gabriella, his hand on top of hers on the table as the family shared stories of him when he was a child.

"Did Hank tell you that he used to sleepwalk when he was a lad?" Andrew asked with a twinkle in his eye.

"Ella doesn't need to hear this story," Henry said with a shake of his head.

"She most certainly does," Johnny said with a waggle of his eyebrows.

"Is this the pee story or the dress story?" Nathan asked.

"Oh, both!" Andrew said with a laugh.

"I'll tell the first one since I was the one who caught him," Betty said with a laugh.

"Bloody hell, mum," Henry sighed.

"When Henry was about five years old, he started sleepwalking. One night I was watching the telly after I put the children to bed. I heard something coming from the kitchen, and I thought it was James in his study, but his door was open, and I could see him at his desk. I went to investigate, and I found Henry in the kitchen, with a cabinet open. When I went to see what he was doing, he had one of my pots on the floor. His trousers and pants down around his ankles with his willy out. I called out his name and asked what he was doing, and he said he was taking a leak. I informed him that he wasn't in the bathroom, to which he shrugged his shoulders and proceeded to urinate in my pot. After he was done, he just went back up to his room and back to bed. I asked him the next morning and he had no recollection of it."

Gabriella bit her lip and tried not to laugh as she looked over to Henry, whose face was pinched together as he tried to hold back a smile. "Well," Gabriella said as she tried to keep control of her laughter, "that is quite the story."

"Nah, that's nothing compared to the next one," Johnny said with a laugh.

"This one is my favorite Hank story," Becca chimed in.

"I must have been seventeen at the time," Nathan began, "Andrew and I were in the drawing room, we had just come back from a party."

"We were pretty pissed when we got home, so we were confused when we saw Hank come downstairs with something in his hands, making his way to dad's study," Andrew continued.

"We called out to him, and he came over to us, one of May's tutus in his hand. We asked what he was doing, and he told us that in order to defeat the troll, he needed to dress up as a princess to trick him," Nathan explained.

"Oh, no. Did you tell him to go to bed?" Gabriella asked.

"Absolutely not! We helped him get dressed. Even found a crown and fairy wings," Andrew cried out.

Gabriella gasped and covered her face as James chimed in, "the boys took a picture of it too."

Henry shook his head. "Do you know how confused I was when I woke up in my bed with a tutu on?"

Gabriella lost her composure and let out a burst of air that sounded like a fart before she succumbed to a fit of giggles. The unladylike noise caused the rest of the family to join in, which filled the house with boisterous laughs. The baby monitor on the table by Millie lit up, and the sounds of a baby's cries came through.

"Oh, we did it now, the slumbering monster has awakened," Nathan said with a laugh as he watched his wife get up and make her way to the stairs.

"At least we were able to eat dinner in peace," Millie said before ascended the stairs.

"So, Gabby, are you seeing a side to your prince charming that you didn't know?" Johnny asked.

"Why are you being such a wanker?" May asked from the other end of the table.

"What are you on about, I'm just taking a piss." Johnny said.

"No, May is right, you're being a bit of an arse. Like you're trying to get Gabby to see flaws in Hank," Shannon said as she called out her boyfriend.

"Alright, enough," James said to quiet them.

"Is there anything you want to ask us, Gabby?" Becca asked.

"Oh, actually, I was hoping to see some old pictures of Henry when he was a child," Gabriella said with a smile.

"We did promise you that," Betty said with a smile, "I think we can make that happen after dessert."

Gabriella smiled at Betty in return. Millie returned to the dining room with an adorable three-month-old girl in her arms, with a tuft of blonde hair and big brown eyes. Everyone cooed when they entered the room. Henry jumped up right away and put his hands out to his niece. The baby smiled as Millie handed the baby to him.

Gabriella smiled as she watched Henry hold his niece, and she could swear she heard her ovaries weep. "Ella, this is my niece, Emma."

"Hi Emma," Gabriella said with an overexaggerated smile as she waved. Emma looked at her and smiled as she hit her tiny hands against Henry's stubble. The family began to talk about Emma's sleep schedule, but Gabriella couldn't remove her eyes from Henry. She could picture him hold their baby, with dark hair and blue eyes. She never felt such an overwhelming need to be a mother as she had in that moment.

Betty cleared her throat and called Gabriella's name. Gabriella snapped out of her daydream and looked over that Henry's mother. "I'm sorry, Betty, did you need something?"

Betty smiled knowingly, her eyes drifted to her son and granddaughter, then back to Gabriella. "I wanted to ask you to help me bring the dessert out, since you were so nice to bake it."

"Oh, of course," Gabriella said as she stood up and made her way into the kitchen as Henry watched her leave.

"It was so nice of you to bake all of this," Betty said as she opened the refrigerator to take the cannoli and cakes out.

"Oh, I love to bake. There is a German chocolate cake, a New York style cheesecake, cannoli, and Florentine and pignoli cookies."

"Wow, you must have been very busy yesterday," Betty said as she set the teapot on the stove.

"Yes, but I find it relaxing, although if you ask Henry, I was anything but relaxed when I was looking for the ingredients," Gabriella said with a laugh.

Betty studied Gabriella as she grabbed the dessert plates from the cabinet. Gabriella grew nervous under the scrutiny, unsure of what to do. She tucked her hair behind her ear, then played with her fingers in front of her burgundy sweater dress.

"I can see why my son is so smitten with you," Betty said as she set the plates on a serving tray.

Gabriella took a deep breath as she made eye contact with Betty, unsure what would come out of her mouth next.

"Henry is a kind soul, he does so much for those he cares about. But he's been burned in the past. I'm sure you know about his ex-fiancée. I never cared for her, very self-centered and snobby. But Henry fell for her regardless. It took him a long time to recover from that relationship."

Gabriella nodded as she waited for the other shoe to drop.

"Just be careful with my boy. I can tell that you care for him deeply, but I'm not sure if he is rushing into things with you. Just make sure that you tell him how you are feeling every step of the way. But I do think the two of you would be very good together."

Gabriella smiled and nodded in agreement. "Henry is amazing, and honestly, he's too good for me. I'm still waiting for him to wake up and realize it. So, I'm just thankful for every day I have with him."

Betty smiled and pulled Gabriella into a hug. "See, that's where you're wrong. And that's why I know you two will make it."

May entered the kitchen and caught her mother hug Gabriella. "Is everything okay?"

"Yes, my dear. Just having a moment with Gabby. Would you help us bring out all of these treats? She made too many for four hands to carry out."

"Of course, Gabby, this all really does look so scrummy, I can't wait to try every single item you made," May said with a smile as she grabbed the chocolate cake. "I have a feeling this one might be my favorite."

"It is you brother's favorite, so I wouldn't be surprised," Gabriella responded as she grabbed the cheesecake and followed May to deposit them on the dining room table. She rushed back in and grabbed the tray of cookies and the tray of cannoli and followed Betty who carried the tray of tea and plates.

"Oh, wow, this all looks so good," Becca said with a small clap as she eyed the food.

"Gabby, would you do the honors of serving? So you can explain everything you made?" Betty asked.

"Of course," she responded as she stood asked what everyone would like after she described everything. Everyone said they would try one of each, so she loaded their dessert plates and passed them around the table. The room was silent as everyone dug into their dessert, which made Gabriella slightly nervous.

"Do you think I messed up the recipes," she whispered to Henry. Henry smiled and shook his head as he shoveled a piece of the chocolate cake into his mouth as his niece watched on in wonder.

Johnny dropped his fork, the clang against the plate caused everyone to look at him. "Hank, I swear to God that if you don't marry this girl, I'm adopting her. No offense, mum, but these might be the best desserts I've ever had in my life."

Gabriella let out a breath that she didn't know she held and laughed. "This really is amazing," Shannon said with a smile as she bit into a Florentine cookie. "You act, you bake, you manage your friends. Is there anything you can't do?"

"Oh, trust me, there is plenty. I just distract you with baked goods, so you don't notice," Gabriella joked.

Each family helped themselves to a second round of dessert, Johnny made his way to a third, and begged Gabriella to share the recipes with them. "This was so good, I want to try to make it myself," Johnny said.

"As long as we don't let Becca attempt to make anything," Andrew joked about his wife. Becca tossed her napkin at him in response.

When everyone was done, they all helped to clear the table and put everything away. "Well, it's getting late, I think we should call it a night," Henry said once the house was back to its original state.

"Are you trying to get out of letting me see your old photos?" Gabriella asked.

"Right on you," he said with a wink.

"We really should get home, Emma will only be up for so long," Nathan explained.

"And she most certainly needs a bath," Millie chimed in.

"I have an early shift at the hospital, so we should leave too," Shannon said as she eyed Johnny.

"Well, I can take a hint as good as any," Andrew said with a smirk as he nodded to his wife. Becca pouted, "and miss out on the old home movies?" Andrew nodded, which earned him an eye roll in response.

Betty stood, which prompted everyone else. "Alright then, on with you."

Everyone said their goodbyes and lingered on Gabriella more than anyone else.

"Mum, can we do one more dinner together before Gabby heads to the States?" Becca asked.

"Of course, but you can always invite them out to you," Betty responded.

"Actually, we are going to do a bit of traveling while we're here," Henry explained, "so I'm not sure how much free time we will have."

"But I would absolutely love to see you all again before we leave," Gabriella added. "And I'm sure I'll be back here in the future. It won't be my only stay in England."

The family walked out of the house together, and Gabriella witnessed who owned the dogs as they jumped into their respected cars. As Millie placed Emma in her car seat, a golden retriever joined them in the back. Johnny was trailed by a jack russell, and the cocker spaniel and beagle followed Becca and Andrew.

The rest of the dogs, which consisted of two border collies, a French bulldog, Leigh, and Scampi sat in the front lawn and watched the departed parade of cars. May turned to her brother once everyone left and smiled. "You know I'm staying to watch the home movies."

Henry shook his head with a smile, "I don't mind you staying, you're not a tart about it like the rest of them."

578

"Gerald, are you going to stay?" May asked.

"Because we have such a far commute? Yes, I'll stay for a bit," he responded before he turned to the French bulldog. "Trixie, come."

"Elton, Freddie, get inside," James called out to the border collies.

Gabriella looked at him and smiled. "As in John and Mercury?"

James' face lit up with a smile. "Right on you. Are you a fan of their music?"

"Oh, here we go," Henry sighed.

"Absolutely!" Gabriella exclaimed.

"I'll have to show you my office. I'm quite the music purveyor." James said as he led them into the house.

***

They spent the night watching home movies of Henry as he grew up and looked through countless photo albums. Henry and Gabriella left early the next morning and headed north to make their way to Scotland for a four-day-long trip. They returned to the Anderson's family home to leave the dogs for a few days while they flew to Ireland for another trip.

Once Gabriella told Henry that she saw everything she wanted to see on this trip, they returned to London. When they entered the house, Henry let the dogs out into the yard, then led Gabriella into the elevator, where they went straight to the top floor.

"Are we leaving our luggage up here?" She asked as the doors opened.

"Leave them here, I wanted to show you something." He responded, then placed his hand on the small of her back and lead her to his study.

They walked into the room filled with deep mahogany built-ins filled with books, an intimidatingly large mahogany desk with a deep brown leather chair behind it, and plush wingback chairs surrounding the fireplace in a deep forest green. The far wall and hallway which lead to the spare bedroom that shared the floor were filled with memorabilia of Henry's career. Gabriella smiled as she took in the framed movie posters and scripts stored in shadow boxes. Photos from the movie sets and red carpets speckled the shelves.

She entered the guest room and gasped at the sight in front of her. Rather than the standard bed and nightstand that was there when she first arrived, a full office filled the space. White built-ins with some standard home office décor stood on the wall perpendicular to wall filled with a giant window covered in sheer window dressings with periwinkle curtains adorning the perimeter of the window. An antique pale white writer's desk with gold accents sat before the shelving with a cream-colored wingback chair.

A feminine chandelier hung in the center of the room, where a periwinkle tufted couch sat against the far wall with two matching armchairs which surrounded an oblong glass and marble coffee table. An off-white plush area rug lined the seating area, and gold-accented floor and desk lamps adorned the space.

580

"What is all of this?"

"Well, I figured you couldn't be taking business meetings in the kitchen all of the time, and I'm hoping that if you have a space of your own to work in will mean that you'll feel comfortable staying here longer. I didn't get you the electronics you need, I wanted you to tell me what you need."

Gabriella cut him off and pulled him into a deep, desperate kiss. Once they pulled away from one another, Henry gave her one of his brilliant smiles. "So, you like it, yeah?"

"I love it. I can't believe you did this. It's amazing. Is this why we were traveling?"

"Maybe. I thought it was a good time to fix up the room. How many bedrooms does one bloke need? What do you say we unpack, get the dogs settled, then come up here and christen your study?" Henry suggested with a wag of his eyebrows.

"Counteroffer, we unpack, get the dogs settled, get some food in my belly, then come back up here." She said with a wink as she walked two fingers up his broad chest, then booped his nose.

With a laugh, the went back to the elevator and dragged the suitcases to the bedroom. As they unpacked Gabriella looked up above the bed and paused at the picture that was now hanging on the wall. There was a 24 x 30 sized canvas print of them in black and white from their Vanity Fair photo shoot. The cropped version of Henry's open lips on the column of her neck. The one that generated many rounds of masturbatory material for her when they were on a hiatus.

"You like it?" Henry asked.

"Where did it come from?" She asked, her eyes remained on the erotic photo.

"It's my favorite photo. I kept it as my screen saver when I was in New Zealand. Besides, I couldn't think of a better photo to have hanging above our bed, can you?"

"No, I really can't."

Twenty-Six

"Are you sure you don't want me to come with you to get your parents?" Gabriella yelled out from the couch in living room with the dogs on the rug next to the driftwood coffee table.

"Yes, Ella, it's fine. Your father is taking me over to the airport in a few minutes." Henry responded as he entered the room from the little yellow kitchen.

"Are you positive your parents are okay staying here with us? The guest room is not the largest."

"They will be fine. They are chuffed to meet your parents. They've only ever stayed at hotels here; they want to experience the beach house." Henry said before he placed a kiss on her forehead.

"I'm so excited to meet you parents, Henry. Your mom and I have been texting, she is ready to be pampered and looking forward to brunch this weekend," Maria said with a smile.

"Right, she's been chatting to me about it nonstop," Henry said with a smile. "I'm going to head out. You have everything you need for tonight and tomorrow?"

Gabriella nodded and smiled. "I think I'm getting a little old for these sleepovers, but yes. I have everything ready. Are you sure you can handle getting the dogs to the sitter?"

"Yes. My dad and G will help, I'm sure. You're positive you are ready for tomorrow?"

Gabriella looked to her mom, then back to Henry and shrugged. "I think so. We have the spa this afternoon, then sleepover at Laurel's. Izzy is bringing my dress tomorrow morning to make sure there are no last-minute alterations. Glam squad is coming by seven. You guys are due to us by two, and we are supposed to arrive at three thirty."

"And you have the jewelry?" Henry asked.

"Yes, babe. I will wear the earrings you gave me only."

"Good girl," Henry said with a wink before placing a quick kiss on her lips. "I'll see you tomorrow, love."

"Okay, babe. And don't forget to drop your mom off to the spa for her appointment today."

Henry gave her a salute, then kissed Maria on the cheek as he left the house to meet Giuseppe in the car. Once they had driven off, Maria sat down on the couch next to her daughter.

"Things seem to be really progressing with you and Henry."

Gabriella smiled brightly as she looked at her mother. "Yeah, things are really great."

"I can tell by the genuine smile that is lighting up your face. You are in love with him."

"I am. I know we've only been together for a few months, but it just seems right. I'm just enjoying it while it lasts, you know? You know how celebrity relationships are."

"Don't be so negative, *Bambolina*. You two really have something special. I know there was a rough start, but you can't deny the chemistry between you two."

"I know, Mom. So, did you have a good time shopping with Caroline?"

"I know you're trying to change the subject. But yes, we had a great time. We got our dresses. Your friend Darius was nice enough to be our private shopper and help us out. I feel terrible for him that he separated from his partner. I can't believe that piece of trash cheated on him." Maria said with a shake of her head.

"I know, it's terrible. But he's doing okay. They sold their place, and he moved in with Max for a bit. He says that he's living his best life, and he's partying with Max and enjoying his newfound independence." Gabriella explained. "But honestly, I think he's sad, and he's just trying to find a silver lining."

"That's all anyone can do in a situation like that. But just because it didn't work out for Darius doesn't mean it won't work out for you." Maria said with a smile as she patted her daughter on the knee. Now, let's get over to the spa. I need a day of rest and relaxation before my daughter wins an Oscar tomorrow night."

***

The soft white and gold walls with the sheer curtains and white furniture and flooring created a carefully crafted ambiance of serenity, which absolutely sold the room's name of The Sanctuary. The soothing music that barely floated through the air cocooned the body in a sense of relaxation. Gabriella smiled as she sat on the soft cushion of the rounded bench and sunk into the oversized decorative pillows behind her. Maria sat on her own bench as they waited for Laurel and Caroline to arrive.

"I'm surprised that Desmond didn't come with us," Maria said before she sipped a glass of champagne.

"He claimed he was going to stick with the guys. I think he was so grateful that Henry gave his extra ticket to Arnie, he's trying to kiss his ass." Gabriella said with a smile.

Laurel and her mother entered the room and inhaled the relaxing scent of eucalyptus that flowed through the room. "You booked the whole spa for us, didn't you?" Laurel asked as she walked over and kissed Maria hello.

Gabriella shrugged and smiled. "Only the best for my A-list, Oscar nominated bestie. But, we only have it for four hours. Trust me, it was a bitch to get."

"Is it just the four of us?" Caroline asked as she settled next to Maria and happily accepted a glass of champagne.

"No, Henry's mother should be here soon. He had strict instructions to pick her up from the airport and drive her directly here."

586

"I'm looking forward to meeting her," Laurel said as she sunk into the bench next to Gabriella. "She must be something else to handle Henry as a son."

"Oh, dear, you don't know the half of it," a British-accented voice said as it entered the room. The women looked over to see Betty in black trousers and a short-sleeved Burberry button down. Her blue eyes sparkled in delight as she smiled back.

"Betty! You made it!" Gabriella jumped up and hugged Henry's mother. "How was the trip?"

"Oh, it was fine. Nothing like a cross-continental flight to get you chuffed for a day of pampering. Oh, you must be Maria," Betty said as she hugged Maria when she approached.

"It's so nice to finally meet you in person, Betty. This here is Caroline, Laurel's mom, and of course you know Laurel." Maria introduced.

"You are stunning! I absolutely love your hair. Very *Devil Wears Prada* Miranda Priestly." Laurel said as she hugged Betty.

"I'm surprised I understood what you meant. Thank you. I have to tell you, I think you are a phenomenal actress," Betty gushed.

"Okay, ladies, I booked us for everything. Get ready for 3 hours of body treatments and facials followed by an hour of mani-pedis." Gabriella said with a smile as their masseurs entered the room to take them to the treatment areas.

After they stored their belongings in the white and gold locker room, the ladies donned their fluffy white robes and slippers and followed the staff into the ladies' lounge, where their masseurs greeted them. Since they were a larger group, they were escorted to a room where five beds with cream-colored plush blankets awaited them. The ambiance of the space quieted the women when they entered the room. Silently, they each took a table and settled into their treatments.

An hour into the full-body massage, Laurel whispered and tried to get Gabriella's attention. "What," she whispered back.

"What do you think is going to happen tonight?" Laurel asked.

"I don't know, we go to the ceremony?"

"Yeah, but do you think we're gonna win?" Laurel asked.

"Hey, ladies, we're supposed to be relaxing," Maria said out loud.

"Seriously, I'm starting to tense up listening to your whispers," Caroline chimed in.

Laurel slightly giggled before she tried to relax into the massage.

After the massages were over and they went through their facials, the five women were sat in the pedicure chairs, where they drank champagne as one person tended to their pedicures and another did their manicures.

"Is it okay for me to talk out here now? Or do I have to be quiet for this too?" Laurel asked.

"It depends, are you going to stress us out again," her mother asked.

"I don't think I could be stressed out after that. I could probably fly all the way back home and still be relaxed. I feel like a puddle," Betty commented.

"It's just, I don't know what to do. How am I going to keep my face neutral if I don't win?"

"You're an actress, Laurel, you act," Maria said with a laugh.

"How are you not freaking out," Laurel asked Gabriella.

"Because I'm going to enjoy the night. I'm not going to win. I'm just happy I get to be there and share this moment with you," she said with a smile, then sipped champagne.

"Are you telling me you don't have a speech prepared?" Laurel asked.

"For what? Laurel, relax. I can help you prep a speech tonight if that's why you're worried. Just thank your parents, the studio, Darius, you manager," she said with a wink.

"Are you kidding me? I have my speech; I've had my speech for years. How do you not have one?"

"Shh, you are raising the stress levels, Laurel. This is a stress-free zone." Caroline said. "Hey Gabby, are we gonna get waxed?"

"I didn't plan for it here. But I can get someone to come to the house tonight if you want."

"Yeah, I think I could go for a wax. What do you say ladies?" Caroline asked.

"What are we waxing?" Betty asked.

"I usually just do my legs and bikini line, but this one over here likes to go full Brazilian," Maria offered.

"I don't think my husband could pick my fanny out of a lineup if I took it all off," Betty said with a laugh.

"No, but it may be a fun way to surprise him. Nothing says you're in America like getting a Brazilian," Caroline countered.

The mothers were reduced to a fit of laughter while Laurel and Gabriella watched on. "Maybe we should all do it, get Laurel's mind off of tomorrow," Caroline suggested.

"If I set that up, and didn't invite Desmond, he'd never forgive me," Gabriella said.

"That little Puerto Rican dips himself in wax every three weeks," Laurel added.

"Bloody hell let's do it. This will be one to tell the girls when I get home."

***

The next day Laurel's home was glam central. There were hairdressers, makeup artists and wardrobe assistants to get the ladies ready for the party. Izzy showed up at the house at seven in the morning with Gabriella's dress. She excitedly trailed after the large garment bag as Izzy was directed to a guest room upstairs. "I can't believe this is the first time you are actually seeing the dress," Izzy exclaimed, her elf-like features lit up with excitement.

"I know it's going to be stunning, you do such amazing work," Gabriella said with a smile.

"Okay, go throw on whatever underwear you're going to wear tonight. And don't forget the shoes!" She called out as Gabriella entered the ensuite.

Moments later, she stepped into the room wearing a strapless bra and matching panties with crystal embellished black satin heeled sandals. "Oh, those shoes are perfection! McQueen?"

Gabriella nodded, then looked at the garment bag filled with anticipation. "I hope you like this," Izzy said as she opened the garment bag, and revealed deep burgundy material. Once the garment bag was removed, the shimmer in the fabric was exposed in the light. Gabriella gasped in delight and awe.

"Izzy, this dress is amazing."

"Let's get it on you to make sure it fits," she suggested.

Gabriella stepped into the dress, as Izzy lifted it up. The full ball gown cinched at her waist, the sleeves hung at the base of her shoulder, and the front and back had the same V-shape, tastefully exposing a small amount of cleavage.

"I feel like a Disney princess in the dress, Iz. Very *Beauty and the Beast*. I'm afraid to wear this and ruin it."

"It's a fairy tale dress for a fairy tale evening. I have to say, I was nervous with the measurements you sent me when I was making this, but you really did shrink a bit."

"It was all the training for the movie I did. Don't you worry, now that I'm not on that strict regimen of diet and exercise, I'll fit back into my premiere dress in no time." Gabriella joked.

"Okay, let me just check a few things and I'll get you down to hair and makeup in no time."

"Why don't you hang out for a while? The caterers just dropped off food, and we've got time before we really need to get ready. Unless of course you have other plans. I don't mean to be presumptuous."

"I appreciate the invite, Gabby. I'd love to hang out for a bit. I will tell you though, thanks to you, business has been booming. There really is a gap in the industry to create beautiful dresses for non-sample sized women."

"I'm so glad, Izzy. You really are so incredibly talented. You deserve all of the recognition for your efforts and your amazing designs."

592

***

Hours later, Gabriella sat at the island in the kitchen, scrolling through her emails as she waited for the arrival of the men in their party. The rest of the women were off in their different areas of the house to make their last-minute adjustments and final prep for their evening out.

Carefully perched on the stool, careful to not crush the ballgown, she hummed along with the music Laurel had playing throughout the house. She subconsciously went to tuck her hair behind her ear when she realized it was all pinned up in a loose braided chignon. She internally cursed herself because she almost ruined her hair, she bit down on her lip, which caused her to roll her eyes and open the front-facing camera to make sure her makeup was still in place.

Her eyelids were darkened with a bronzed smokey eye, which were highlighted at the inner corners to make her eyes brighter, and the fake lashes fringed them, which made them impossibly long. The thicker camera-friendly makeup that was brushed onto her face always made her feel like an imposter, but she had to admit that the makeup artist did wonders to make her face look more chiseled than usual. She showed her teeth to make sure the deep wine color that made her lips look extra pouty did not transfer onto her whitened teeth.

The clacking of heels drew her eyes away from her image as Laurel entered the kitchen dressed in an antique bronze one-shoulder dress with a high slit on the left, the fabric looked like it was poured liquid destressed leather on her body but flared into an A-line silhouette. Her honey-highlighted locks were tucked into a low bun, opposite the ruffled petal-like fabric decorating the covered right shoulder. Her eyes shimmered in hues of gold, and her lips were painted a nude. She looked as though she was channeling the Oscar award.

"They are on their way," she announced as she entered the room. "Matt texted that they are almost here."

"You look amazing, Lau," Gabriella said as a smile of pure joy split across her face.

"Yeah?" Laurel asked timidly.

"Absolutely! You are going to look amazing accepting on the stage tonight."

"Stop it. Can you tell I'm a nervous wreck?"

"To the untrained eye, you can't tell at all. As holding a doctorate in Laurel studies, I think I need to make you a drink." Gabriella said with a laugh as she stood up and moved from the island to the refrigerator. "Lau, why do you have so many bottles of champagne in here?"

"Gabby, that dress is amazing!" Laurel gushed.

"Oh, thanks. Izzy really is something else," she responded as she reached past the champagne and grabbed the chilled bottle of grey goose. "Is a shot okay for you, or do you want a glass of wine?"

"I'll grab the shot glasses," she said as she made her way to the bar in her den.

"What's up with the music?" Gabriella asked as she took the two shot glasses and poured the vodka.

594

"I'm trying to pump myself up for tonight. Is there a problem with that?"

Gabriella shook her head as she smiled, then handed her the shot. "I'm surprised that Lionel Richie was in your playlist." She held her glass up to Laurel and said, "to my best friend, killing it and taking home a trophy."

Laurel clinked her shot glass to Gabriella's and responded, "to both of us taking home trophies, and keeping it together tonight."

The took their shot and laughed as the music changed to Salt-N-Pepa's *Push it*. "Now this can get anyone pumped," Gabriella said with a laugh as the two of them stared their best impressions of the nineties trio as much as they could in their designer gowns.

"What is this shit?" Desmond yelled from the entrance of the house, then marched through the main hall until he spotted his two friends as they made fools of themselves in the kitchen. "Shots and dancing without me?"

The girls threw their arms open and hugged Desmond, then pulled him in between the layers of fabric and white girl dancing. His smile was a bright as the purple and silver paisley tuxedo jacket he wore, with a matched bowtie, white dress shirt, black vest and black pants. His usual wild black curls were gelled back, and his face was dusted with a manicured shadow of a beard.

"You look very debonair," Gabriella said with a smile as he danced his way from them and poured himself a shot.

"Bitch, I always look good," he said with a wink, then swallowed the vodka. "Speaking of, Laurel, you need to take a look at what Matt is wearing."

"Oh no, please tell me his didn't do the white tux."

Desmond mimed a zipper across his lips, then nudged his head towards the hallway. Laurel grunted and rolled her eyes as she grabbed Desmond's arm and dragged him out of the kitchen. "Excuse us, Gabby, I might have to kill my fiancé before we leave."

Gabriella saluted her friends, "okay, just no blood on your dress and remember we need to leave in thirty minutes!" She laughed as they stomped out of the kitchen, then grabbed the shot glasses and placed them in the sink, then grabbed the bottle and put in back where she found it. She started to hum along to *Just My Imagination* as it played on the speakers.

"What is it with us and this room and The Temptations?" A deep, British voice asked from the entryway of the kitchen.

Gabriella turned around and smiled to see her boyfriend in the entrance to the kitchen with his hands in the pockets of a sharp, well-fitted, traditional black tuxedo with black bowtie and white pocket square. His face was clean-shaven, and his hair was styled slightly parted on the side and gelled back, his eyes sparkled in their unique blue as he took her in.

"I might need to go change my underwear if you keep looking at me like that while you are looking like that," Gabriella said with a smirk.

"And just when I thought you couldn't be more perfect, there you are, looking like a goddess with a dirty mouth." He said as he made his way across the kitchen and met her at the island, pulled her into his arms and kissed her deeply.

596

"Watch it, Mr. Anderson, you're going to ruin my makeup and my panties."

Henry's eyes rolled up into his head as he let out a growl. "Behave yourself, Miss DiStella, we have a long night ahead of us."

Gabriella nodded somberly as she tried to suppress a grin. He studied her face and took in how beautiful she looked. One of his eyebrows arched up as he asked, "where are your earrings, Ella?"

"Oh!" She exclaimed as she removed herself from his embrace and walked around the island to reach her evening bag. "I kept them in here so they wouldn't get pulled or anything by the hairdresser. I'm so glad you reminded me," she said as she fetched them from her bag and put them through her ears.

"I do have something else for you to wear tonight," Henry said from behind her.

"Henry, you don't have to give me anything," she said as she secured the second earring. A black velvet box was placed on the island and slid in front of Gabriella. She looked down at the small box and tilted her head a bit, unsure what he could have purchased her since she already had the earrings in. She reached for the box; her hands slightly shook as she grabbed it and held it completely covered in her hands.

She held the box close to her stomach, took a breath, then looked down at the box and slowly opened it, a gasp escaped her lips as she revealed a four-carat solitaire diamond ring in a six diamond-encrusted-prong setting on a cathedral-style diamond band. She stared down at the ring, unable to move or breathe.

"Do you not like it? Is it too much?" Henry asked from behind.

"Henry…" she breathed out. "This is… is this?"

"An engagement ring? Yeah." He answered.

She began to turn around as she saw him drop to one knee in the middle of Laurel's kitchen, completely unaware of the crowd that gathered at the entryway.

"Gabriella DiStella," Henry started when she went to say something. He held up one finger to quiet her, then continued. "You are the most amazing person I have ever met in my life. You are the breath of fresh air that I need to survive. You are compassionate, loyal, and true to yourself and your beliefs.

"You are a good person, Ella, truly good down to your core. There is no future for me without you being the main component in it. I knew it from the first time on set when you gave me an earful about assuming you were the help that you were it for me.

"I know our relationship may not have been a traditional one, but I think the best love stories are the ones you write by following my heart, and mine always leads to you. I kneel before your, Ella, not as an actor or some fodder for the press, but as the man who is madly in love with you. Spend the rest of your life with me as my wife."

Gabriella looked down at the love of her life knelt before her through blurry eyes. She dropped down onto her knees in front of him and threw her arms around his shoulders. She clung onto him and buried her head in his neck as she shook with emotion.

After a few moments of holding her tightly, Henry asked, "is that a yes?"

"You can't be serious, Henry," she muttered into his neck.

"Of course, I am, Ella. You think I bought you that ring as a joke? I love you. You're bloody brilliant. I want you to be the mother of my children, love. I want to grow old with you and share our lives together. It doesn't hurt that I think you are stunning and can't wait to get you out of those panties later."

"Christ, Henry," James said from the doorway.

"Sorry Dad, that was not for you to hear," he said as he turned his head back to address the crowd. He turned back to Gabriella and smiled as he gently held her chin. "So, what do you say, Ella?"

Gabriella looked him in the eyes and smiled and nodded her head. "Yes, Henry. I want to marry you."

Henry stood up and lifted Gabriella into a hug before he placed her on her feet and took the box from her hand. He removed the sparkling ring of platinum and diamonds and placed it on her left ring finger. She pulled him close and kissed him desperately.

The crowd in the doorway cheered and gathered into the kitchen as they waited to congratulate the couple. Laurel made her way to the fridge to take out the bottles of champagne while Matt retrieved the flutes. The song through the speakers changed to *My Girl* as Henry and Gabriella parted to address their parents. Maria pushed her way between the two of them and threw her arms around them both and kissed them both on the cheek.

"Congratulations! Welcome to the family, officially, Henry. I'm so excited for you!" She said, then released Henry and focused on her daughter. "*Bambolina*, I'm so happy. Are you happy?"

"Of course, mom. I'm shocked, but yeah, really happy."

When Betty released her son from a tight hug, she turned to Gabriella and placed a hand on her cheek. "You, my special girl, are the piece not only missing from my son's life, but from mine as well. Get ready to be a part of the Anderson clan." Betty then enveloped her in a warm hug before she released her to the fathers.

James approached next to congratulate his son and then his future daughter-in-law. Giuseppe waited until James was done before he spoke. "Good job, H."

"Thanks, G."

Gabriella looked between her father and her fiancé and studied them. "You knew," she accused her father.

"Sure did." He responded.

"When," she asked.

600

"Christmas. Well, he told me he planned to marry you back before Christmas. But he spoke to me yesterday on the drive to the airport to ask of my blessing. Wanted to make sure he lived up to all of the promises he made to gain entrance to our house on Christmas Eve." Giuseppe explained.

"Really? What were the promises?"

Her father shook her head. "Can't tell you, Gabby. That's between me and H. But I can tell you that he has, and I trust him to take care of my baby when it comes time that I can't do it anymore."

Gabriella teared up and hugged her father. "Thank you, Dad, I love you."

"I love you too, Gabby. Always have, always will." He said before pressed a kiss to her forehead.

A hand with a glass of champagne reached in front of Gabriella. She took it and looked at Laurel, who winked and then handed a glass to Giuseppe. "Congratulations, bitch!" Desmond said as he jumped in front of Gabriella and kissed her cheek. "I'm so freaking excited for you! Let me see that rock."

Gabriella extended her left hand and Desmond squealed. "Fucking blinding and stunning, good work Hanky-poo."

"Oh, let's not make that one a thing," Henry said with a laugh as he shook his head and accepted a glass of champagne from Matt. Matt patted him on the back and clinked their glasses together. "Congrats, bro. Welcome to the club. Do you feel ready to part with your balls? Because you just handed them to that woman right there," Matt said as he gestured with this glass towards Gabriella.

"Real nice, Matt. Be sure not to spill any of that champagne on the white tux," Gabriella said with a smirk.

"It might be an improvement," Laurel said with an eye roll as she rested her head on Gabriella's shoulder. "Congrats, bestie."

Gabriella eyeballed her friend, then stated, "you knew, too. Didn't you?"

Laurel shrugged and smiled. "Someone had to have the champagne ready. And he said it needed to be somewhere special for you two, which is apparently my kitchen."

"And the music?" Gabriella asked.

"It was him; you know I'm not a music person. That's always been you."

"You're a good friend, Lau."

Laurel winked and then clinked her nails against her glass. "Does everyone have their glasses? Good! I want to propose a toast to Gabriella and Henry. Congratulations on your engagement. We know that things may not always be easy but know that the people in this room right now, and some others back in New York and in England, will always be here for you. To a long, happy, and healthy relationship! Cheers!"

Everyone toasted and drank their champagne, the music changed from the Motown music to DJ Khaled's *All I Do is Win*, which made Matt to start sing along.

"So," Dino said as he addressed the younger members of the group, "now that all of you are engaged, who is going to be the first one married."

"Desmond," they all responded.

Caroline laughed, "isn't Arnie included in that too?"

"Well, sure, but we all know that wedding is all about Desmond. Arnie is just the sweetheart making it happen," Laurel said before she pinched Arnie's cheek.

"Any idea of when you want to get married, Hank?" Matt asked. "Because Desmond already has his planned and I can't get this one to even commit to a year."

"Wow, really?" Laurel said as she started at Matt. "He literally just proposed like five minutes ago."

"We're getting married on our anniversary in January," Desmond volunteered. "We put down deposits a few weeks ago."

"And you didn't say anything?" Gabriella asked.

"I wanted more things firmed up before I said anything." Desmond explained.

"Maybe we can get married next year?" Henry suggested, which surprised Gabriella and Laurel.

Laurel looked to Gabriella with panic in her eyes. "Let's get through tonight and then we'll talk about it." Gabriella said in response.

"I think it's time we start heading over, it's time for the three of you to do what this song is talking about," Desmond said.

"I'm taking Gabby to the bathroom to touchup her makeup, thank God for waterproof mascara. Then we can head out." Laurel said.

"Okay, we're all in one limo. If you all want to start heading in, we'll be out in a few minutes," Gabriella informed the group, as Matt collected the glasses from everyone, and Arnie directed everyone towards the main entrance.

***

On the limo ride to the awards show, Gabriella sat next to Henry, unable to pull her eyes away from the shiny object that decorated her finger. The events that took place at Laurel's were a whirlwind, and she hadn't had the time the appreciate the beautiful piece of jewelry that adorned her hand.

"Are you sure you like it?" Henry asked softly in her ear.

"Henry, it's amazing. I mean, it's way too much for someone like me."

"No, it isn't. I was going to get a bigger one, but I know that isn't your style. I knew you would want something more traditional than Laurel's ring."

"You know me well," Gabriella said with a smile before she placed a soft kiss on his lips.

604

"I will say that I can't wait to see you wearing only that ring tonight," he whispered into her ear before his phone distracted him.

"Hello?"

"Did you do it? Did she say yes?"

"May? Are you mad, it's nearly midnight?" Henry asked as he put the call on speaker.

"Don't be daft, Hank. Mum told us earlier today what you were doing, you cheeky bastard. You're a right tart for not telling us yourself."

"Well, what happened. Did she tell you to fuck off?" Johnny asked.

"What are you all together?" Henry asked while Gabriella held in her laughter along with the rest of the limo.

"Yeah, mate, we're all at my house. The girls thought they could have a sleepover and stay up to watch the awards ceremony," Nathan responded.

"It probably won't be over until 3 in the morning," Henry said.

"We know. Millie and Emma already turned in for the night," Nathan said.

Andrew chimed in next, "the other three are drinking espresso martinis to keep themselves awake."

"Stop dodging the subject. Did she tell you no?" Johnny asked again.

"No, I didn't tell him no," Gabriella responded to the sound of high-pitched cheers in response.

After a symphony of "oh my gods" and "congratulations" the Anderson clan finally calmed down. The group in the limo laughed at their antics.

"That was a mistake, Gabby," Johnny said gravely.

"Was it now," Henry asked as he looked at his parents. James shook his head while Betty chuckled.

"It's going to be heartbreaking for you when your fiancé leaves you for me," Johnny said with a laugh.

"Hey Johnny," Gabriella called out.

"Yeah?"

"Bugger off, mate."

Johnny began to laugh with the rest of his siblings after a moment of shock. "Welcome to the family, sis."

Twenty-Seven

Once the group departed from the limo, Laurel, Matt, Gabriella, and Henry were separated from the rest of the group. Their families and guests were led down the shorter path of the red carpet and led into the Dolby Theatre to take their seats. The workers instructed Laurel and Matt to start down the carpet, where Gabriella watched her best friend transform from the bundle of nerves, she was earlier in the day, to the professional actress she portrayed herself as to the world. She watched as Laurel graciously answered questions for the press, posed for her solo and couple photos with Matt, and stopped along the way to greet fellow actors and others in the industry.

"Is it weird that I feel like a proud momma watching her baby grow into the woman she is now? Like I've witnessed her transformation into a full-fledged hopefully award-winning actress?" Gabriella asked as they waited for their cue to start walking the carpet.

"Not at all, because you are nurturing person, Ella. Good to the core, and you want nothing but the best for those close to you. You should also be proud because you have been with her, helping her, every step of the way."

Gabriella looked up at her fiancé, which was an adjustment to think of him in those terms and smiled at him. "I really do love you."

"I love you too, and it looks like we're up." Henry said as he placed his hand at the small of her back and helped navigate her to their first stop. They paused at the Oscars backdrop where they were asked to pose both separately and then together. Henry placed himself at her right side with his arm around her back. They looked to the cameras and smiled.

After a few photos, some of the photographers started to yell questions if they were engaged. Gabriella looked up at Henry with a puzzled look on her face as he looked back, a genuinely large smile spread across his face. He gazed down at her ring, and when she followed his gaze, she noticed the flashes made it sparkle and come to life.

"You stood on this side on purpose, didn't you?" She asked. He winked at her, then pulled her closer and kissed her on the lips, while the cameras snapped and flashed quickly to capture the rare moment of PDA from them.

They made their way further down the carpet where they were in the queue to speak with the journalist. The first person to greet them was Spencer Johnson from Access Hollywood. "Henry, my man! It's good to see you," he said with a genuine smile, "and Gabriella, it's a pleasure to see you again."

"Hey, mate," Henry said with a smile as he shook his hand.

"So, Oscar night. How are we feeling?" Spencer asked with a smile.

"I feel great mate, happy to be here, especially with this beauty on my arm."

"I'm excited. It's amazing to be included, but I'm hoping that The Edge of Time takes home some awards," Gabriella said with a smile.

"Any awards in particular?" Spencer asked with a wink.

"Well, any award would be amazing for the film, but I'm really rooting for Henry and Laurel."

"You two seemed to cause quite the commotion with the photographers down there. I try to keep it professional when I'm doing my interviews and stay focused on who I'm talking to, but I thought I heard something about an engagement?"

Gabriella looked up at Henry who winked at her, which cause Spencer to lean in a bit with the microphone. "I may or may not have asked this woman next to me to be my wife earlier today."

Spencer's mouth dropped open as his eyebrows shot up in surprise. "Really?"

Gabriella smiled and wiggled her fingers up by her face. "I may or may not have agreed."

Spence was shocked, then offered his congratulations. "How much earlier today did this happen?"

"About an hour ago," Henry said after moved his head slightly as if he had to think of the answer. "So, congratulations, you are the first to officially know."

"Oh, wow," Spencer said as he looked to the camera, "did you hear that, Hollywood Access exclusive, Henry Anderson and Gabriella DiStella are engaged." He turned back to the couple and smiled, "wow, that's amazing. Congratulations again. And good luck with the awards tonight."

"I don't need an award tonight, her saying yes was the best prize I could ever win."

They said their goodbyes and started to head to the next interview when Spencer pulled Henry to the side. "Henry, really, you have no idea how big this is for me to be the first to report the news."

"I know mate. You've always been really kind to me, and to Ella. You never ran any of the garbage some of the other stations did. That means a lot to me. I hope you can get somewhere with the information. I promise not to confirm the news to anyone else on this carpet," Henry said with a wink as he joined Gabriella in the queue for the next reporter.

"Henry, I don't really want to talk to the next one. She was a huge bitch to me the at the premiere." Gabriella said as she clutched his arm.

"Felicia? Really? She's always been quite the charmer with me," he retorted.

Gabriella arched and eyebrow at him and he laughed. "Okay, we don't like her. We'll make it quick." They made their way over as Henry mumbled, "I guess I did hand my berries over to you," which made Gabriella laugh as they approached the Hollywood Reporter area.

"Henry, doll," Felicia said in her fake sugary voice, "it's so good to see you again. You look very handsome."

"Thank you, Felicia."

"I know I'm supposed to be impartial, but I'm really hoping you win. You definitely deserve it."

"Well, I don't want you doing anything you shouldn't be doing," Henry responded, which made Felicia giggle.

"I won't tell if you won't tell."

"But I might," Gabriella said, not as quietly as she intended to, which made Felicia's attention to snap to her.

"Oh, nice to see you again. It must be exciting for you to be attending with Henry."

"Gabriella is nominated for supporting actress," Henry informed her.

"Oh, I know, I was just saying it must be exciting to be on your arm attending the awards. That dress is nice, very large."

Gabriella's head snapped back as if she was struck, and Henry's eyes grew in shock at the comment. "I truly hope you are speaking to the size of the skirt and not the size of the person wearing it."

"Oh, of course I mean the skirt. The ballgown and the material are amazing. Who made it?" Felicia tried to recover.

Gabriella looked to Henry and shook her head, to which Henry told Felicia, "We need to be moving on." He then placed his hand at the small of Gabriella's back and directed her away.

"See?" Gabriella asked as they made their way to the Entertainment News area, which had a large overhead camera near their station.

"Twit," Henry agreed, then approached Loretta Owens.

"Gabriella, Henry! It's so nice to see the two of you. Congratulations on the nominations. Both of you are nominated in your own category, plus best picture. It must be quite a night for you two!" She said with a bright, professional smile.

"Absolutely, we're excited to be here," Gabriella commented.

"You two look stunning. You know I need to know who you are wearing," Loretta encouraged.

"Tom Ford," Henry responded with a smile.

"Another Isadora Knight original, and Alexander McQueen shoes," Gabriella responded.

"I have been seeing a lot of Isadora's dresses recently. They are beautiful," Loretta responded.

"Absolutely. She is a genius. She knows how to design for every body shape and size." Gabriella agreed.

"I wish you both luck tonight. Would you mind stepping over here to our 360-photo booth?"

They followed Loretta where she instructed them to pose for a picture, and photos would be taken from all around them. Henry pulled Gabriella close, her engagement ring hidden behind his body. She placed her right hand on his cheek and his left hand rested on her waist. As the photographer counted down for the photo, they stared loving into each other's eyes with genuine smiles plastered on their faces.

As the photographer snapped the photo, Henry's hand slid from her waist to her butt and he grabbed it through the ball gown, which Gabriella followed suite and gripped him back. Gabriella began to laugh when the photo was over and swatted at Henry's arm, who was in the midst of his own laughter.

When they came out of the photo area, they met with Loretta who stood by the screen to review the photo. She fawned over how cute they looked in the picture but then gasped when the rear view when they both hand a handful of each other's asses. "Oh my, you two are something else," Loretta laughed.

"Wait a minute," she said as she studied the photo, then touched the screen to zoom in on Gabriella's hand on Henry's behind.

"I'm flattered, Loretta," Henry said with a laugh.

"Is that an engagement ring?" Loretta asked.

"Loretta, Riona Murphy is ready for her interview," a man with a headset dressed in black announced.

"It was a pleasure speaking with you Loretta," Henry said with a smile as he began to lead Gabriella away.

"Wait, but is it an engagement ring? Are you two engaged?" Loretta called out.

They continued on their way down the red carpet and greeted a few people as they made their way to Laurel and Matt, who waited by the entrance of the theater.

As they began to climb the stairs, Gabriella turned to Henry. "Why didn't you tell Loretta that we are engaged?"

"I wanted Spencer to have the exclusive. Let Loretta speculate until it is confirmed by Spencer."

***

They all sat in their assigned seats; Henry and Gabriella sat with their parents and Desmond and Arnie in the third row from the front with Laurel and Matt sitting directly behind them with the Dolces. Peppered throughout the rows around them were some of the stars who were up for the same awards, some of their co-stars, and Don Starr was nearby as well.

Henry looked down at his phone and pulled up Spencer's social media. "It's official, he posted it on twitter as soon as we walked away." Gabriella glanced at his phone and smiled. "As long as it wasn't that Felicia woman, I'm happy."

The host of the awards show, a popular comedian with specials on all the streaming networks named Willie Lewis, took the stage and began his opening monologue, which made jokes about all of the movies nominated for best picture. After he spoke about the space movie and the horror movie, the host focused on The Edge of Time. "I got to say, Henry, my man."

The camera focused on Henry in the crowd as he watched the host pace back and forth across the stage. "I don't get you man. Three hotties. Three. You selfish bastard. Why don't you just stay dead?"

The audience laughed as Henry chuckled and shrugged his shoulders.

"And Gabby," Willie called out and the camera focused on Gabriella. "How you doin' baby? If I had a smoke show like you as my wife, no way would I be going after anyone else. But since you're not, how you doing Laurel? Riona? Call me." He said with a wink as the audience laughed. After he said something about all ten nominated movies, Willie moved on to bring out the presenters for the performance by an actor in a supporting role. After the nominees were called, Jake Wilson was announced the winner of the category.

They cheered for their co-star as he approached the stage, dressed in a deep charcoal grey suite with a deep navy-blue tie. His blonde hair was longer, and he had grown out a beard for a role he was currently working on. After his acceptance speech, where he shouted out his co-stars for making it such a memorable movie, they moved onto achievement in costume design, where Darius won. Gabriella's heart soared for her friend as he walked onto the stage.

He grasped the award in his hands and looked down at it lovingly. "This hasn't been the easiest year for me," he stated. "I had a lot of personal trauma and changes in my life. But standing on this stage in front of you all makes me realize that I can rise above anything. I earned this with the help of my staff. I want to thank the studio for taking a chance on me. This film challenged me in a way I loved. I want to thank the staff and everyone who I dressed on the set. Thank you for trusting me to bring the vision of the movie to life."

615

After the awards for makeup and best foreign language film were given, there was a commercial break. Gabriella stood with Henry to stretch their legs as Kaitlyn McGrave, an actress in the upcoming Amazonian film came down the aisle to say hello. After they chatted for the few minutes, she left and Gabriella asked Henry, "where is Darius? I wanted to congratulate him."

"You're going to have to do it later, love. He's stuck backstage now. You can't come back here." Henry explained.

"I didn't know that," Gabriella said as they sat back down. "Are your parents and Laurel's parents aware of that?"

Henry nodded, then turned his attention to the stage as Willie Lewis came out dressed as an astronaut as they played a clip of one of the films nominated for movie of the year. The next awards to be given out were best live action short film, best documentary, and best sound mixing. The next introduction to a movie was presented, when Willie came out on stage dressed as the murder from the nominated horror movie. Another commercial break took place, then Willie came out on stage dressed in a red saloon girl outfit like the one that Gabriella had worn during the movie as he introduced The Edge of Time, which the audience laughed at before the clip ran.

Gabriella was trying to keep it together from laughing at Willie in her costume when the award for achievement in sound editing was announced. The next presenters were brought on stage to announce the performance by an actress in a supporting role. Riona's name was announced along with Gabriella's, Samantha's and two other high-profile actresses. Gabriella wiped the tears away as she held in her giggles from Willie's outfit when the envelope was opened. She heard one of the presenters make a joke about it being another The Edge of Time winner and had in her mind that Samantha won. "Gabriella DiStella, the Edge of Time!"

She clapped along as Henry turned to her. "Ella, they called your name." She looked at him confused, then in shock as he stood up to step out of her way. Her mother and father jumped up along with Desmond and Arnie to hug her. Maria pulled her out of the chair, and she hugged everyone, including Laurel and Matt before she exited the row. Henry grabbed her and kissed her, which caused the crowd to coo at them, then she was escorted to the stage.

She was handed the award and lead to the podium where the two presenters congratulated her. She stood at the podium, and stared down at the award, then looked out to the over three thousand people in the theater. "Um, I didn't write a speech." She breathed out, which caused the audience to chuckle.

"No, I'm serious. I shouldn't be standing up here. I was a last-minute extra. I... I...have no words for this. This is a joke, right?" She asked as she looked around.

"I don't deserve this award. The other women nominated, they should be up here," she said before took a breath and licked her lips. "I want to thank my parents, who always believed in me and raised me to know right from wrong and to stick to my convictions. To my nonna, who I'm sure is smiling down from heaven right now, who pushed me out of my comfort zone and encouraged me to take risks. My best friend Laurel Dolce, who I owe this crazy, amazing life I've been living to, and to my best friend Desmond, who always believed in me. I need to thank Don, April, Gina and Lloyd at the studio, Nicole and Lily, Darius, Max, Jem, Bob, Patti and Joshua. And of course, I have to thank Henry, for so much that I can't say. I love you. Thank you."

She was directed off the stage to a round of applause, then handed a glass of champagne. After she took a moment to stare at the gold man in her hand, she was instructed to walk to the hotel next door where she was bombarded with photographers who had her pose with her award.

After a session with journalist who asked about how she feels about her win and her thoughts on the movie and what she thinks she might do next, she was brought back to the theater and escorted to the green room where Darius and Jake were. "There she is! Miss best supporting actress!" Darius said as he ran over and hugged her.

"Oh my god! Have you guys been hanging out here the whole time?" Gabriella asked she moved from Darius to Jake.

"Yeah, we were offered to head to the afterparty, but our guests are still out there, and we want to be here if we win best picture," Jake explained. "But at least we get champagne back here, and I may or may not have ordered some appetizers from the hotel next door."

They sat on one of the couches as they watched the rest of the show. "How much of the show did I miss?"

"Three awards, four movie intros, and a commercial break." Darius responded.

"Do you think I should go out there for Laurel and Henry?" She asked as the award for animated feature film was being announced.

"No. You can't celebrate out there like you can here. You have to be all proper. You should have heard the two of us cheering when you won," Jake said with a smile. "Actually, you'll probably see it at some point, they have cameras back here to record any crazy reactions."

"And the camera guys that follow you as you walk of stage and walk over to the hotel," Darius added.

"There was a camera following me?" Gabriella asked.

"Yup, behind the scenes stuff and what not."

The Edge of Time won for film editing and best original screenplay. Gabriella cheered for April Brown when she accepted her award for writing the script to the movie. After two more introductions to the nominated movies, and the best adapted screenplay award, they cut to another commercial break. Gabriella opened a group chat with Henry, Laurel, and Desmond.

Gabby: are you guys okay with me staying back here?

Henry: yes, love. We'll all meet after this is over to take the limo over to the afterparty.

Laurel: just relax and enjoy miss Oscar award winner!!!

Desmond: I can't wait for the after parties, I'm starving.

Laurel: did you tell her the tickets you scored for everyone tonight?

Henry: no, belt up Dolce.

The last two films for best picture were shown, then Best Director was announced, which Don won. The three of them cheered Don on as he walked off the stage, and they stuck their heads out of the green room as he passed them. He was held off to the side since the best picture would be announced shortly. The next set of presenters made their way onto the stage to announce the performance by an actor in a leading role.

Gabriella paced nervously as they announced the nominees. She mumbled words of encouragement under her breath as she watched them open the envelope. "Henry Anderson, The Edge of Time!"

Gabriella began to scream in excitement as she watched Henry kiss and hug his parents, her parents, Desmond, Arnie, Laurel, Matt and Caroline and Dino before he made his way up the stage. He hugged both presenters, then held up the award as he approached the podium.

"Wow! I'm not sure if you are all aware of this, but this is the second-best thing to happen to me today. What is the best thing, you ask? I asked Gabriella DiStella to marry me, and she said yes."

The audience went crazy as Darius grabbed Gabriella's hand and studied her ring. "I can't believe you didn't tell me!"

"It happened right before we came here, I swear," she whispered back as Henry resumed his speech.

620

"I have to thank the academy, my mum and dad who have put up with my desire to act for ages. The whole Anderson clan for their support. Ray, Jimmy and the team back at the agency. Don and April for this brilliant movie. My Edge of Time family who made all of this more than just a movie. I want to thank my beautiful fiancée, who may have put me through the ringer, and maybe I did some of that to myself, for loving me and taking a chance on love. I'll make it worth it, my love. To all of you gents out there, I don't care what you do or what you look like, if you love the girl, go for it, but make sure your worthy of her love. Just because the package looks good on the outside doesn't mean you can be rotten on the inside. Thank you!"

Henry was escorted from the stage and handed his glass of champagne, where he was greeted by Don. After his drink was done, he was escorted a little further down the hall where he was asked to wait until end of the show. Gabriella stuck her head out of the green room and spotted Henry, then moved as fast as she could in her heels and dress and threw her arms around him. He reciprocated and dipped her, then gave her a screen worthy kiss, which made April, Jake, Don, and Darius whoop in excitement.

"Congratulations, fiancé," Gabriella said with a smile as she smoothed the lapels of his tuxedo.

"Congratulations to you too, fiancée," Henry retorted.

"Oh, I have to run back in there, I want to see if Laurel wins," she said before she scrambled into the green room just in time to watch the presenter open the envelope. When Laurel's name was called, Gabriella teared up, cheered at the top of her lungs, as Darius and Jake celebrated with her. Laurel was kissed by

Matt, then hugged by her parents, Desmond, Arnie and Gabriella's parents before she made her way up to the podium.

"Well," Laurel said as she looked down at the award, "at least I don't have to hear it that my manager got an Oscar I didn't," she said with a laugh. "It's funny, I had a whole speech planned out to thank every single person. Do I want to thank the Academy? You know I do. Do I want to thank my parents for always supporting me? My best friends for sticking by me when others didn't? My fiancé who shares our unconditional love? My team who makes me who I am? Absolutely. But I'm going to do that on my own time. I want to thank you. All of you sitting in this theater, and all of you watching at home. Thank you, from the bottom of my heart, for making a little girl's dreams come true. Without your support, without you going to see these movies and supporting us like you do, we wouldn't be able to do what we do. So, thank you for allowing me to keep doing what I love, to make things that you love. I'm truly humbled and honored to accept this award among the power houses that were nominated. I hope that together we can keep making magic together."

Laurel walked from the stage, completely poised until she downed the glass of champagne handed to her. She turned to Henry and threw her arms around him in celebration as Willie made his way onto the stage to wrap up the night and keep it moving to the last award. Gabriella, Jake, April, and Darius left the green room to congratulate Laurel in the brief moments they had before the presenters read off the ten movies.

They all joined hands as they waited for the winner. When The Edge of Time was announced, they all began to celebrate. They were asked to join the rest of the actors involved on the stage. A massive group of all the members of the movie that were in attendance collected on the stage. Don moved to the podium and accepted the award.

"You've all heard from me already. I want to have our own legend come up and say some word. Bernie?"

The audience stood and applauded as Bernie approached the podium. He looked around and smiled, then motioned with his hands for the audience to sit down. "I feel like this might be a consolation prize, Don. Losing out to that Jake guy," he said with a wink as he looked back at Jake.

"I've been in the business for a long time. More decades than I like to admit. I've seen my fair share of changes in the industry. From how we film to what we film and refilm as some cases may be. I've witnessed some great actors in my career, and I've witnessed some temper tantrum throwing children crash and burn. This movie, this cast, some of the greats. I knew it from when I read the script and when I met the cast. This experience will stay one of the best of my career. Thank you to everyone involved with the film and thank you to all of the fans who made it such a hit. And thank you to the academy for recognizing the talent in this film."

***

The Governor's ball was full of stars by the time their limo arrived. After dozens of photos, they headed to an area where tables were available and settled down for a breather. Within minutes, people approached the table to congratulate Laurel, Gabriella, and Henry on their wins, and then focused their congratulations to the latter of the two on their engagement.

Gabriella looked over the shoulder of one of Laurel's friends at her parents. "Can you excuse me for a moment?" She smiled and made her way over where Arnie and Desmond chatted away with the others at the table.

"Are you okay, *Bambolina*?" Maria asked as she saw her daughter stand nearby with her award still clutched in her hands.

"Yeah, mom, I'm fine. Overwhelmed, but I feel bad that I'm not even with all of you. There are just so many people wanting to talk and all of the pictures. Are you all sure you're alright?"

"Yes, Gabby, we're fine," Giuseppe said with a reassuring smile. "You're not going to have many nights like this. You won an Oscar. You got engaged. Don't worry about us. Just soak it up. This is going to be one of those moments that you'll look back on when you're old and gray, and you'll smile. You don't get many of these life affirming moments, so enjoy it while it lasts. Your mom and I are professionals at partying. We've got Desmond and Arnie to keep us company. Not to mention Dino and Caroline are here, and we are making plans with your future in-laws. We're fine, Gabby. Go enjoy yourself."

Gabriella smiled at her parents, then leaned in and kissed them both on the cheek. She looked at the award in her hand, then looked at them and handed it to her mother. "Do you mind babysitting? I can't keep dragging it around all night."

"You got it, *Bambolina*. Not exactly the grandchild I imagined babysitting, but sure."

Gabriella laughed and headed back over to where she left Laurel. "You are a genius," she said as she looked at the award on the table, then ran over to deposit hers with her parents.

"So, Gabby," a voice approached her from the right. She looked over to find Kaitlyn McGrave approach her in a slinky sliver dress that hung off her body like the supermodel she looked like. "What do you think, maybe we can be standing here next year with some awards for Ortera Descent?"

She smiled at her costar and shook her head. "Not me. I mean, I'd love to be at the party as a guest, but my once-in-a-lifetime moment already happened. But I'll be cheering you on."

Kaitlyn smiled and tossed her golden-brown hair over her shoulder. "You're too modest. So, I'm totally staring at your ring, and I need to know how he did it. It's stunning."

Gabriella looked down at her hand and smiled, a blush crept on her face. "He did it right before we left for the ceremony. He said he has something for me to wear tonight, and then he was down on one knee asking me to marry him."

"Did you know it was coming?"

"No, not at all. I still can't believe it's real. I feel like I'm going to wake up and all of this was just some amazing dream."

Kaitlyn arched an eyebrow at Gabriella, then quickly reached over and pinched her arm. Gabriella pulled back and yelped. "Yup, not a dream, Gabby," she said with a wink and a smile.

"Yeah, thanks for that one, Kait."

"So, where are you going to be until your next project? I don't have to be in Vancouver until July."

"Oh, no more projects for me," Gabriella said with a shake of her head. "I'm totally committing myself to management duty full time."

"You can't be serious. Gabby, people are going to be knocking down your door to get you in their projects now."

"Can you believe her? I think she is making a huge mistake too," Laurel chimed in. "Hi, I'm Laurel Dolce."

"Kaitlyn McGrave, it's nice to meet you. I was with Gabby in Greece."

"I loved you in Little Jane," Laurel said with a smile.

"How do you even know that movie?" Kaitlyn asked with a laugh.

"I had a huge crush on Robert Lockhart growing up. I've seen everything that man was in."

"He played my dad in that movie," Kaitlyn laughed.

"Yeah, I had a thing for older men," Laurel said with a laugh.

"I'm going to be in California for a few weeks at least. Henry's parents are going to be here for a bit, so we wanted to spend some time with them. After that, I have no idea what we are doing. He has a project in England in the fall. We really haven't discussed the logistics of where we are going to live yet."

"Wow, that seems like a big discussion," Kaitlyn said wearily.

Laurel scoffed and waved off Kaitlyn's comment. "Those two lovebirds will be fine. I absolutely adore your dress. Who designed it and where can I get one?"

Gabriella zoned out a bit until a deep country drawl pulled her attention. "Pardon me, Gabriella?"

She turned to find herself looking at a wall of muscle in a light grey suit. She glanced up and was met by a strong jaw, slightly crooked nose, bright green eyes and dirty blonde hair pulled back into a bun. "Um, yes."

He smiled brightly and extended his hand, "Hi, I'm Brighton Ashley. I wanted to come over and introduce myself. I loved you in Edge of Time."

"Oh, thank you, it's nice to meet you Brighton."

"He never mentioned me, did he?" He asked as he cocked his head to the side.

"Who?"

Brighton laughed in response. "Henry. I play Perceval to his Galahad. I asked him to introduce me to you back when we were first filming. I was kind of enamored with you on social media."

"Oh, wow, um, I'm flattered. Henry and I weren't really speaking when he was in New Zealand."

"Yeah, and the selfish bastard kept you to himself, and now I hear a rumor that I'm too late." He said with a friendly pout.

Gabriella laughed and shook her head. "Not a rumor."

Brighton looked down at her hand as whistled. "Wow, Hank did good. Congratulations. On the engagement and your win. Where is that selfish bastard?"

Gabriella looked around the room and spotted her fiancé beyond the tables towards the back of the room. As if he could feel her eyes on him, Henry looked over from the group of people he spoke with and made eye contact, his eyes lit up as he smiled at her.

She returned his smile, the gestured towards Brighton with her eyes. Henry turned his attention back to the group of people and bid his farewells, then made his way over.

"That siren call works wonders," Brighton said with a laugh as he watched Henry approach them. "Well, well, well, look who it is, Mister Best Actor."

Henry laughed and embraced his coworker. "Brighton! Who the bloody hell let you in here, mate?"

"Had to make introductions myself since you're so selfish, keeping her to yourself."

628

"I couldn't let you near my woman when she wasn't really mine," he said with a smile, then looked at Gabriella, "she was always mine, she was just being stubborn about it. Couldn't let you try to steal her away."

"And now you've made it impossible," Brighton said with a sigh, then a laugh. "Congratulations, man."

"So, will you be joining us when we film the next season?" Brighton asked Gabriella.

"Oh, I'm not sure. Maybe?" Gabriella responded as she looked up at Henry.

"We're still ironing out all of the details, but I hope she will. Now that I have her, I don't think I want to be away from her." Henry said as he wrapped his arm around her waist and pulled her into him.

"Hey, sorry about that, Laurel was telling me about the serial killer series and wanted to introduce me to one of the producers," Kaitlyn said as she returned to Gabriella.

"Wow," Brighton said as he looked at Kaitlyn.

"I'm so sorry, I didn't mean to be rude and interrupt," she responded defensively.

Henry looked at Brighton and saw the interest spark in his eyes as he stared at Kaitlyn. "I don't think he meant it in a rude way," Henry said with a chuckle. "Kaitlyn, this is Brighton Ashley, we work together on a series. Brighton, this is Kaitlyn McGrave, she co-starred with Ella on the Ortera Descent film."

"It's nice to meet you," Kaitlyn said with a smile as she shook his hand.

"You too. You are stunning."

Kaitlyn smirked and responded, "you're pretty nice to look at yourself."

"I was going to head over to the bar for a refill. Could I get you a drink?" Brighton asked.

"Sure, I'll take a walk with you. I'll see you guys later," Kaitlyn said before she walked away.

"Matchmaking, Henry?" Gabriella asked with a smile.

Henry looked down at her and wrapped his other arm around her, then dipped his lips to her ear. "I know we are surrounded by people here, but I can't wait to get you home and see you just wearing that ring."

Gabriella smiled. "That would be amazing. All I want to do is strip you out of this delicious tuxedo, get you naked, and lick my fiancé all over his body until he can't take it anymore."

"Go on, I'd love to hear what you are going to do next."

"Actually, I'm not going to do anything, because both of our parents are staying at the beach house. It's going to be a long week of sexual buildup."

"Bollocks. I got us a hotel room for tonight."

Gabriella arched an eyebrow, "did you really?"

Henry smiled and nodded, then lightly sucked on her neck. Gabriella moaned and gripped the back of his head. "Can we go now?"

Henry didn't respond and continued to kiss her neck.

"Henry, please. I need to get you alone, like now."

"We can't yet," he said as he continued the assault on the column of her neck.

Gabriella whined and pushed Henry away, "seriously? Then you can't keep getting me worked up."

"Is that what I'm doing?" He asked as his thumb grazed her cheek.

"Yes, and you know it."

"Mm. Well, I think I have something that might help."

Gabriella looked down at his groin, then looked around the room for somewhere for them to sneak off to. Henry laughed and shook his head. "My naughty fiancé. That we can address later. I have something else. Something that involves your parents, my parents, and everyone else that we are with."

Gabriella pulled back and looked up at Henry, the desire that lit up inside her quickly doused by the mention of their parents. "I don't think they work into what I want to do."

"Trust me you'll love this even more than me ravaging you right now."

"Doubtful," she pouted.

Henry leaned in whispered into her ear. "I got us tickets to Elton John's Oscar party, let's get everyone and head over."

Gabriella's mouth gaped open as her eyes went wide. An excited squeal escaped her lips as she performed a little happy dance. "You are the most amazing man ever!"

"Ah, there is the squeal, he told her, let's head out," Desmond said to the table when he heard the shriek.

Twenty-Eight

5 years later.

"Oh, Henry, uh, yes… right there," Gabriella moaned as Henry's fingers expertly worked her body. She moaned loudly and bit her lip to try and stifle the sounds.

"Does this feel good, Ella?" Henry asked as he looked up his wife's body to her face. She looked down at him and nodded as she bit down on her lip in attempt to muffle another moan.

Henry smiled, then adjusted the pressure, which caused her head to drop back and her mouth to open. "Oh, fuck, Henry. Just like that. Fuck! That feels so good."

His eyes peered up and caught her as she stared at him. He smiled up at her and enjoyed the symphony of her pleasure. "Right there, oh my god, Henry, right there."

A sound in the room brought them both to a stop. Henry exhaled, then lifted Gabriella's legs off his lap. "Sorry, love. Let me check on that. I'll be back in a bit." He leaned over and kissed her briefly and studied her face. "You look tired, Ella, why don't you go up to bed?"

Gabriella shook her head and adjusted into the cushions of the oversized mocha couch. "I have a call with Laurel and Desmond."

"It's nearly midnight," Henry countered.

"I know, but she's waking up early. We haven't all spoken in weeks."

"Alright, I'll be back," he said with a wink, then headed towards the stairs, the two dogs looked up from their dog beds, no longer the spry pups they once were. After nine, they seemed to just want to cuddle in their beds and sleep.

Her phone rang minutes after Henry left, and she answered the facetime call. "Hey!"

"Hey bitch. How's in going in jolly old England?" Desmond asked with a pink raised.

"Just lovely. How's the city?"

"Hot and disgusting. The summers are always terrible. At least I'm able to escape to the island on my days off."

Laurel joined the call, still in bed. "Morning."

Desmond laughed. "Look at you two, in bed."

"I'm not in bed, I'm on the couch in the den." Gabriella retorted.

"Whatever, you're lucky I set an alarm for this," Laurel said with a yawn. "How's my godson?"

"Sleeping. His baby monitor went off before while Henry was rubbing my legs and feet. They are so swollen," Gabriella complained.

"How's my goddaughter?" Desmond asked.

634

Gabriella smiled and aimed the phone down at her swollen belly. "She's baking, kicking, and making me pee constantly."

"You never complained about your legs and feet swelling when you were pregnant with JJ," Laurel commented.

"They claim that girls steal your beauty when you're pregnant with them. And this little one is doing just that," Gabriella said with an eye roll while she caressed her stomach with her free hand.

"When are you coming back home?" Desmond asked.

"The house is going to be ready in two weeks. The whole kitchen was remodeled, and Henry had the gym redone to his specifications. Plus, he needed his sauna added."

"I can't believe you're going to be living in Centre Island. That's like big money," Desmond said.

"She's married to Henry Anderson, they have big money," Laurel joked. "I heard Billy Joel lives over there."

Gabriella smiled. "He does. How amazing would it be to meet him? Maybe JJ can become friends with his younger kids."

"Is it safe for you to travel?" Laurel asked.

"Yeah, my doctors already approved it. I'm only six months, and they said everything looks good, and my doctor here already informed my doctor in New York."

"I can't wait for you to be home. You're like twenty minutes away from me when I'm at the house," Desmond said excitedly.

"I know. As much as I love it here in England, I'm ready to be in New York. It's going to be hard for JJ, he has all of his cousins here."

"I'm sure Giuseppe and Maria are excited for you all to come home," Desmond said.

"Yeah, but they were here a few months ago. They took over one of the floors here, claimed it as their own."

Henry entered the room and placed the baby monitor on the coffee table, then sat down next to his wife. He put his arm around her and looked into the phone. "Hey Laurel, Desmond. How are you?"

"Oh, if it isn't the sexiest man alive," Desmond teased as he fanned his face.

"For the second time," Laurel followed up.

Henry rolled his eyes and laughed. "Come on now. That's all rubbish. I could understand maybe the first time, but now? I'm married. I've got a dad bod."

"Fuck you and your dad bod. If dads had your body, no one would go to work because they'd be too busy fucking all of the time," Desmond scoffed.

"Which is why our bestie is pregnant again," Laurel said with a laugh.

"You make it sound like I got knocked up right away. JJ is almost two," Gabriella retorted.

"Eh, you're right, Ella can't keep her hands off of me. You should have heard her earlier, moaning and telling me not to stop." Henry teased.

"You were massaging my feet, you jerk," Gabriella said and elbowed Henry in his dad bod.

"Laurel, will we see you and Matt at the housewarming party next month? It's been ages since I've seen you two." Henry asked.

"Yeah, we'll be there. Jem said that she and her boyfriend are coming out for it too. We're going to fly out together."

"What about Max and Darius?" Henry asked.

"Yeah, they are coming out a week earlier and staying at the house with Arnie," Desmond answered.

Henry shook his head. "I still can't believe those two eloped."

"It's been over a year, get it over it," Laurel said with a laugh.

"I just never saw those two getting together," Henry said.

"Max really helped him out after the separation. It's not like it happened overnight. The two of them were dating other people for a while before they got together," Desmond said.

"How about Joshua and Patti?" Henry asked.

"Patti, yes. Joshua, no. I think Patti got us in the divorce," Gabriella said.

"That sucks, but it will be nice to see everyone," Desmond said.

"What about Bob?" Laurel asked.

"He is coming and bringing his girlfriend with him. She's exactly the kind of girl you would think Bob would date," Henry said with a laugh.

"Country bumpkin?" Desmond asked.

Henry laughed more and shook his head. Gabriella looked over at her husband and smiled. He kissed her forehead and looked at the phone. "That's my cue to leave. I know you need your gossip time. I'm going to head to bed, love, I'll bring the dogs up with me."

Gabriella smiled as she watched Henry make his way to the stairs and called Scampi and Leigh to follow. Once they were gone, she waited a few moments and then looked back at the camera. Her friends stared at her and waited for the signal that it was safe to talk.

"So really, what is it like having Henry voted sexiest man alive?" Desmond asked.

Gabriella sighed, then looked to the staircase. "It's really hard. I mean, I knew since day one that he was super-hot and lusted after. Hell, he was voted sexiest man alive before I met him. But being married to him and then being this whale of a pregnant person at the same time has not been fun. I never lost all the baby weight from the first time, and now the sexiest man alive has this beluga on his arm?"

"You're not looking at the gossip sites, are you? Nicole will kill you if you are," Laurel asked.

"No, I know better than that. He's been doing all the interviews and shit that goes along with it. He always talks about his family and how happy he is. But the whole thing is about sexualizing my husband."

"I'd eat that shit up with a spoon if my husband was being sexualized all over the news," Desmond said with a laugh.

"You know he loves you," Laurel said.

"I do. It's just, when we're in our own little bubble, everything is wonderful. I just hate when the press gets into stories about him. It was bad enough when we filmed The Edge of Time sequel the gossip columns were saying that he was cheating on me with Riona."

"And you guys stuck it to them by revealing that you got married months before filming started," Laurel countered.

"And then you showed up pregnant at the premiere," Desmond added.

"I'll get over it. I'm hoping everything will be back to normal when we move. The house is gated, so we should be fine."

"So, how are you feeling, pregnancy wise?" Laurel asked.

"I'm good, just swollen legs and feet."

"Any more nausea?"

"No, it all subsided after the first few months."

"Both times?"

"Yeah, why do you ask?"

Laurel took a deep breath, then looked around the room before answering. "I'm pregnant."

"What?" Gabriella and Desmond screamed at the same time.

"Yeah, um, I thought that I was late from the stress of that last movie. I was feeling really sick for a while, but it eventually stopped, and I thought I just had a bug. I realized the other day that I hadn't gotten my period in a while. I went to buy a test, and it was positive. I checked my tracking app and realized it had been months since I had my period."

"How far along are you?" Gabriella asked.

"Four and a half months." Laurel answered as Desmond let out a shocked gasp.

"I guess you're having a baby," Desmond said slowly.

"What did Matt say?" Gabriella asked.

"I haven't told him yet," Laurel winced.

"Oh my god, why haven't you told him?" Desmond asked.

"Things have been a little off with us. He's annoyed that I keep pushing off the wedding. I still can't bring myself to do it. And now this? He's definitely going to want to get married now."

"Why haven't you married him yet?" Desmond asked.

Laurel took a deep breath and sighed, then dropped her head to her hand. She looked up at her friends and felt completely defeated. "I don't know. It just doesn't feel right. I don't know if I ever want to get married. I like my life the way it is. I like traveling the world and having my freedom to do what I want. I love Matt, he's a great guy, and our sex life is phenomenal, but I just can't wrap my head around being married."

"And what about being a mom?" Gabriella asked.

Laurel blew out a breath and tried not to cry. "You make it look easy, Gabby. You still work, you have a husband who worships you, and you have this adorable little clone of Henry. I just don't see myself being a mother. If I had known about this earlier, I may have done something about it." She looked up at the camera and gave a sad smile. "Hey Des, you looking to adopt? I'd give you my baby."

"Oh, hell no. Uncle Desmond is all about spoiling my nephews and nieces, but I'm not made out for fatherhood."

"I feel the same way," Laurel cried.

"Laurel, Matt is a terrific father. He and Matty have the best relationship. I think he would be ecstatic if you told him you were pregnant. Just tell him that you still aren't ready to tackle marriage and parenthood but take it one step at a time." Gabriella advised.

"She really makes it sound so easy," Laurel said to Desmond.

"Girl, you are in the land of the rich and famous. They have au pairs and day cares and all that other stuff. You won't have to completely change your life," Desmond said.

"You don't think your parents wouldn't be on the first flight to L.A. to help you?" Gabriella asked.

"Gabby's right. Your parents are pretty much retired at this point. Arnie took over the whole business." Desmond concurred.

"Ugh, I know. You're both right. I just have to wrap my head around this. It's just so out of left field. I wasn't planning any of this."

"When did you find out?" Gabriella asked.

"Yesterday. I've just been in a state of shock. I knew we had this call, so I figured I'd just wait to tell you both."

"Do you need me to fly out there?" Desmond asked.

Laurel smiled and shook her head. "No, I'll be okay. I should probably tell Matt today, see what he says. Plus, I'll see you guys in a few weeks at the Anderson's big housewarming extravaganza."

"You make it sound like were having a huge party. It's just family and some close friends."

"Aren't all of your in-laws coming for the party?" Laurel asked.

"And the extended Christmas Eve family?" Desmond added.

"It's a really big house. And it's the summer, and there is a pool," Gabriella tried to reason.

"Yeah, sure. Lau was right with extravaganza," Desmond said with a laugh.

Gabriella tried to hide her yawn as the two of them spoke about when they all get together. "Gabby, you must be exhausted," Laurel commented.

"I'm fine," she said through another yawn. "Keep talking."

"She's going to fall asleep on us, I think we should hang up." Desmond said.

"No, no. Laurel needs us."

"Laurel is fine. Laurel is going to put her big girl panties on and tell her fiancé that she's pregnant," Laurel said, as she spoke about herself in the third person.

"And then Laurel is going to text us about how it goes," Desmond tacked on.

"Right. I absolutely will. Get some sleep Gabby. I love you guys."

"Love you too. Please let me know if you need anything."

"I will. I'll text you guys later."

Gabriella hung up, then pushed herself off the couch and made her way upstairs. She walked up two flight of steps and gently opened the door to her son's room. He was fast asleep in his crib, his stuffed dog clenched in his little fist. Gabriella stared down at JJ, who was really named James Joseph after her and Henry's fathers. His long lashes rested on his chubby pink cheeks and his breath puffed through his pouty, open lips. She gently brushed back his thick, straight, nearly black hair, the only feature of hers that he had, from his forehead. Not to wake him, she crept out of the room and gently closed the door.

She walked down to their bedroom to find it empty, except for the dogs curled up in their beds. Before she settled into the bed, she grabbed a photo album from the shelf in the reading nook. She fluffed her pillows against the headboard and made her way under the light summer sheets.

She opened the cover and gazed down at the start of their wedding album. She smiled at the memories the book held, although it was only three years ago. The gorgeous outdoor setting on the cliff that overlooked the water was what Gabriella fell in love with when Henry had taken her to a bed and breakfast in the south-western section of England. It was exactly where she pictured where

644

they would say their vows, away from the prying eyes, in front of their close friends and family.

They had booked the venue and the grounds for a week and had less than a hundred guest in attendance. Laurel, Desmond, May, and Johnny made up the bridal party. They kept it casual and low key and opted to get married outside in the late afternoon. Gabriella had worn a light and airy dress; the bodice was lace with thin straps, which transitioned into a tulle over satin A-line skirt. Her hair remained loose and hung in waves down her back with a small, white beaded headband tucked on the top of her head. Henry was equally as casual, wearing a three-piece suit in a cream color with a crisp white shirt and light blue tie.

It was the perfect opposite of the wedding they filmed. They danced under the stars, into the early hours of the morning. Their guests celebrated with them for almost the entire week, to make it worth the trip to travel to England for the festivities.

"Hey, love, what are you looking at over there?" Henry asked from the doorway as he watched his wife in the bed with a smile stretched across her face.

"Our wedding album," she replied to find her husband in a pair of gym shorts, his body glistened with sweat. "I guess you were down in the gym?"

"I got some cardio in. Can't lose the sexiest man alive title after just receiving it," he said with a smirk and a wink.

"Keep standing there looking like that and I might get pregnant again," Gabriella said with a lustful glance.

"I'm not sure if that's possible, but I sure would like to try, Mrs. Anderson," Henry said as he made his way across the room to their bed and added some extra swagger in his steps.

"Na-uh. Go shower. As much as I love you all sweaty and reeking of testosterone, I just changed the sheets this morning."

Henry leaned over and kissed his wife before he stripped down next to bed to give her and eye full, then sauntered over to the ensuite. Gabriella laughed at his antics as she placed the photo album back on the shelf. Henry came out in his boxer briefs and got into the bed next to his wife.

"What had you pulling out the photo album?"

Gabriella shrugged. "Not sure. I think it was bringing up Patti and Joshua that made me nostalgic."

Henry raised an eyebrow in response. "It has nothing to do with Laurel being pregnant and still not wanting to get married?"

Gabriella gasped and then smacked her husband on the chest. Henry breathed out an "oof" as she shook her head in disbelief. "You were supposed to be in bed, not eavesdropping on my call."

"You always save to good stuff for when I'm out of the room. And I did come to our room, but I decided to get changed and work out. I heard it as I walked past to go to the gym."

"You're unbelievable."

Henry wagged his eyebrows at her. "But you love me anyway. So, what is going on with them anyway? They've been engaged for six or seven years already."

"I don't know, Henry. I'm exhausted. I want to go to bed. I'm hoping your daughter doesn't break out into her one-woman interpretation of Lord of the Dance tonight."

Henry chuckled in response. "I love you, gorgeous. You make life worth living."

***

It was late July, and the summer heat on Long Island was tolerable because of the breeze that came in from both Oyster Bay Harbor and Cold Spring Harbor. The waterfront estate was full of life as the catering company setup the food on the open patio that led from the main house to the pool and pool house. The massive outdoor kitchen grills were prepped as extra seats was being setup for the guest.

It had taken nearly an entire month to get settled into the house, if the compound they moved into could be considered a house. The six-bedroom, seven-bath sprawled over three and a half acres. Gabriella was hesitant when the realtor sent them the listing, but Henry insisted that they needed the space.

"Gabby, are you sure you are okay with all of us staying here for the week? It seems like an awful lot of hassle," Betty asked after Henry showed his siblings to their respective areas.

"As long as you are all okay with sharing rooms and staying in the theater room and the living areas. We love having you all here. JJ was shrieking with excitement when he saw his cousins."

"Those movie room loungers are more comfortable than our bed," James joked.

"You're sure your friends don't need to stay here as well?" Betty questioned.

Gabriella shook her head. "No, Laurel and Matt are staying with her parents, and the rest of them are staying with Arnie and Desmond at their house. Patti is the only one staying here, and she already claimed the pool house."

"What can we do to help? You really should rest, you've gotten bigger since we last saw you," Betty said as she placed her hand on her daughter-in-law's belly.

Gabriella smiled, "I'm good, Betty, I promise. Henry hired so much help, I feel like I'm in the way if I try to do anything."

"Party's here!" Desmond shouted as he walked into the house. "Gabby, this house is amazing. The pictures didn't do it justice. You need to show me around, like now."

Gabriella kissed Desmond and Arnie hello. "I think Henry is going to be doing the tours when everyone gets here."

"Where is JJ? I need to get my hands on that little monster." Desmond asked.

"He's in the playroom with his cousins. Poor Millie and Becca are on child patrol for the first shift."

"Where is everyone else?" Arnie asked.

"Out back, Shannon and May b-lined it to the outdoor bar. I think the boys are with them."

Arnie nodded, "then that's where I'll be. Excuse me. Betty, James, so nice to see you again."

Gabriella looked at Desmond and arched an eyebrow. "Work stress?"

"You know it. Long hours, lots of pressure, but he loves it."

They made their way to the playroom in the wing opposite the living area. The sounds of toddler talk and laughter filled the hallway before they made it to the door. They walked into chaos, where six children all under the age of six ran around an indoor play area. Millie and Becca sat on oversized bean bag chairs in the corner of the room while they watched the little ones run around and expel some of their bottomless energy.

Gabriella called out to her son, who froze mid-run while he chased his cousin, and looked over to his mother. "Momma!" He yelled out as he ran towards his mother's legs.

"Uncle Desmond is here," Gabriella said as he crashed into her.

JJ's bright blue eyes lit up as he looked at Desmond. "Dee-Dee!" He yelled out, then threw himself into Desmond's arms.

"Hey, JJ monster. What are you doing?" Desmond asked as he lifted the child into his arms.

"I play." JJ told him.

"Are you having fun?" Desmond asked. JJ smiled and nodded his head. "Dee-Dee play?" JJ asked as he looked up at his uncle.

Desmond looked to Gabriella and shrugged. "Sure, JJ. Want to play in the ball pit?" JJ cheered in response. "Come get me when Laurel gets here."

***

A few hours later, everyone had eaten their body weight in grilled steak, seafood, and ribs. People were spread all over the yard; some were in the pool, others lounged in the pool chairs. Some were crowded around the bar while the parents sat around the table chatting. Henry and his brothers had the children in the newly fenced section of the yard where the swing set and sand box were safely tucked away from the open yard that butted the bay.

650

Desmond approached Laurel and Gabriella, who sat with their feet in the pool while they chatted with Max, Darius, and Arnie, who floated around on the inflatables. "Ladies, I need a word."

They followed Desmond into the house, who stopped in the den with the large window that overlooked the bay and grabbed a bag. "Lead the way to your room," Desmond instructed.

Perplexed by his request, Gabriella took them up the grand staircase and down the hall to the master suite. Desmond made his way to the oversized bed and made himself comfortable. Laurel looked at him and then laughed. "There is a sitting area right over there."

Desmond shook his head. "Did we ever settle into a sitting area in Gabby's room before?"

"Pretty positive I never had a sitting area in my room," Gabriella laughed as she and Laurel followed Desmond's lead and sat down. Desmond handed each of them a thermos.

"Since you bitches are both knocked up and are spoiling my sangria time, I made you guys a non-alcoholic version."

Laurel sipped the drink and crinkled her nose. "It's watered-down juice."

"Talk to me in four months and I'll get you the real thing." Desmond said with a smirk.

"So, are we having Christmas Eve in July?" Gabriella asked.

"How are you, Laurel?" Desmond asked.

"Pregnant." Laurel said as she looked down at her rounded belly. "And getting to the point that I can't hide it anymore."

"Like from the press?" Gabriella asked.

"Yeah, I just don't want them involved. Part of me is thinking of staying with my parents for a while. I don't have a project until after the new year, and the press for the last project is over. But I don't think Matt would go for it. It would be too hard to stay away from Matty for that long."

"How are things with Matt?" Desmond asked.

Laurel shrugged. "Good. I mean, he's really excited to be a dad again. He said he completely understands me not wanting to get married while pregnant, so he said we'll talk about it when the baby is like six months old. We can talk about it, but I don't think I'll change my mind." Laurel took a swig from the thermos and then shook her head. "Juice does not have the same effect as booze."

"Maybe it wouldn't be such a bad thing to stay here for a while," Gabriella said. "I'm not saying to stay until you have the baby, but maybe for a month? Get away from the drama that is L.A.?"

"Can I swing it, manager?" Laurel asked.

"Matt aside? Yeah. The only thing you have coming up is the audio book you are supposed to narrate. We can get that done here at a studio in the city." Gabriella verified.

"Have you wrapped your head around the whole motherhood thing yet?" Desmond asked.

Laurel shook her head. "Not really, no. It's like there is an alien in me. I don't feel like myself. I don't feel attached to it. Did you?"

Gabriella placed her hands on her belly. "Yeah, when I first found out I was pregnant with JJ, I was shocked. I just remember being so thankful that we finished filming the sequel. The amount of physical fighting I did with Henry in that movie would have been horrible to do while pregnant.

"But I spoke to him all the time. I probably seemed like a crazy person, but anytime I was alone, I was talking to JJ. Henry eventually started doing it too. But I did hide it from the press. It helped that we weren't in L.A. for most of my pregnancy. I think the first time I was in L.A. was for the premiere, and I was already seven months pregnant, so there was no hiding it at that point."

"But you looked adorable with your baby belly in one of Izzy's dresses," Desmond said with a smile.

"You always felt the connection, I still don't. I feel the baby kicking and stuff, but I still feel nothing. Don't get me wrong, I'm doing everything I have to do. I go to my visits, I take my vitamins, I eat healthy, I still work out. But I just don't feel the whole maternal instinct. It's like I'm broken."

"Maybe you should talk to your mom. Or maybe see a therapist? My therapist is a lifesaver," Desmond suggested.

"Maybe," Laurel said non-committedly. "Maybe I'll feel the connection when they are here."

"Are you going to find out what you are having?" Desmond asked.

"No, I don't want to know. It will make it more real." Laure responded.

Gabriella and Desmond shared a look of concern before they took sips of their mocktails.

***

"Hey Patti-cakes," Gabriella said as she laid down in the pool chair next to where Patti sat. The sky was dark, but the stars were barely visible from the light pollution. Lanterns and tiki torches lit up the backyard from their strategic placement hidden amongst the décor.

"Hey Gabby girl. Did JJ give you a hard time going to sleep?"

"Not at all, out like a light. I might need you all to live here full time if he goes down for the night like that every night," she said with a laugh.

"This house is amazing, Gabby." Patti said wistfully.

"Thanks. It's very overwhelming. But Henry fell in love with it, and if this is what it takes to get him out of England, so be it," Gabriella said with a laugh, her eyes drifted to the guests in the yard. "I can't believe Bob. He's like a real adult. In a real relationship. I can't deal. Isn't he still supposed to be a teenager?"

Patti laughed. "I wish, but unfortunately, it's been half a decade. You're in your thirties, and a mom. I'm not going to reveal my age and divorced. As much as I loved that time in our lives, I wouldn't want to be back there."

"How are you holding up?" Gabriella asked.

"I'm okay. We each took over a restaurant, and we're still business partners, but it's easier for us to communicate through the staff and keep our distance in our own establishments. It wasn't a long marriage, but it's never easy to go through a divorce. Especially since we were friends for so long."

"What actually happened? You guys never really disclosed why you divorced."

"I'm not sure how it started. Maybe we spent too much time together and we started to resent each other. We began to drift apart, only really speaking to each other if it was work related, otherwise he would disappear into his study or just watch television.

"There were some issues going on in our second location, and he said he'd head over there and see what the problem was. It was supposed to be a few days, but he stayed for a week. He reported back every night to let me know what was going on. We had to replace some of the staff, including a new manager.

"Over the next few months, Joshua was spending more and more time at the second location. When I asked him about it, he said that he felt more comfortable at that location and said that the place was really turning around. The numbers didn't lie, I saw that business was improving there. What I didn't see was that he was sleeping with the new manager. A mousey looking thing with a skinny waist. One of the staff called me one night and told me that she caught them in the office.

"When I confronted him, he didn't deny it at all. Said that he fell in love with her, and that our marriage was one of convenience and friendship. Told me that he was going to move in with her, and that we could stay business partners, but he'd be filing for a divorce.

"A year later, here I am. Divorced at my undisclosed age, still working with the man that betrayed me in so many ways."

"Jesus, Patti. Why didn't you tell us?"

"It wouldn't change nothing. Bob found out about all of it, told Joshua to stay away from everyone. Said he didn't deserve to be around everyone for being such a piece of shit. That kid is something else." Patti said with a shake of her hand and laugh, then tipped back the bottle of beer in her hand.

"I'm so sorry you had to go through that. I really thought Joshua wasn't like that. I'm sick to my stomach for you. I'm so glad you're staying here this week."

"Me too, Gabby girl. I'm glad things are going well for you. I've been worried about you ever since the sexiest man was announced."

Gabriella smiled at her friend. "I had a bit of an issue with it, but in four months, it will be someone else, and I won't have to deal with it."

"Have you spoken with Jake or Riona at all?" Patti asked.

"No. The last time I spoke with Jake was after Bernie's funeral. I think JJ was six months old? He's been so busy with the spy franchise. As for Riona, last time I had any interaction with her was at the premiere of the sequel. I don't think she really got it through her head that Henry and I were serious until she saw me on the red carpet pregnant. Even us being married didn't deter her from feeding into the rumors while we were on set."

"She's a real piece of work. So, do you have a name all picked out for little miss Anderson when she arrives?"

"Yeah, we decided on Marybeth. JJ was named after our fathers, or at least the American version of my father's name. So, we thought we'd do the same for our daughter. Mary for my mother, Maria, and Beth for Henry's mother, Elizabeth."

"I think that is beautiful," Patti said with a smile. "How many more do you think you'll have?"

"Oh my god, Patti. Let me get through this pregnancy," Gabriella said with a laugh.

"It's a big house you have here, Gabby, you gotta fill it up, don't 'cha know."

***

Henry clinked his dessert fork against his beer to get the attention of all his guests. It took some time for everyone to quiet down, which included Johnny when he yelled at everyone to shut up or piss off. Henry shook at his head at his brother's antics and laughed when Andrew walked over and hit Johnny on the back of his head.

"Wanker," Johnny mumbled as he rubbed his head, which made Nathan start to laugh.

"Right then," Henry started. "I wanted to thank all of you for coming here for our housewarming. It's rare that we all get to come together, the last time may have been our wedding.

"I've known some of you for a few years, others I've known all my life. But you are all important to me, and to my beautiful wife. Blood or not, you're all a part of my family. I know it's not easy to get together, especially for you Brits. But it means the world to us that you are here now.

"I wanted to raise a glass to all of you and thank you for being such an important part of my story. As actors, we play roles in other stories, but the story that counts is life. I wouldn't be who I am, or where I am without you lot. I love you all, and I want you to know that our home is always open to any of you, for whatever reason. You may need to get through the gates, but the home is always open. Cheers, mates."

Everyone lifted their glasses in response. Gabriella sat next to her husband and looked up at him with a heart full of love. He looked over to her and winked, then leaned in and kissed her like she hung the moon in the sky. She looked around the table and watched as the family she was born into, the family she married into, and the family she chose all congregated in the yard of the house that she would raise her family in.

She observed as her parents, who gave her all they could while she grew up, and molded her into the woman, mother, and wife she had grew into, laughed and joked with her best friends' parents and in-laws. She watched Henry's sister and sisters-in-law gossip with Darius and Marcus, while Patti and Bob challenged Henry's brothers to a game of flip cup.

Desmond and Arnie spoke with the newcomers, Bob's girlfriend and Jem's boyfriend while Jem sat on the stonework and gave belly rubs to Leigh and Scampi.

Overwhelmed by the love around her, and a huge blame to her pregnancy hormones, Gabriella sat there with a smile on her face as tears of complete happiness rolled down her cheek. Henry squeezed her hand while he spoke with Gerald about a new book series he was into. No matter what the outside world could throw at her, she knew that everything would be okay.

Giuseppe threw his arm around his wife's shoulders and laughed at something Sierra said, then looked over and made eye contact with his daughter. Gabriella smiled at him as he sent her a wink. And she knew what he was thinking. This was one of those moments that she would remember when she was old and gray. It was one of those life affirming moments, and she was going to enjoy it while it lasted.

Twenty-Eight

Forty years later.

"Hey, mom, are you almost ready to go?" Marybeth asked from the entrance to the California home that they purchased over twenty years ago.

Gabriella looked past her reflection in the full-length mirror and caught eye contact with her daughter. "Sure, S*tellina*, just making sure I look okay for tonight."

Marybeth sighed and smiled at her mother, Gabriella's own face looking at her through her daughter's, except she had the dimples and blue eyes of her father. "You look beautiful, Mom."

Gabriella looked back to her own refection and studied the silver hair that ended at her chin and framed the face that lines of laughter and wisdom woven into her skin. She looked down at the plum-colored long-sleeved dress, with its high neckline and tiny train and questioned if it was the wrong choice. She looked at her arms in the mirror to ensure that her loose, flabby skin couldn't be seen.

"Are you sure this dress is alright? I just know your father is going to be photographed and those tabloids love to point out how plump I am."

"You're seventy-one years old, you're not supposed to be shaped like some supermodel," Marybeth countered.

"Tell that to your Aunt Laurel." Gabriella said with a laugh.

"Aunt Laurel has always been tiny. Plus, she has that weird relationship with Uncle Matt," Marybeth responded. "Besides, you know how much everyone loves you and Dad. You're like their golden Hollywood couple."

Gabriella rolled her eyes and smiled at her daughter, then went over to the closet and slipped on silver low-heeled shoes. "Are you sure Emily, Donna, and Kirk are okay missing the ceremony?"

"Yeah, all of the kids would never sit through it, we can barely sit through it," Marybeth joked. "But seriously, Emily and Donna are watching your grandchildren. Kirk is at the venue making sure everything is ready for the afterparty. Are you sure Dad wants to skip out on the official afterparty for this one?"

"Yes. Your father wanted to celebrate with his family. Are you positive Kirk didn't want to come? Won't it be strange not having your husband next to you on the carpet?"

Marybeth laughed. "Mom, he's been to so many with me. Occupational hazard of marrying an actress. You should know better than most. As much as Chloe loves her aunts, she doesn't get to see them very often, and she'll be more comfortable with her father being there."

"Okay, as long as they aren't insulted. I know we only had ten seats." Gabriella said as she followed her daughter out of the bedroom and headed down the stairs to the main living area. She watched as her thirty-nine-year-old daughter floated down the stairs in her stilettos and open-back evening gown. She was

668

the mother of a four-year-old and followed in her father's footsteps and became an actor. She married her husband, Kirk, a professional party planner, six years ago, and they settled down in Bel Air.

JJ was waiting in the hallway with his wife and his younger brother of five years, Sean. JJ looked up at his mother and sister with a smile and met them at the bottom of the stairs as he offered his arm to his mother. Gabriella looked up at her son, whose looks still favored Henry's, and smiled as she tucked her hand into his elbow.

"You look beautiful, Mom," he said as he walked her over to the rest of the family.

"Thank you, *Tesoro*," she said with a smile. Her oldest son, who was a lawyer based in New York, had married his high school sweetheart, Emily, and had three children of his own. Rosa was nine, Arthur was seven, and Maria was four.

When Gabriella's father passed away fifteen years ago, her mother couldn't bear to live in their house anymore. JJ had purchased the home from his grandmother, and he raised his family in the home that Gabriella grew up in. When Maria found herself a part of the widow's club, she and Caroline headed to the west coast and moved into the beach house. Five years later, Sierra joined them. They lived out their own version of the Golden Girls until Maria passed away three years ago.

Gabriella looked at her daughter-in-law and smiled, "you look beautiful Emily. That dusty rose color complements your skin tone and blonde hair. Are you sure you don't want to join us at the ceremony?"

"Thanks, Mom. Donna and I are on kid patrol. We are going to head over to the venue a little before you are due to arrive so the kids can get the running around out of their system."

Donna came out from the back of the house, where you could hear the kids as they watched a movie. Her auburn hair was twisted up, and the emerald-green cocktail dress kissed the top of her knees. She let out a deep breath, then smiled as she walked over.

"Are they giving you trouble?" Marybeth asked.

"Bit of an argument over the movie, but it was nothing that some pretzels couldn't fix," she said with a smile, before she stopped in front of her husband and kissed him sweetly. Sean smiled at his wife; his closely clipped brown hair made the features on his face seem larger than his siblings. He had Gabriella's almond shaped brown eyes, Henry's nose and chin, and Gabriella's smile. He was the largest of the siblings and stood at six foot five with the build of his father during his superhero movie phase. Sean went into the military after high school, and was stationed overseas in England, where he met his wife.

After he served for eight years, Sean settled in England and worked for a private military company. They often spent their summers in the States to spend time with the family. Their two-year-old son, Ethan spoke with an adorable British accent.

"You look stunning, Mum," Sean said as he looked at his mother.

"I'm so happy that you all were able to make it. I know it means the world to your father. Speaking of, where is he?"

670

"He was back in the study," Donna said. "And he looks very dapper."

"Well, it's not every day you receive a lifetime achievement award," JJ added.

Henry finally emerged from the back of the house with a large smile on his face. His gray hair was neatly styled away from his face, and he wore a traditional black tuxedo, complete with a bowtie. He wore his black-framed glasses, and his signature trimmed salt and pepper beard.

"Well, someone is looking happy," Marybeth said as he entered the room.

"What is there not to be happy about? I just got tackled by my five grandchildren, my children and children-in-law are all here under one roof, and I have a wife who looks like that," Henry said with a wag of his eyebrows at Gabriella, which caused her to blush and roll her eyes.

"It really is sickening how cute they are," JJ said to the rest of the room. Emily hit him on the arm. "Stop it, I love them," she chided.

"I don't know how it's possible, Ella, but I think you get more beautiful every day," Henry said as he swept his wife into his arms and kissed her.

"Uh-huh. I think you need to get that eyeglass prescription checked," Gabriella said with a laugh.

"Okay everyone, the limo is here. I'll be heading to the venue to make sure everything is ready. I have transportation for all of the guest to arrive. Enjoy the ceremony. You really do deserve this, Hank," Kirk said as he directed the group out of the house.

**

The family was seated at their table and waited for the ceremony to start. Industry heavy hitters approached the table to congratulate Henry and say hello to the rest of the family. JJ and Sean sat next to one another and looked at the remaining five chairs.

"So, who else is sitting with us?" Sean asked and JJ shrugged in response. "I know Aunt Laurel and Uncle Desmond are two of the seats. Don't know about the other three."

"Rachel is coming with her mother," Marybeth informed her brothers.

"Now we know why she took that seat, she needs to sit with her bestie," JJ taunted.

"How are you two not sick of each other after living together for so many years?" Sean asked.

"We haven't lived together in almost seven years," Marybeth responded.

"That apartment must have been a nightmare with the two of you in such close quarters," JJ teased.

"You two need to get over it that Rachel never gave either of you the time of day," Marybeth teased in return.

"Does your mother have to yell at you three?" Henry asked with a smile and acted as he did with them when they were young.

"Still trying to make me the bad cop?" Gabriella asked with a smile.

"Only because you couldn't be the sexy cop in front of the kids," Henry said with a wag of his eyebrows before he placed a kiss on Gabriella's lips.

"Oh no, these two are still doing that lovey dovey bullshit? Knock it off, already. It's been forty-five years," Laurel said as she approached the table with Desmond and Rachel. Gabriella laughed as she stood up to greet her friends.

Laurel looked as though she was frozen in time, thanks to her extensive plastic surgery tune-ups over the years. She had taken up yoga and had the svelte physique to prove it. Her hair was platinum blond and was styled in an angled bob. She wore a sleeveless mermaid gown in a pale blue satin, and did not look a day over fifty.

Desmond made his way over to Gabriella next, dressed in a salmon pink suit with a white shirt and black tie. His curly hair was wild, with more salt than pepper over most of his head. Gabriella held Desmond close and squeezed him. "How are you doing, Des?"

Thirteen years after Desmond and Arnie got married, Arnie started to lose weight rapidly and suffered from stomach pain. After he confided in Brad, Desmond convinced Arnie to see Brad for an exam. He was diagnosed with pancreatic cancer. Since he chose to not go through any chemotherapy or radiation, Arnie passed away three months later in the master bedroom of their Long Island home. Desmond was devastated, and tried to throw himself into the theater, but his heart wasn't in it anymore. He sold the house and moved into Gabriella's pool house for a few months but ultimately decided that he needed a drastic change.

He moved across the country to live with Laurel, who went through her own crisis. After her daughter, Rachel, was born, Matt had finally worn her down, and they eventually got married. Rachel was the seven-year-old flower girl at their wedding. Although Laurel finally felt a connection when her daughter was born and blossomed into motherhood, her transition into wife was not as easy.

The longer Laurel and Matt were together, the more they fought. Every little inconvenience exploded into an argument of epic proportions. They had become so awkward to be around, that many of their friends steered clear of them. Whenever Gabriella was in town, she would try to spend time with them separately to keep the peace during her visits.

When Rachel turned twelve, they decided to call it quits. The two of them lived on opposite ends of the house and lived separate lives. After Matt moved out of the house, Laurel invited Desmond to move in with them. Desmond packed his bags and headed out west and left Broadway behind. Gabriella was able to find him work as a host for cooking competitions and eventually became a staple in a round table daytime talk show hosted by all LGBTQ community members.

Laurel and Desmond still lived together. Over the years they had lived a very single, party lifestyle, which was a rotating door of relationships. Desmond had as close to a taste of fatherhood as he wanted as he helped Laurel raise Rachel, and Rachel adored Desmond. She often joked that she was raised by two mothers.

"I'm fine, you fabulous bitch. The designer I was sleeping with was boring me, so I'm back out on the market," he said with a flick of the wrist. "I'm loving this color on you."

Gabriella looked down at her dress and smiled at one of her best friends. "Thanks, I wasn't too sure of it, but Marybeth assured me that it was okay."

"You know none of your children would allow you to walk out of your house looking a mess," Desmond retorted.

"But Henry would?" Gabriella asked with a laugh.

"The man is still so blinded with love for you, you could be walking around in a hospital gown with your ass hanging out and he'd still tell you that you're gorgeous." Desmond said with a laugh. "I know I would have said the same thing about Arnie had he made it with us."

Gabriella grabbed Desmond's hand and gave it a squeeze. It didn't matter that twenty-seven years had passed, Arnie had always been, and would always be the love of Desmond's life. It broke Gabriella's heart whenever she thought about the hand that life had delt Desmond, but she was always so proud of how he still lived his best life for the two of them. Desmond took the seat next to JJ after he said hello to the rest of the table.

Rachel took the seat next to Marybeth as Laurel and Gabriella spoke. "You will never guess who asked me to dinner next week," Laurel gossiped.

"You know I'm terrible at this game. Who was it?" Gabriella asked.

"Jake Wilson. I ran into him a charity golf event two weeks ago. He and wife number two divorced a year ago. And he looks pretty good for his age. Still has a full head of hair and still had the same sense of humor from all of those years ago."

"Wow, I haven't thought of Jake in so long. He's doing well?" Gabriella asked.

"He's going to be doing even better next week," Laurel said with a wink. Gabriella laughed and shook her head.

"What?" Laurel asked with a chuckle. "I don't work out and get my nip/tucks done to hide this body under frumpy clothing. In the words of Nonna Rosa, I'm not dead yet!"

Gabriella blushed and broke out into a full laugh. "Don't even act like you two still aren't screwing." Laurel challenged.

"You know we are," Henry called out from his seat as he wagged his still dark eyebrows, which made his adult children groan in response.

"Come on, Dad, not in front of the children," Sean joked.

"Your father was voted sexiest man of the year twice. And then again in the over fifty category," Desmond chimed in.

"Yeah, we don't need reminders of that, Uncle Desmond," Marybeth said with a groan.

After they settled in their seats, Laurel's attention was pulled to the two empty chairs at the table. "Who else is coming if all of your spouses aren't here?"

"Oh, hey Dad," Rachel said as Matt approached the table.

"Hey, baby girl," he said as he greeted his daughter. Matt was still in great shape; he wore navy blue suit with his head shaved bald and wrinkles around his eyes and on his forehead. Laurel hit Desmond then stood up and made him switch seats with her so she wouldn't have to sit next to her ex.

Matt watched as Laurel swapped chairs and scoffed. "Real mature, Lau." He then brought attention to the young blonde that hung on his arm, draped in a barely-there dress. "Everyone, this is Natalie. Natalie, this is my daughter, Rachel. That is MaryBeth, Gabriella, Henry, Sean, JJ, Satan, and Desmond."

Laurel rolled her eyes as Sean stifled a laugh. "Speaking of mature, Matt, is she younger than your daughter?"

"I don't think that's any of your business," Matt snapped back as he pulled out the chair next to Desmond for his date.

"What happened to wife number four, Matt?" Laurel continued to needle.

"Also, none of your business," Matt bit out between his teeth.

"Well, if this one is gunning for number five, make sure she's legal. It would be really embarrassing for Rachel to have her father arrested for being a child predator." Laurel threw back.

677

"Not any more embarrassing than her mother being a whore," Matt clapped back.

"Okay, enough with the two of you. If you guys can't be civil for Uncle Henry's big night, then one of you have to leave. This is ridiculous. Your blip of a marriage is ancient history. Get over it," Rachel snapped at her parents, which caused them to quiet down.

***

After a semi-awkward dinner, the awards started. When it came time to announce the lifetime achievement award, the lights went down, and a highlight reel of Henry's career played on the screen. It started out with one of his first acting roles on a British network. It flashed through a few of his other early projects and then focused on some of his well-known parts. There were clips of him from the superhero franchise, clips of him as a knight on horseback, then a few clips from the Edge of Time movie. Many of those clips focused on the wild west scenes and showed the famous saloon bedroom scene. There was a montage of him without his shirt on from various projects and then moved onto some of the more dramatic roles that he played as he aged. They focused on a limited series he worked on as the head of the IRA and ended with the latest film that he starred in as a therapist who obsesses over the problems of his clients, and takes punishments into his own hands when they revealed horrible things they did in their past.

When the film ended, Henry was asked to come to the stage. He stood up, hugged his sons and daughter, then leaned in to give Gabriella a kiss. He gently brushed his thumb against her wrinkled cheek and winked at her before he made his way to the stage through a standing ovation.

He stood at the podium with The Actor award in his hand. He looked around the room and took in the revelry. Once the audience settled down, he stood at the podium and observed the room. After a few beats of silence, he began to speak.

"A wise man once said that we don't have many nights like these. You need to take the time to soak it up. That it's one of the moments that will make you smile when you're old and gray. Well, I am old and gray, and I am absolutely smiling. That man was my father-in-law, and he was so right.

"Watching that highlight reel didn't just remind me of my career for the past fifty-some-odd years. It reminded me off all the moments off screen that made my life what it is. It brought back the memories of people and names long forgotten. Of friendships and bonds made working on projects together. It reminds me of the support I always received from my parents and siblings. Of the good advice I got from working with my heroes, and the ability to pass that knowledge onto the younger generation of actors.

"I'm a lucky man. I've gotten to live so many lifetimes in this line of work. The magic created to entertain the masses is amazing. But the most amazing lifetime out of all of them, the most magical of all, is the one where I met the love of my life, and from this amazing love we created a family. Not only biologically, but through years of friendship, heartache, love, and loss. I stand before you, a humble man whose greatest accomplishments aren't what you saw on the screen behind me, but at the table at the back of the room in front of me.

"I want to thank you all for this honor. This here isn't meant for me. It's for my five beautiful grandchildren, my three amazing children and their spouses, for my life-long friends who have become family, and my family overseas. But most of all, my beloved Ella, it's for you. Without you, nothing makes sense. Our life, our love, our story... it's my favorite one. Epic enough to be on the big screen. Thank you."

Henry left the stage to another standing ovation, and many teary eyes. Gabriella tried to compose herself at the table with their children as she watched the most amazing man say the most heartfelt speech. Marybeth hugged her mother as she tried to stop her tears. The cameras caught the emotional moments, which Laurel pointed out as she handed Gabriella a napkin for her eyes.

***

They arrived at the venue soon after the ceremony was over. Kirk did a phenomenal job when he planned the party. The children had a designated area to play in, which had over twenty children running around. Henry entered the room to much fanfare from the guests. He made sure he took the time to say hello to everyone. He was thrilled that Johnny, May, and Gerald made the trip, along with all his nieces and nephews and their children. Nathan and Andrew weren't fit to travel, but they sent their love and regards through their children.

Elise and her family made the trip from New York as an excuse to visit with Desmond. Jem sat with her family and were joined by Darius and Max. Bob was there with his wife and two out of the seven children they had. Gabriella made the rounds with Henry, making sure to say hello to every guest that came to the party. It had been decades since all of them had been together. As they walked around the room, they noticed little touches that Kirk had added to incorporate some of their traditions. There were tables in the back of the room with flip cup and beer pong set up, and even in his sixties, Bob was parked at the beer pong table and challenged their children to games.

They stopped at the bar to get a drink, where Laurel and Desmond were stationed. Gabriella tried to decide what to order when Desmond nudged her arm to draw her attention to Laurel, who held a bottle of sangria. "You have to be kidding," Gabriella said with a laugh.

"That Kirk is one really good party planner. What do you say, want to sneak off and drink the bottle?" Laurel asked with a wag of her eyebrows.

Gabriella laughed as she weaved her arm with Laurel's. "I'm pretty sure I can't mix that with my medication."

Desmond scoffed in response. "Wow, it just hit me, we really are old."

"Speak for yourself," Laurel joked.

"The saying is you're only as old as you feel, not as you look, bitch," Desmond said with a wink.

Laurel shook her head as Gabriella tossed her head back in a hearty laugh. "I should have never let you sit near Matt tonight; his snark is rubbing off on you, you old queen."

"Hey, Mom, Uncle Des, come over here, we need more players for flip cup," Rachel called over.

"Duty calls," Desmond said as he grabbed Laurel's arm to pull her away while he blew an air kiss to Gabriella.

Gabriella watched as her two best friends made their way over to join the most disjointed flip cup teams prepare to play a game. She moved away from the bar and walked around the perimeter of the room and stopped for small talk as she passed people. She made it to a corner of the room that she didn't get to before and noticed a table full of photos with empty chairs around it.

The photos were of the family members and friends that were no longer with them. Gabriella got choked up as she looked at the faces of her parents, Henry's parents, the Dolces, the Balvins, Arnie, Patti, and a photo of Leigh and Scampi together. There was a candle lit in the middle of the table with flowers around it. After a moment, she moved onto a longer table next to it, which had photos in frames from their lives. There were group shots from the beer garden when they filmed The Edge of Time. One from Gabriella's graduation. Some from their wedding, others from their children's first birthday parties. There were at least thirty frames on the table, each one signified a life event worth celebrating.

"Hola, senorita," Henry said as he snuck up from behind her, and he wrapped his arms around her waist and rested his chin on her shoulder.

"Asshole," she responded with a laugh. "I wasn't expecting any of this," she said as she gestured to all the photos.

"We have some really amazing children who put this together."

Gabriella nodded in response as she tried to hold the tears back. Henry kissed the tear trail on her cheek and understood the emotions she felt. "I'm really proud of you Henry. And that speech was…"

"The truth." Henry finished her sentence for her. They stood together as they looked at the framed memories and how they evolved over the years.

"We've really had an amazing life," Gabriella said softly as she smiled at each life affirming moment displayed on the table.

"We have. And we aren't done yet." Henry agreed.

Gabriella nodded her head as her eyes drifted over to the picture of her parents and fondly remembered her father's advice to soak in the moments.

Henry brought her attention back to the table, to the first picture of them from the storm in the trailer. "If you could go back and change anything in your life, would you?"

Gabriella thought about it, back to her awkward teen years to the rocky start to their relationship, all the way to how they raised their family and dealt with the press, to the very moment they were stood in now. She shook her head. "No, I wouldn't. It was all worth it."

"Not even to when we first met, and I got your panties in a twist when I thought you were the help?" Henry asked with a smile.

"No, not even that."

"Really? You were bloody pissed at me for that one." Henry said surprised.

"Yeah but look at all the sexual tension it had created." Gabriella said with a laugh.

Henry wrapped his arms around his wife and pulled her close to him as he responded, "oh yeah, we had a lot of that," then kissed her.

"Henry, we've a lot of everything."

The End.

Author's Note

I hope you enjoyed the conclusion to Gabriella's story. The way this book entertained me and took over my mind while I was writing it is comical. I dreamt about these characters. I'm sad to see their story end, but I'm excited to see what I dream up next.

I want to thank everyone who has supported me on my indie author journey. Between the encouragement to keep creating, to those who read my books, I appreciate everything!

I have some ideas brewing for a new novel, but I'm sure it will take a while for it to be ready for the masses. In the meantime, follow me on social media. Feel free to reach out, I love connecting with other readers and discussing all things books!

About the Author

C.E. Maras is a Long Island native, who lives with her husband, Tom, and their two Scottish Fold kittens, Hermes and Freya. She is a technical writer by day and inspired by her dreams and past experiences to write fiction at night. She has been writing fiction since elementary school and was told by her first grade and seventh grade teacher that she was meant to be a writer. With many stories written and shared with her friends growing up, C.E. decided to take the plunge-publishing her first novel, Burgundy, in the summer of 2024; and fulfilling the answer to the question in her elementary school yearbook, what do you want to be when you grow up? Aside from writing, C.E. is a voracious reader, consuming around 150 books per year. She also enjoys knitting, crocheting, cooking, baking, spending time with family, and spoiling her niece and nephews.

Follow on Facebook and Instagram: C.E. Maras Books

Follow on Amazon: C.E. Maras

www.ingramcontent.com/pod-product-compliance
Lightning Source LLC
Chambersburg PA
CBHW050837030726
47503CB00007BA/2206